The Pearls That Were His Eyes

a Tale of Cittàvecchio

By Ian Andrews

First published in the UK in 2008 by

TATTERDEMALION PRESS

Red Door, 12 Ardencote Road,

Birmingham B13 0RN

ISBN **978-0-9558524-0-4**

Typeset in Garamond. Printed and Bound in Great Britain by Lulu.com

Prologue: Unreal City

Unreal City

Under the brown fog of a winter dawn,

A crowd flowed over London Bridge, so many,

I had not thought death had undone so many.

Sighs, short and infrequent, were exhaled,

And each man fixed his eyes before his feet.

T.S. Eliot, The Waste Land, 60-65

The night mists of Cittàvecchio are legendary.

It's said (by those who live safe and far from the oldest, waterlogged quarters) that every night the Tattered King throws his cloak over the ancient and crumbling city, his constant lover and royal consort. Centuries ago, those gossips and harpies say, the Old Gods tried and failed to wash her iniquities away with their great deluge; she endured, half-drowned, half-dead, knee deep in silt and floodwater, a sunken shadow of her Imperial past. Half one thing and half another; astride the divide between *what is* and *what could have been*. Such borderlands are the places where the eldritch and wondrous can sometimes slip through the cracks; the place where the realm of the Tattered King touches our own more mundane world for good and for ill.

And in his ragged winding-shroud, in the fog that clings to the water of her flooded streets and mossy canals, things not wholly of this dull and dreary world sometimes occur.

The pious call them miracles and gloss over their more sinister connotations. The old nobility of the Cittàvecchi are skilled at putting masks on things. Indeed, they are famous for their masquerades and their carnivals; the polite diplomacy; the inevitable stiletto clenched in the iron fist – velvet glove optional, but it had better be of the most *exquisite* fashion. Famous, if not infamous, for the beautiful and terrible history of their drowned and undying city. And, of course, famous for their elegant masks.

Old Cittàvecchio, the ancient Imperial capital. Now in drowned and faded splendour; with its bells and towers and flooded streets, with its mossy statues and its mournful cloak of night mist. A city of quiet magic, unregarded by those inured to the miraculous or determined not to see it. But for every haughty and disdainful mask in the salons of the upper city, turning their back on the traditions and the quiet sorceries of the city for the new sciences, there is another who remembers to bow before crossing a bridge and who pays respect to the spirits of deep water.

If you know where to look, they say (and who are you to argue with Them?) there is a courtyard where late at night the statue of a lion in combat with a snake dance in battle for their own secret amusement. Up a tiny and disregarded canal there was once a walled garden in Imperial times; there you can find a small pool where the Undines come to wash the long weeds of their hair in the dark of the new moon. And if you scramble over the right rooftops when that selfsame moon is full, you can find a walled courtyard with no entrances or exits - within, silent dancers trapped forever in a slow and stately measure like the marionettes of the city's famous *commedia* puppet plays dance a solemn and mournful pavane, in clothes that were the very height of fashion three hundred years ago. In the catacombs and cellars of the Palazzo d'Annunzione on the Grand Concourse, legend tells of a great war of frogs and mice, every year, conducted with cavalry charges, military uniforms and pipers. To see it, they say, is to be granted a free and full passport into Cittàvecchio's secret world of wonder. But be careful: once the unreal has brushed your shoulder, the real is never quite sufficient again.

There are temples, everywhere, old places of devotion, if one only knows where to look (and looks with the eyes of a native of Cittàvecchio). Ten places within a minute's walk of the docks where old gods were once worshipped – the old fane to Apollo; the stone sacred to Poseidon now half-drowned on the edge of the lagoon; the weathered crypt sacred to Erebus and Nix, the sons of Chaos, deep below the Cathedrale; the ancient Mithraeum, temple to a soldier's god, on the edge of the

Rookeries. It is rumoured that if you walk three times round the Pillar of the Winged Bull in the Piazza, between the tenth and twelfth strikes of the campanile at midnight, you can see the Cathedrale as its Imperial builders intended –and you can behold with your inner eye the sacred geometry of the city's holy places. It is also said that such a sight will cause you to run mad. And everyone knows someone who knows someone who ran mad. Or so they say.

(And who are you to argue with Them?)

And of course, everywhere you look - from the name of the ruling House to the skewed trident symbol of the Trinity; from the fortune-telling cards made in imitation of the legends, to the sacred spaces of the city laid to his design; even in the masks that all the Cittàvecchi wear - there are echoes of the *Re Stracciati*, the Last King, the King in Tatters. Like the proverbial ghost at the feast, there are signs of his passage everywhere; hints of his presence. Though one never catches a glimpse of anything more than his ragged mantle vanishing around a corner, or his mocking mask seen from an ancient carving, weathered and worn but still watchful. Some things in its past Cittàvecchio is not proud of, but the city does not forget.

This, though, is an Age of Reason. Such myths and legends are dismissed by the intelligentsia in their salons and their cafes on the edge of the Grand Piazza. The mists come up in the spring from the marshes and smother the city for a while on their way out to the open sea. *Simply weather, nothing more*, they say, and raise laughing masks to hide their faces from their fellows. But to the folk of the Old Quarter, crammed together ten to a room in the warren of decrepit and decaying buildings they call the Rookeries, the night mists bring more than a whiff of old legend and a promise of mystery. To them, the cloying fog is a pillow pressed over their face, a distemper creeping into their souls and colouring them grey.

Or, on occasion, red.

* * *

The actor cursed richly and with fervour as the last of his coin was swept up from the gaming table by the laughing Dane. Fortunately for propriety, his profanity was largely lost in the tumult of the crowded gambling-house, and in any case, swallowed whole by the Dane's laughter, an avalanche from behind a great quivering red beard. He and his shipmates had openly boasted that they had washed their dice in the fountain below the statue of Merkuri with his staff and had prayed to the old pagan god for the luck of the bones. Perhaps the old trickster was listening, for they had taken on the entire clientele of the *Red Lion* over the course of the evening and thus far at least they had profited richly from their endeavours. The dice had been changed three times, when complaints at the Danes' luck became too strident, and what's more it was said that the *Lion* was under a *benedizione*, a charm that prevented the tricks of gamblers. Rumour had it that the Duca's brother, the Lord Seneschal, had paid for the *benedizione* himself after nearly losing his favourite horse to a card sharp in the back-room salon there a few years ago, but like many such rumours it may just have been clever promotion by Barocchio Iron-Gut, the proprietor. A man with whom wise men did not trifle, and a man who kept a most accurate and detailed tally of all wagers and debts made in his establishment. Barocchio had become one of the city's most successful bookmakers by extending lines of credit to those who could ill afford to take them – such as actors with a compulsion to gamble against those enjoying a lucky streak - and then pursuing a most vigorous and on occasions quite visceral schedule of repayments. He was into Barocchio for forty ducats, and both of them knew that tomorrow would be a desperate scramble for funds. Barocchio was not known to be tolerant of debtors for long and his reach was impressive.

It had been a long night and he had been spending faster than was prudent, trying to bury the memories of the afternoon performance. Of all the times to dry, when the Donna Ophelia di Gialla was in the audience... the Duca's sister and, it was whispered, the real power behind the throne; orbited by her suitors and hangers-on. Half the court had come to see his

Lussurioso in *The Revenger's Tragedy* but his performance had been mediocre; his cues mistimed, his attention elsewhere. What should have been a chance to make a mark, to expand his patronage outside the circle of the Lord Seneschal's Men had been carelessly squandered.

The mood in the city wasn't exactly conducive to theatre at the moment. Even a group as well-connected as the Seneschal's Men needed to be careful; they had been advised against showing *Revengers* but had gone ahead anyway – and now, mirroring the events of the play, it seemed, one of the leading lights of the city's political scene, Lord Feron, had been arrested for treason by the feared and infamous Tartary Guards and swiftly tried and executed before his supporters could muster in any numbers. The Duca, it was said, was watching the theatres and the old city carefully, waiting for signs of the promised rebellion; such things often began among the *intelligentsia* and Feron was much loved among the poorer sections of the populace.

He had not died well, or easily, according to the rumours.

The city's mood was hard to read, now; but every night the play went on, the actors had watched the audience nervously. The nobility avoided the play; the Captain of the Guard was seen in the upper circle hard-faced and clearly not there to appreciate the art. It is a bad time to be an actor in a political satire, when the events of the real world are more fantastic than anything you portray. So the arrival of the Duca's sister and her hangers-on... well, that could have meant a number of things. And, whichever of them it meant, it had not done wonders for his performance.

He felt around in the bottom of his pouch, hoping to find a loose *piastre* coin caught in the seam; to no avail. A long walk back to the theatre lodgings, then, no comfortable boat ride and no whore. And through the Rookeries, not exactly the safest part of the city nowadays...

The leader of the red-haired sailors, a mountain of a man whose speech was fiercely accented but intelligible, raised his tankard, and called for another round of drinks for all who had lost money to him that night; "*Gut sport, no ill feelinks, gut sport!*"

One more drink then. Can't do any harm. Recoup a little of the lost coin...

"Abelard, isn't it? Gianni Abelard, of the Lord Seneschal's Men?"

He turned to regard the man next to him at the bar who had spoken. At first glance he was dressed much as most of the rest of the clientele of the gambling-house; plain blacks and greys in heavy wool and leather; sensible dress for a cold wet night. It was the quality of the clothes that gave it away; tradesmen and artisans could seldom afford silk shirts or soft leather gloves tucked at a jaunty angle in the belt. And few in the lower city wore their hair pulled tightly back into the aristocratic topknot nowadays. Good enough to deflect a casual glance, but to an observer, far too fashionable for dockside. One of Barocchio's *special* customers, a patron of his fabled Blue Room. Abelard stood up straighter.

"My Lord d'Orlato; I had no idea you would be here."

The young nobleman smiled, but it never reached his cold blue eyes. "There is a... private game in the back room; Lord Prospero is once more wiping the floor with all comers at cards. I prefer to gamble when there is at least a small chance I will not lose; and of course Prospero's forfeits can be *quite* the spectacle." The nobleman's eyes flicked across to the sailors, loudly and raucously distributing their alcoholic charity to the crowd. "I see I am not the only one whom the Lady has not smiled upon this evening..."

Gianni assumed a carefully schooled, neutral expression. "Alas too true, my Lord. Dame Fortune's face was turned away from me this eve; coin has fled from me like a sailor from a pregnant whore. I rely now upon the charity of those who vanquished me for even the simple pleasures of a beer."

Again, the smile that left the icy eyes untouched. "I hardly think an actor of your calibre will want for employment or the gold it brings for long, Abelard. Those who patronise the stage speak highly of your talents."

"But not you, my Lord?"

Lord d'Orlato's eyes were moving, his interest in the conversation seemingly spent. "No, Abelard. Not me. I prefer my pleasures more honest." He gestured to the curtained door into the back room of the *Red Lion*, from which a great commotion could be heard. "Go with the Father, Gianni Abelard, and buy yourself a drink." He flipped a *ducat* in the air; Abelard snatched the coin with well-practiced ease before it reached the top of its arc. "You never know when your next one might be."

Abelard watched the nobleman make his way across the crowded floor to the curtained doorway of the fabled Blue Room and nod to the burly minders before passing through. It was said that the young Lord Gawain d'Orlato was the favoured protégé of the Lord Seneschal himself; perhaps even a possible successor to the famously childless Old Man. But the Lord Seneschal was well known as a patron of the arts, especially of the stage. Lord Gawain was more famous for his appetites than his patronage. Why would he notice, much less recognise, an actor?

I have been marked, thought Abelard. *Marked for great things in the future. Perhaps today has not been a complete waste...*

He turned to the bar, and ordered himself another beer. The night was young, and provided he avoided any further flirtation with Dame Fortune, the change from a ducat would provide a full night's sport if husbanded with care...

* * *

Gawain made his way into the back room to be met with a wall of raucous noise. A beleaguered string quartet competed gamely for attention with the cries of several large caged birds and the laughter and shouting from the centre of the room, where perhaps a dozen people stood around a sunken area from which came howls and snarling. Off to the side were several smaller tables positioned to give a good view through the large bay windows onto the canal; all they displayed at present was a milky whiteness as the fog from the streets rolled up against them, and the occasional shadow of a reveller passing outside.

Around one of the tables a cluster of well-dressed figures shouted and passed wagers between themselves; he elbowed his way between two of them, and surveyed the crowd.

Here, sat at one side of the table, powdered, his wig slightly askew and the hint of a drunken flush on his cheeks, was Prospero. Nowadays he carried a little more weight around the waist than in his youth but he still looked better than most of the observers around the table and the drunken flush was almost certainly a clever combination of acting and makeup. Nobody in Cittàvecchio could hold a candle to Lord Prospero of the Three Lions when it came to parties, excess, or shrewdness at the card table and everyone knew it; well, almost everyone. Sat opposite him, hunched over his cards as if shielding them from the attentions of the hostile fates was young Gratiano dell'Allia, boyish face screwed up with concentration. The stack of coin before him was significantly smaller than the mountain before Prospero, and the general run of the betting in the crowd was not who would win the hand, but how long young Gratiano could stay in the game. Prospero blinked once, slowly, and licked his lips, his eyes never leaving Gratiano's face. Gawain was put in mind of a lizard; the large kind that swallows its prey whole and then, a few months later, disgorges a small, sad bundle of dried and splintered bones.

Prospero's eyes flicked once to Gawain, then back to Gratiano. His expression of slightly unfocussed geniality didn't change, but his refined and slightly effeminate voice cut through the surrounding chatter, pitched exactly right.

"Gawain, *darling*, do remind your kept boy there that he's supposed to be playing cards, not dreaming of coitus with farm animals. I am growing old and fat here waiting for him to reach his climax."

Gratiano flushed crimson, but did not look up. Gawain inclined his head to Prospero, but did not smile. "To my practiced eye, my lord Prospero, you grew old and fat long ago, and a moment or two more will come to no account either way. And nobody would seek to question your clear pre-eminence in the matter of farmyard sexual escapades after the business with the crocodile. How is your mistress of late? Still biting?"

Prospero laughed, a deep sound that began somewhere down in his belly. "Oh, Lord Gawain, you do cut me; you do cut me hard. She is a fine pair of boots, two travelling cases and an elegant clutch purse, and I have kept her teeth to remind me that there are some things on this earth sharper than your wit, but few and far between. A side wager that I can clean the whelp out in two hands?"

"Oh, no. You've taken enough gold from me for one lifetime, Prospero. I want a waterman's fare and the cost of a good whore in my pocket when I leave, not a void full of good intentions."

Gratiano threw a handful of coin into the pot. "You bluff, Prospero. You always hold your head like that when you bluff. I will see your cards."

Prospero smiled the gentle smile he reserved for marks and congenital idiots, and laid his cards down face up. "You, my young pigeon, have a lot to learn, and you had best learn it with some despatch or you are going to end up in a *pie*."

Gratiano groaned, and put his head in his hands. Prospero swept the pile of coin in the centre of the table into his lap with a grin of sheer innocent pleasure. "Another hand? Or have you learned your lesson yet?"

"I'll pass, my Lord. I'd prefer to keep my shirt." Gratiano stood, bowed to Prospero and left the table, the very picture of slump-shouldered dejection.

"How much?" queried Gawain.

"He took me for near a hundred ducats. I was *certain* he was bluffing."

Gawain smiled his cool smile. "Prospero laughs like a jolly grandfather but within that breast beats a heart of blackened flint, and only a fool forgets it. He's taken wiser heads than you for everything they own, and youthful overconfidence is the food he lives on. Note, I never play cards with Prospero, even when I'm in my cups. *Especially* when I'm in my cups."

Gratiano smiled dolefully to himself. "I'll crack him eventually."

"By which time you will owe him the Earth and the stars in the heavens above and your immortal soul too. Give it up, Gratiano, while you still have your freedom. Don't imagine Prospero won't sell you into slavery for bad debt; I've seen him do as much – and worse - to gentlemen of higher status than you before. Now, set aside this lunatic urge to gamble your way straight into Hell and tell me of what you've seen in here this evening. I've been out on business and it doesn't do to be behind the times on the gossip…"

Gratiano took a seat in the wide window bay and leant forward conspiratorially, nodding toward a small group close to the fireplace. Two women, one older, soberly dressed, veiled and watchful behind a fan; the other much younger, dressed impeccably in silk and velvet and wielding a full-face mask on a beribboned stick as adroitly as a fencer with a rapier. Lurking behind them were several swarthy men, stocky, thick-set and clearly ill-at-ease in their finery. Though they appeared unarmed, they had the constantly alert and shifting air of men who expected trouble at any moment, from any direction – the universal demeanour of the bodyguard in a crowded room. Stood in front of them, attitude attentive and politely interested, an athletic man of middle height in an elegant tailored black coat, his dark hair loose and untied falling to his collar, with vivid, luminous grey eyes. Occasionally, he'd make a remark or gesture with his own half-mask, which spent more time in his hand than before his face, to the disguised woman; servants hovered discreetly in the background making sure that neither suffered the indignity of an empty glass. A long black kerchief was tied around his left arm above the elbow, hanging down past his waist.

Gratiano chuckled to himself and launched breathlessly into his carefully hoarded trove of gossip. "I see you have noticed our friends from the Tartary Guard over there. That, apparently, is what passes for incognito nowadays; and even though they are plainly here to bodyguard the Duca's sister, it hasn't escaped anyone's notice that since they arrived, a number of the more outspoken among Barocchio's customers have quietly made their excuses and left. Barocchio can take no offence, for the Donna Ophelia patronises his establishment and it is not prudent to turn away the favour of the ruling family; but she does so with an armed mob that watches everyones' faces, eavesdrops clumsily on everyones' conversations and generally *lowers the tone.* He hides it well, but Barocchio is not well pleased."

Gawain inclined his head slightly toward the elegant black-clad man by the fireplace. "If all of the troublemakers are scared off by a clumsy military presence then what on earth is di Tuffatore doing dancing in front of their very noses? It's no secret he was a friend and ally to Lo- to Feron, whom we are told is now to be called traitor." His face remained expressionless, but Gratiano scowled.

"Lord Xavier has been paying court to the Donna Ophelia all evening; one would almost think that he imagines himself in with a chance there. He's been strutting like a peacock before the fireplace since eight, and he has monopolised her shamelessly. Not that she seems to be complaining of it, of course. Xavier may well have dubious politics but he is always ready to lay them aside, it appears, in favour of a bout of social climbing. Perhaps Feron's fate has changed the wind to which he angles his sails; certainly this evening you would think him a true supporter of the Ducal faction. Indeed, he's been like this for a week or so; chasing the Donna like a dog in heat. Perhaps she likes the undivided attention, but most here think it scandalous so soon after what happened to his last paramour..." Gratiano leaned forward and dropped his voice to a bare whisper. "Donna Sofia, it is said, hurled herself from her tower window last month into the canal and drowned when she heard tell of his abandonment of her and his suit for Donna Ophelia; and now look, the shameless fellow has the gall to wear black and carry a mourning colour around his arm! One can only admire such – Gawain; Gawain, are you well?"

Gawain tore his eyes away from the group by the fire. "I am fine; why?"

"Oh; you went the most peculiar colour just then. Sort of mottled. Are you sure you feel all right? My aunt went just that way; mottled, then carried off by the flux a week later. Healthy as a horse before that –"

"Your aunt was never as healthy as a horse. Especially not after you discovered what she was worth and how much you were into her for in the will. Why young Gratiano! I do believe you've gone *red!* Surely not..." Gawain barked a laugh and feigned shock at Gratiano's unmistakably crimson cheeks. "Clearly we have hit upon a family skeleton here. We shall crack the bones and examine the marrow a little later, perhaps; but for now, I have a pretty-boy's evening to ruin. Watch and be educated in the field of social and political engineering, young man."

Gawain stood and smoothly whipped a glass from a tray in the hands of a passing waiter, taking a mouthful, pulling a face and heading for the fireplace, leaving Gratiano to observe from his window seat. He circled for a moment and then approached from behind Lord Xavier, clearly in view of the lady and her bodyguards, who watched him with the cold and emotionless eyes of reptiles. At the last moment Gawain dodged to the right, slid his hand into the small of Xavier's back and nudged him around so he was suddenly a natural part of the conversation between Xavier and Ophelia. Xavier tensed abruptly and eyed Gawain coldly. Donna Ophelia regarded him from behind her emotionless porcelain mask and kept her own counsel.

"My Lord, My Lady, how marvellous to see you both here and in such fine spirits given the recent tragedy to afflict Lord Xavier. My *condolences* on the terrible turn of events, my Lord. I'm sure the pain is still very sharp..."

Xavier shifted uncomfortably, aware that Gawain's hand was still in the small of his back. Gratiano, watching from the window, smothered a snigger. Gawain smiled a solicitous smile and pressed on regardless. "Still; some jollier news, to lighten the sobre tone. I just had the most excellent good fortune whilst coming through the main bar. I ran into that fellow whom everyone speaks of on the stage; Gianni Abelard, of the Lord Seneschal's Men. The actor fellow. I understand you follow him quite closely, Donna?"

Ophelia nodded, once. "Indeed, Lord d'Orlato. Lord Xavier and I watched him perform at the Compass this very afternoon. The *Revenger's Tragedy*, a most bloody and disquieting piece, and one which I cannot help but feel was speaking more to our own poor city's politics than to any fantastickal setting. . I thought him the very essence of acting, but Lord Xavier was just saying that he disagreed." The porcelain mask turned to Xavier.

Gawain smiled. "Please, my Lady, call me Gawain. Only my creditors and my tailor call me Lord d'Orlato."

"We shall not discuss in polite company what names his friends or his sainted mother call him by." Xavier's smile was equally as cold as Gawain's, but his eyes crinkled at the corners in a way that suggested he was seeing more humour in the situation than might at first appear. "And yes, I must confess, having had Abelard described to me as one of the great actors of the age, I was expecting a man who could transform the very world in my imagination. All the city talks of this play as if it were some kind of Sybilline prophecy that maps out the future; some kind of seditionary blueprint for a republic and the fall of the Duca." Xavier's eyes flicked across the guards ranged behind Ophelia; they were watching him with open attention and he smiled to himself, paused, and chose his words with exaggerated care. "If such were true, the play would indeed be dangerous. And because so many have assumed this play to be some kind of wonder, I went along to see what kind of genius, what sorcerer of the stage could have taken such base clay and transmuted it through theatrical alchemy into sedition and treachery. Such an actor would be, I thought, the greatest man of the age to so ensorcel the people of the city. Instead, I found an unremarkable hack who stumbled over his lines and was far from the best thing in the play. I go in pursuit of rumours of rebellion and treason, expecting to find a great leader of men ready to create an uprising from the very stage, and instead I find an innocent man free of all the talents and crimes I so blithely accuse him of. A disappointment. And I do so *detest* disappointment..." His eyes flicked from Gawain to the cold porcelain mask and back. "…as I was just saying."

Gawain stepped back, his eyes not leaving Xavier's. "Only yesterday, I was speaking with the Duca, and I am sure he expressed a quite similar sentiment – disappointment that a great leader turned out to be, in the final analysis, quite ordinary and not at all what was expected. Disappointment can be a terrible thing. It can completely ruin your day."

The room had abruptly become much quieter; many of the patrons were not even trying to disguise the attention they paid to the conversation. Even Prospero had risen from his gaming table and stood, one ear on the conversation.

Xavier met Gawain's gaze unblinking. "It certainly can. One should guard against disappointment and build up strong friendships and alliegances to shield oneself in times of sudden misfortune. Don't you agree?"

"Ah, wise counsel indeed. If only poor Lord Feron had followed it, perhaps he would still be with us today. He was, like you, a patron of unconventional theatre. And, of course, a good friend of yours, no?"

Xavier's reply, whatever it might have been, was lost in sudden shouting from the doorway: Barocchio's man, Pasquale, loudly announcing the next pit-fight and requesting that patrons take their places if they wished to bet. Ophelia dropped her mask from her face and regarded Gawain coldly. "Lord d'Orlato, I do believe you are going out of your way to be disagreeable. Do you have some quarrel with Lord di Tuffatore? If so, take it elsewhere; this is not a night for quarrels."

Gawain bowed low and formally to the lady, and with a flick of his cloak vanished into the growing crowd. Ophelia turned to Xavier and arched her eyebrow. He responded with an expressive shrug. "It is no easy thing to fathom my lord Gawain's moods, Donna. Clearly I have somehow offered him some offence, and equally clearly, he will make its nature plain to me in due course, but I think you need not worry."

Ophelia smiled demurely. "I do not worry, Lord Xavier. I merely wonder at the strangeness of it all. Shall we watch the bloodshed?"

Xavier reached round and felt in the small of his own back, and then examined his fingers closely before surreptitiously wiping them on the dangling mourning-cloth. "It has already started for some, Donna."

"My Lord?"

"No matter." Xavier offered Ophelia his arm. "Shall we?"

∗ ∗ ∗

Gianni Abelard pulled the collar of his cloak higher and quickened his pace. The pavement alongside the canal was clammy and the mist brought with it an unseasonable chill, blurring the edges of the buildings and making footing uncertain. Not the best time to be in one's cups. Still; a late rally on the dice had made him another fifteen *ducats* and that would at least keep Barocchio off his back for another few days.

He stumbled as abruptly something black and fast, low to the ground, danced between his feet in the mist and then shot up a wall, all bristling fur and great green eyes like a lantern. A cat, its back arched, was watching him with fierce and hypnotic intent. He made as if to stroke it, then held back; the animal did not look well-disposed. Instead he made the sign of warding to fend off ill luck and hurried on over the slippery cobbles.

Another mile to the Lovers' Bridge, then up and onto higher ground and out of this fog...

Like most of Cittàvecchio's late night revellers, Gianni knew his way across the city with his eyes shut. When one grows up in a city where many of the main streets are flooded by subsidence and others are canals by design, a city where ground mist is common, then one learns where to put one's feet or one does not live to see adulthood. So when he felt not the expected cobbles of the *Via Mattone Gialla*, which should lead him straight to the *Ponte Amanti*[1], but instead cold marble slabs of unfamiliar ground he froze, instantly. Failure to do so could lead to anything from an unexpected dip in the harbour to a fall of many feet onto hard and unforgiving stone.

All around him the fog swirled like milk. He closed his eyes and listened carefully for any sound of water lapping; nothing. No; wait...

Movement? Movement off to the right. Visibility was almost nothing, even an outstretched hand indistinct in the mists now, and Gianni suspected he would not be the only man feeling his way home tonight. But how had he come to stray off the path? The route from the *Red Lion* back to his lodgings was so familiar to him that he could do it in his sleep, yet nowhere along that route should there be an open area far from water with a marble flag floor...

Movement, again. The faint sound of a footstep, the swish of a cloak. Gianni called out, but the fog muffled and deadened his voice, sending his halloo back flat, damp and dead. He stumbled forward, both hands held out in front of him, and nearly shrieked when he felt someone take his hand.

She loomed out of the mist like a haunted wreck in a tale of pirates and corsairs; the long nose of the *Vappo* mask, eye sockets black with mystery; the mist forming a silver lace of dew on her great black wig; her dress seemingly part of the fog itself. She took Gianni's hand and held her other to his lips, theatrically, finger raised.

---

[1] *Ponte Amanti*, or the Lovers' Bridge, the main connecting thoroughfare between the flooded north and west of Cittàvecchio and the mainland and harbour area. The bridge is one of the oldest structures in the city, and legend has it that inside each of the curiously carven support pillars of the bridge's span there is a pair of lovers entombed, their blood sacrifice appeasing the old god Poseidon. Most nowadays do not believe in that sort of thing, but it is worthy of note that all of the other major bridges of Cittàvecchio have had to be rebuilt over and over as the city has subsided below the water, whereas *Ponte Amanti* remains on solid ground. This is the source of the Cittàvecchio saying: *"If you wish to build to last, build on love and death."*

Shhhhh…

He felt a shiver run up and down his spine at the touch of her finger, delicate as moth wings, on his lips. He felt at his waist for the knotted ribbon that held his own mask, the *Bauta* favoured by those seeking general anonymity, and raised it to his own face in tribute. One does not go barefaced into the heart of the City and expect to return unchanged.

She disappeared into the swirling mists that seemed to form into a train for her, tugging him onwards, surefooted in the milky air. Gianni felt the hand disengage from his own, and then the long nose of *Vappo* loomed out of the fog once more and he caught a flash of amusement and perhaps malice from the eyes of the mask before she whirled away, again, the fog billowing around her like a familiar spirit. As it did so, the shapes of the buildings around Gianni assumed a ghostly substance; with the masked figure's departure, the fog thinned and sank back down below eye level. And as he looked around, he realised where he was.

The Rookeries; a warren of tall, narrow houses of varying stages of decrepitude and interconnectedness that stretched from the Church of the Mother and Child at dockside all the way to the foot of the Ponte Amanti. One of the most sunken areas of the city, in some places the Rookeries were submerged up to their second-storey windows, the remaining floors rising from a maze of tiny canals and boardwalks constructed of rickety wooden laths stretched from windowsill to windowsill or supported by rotten rope and cables. In others, the Rookeries remained above the water table, and tiny, cramped courtyards with looming tall buildings on all sides clawed for space, their corners drifted with filth and debris.

Into one such courtyard had he stumbled – how, he knew not, save by the grace of the mysterious masked stranger who was now nowhere to be seen. He was a clear half-mile off course by his estimation and the realisation that he was alone, past midnight, in the Rookeries was a more sobering thought than a bucket of cold water in the face.

Click.

Gianni froze, and slowly moved his hand toward his knife, tucked in a scabbard in the small of his back. He scanned the courtyard, slowly. Paranoia gave every gaping window watching eyes and each shadow bore malice entirely absent a short moment before.

"Hello?"

Gianni whirled in response to a sound; but it was only a cat, all black like a shadow with amber eyes, perching atop a shattered barrel, watching him. His shoulders slumped in relief. "Perhaps you are lucky for me tonight, hmm?"

He made to move toward the cat, but as he was about to do so, heard the soft whisper of cloth on cloth, the muffled creak of leather, and the soft crunch of boots on gravel. He turned to confront the presence, but by then, of course, the blade was already in motion and it was far too late.

*　*　*

They found the body and called Captain Visconti of the Night Watch. Only the Captain could spur the Night Watch to enter the Rookeries after midnight and even then, they arrived in a group of ten and did not let any of their number stray out of sight as the sullen and red-eyed inhabitants of the crowded and derelict buildings formed a ring around what had been made from a human being. This was not the first such death in the Rookeries and the natural antipathy of the locals for the Watch was counterbalanced by the desire to ensure that they themselves were not next...

Visconti, a narrow-eyed man with a goatee who knew his city well enough to always carry a naked sword when he was on duty, ordered the stained sheet covering the remains pulled back. His sergeant blanched and turned his face away, but Visconti hunkered down and looked more closely.

"It's the same one. He's burst the eyes again, and again, with the face. Has anyone found the face?"

One of the junior watchmen cried out, and then vomited copiously. A black cat with great amber eyes clambered up a porch and sat atop the ramshackle roof, hissing at the watchman as he lifted a shapeless mass of chewed and lacerated flesh from the gutter.

"Here, sir. The cats have been at it."

Visconti turned away from the naked bones and sightless stare of the corpse. "Stretcher duty. Cover him up and get him down to the watch house. I want the body identified as soon as possible."

The watchmen scrambled to lift the ruined body; as they did, Visconti looked narrowly round the courtyard.

"The same as usual. Gold for useful information. A flogging for wasting my time. We want this stopped just as much as you do."

The response was a silent and sullen gaze from the locals. Visconti watched them until the last of his men had left the courtyard, and then he followed them out.

The amber-eyed cat sat unblinking and watched as he and his men retreated from the courtyard, and slowly licked its lips.

Part One: One Must Be So Careful These Days

I see crowds of people, walking round in a ring.

Thank you. If you see dear Mrs. Equitone,

Tell her I bring the horoscope myself:

One must be so careful these days.

T.S. Eliot, The Waste Land, 56-59

Flanked by guards no longer making any effort to be subtle, Xavier escorted Donna Ophelia to the canal side and saw her down the marbled steps into her barge, while her veiled attendant lurked watchful in the background.

"Shall I have the pleasure of the Donna's company tomorrow night?"

"I am sure, my Lord, that you will have the pleasure of *somebody's* company tomorrow night; but I fear it will not be mine. I have given a commitment to my brother that I will attend him during the Courts of Justice tomorrow evening, and matters of policy must come before my own amusement."

"It gratifies me nonetheless that you regard me as an amusement and not as a matter of policy…"

A flash of a smile beneath the mask and Ophelia inclined her head as if to say *a point to you, my Lord. A point to you.* Then she stepped into the barge, steadying herself on Xavier's arm.

Xavier saw her seated and then turned away, to find her veiled attendant face to face with him, blocking his route back up to the main thoroughfare from the dock. The Mater Calomena; spiritual advisor, nursemaid and some said sorceress; she never let Ophelia out of her sight, as many frustrated suitors had good cause to know. She stared at him silently until, reluctantly, he offered her his arm as well. She took it, and clambered down into the barge, composed herself and inclined her head with bare civility. Underneath the lace veil, eyes like black marbles watched his every move with an attitude deeply unsympathetic.

"Lord di Tuffatore…"

Xavier bent forward to catch her whispered words and as he did so, she grasped the mourning cloth hanging from his arm, pulling it tight and threatening to overbalance him. As he struggled for balance, she moved close to the side of his head and whispered "*I know what you are up to, you and your friends. I am watching you. Do not give me cause to* act."

Xavier shook free and took several steps back, watching the veiled woman warily. She remained standing in the centre of the barge as it pushed away onto the canal, and her gaze never left Xavier until the mists rolled in and claimed it for their own.

Xavier watched the barge vanish into the mists, until he was certain it was gone. Then he turned and ran up the steps to the pavement two at a time, grabbed his cloak and mask from one of the gambling-house servants and set off into the darkness himself, a grim set to his face.

*　*　*

"What did you say to him, Mater?"

Calomena sat and composed herself. "I offered him a warning about overreaching ambition, and told him I'd have his balls in a vise if he tried anything on."

Ophelia laughed. "Mater, your language is shocking and your methods as subtle as a charging bull! How am I to ever marry if you keep scaring off my suitors like this..."

Calomena shrugged expressively. "Charging bulls seldom have to gore anyone twice. Most learn the first time. And if you think I'm capable of stopping you from doing anything you take me for an even bigger fool than di Tuffatore does, and he thinks I'm the biggest idiot in the city."

"But are we even certain, at this stage, that it's him?"

Calomena flicked her veil back over her head revealing an old, weathered but not unhandsome face framed with iron-grey hair. "I was watching for most of the evening, and I'm still not certain. It might be him. Or it might be Lord Gawain, though I count that less likely. Or it might be Lord Prospero. But one of them at least was up to their pampered necks in it with Feron, and even if it's not Xavier, I've given him a good scare that should keep him honest. Besides, it serves a dual purpose. His track record with ladies of the Court does not encourage me..."

Ophelia set aside her own mask, revealing a heart-shaped face that projected an entirely duplicitous impression of innocence. "And Gawain?"

Calomena smiled a grim smile. "And him. We have to take into account what influence the Lord d'Orlato exercises over young Xavier as well, and in turn what influences the Lord d'Orlato."

"Is it worth taking this to the Lord Seneschal yet?"

Calomena shook her head vigorously. "No. Cittàvecchi society is riddled with secret societies, clubs, political movements and the like. Masks breed them like flies. For the moment we have nothing more than my disquiet and a series of coincidences that seem too convenient to go on - that is not enough for any kind of legal process. If we have nothing but innuendo and we take it to the Seneschal, then *he* will take it to the Duca, and the first thing the Duca will do is order another round of hangings and gibbetings for no better reason than it is you and I who raise the matter. And if he executes any more members of the nobility on our say, it will probably trigger the very open revolt we seek to avoid at the moment and, worse, will make our own position untenable. Everything is finely balanced and I do not want to try and provoke another of the Duca's *funny turns*. They are inevitably bloody in consequence."

"So for now we continue to gather information?"

"For now, at least. Your man Gratiano remains close to Gawain and Prospero both. Continue to cultivate him, Ophelia; learn what he has learned of the activities of those three. I have a meeting with the other members of my Order at dawn tomorrow; I'll be better able to take the temperature of the political wind then. And carry on your dalliance with Xavier –

for now. But have a care you don't lose your head, young madam."

Ophelia looked affronted. "I am not some milkmaid to have my head turned with fast words and a title..."

"And neither was Sofia d'Amato. And now she lies drowned in the morgue because he cast her off to pursue you. At best, Xavier di Tuffatore is a rake and the worst kind of cad. At *best*."

Ophelia raised her mask swiftly to her face and looked out over the water of the canal, but not before Calomena caught the tiny look of defiance. The older woman sighed, but kept her own counsel.

*　*　*

Gratiano hailed the boatmen from the edge of the water and gratefully collapsed into the well of the boat. "The Bridge at the bottom of *via Fiore della Ciliega*, boatman. By the Court of the Dragon."

"Ho, hold! Hold the boat, you wretched villain!"

Prospero jumped the short distance from the quayside into the boat, causing it to rock alarmingly; cold canal water slopped over the gunwales and splashed Gratiano's legs. Prospero, in apparent defiance of the laws of both gravity and probability, remained on his feet.

"Prospero! You could have killed us both!"

"Half a tragedy averted, then. Surely you are not calling it a night already, young man? Just because you are afraid of losing any more gold doesn't mean the gambling has to stop..."

"Prospero, I would love to give you the opportunity to take yet more of my money, but I have agreed to meet Lord Gawain at the *Priest's Hole* in the Court of the Dragon to take a late supper."

"Mother and *Child*, man! Are you so under his control that you cannot even think independently?" Prospero pulled an exceptionally rude face, and made a hand gesture which left Gratiano in no doubt as to his opinion of Gawain, or indeed of his opinion of Gratiano. "Gawain's gone to speak to the Seneschal, as is his duty; he'll be back in town in an hour. And that's time to take in one of the big pit-fights and be back at the *Priest's Hole* in plenty of time. You might even win back some of the handsome sum I have extracted from you this evening. Come on – I'll stand you your drinks."

Gratiano dithered helplessly, his determination withering like a moth in the fierce heat of Prospero's enthusiasm. Prospero put on his best grin, the one which caused walls to fall, virtue to be abandoned and good sense to drown its sorrows for the evening.

"Come now, Gratiano. I have brought the *best* beast from my menagerie tonight, and Barocchio has wagered a flat thousand with me that his beast will have the better of mine. A one thousand ducat wager, Gratiano. Is that alone not worth seeing? Such opportunities simply do not come along every day!"

Gratiano grinned. "What are you putting up for the fight?"

Prospero smiled the broad smile of a shark in ambush. "Something a little *unusual*. I have had the beast sent directly to me from my factors in Calicut. They spent near a month hunting it in the interior and I am informed on good authority that it's a man-eater. Well; allegedly at least it ate four of my agents, the bloody thing, so it's good and ready for the bout. Tonight, young Gratiano, you will witness a clash of two true *monsters*. Barocchio says he has been saving a prime contender for weeks for a fitting competition, and he is confident, yes, very confident. I will look forward to taking his money."

"So this is a sure thing, then?"

"Absolutely. We've even got Fra Ottavio to come and witness the oath under the Trinity, and to give it his *benedizione* and ward off ill intent from the beasts. Now are you going to scuttle off to the *Priest's Hole* and sit meekly awaiting the return of your stern and humourless sponsor, or are you going to *party* a little?"

Gratiano's shoulders slumped in defeat. Prospero just smiled, and waved his hand in the air at the boatman, who dutifully turned his prow back to the Red Lion's quay.

* * *

The Pit, below the Red Lion, was one of the best-known venues in Cittàvecchio for such fights; of dubious legality, the Watch had historically avoided paying too much attention given the number of nobility and courtiers involved in the sport. That, and Barocchio's handsome inducements to senior watchmen to look elsewhere for their trouble. It extended down into the old cellars beneath the Red Lion – indeed, into what was, before the subsidence of the city, the ground floor. Around the top of The Pit, a broad wooden rail had been constructed – broad enough to prevent most drunken revellers from falling to a hastily hushed-up death below, though such things were not unknown.

Pit fights drew a somewhat more raucous crowd than the more refined games of card and dice that Barocchio ran during the earlier part of the evening and as Gratiano made his way in through the main double doors, many of the circular benches ringing the Pit were already filled and the noise level was high, though nowhere near so high as it would shortly be. Prospero had gone below to see to the arrangements for his contender; Gratiano made straight for Prospero's favoured seat, right at ringside over one of the two entrances to the Pit.

On the opposite side of the railing, Barocchio sat in court like a medieval potentate, surrounded by his hangers-on. Though he still described himself as a "…humble innkeeper and host who has had the good fortune to hit upon a popular idea", there was little humble or indeed bourgeois about Barocchio Iron-Gut. Easily the wealthiest proprietor in Cittàvecchio's crowded and colourful gambling scene, his wealth was more what was expected of rich and prosperous merchants or minor nobility, and it pleased Barocchio, whose origins were far from noble, to mix with such people.

But some habits are hard to break, even for one with pretensions to the upper classes and Barocchio's hands and arms and his barrel physique still showed the badges of a man who was unafraid of hard work – whether that work be hefting casks, or strangling debtors until their eyes bulged out of their sockets. He caught Gratiano's eye and bowed; just brief enough to display mild contempt, just deep enough to display required respect for noble blood. *He could buy my family ten times over and he knows it.*

As Gratiano's eyes flicked over Barocchio's court, he caught sight of a distinctive mask; a bejewelled silver crescent moon, inlaid with opals and chips of marble. From behind it, eyes of the most vivid green watched him, and then crinkled with amusement. The Donna Elizabeta Zancani; art collector, gallery owner, patron of the theatre and the arts, socialite and, just occasionally, serious player. It was said that she was one of the few women in the city who would play cards with Prospero, and what's more she was the only one who had beaten him and taken his shirt.

An unmarried woman of independent means was a rarity in Cittàvecchi society, but the Donna Zancani filled the role with élan. Some said that she'd poisoned her first husband and strangled her second; others that she was simply yet to find a man who could keep up with her appetites. Gratiano could certainly speak for those; he had on more than one occasion spent a pleasurable evening in the company of Donna Zancani, though she always seemed to return to her first and favourite lover eventually, her factor and "servant" Mercutio del Richo. A quick scan of the room showed no sign of del Richo; Gratiano's pulse leaped for a moment with the prospect of potential passion. He bowed; across the ring of the pit, she inclined her head in response and tilted the mask to conceal a smile. The fan snapped, abruptly, into line of sight and she watched him over it. He knew the signals.

He bowed to the lady again, deep and low, and mouthed a promise to her; she flicked the fan shut with a minimalist gesture and was seated, her maids fussing around her like tiny boats steering a great galleon into port. She leaned over and said something behind her fan to one of her maids; the young girl looked straight at Gratiano and giggled. He felt himself colour with embarrassment; the lady could have said one of a hundred things, all equally injurious to his pride and dignity, or one of another hundred, all good.

Her eyes shone behind the mask, and he knew he was summoned; it was just a case of how long he could resist. It was all part of the game.

The benches around the ring were crowded now and the scent of money and expectation was heavy on the air when Prospero suddenly appeared at Gratiano's shoulder. He was slightly flushed, his clothes were in some disarray and he has a faraway sparkle in his eye.

"Magnificent. Magnificent. What. A. *Magnificent*. Brute."

"Prospero, are you well? Is everything alright?"

Prospero grinned broadly. "Oh yes. *Oh*. Oh yes. Everything's just *fine*." He stood, and stretched his arms out wide. "Lords, Ladies and Gentlemen, tonight, as you know, we have something *special* for you. Something a little unusual."

Barocchio rolled to his feet, not to be outdone. "Indeed. A pair of rare beasts, so I am told, ready to compete unto the bitter end for your delectation and delight this fine evening. I would-"

Prospero cheerfully rode over his co-sponsor's opening speech. "I am so confident – *so* confident of my own beast that I will, sight unseen of my opponent's entry, wager one hundred ducats against any one of you in the room that cares to take the bet that I shall emerge victorious!"

Barocchio's face screwed up into a picture of agony. Here, thought Gratiano, is a man caught between the twin horns of miserliness and loss of face. Which way would he jump?

"As will I", snarled Barocchio through gritted teeth. The hubbub became a tumult as factors hurried to record the bets of the eager punters.

Barocchio made his way around the railing of the Pit to Prospero. "Are you trying to bankrupt me, you rogue?"

Prospero pursed his lips and looked shocked. "Why, Barocchio! I was sure you would have sufficient confidence in your beast that you would not even *entertain* the thought of losing money! It's not too late to back out of our little wager, you know – Fra Ottavio isn't here yet, you could always accept defeat with good grace and no loss of coin..."

"Oh, I am here, Lord Prospero. Just a little quieter than you."

Prospero turned; stood just behind him, a man of middling height, with vivid golden eyes, black hair swept back from a widow's peak and a neatly-kept beard and moustache. He dressed in the formal black velvet of a Priest of the Trinity, and carried an ebony walking-stick more in the fashion of a military commander than a gentleman. He tucked the stick under his arm and pulled off one of his gloves, businesslike. "Come, gentlemen. Time is passing. Are you going to wager, and are my services required?"

Prospero shook off his right glove and stuck his hand out cheerily. Barocchio, with much scowling and reluctance, took the proffered hand and Fra Ottavio placed his own atop theirs and closed his eyes.

"I wager a thousand ducats that my beast will indeed slay yours in the pit this night. Do you accept?"

"I accept your wager," rumbled Barocchio.

Ottavio opened his eyes. "In the eyes of the Father, the Mother and the Holy Child this wager is now sacred. Do you accept my right and duty as adjudicator of this matter?"

"We do," both intoned. Ottavio let both hands free and smiled brightly. "Right; let's see some sport then, gentlemen."

All three took positions close to the railings. Barocchio signalled to his staff to begin the evening's main event and gestured to Prospero. "The honour is all yours, my Lord."

"From the darkest depths of the Sindi interior comes my contender. A man-eater, and one that has consumed the living flesh of four of the brave agents I sent to capture it – ladies and gentlemen beware, leaning too far into the pit, for its deadly spines might reach even to such a height!"

Below Prospero, a large portcullis started to rumble upwards, and from within the darkness beyond it came a deep-chested roar... Prospero closed his eyes a moment and supped deep of the cheering and the noise from the pit below; when his eyes opened again there was an almost unholy glee lighting them like lanterns from within. "Lords, ladies; it treads soft in the darkness of the Sindi night and its teeth and tail are legend in their own right. Fed on the soft flesh of children and my own dear agents it comes to you now lean and athirst for the blood of its foes... I give you the *manticore!*"

Thick-set and square the beast stalked into the arena, muscular and squat. The great leonine head swung left and right, the jaws still bloodied from whatever unfortunate animal had served as its last meal. A long, sinuous tail ending in a spined club whipped back and forth, and from its back hung two large wings, clipped and de-feathered to hobble the beast and keep it in the pit. It roared, and the very walls of the Pit shook with the sound; as it roared, it reared and was brought up short by the thick iron chain padlocked to its collar. Prospero gave a broad and happy grin at Barocchio and the betting and waving of wager slips reached a tumultuous level.

Gratiano stood and raised his hand to Barocchio. "A hundred says Prospero's beast will triumph!"

He felt Elizabeta Zancani's eyes on him; he carefully avoided her gaze. Barocchio nodded graciously, and when he looked back up at Gratiano, there was a gleam of malicious amusement in his eye. Gratiano tugged Prospero's sleeve, but he was already watching Barocchio through narrowed eyes. The revelation of his beast had not had the profound effect upon his rival that he had hoped...

Barocchio stood. "Worthy gentles, patrons and pit fight fanatics all, I am gratified that Lord Prospero has gone to such lengths to give us a fight to remember. I had worried that my own beast was of such overriding puissance that nothing he could find would compete fairly. Now I see I misjudged Lord Prospero, and we shall have a fair fight indeed!"

Gratiano looked to Prospero, who had blanched.

"In the depths of the Pripet Marshes in the pagan North my agents followed rumour and legend for months until they came upon the nest that I had been told of; and from therein they took but one egg. That egg have we nurtured and pampered in preparation for this very day. Its venom is so potent, that legend tells of its ability to strike its foes to stone with but a glance; and I do not imagine that even so mighty a foe as a manticore will long prove the equal of such ferocity!"

"*Do* get on with it..." hissed Prospero.

"Ladies and Gentlemen, I give you the *basilisk*."

The lizard was perhaps a third of the size of the manticore, but lightning-quick on its spindly, splay-toed legs, and whip-thin. Its eyes were an almost luminescent orange and as it swept its gaze over the railing there were screams and several of the more impressionable patrons fainted clean away. Barocchio raised his hands and called for calm. "Ladies, ladies. The deadly gaze is, we discover, a myth; it is the venom of the bite that causes the effect the basilisk is famed for. You may meet its gaze in safety. Safety of our patrons is as ever our paramount concern... Lord Prospero, are you content that we have a fair match?"

Prospero braced himself with both hands against the railing and leaned over the edge as far as he dared. "I am!"

"Then *release the beasts!*"

The collar-chains on both beasts snapped free and instantly the basilisk was moving like lightning up the wall of the Pit, heading straight for Prospero. It was fended off only by the ring of inward-pointing spikes at the Pit's mouth. It made as if to try and leap for him through the spikes but a thunderous roar from below distracted it, and the warning came just in time as the manticore whipped its tail sharply and spat spines at the basilisk, which scuttled adroitly out of the way. Gratiano felt the thud as the spines embedded themselves in the Pit's wooden walls.

"Barocchio had his trainer wear one of my cast-off cloaks while it taunted the beast," said Prospero, tipping a salute to Barocchio. Barocchio was in no position to return the salute as he ducked below the railing to avoid a spray of spines that thudded into the rail where he had been standing moments before. "I, on the other hand, would never even *consider* such blaggardly behaviour."

The basilisk stayed on the walls, dodging the whistling club of the manticore's tail and staying well beyond the range of its jagged bite. Occasionally, the manticore would risk another spine but the nimble lizard was more than equal to the task of dodging the missiles. The tumult around the Pit raised another notch when, unexpectedly, the manticore leapt a full fifteen feet straight up and caught the basilisk completely by surprise, landing one paw right on the lizard's hindquarters. The basilisk shrieked with alarm and fled higher up the wall, leaving its still-twitching tail in the manticore's claws. Prospero roared in triumph. "First blood! First blood!"

Barocchio just smiled, untroubled.

The basilisk reared away from the wall, and spat a stream of black spittle at the manticore below. The larger beast dodged, but a few drops landed on one of its clipped wings; where they fell, smoke rose and a dark shadow spread over the hobbled limb. The manticore roared in pain and shook itself as if trying to shed some sudden and unexpected weight; the wing where the venom had landed was noticeably slower and heavier. Prospero, to all intents and purposes, had ceased breathing.

The basilisk scuttled closer to the floor, circling the manticore, which now dragged one wing, sluggish and useless, on the floor. A spray of spines thudded into the wall around the basilisk but the agile lizard dodged them and darted out onto the floor hissing wildly. Clearly it measured the manticore as wounded prey and was closing in for the kill. The manticore, however, was having none of it. The basilisk darted in toward its face, but it was not quite quick enough and another of those jagged, claw-studded paws crashed down, this time trapping the entire hindquarters of the lizard. It writhed like an eel, and sank its fangs deep into the manticore's paw – and, like a racing shadow, blackness started to spread up the animal's forelimb and across its chest. The manticore barely had time to let out a roar of frustrated rage and whip its tail over its head for the coup de grace before the venom of the basilisk had taken full effect. From the paw upwards, the great beast began to freeze and the blackness gave way to the off-grey of stone.

Barocchio leapt to his feet and punched the air, but Fra Ottavio was watching the Pit keenly, as was Prospero.

The basilisk was still trapped under the manticore's stone paw, wriggling frantically as the venom did its work and more and more of the manticore's body vitrified. Poised over the basilisk, about six feet in the air, was the great spined club at the end of the manticore's tail; it had been caught in mid-strike, just about to crash down on the pinned basilisk when the venom hit. And as the effect of the basilisk's venom spread along the whip like tail, it cracked ominously. The slender arch of flesh and bone was not equal to the task of keeping the weight of the tail club in the air when that flesh was replaced with brittle stone. The basilisk redoubled its efforts to break free, but with one final crack the club broke away and crashed down on the lizard with a very final crunch.

Prospero rocketed to his feet and cheered. Barocchio's face crumpled sourly. The roaring around the pit-side continued; both beasts were clearly dead. Adjudication was required!

Both owners closed on the serene Fra Ottavio, who rose to his feet with an expression of mild amusement. "I am only here to adjudicate your personal wager, gentlemen, not the outcome of the bout for the entire room. I did not personally witness any other wagers and cannot speak to their terms and conditions."

Prospero shrugged. "I know how I would call the result; but I await your adjudication as agreed. The room can wait a moment. Settle our wager first."

Barocchio growled under his breath. "The basilisk *clearly* struck the first killing blow."

Ottavio shook his head. "Irrelevant, my furious friend. Irrelevant. Prospero said 'I wager a thousand ducats that my beast will indeed slay yours in the pit this night.' Your reply was 'I accept your wager'. By my reckoning, Prospero's beast did indeed slay yours, by dropping a large chunk of stone on it. Hence, Prospero wins the wager. As to the wider fight – I agree, the basilisk clearly had the first killing blow and were I in a position to declare, I would declare for that beast. But I am not. Barocchio, you owe the Lord Prospero as agreed on this matter. Do you accept my adjudication?"

Barocchio ground his teeth. "Does my Lord Prospero accept the adjudicator's suggestion regarding the overall bout?"

Prospero assumed a lugubrious face. "Well, Barocchio, I don't know. I mean, the basilisk is dead..."

Barocchio's colour sank through vivid crimson to beetroot, and the muscles of his neck stood out like a ship's rigging. Prospero threw his hands in the air in mock surrender. "I *jest*, Barocchio! I jest! Calm yourself. The bout is yours and well-fought. Good fortune alone prevents me from walking away at a complete loss this evening. I concede the bout, but claim our personal wager."

Barocchio nodded, once, slightly mollified, and extended his hand. "Agreed." Prospero took the proffered hand and again, Fra Ottavio placed his own over the top of theirs. "Your wager is discharged honourably in the sight of the Father, the Mother and the Holy Child. No *maledizione* will fall upon you over the conduct of this wager. Go with the Father, gentlemen."

Barocchio nodded, and turned to the baying crowd. "The basilisk wins by virtue of first fatal blow!"

Amidst the cheering and booing, Prospero made his way back to his box where Gratiano sat slumped in disbelief.

"You said you had a *sure thing!*"

Prospero looked at him blankly. "I did! And I won my wager with Barocchio, which is what matters, after all. My dear boy, if you look like that after losing a measly hundred then you really should try and get this gambling problem of yours under control!"

And with a bright and cheery smile, Prospero whirled off into the night to collect his winnings and pay his debts with good grace. Gratiano, bereft, looked across the pit to where Elizabeta Zancani had been standing - but she too was gone.

*   *   *

Xavier, hooded and masked, hurried across the darkened Grand Piazza, the low-lying mist swirling like smoke in his wake. Rising before him, the great bulk of the Cathedrale, the centrepiece of Cittàvecchio's spiritual life; the low-hanging moon cast the shadow of the trident surmounting the spire – once the symbol of the Tattered King, now that of the Father, the Mother and the Child – across the broad open space of the piazza like reaching claws.

He nodded courteously to a few other late-night revellers on their way back home, masked and cloaked as he was; at this time of night in Cittàvecchio anonymity was the only certainty. Overhead, the Cathedrale campanile began chiming for midnight, low, sonorous and echoing through the billowing mists. Xavier cursed softly. *Late, again.*

Hugging the wall of the great building he glanced around to ensure he had not been followed, and approached the alcove with the portly and chuckling statue of Saint Niccolo, keeper of secrets. In the saint's left hand he held a toad; Xavier pressed down on the animal until he heard the soft click of a well-maintained mechanism, and old Niccolo rolled backwards into the darkness revealing a staircase descending into the depths. With a backward glance and a swirl of his cloak, he was gone, and old Niccolo with his secretive smile was back in place.

Xavier hurried down the spiral staircase to the anteroom; this was the route to the secret chamber that he had been taught and which he would in due course teach to his own successor as his own father had taught it to him. The anteroom contained a table on which lay long shapeless black robe with a deep hood and a large leaden carnival mask in the shape of a Grecian tragedy face. He hastily donned the robes and the mask, and moved on down the remaining steps to the main chamber beneath him.

The chamber, lit by burning torches in sconces, was octagonal with archways in each wall leading into the darkness. The one from which Xavier emerged was the route that was vouchsafed to him by his predecessors; each of the other archways had a keeper and a secret route, no doubt, to somewhere in the city. Of such convoluted conditions and precautions is true secrecy maintained.

In the centre of the chamber, eight chairs in a circle. Over the past few years, as the Duca's madness had gripped him more tightly and the senseless executions had continued, chairs had been vacated – sometimes by age, sometimes by more abrupt and unexpected methods - and no successors turned up to claim them. Now there were five left, and four of them were already occupied. The masked faces turned to him; a great cruel black sun limned in crackling veins of gold; a laughing silver moon; a green-bearded old man of the sea beaten from copper all green with verdigris and a bronze face composed all of autumn leaves. The moon passed a tray bearing two great goblets to the sun, goblets that steamed like the mists of the city. She, Autumn and the Old Man of the Sea raised their own to him in greeting.

The sun face regarded him and held out the tray. The voice was young-old, male-female, quiet yet echoing in the dark smoky chamber.

"Take the sacrament of the city's blood, Tragedy. We have much to discuss, and a lost Senator to toast."

Xavier took his goblet, and Sun took the remaining one. All five stood, and turned their backs on their compatriots. Looking at the ancient carvings on the wall, Xavier steeled himself, lifted his mask, and took a mouthful of the smoky liquid, feeling it burn the back of his throat and warm his chest like a good brandy. He set the goblet aside and, lowering his mask, turned back to his fellows as his vision blurred, his wits sharpened and the sacrament gripped him.

Madame Sosostris, famous clairvoyante,

Had a bad cold, nevertheless

Is known to be the wisest woman in Europe,

With a wicked pack of cards.

T.S. Eliot, The Waste Land, 43-46

Officially, of course, Xavier was supposed to be ignorant of the identities of the other Secret Senators – that was part of the reason why the Senate meetings always began with a draft of mulled wine spiced with *Methi*, the blue fungus which blurs the senses while focussing the mind. The precautions were as much for the safety of the members of the Senate as for anything else – what was discussed in these meetings nowadays was at best sedition and under the regime of the Duca di Gialla, sedition, especially among the wealthy and influential, normally resulted in a slow, lingering death.

Membership of the Senate was hereditary in certain family lines; the masks were passed to the scion of the line by their predecessor, just as Xavier had received the mask of Tragedy from his old uncle Giuliano before he left the city to go travelling. Like most Cittàvecchi secret societies, its purpose varied through the ages: watchdog on the powers that be, secret committee of nomination for the civic leadership, star chamber for those who thought themselves beyond the justice of the republic. But since the recent descent of the Duca into irrationality and paranoia, increasingly the purpose of the Secret Senate was to find a way to replace him and to return the city to the perceived glories of its past, before the Gialla came to power. That alone would be sufficient cause for caution in displaying one's identity.

Of course, Cittàvecchio had quite a lot of history prior to the rise of the Gialla family, and not all of it could be defined as "better" than the current regime. Opinions that were socially... inappropriate might be expressed with impunity in such a setting. And when dealing with the nobles of the Cittàvecchi, one does not normally need much in the way of an excuse to wear a mask.

So, in theory the Senate met in anonymity, where all could speak openly without fear of their identity being exposed, compromised or even taken into account during their deliberations. In practice, when dealing with the figures of high society one came to recognise mannerisms, turns of phrase, voices, now and then. Take the figure behind the Old Man of the Sea mask – Pater Felicio, the Keeper of the Keys of the Cathedrale. His voice was unmistakable to anyone who had sat through one of the Pater's blood-and-thunder orations from the Father's pulpit in the Cathedrale, and he conceded that point to the other Senators with good grace. The Pater's mask was an affectation, and everyone knew it. Xavier nodded to him, slowly and graciously, from behind Tragedy's mask. And of course, it had been an open secret among the Senators as to who had worn the mask of the Pole Star – the mask that now sat, unworn, on one of the empty seats, with black mourning ribbons adorning it.

The five of them assumed their seats, facing one another without preamble. Moon began the night's sedition, pointing to the vacant chair opposite Sun Face.

"The Pole Star shines no more." The Moon was a woman, tall and acerbic. He had wondered, once, if Ophelia di Gialla herself hid behind that mask, but Moon was older and more self-assured than Ophelia. He was pretty sure *she* knew who *he* was, and his curiosity burned to get behind her mask in turn. He caught her green eyes on him, a gleam of amusement behind the mask of the moon before the conversation moved on. She gestured to the vacant chair, and to the mask of the Star, lying on the cushion of the chair.

"The Pole Star shines no more and everyone knows why. Another execution ordered. Lord Feron, dead; and that suggests to me that the Duca's spies are closer to us than we thought. Any one of us might be the next that the Duca's attentions turn to; for the list of possible successors to the Duca grows ever slimmer." Her voice soft and quiet, belying the seriousness of her words.

"Feron's arrest was inevitable; he was popular among the working poor; he spoke against the Corn Tax and portrayed himself a *hero*." Xavier could hear the curl in Autumn's lip on that last word. Autumn was a big man, well-muscled and carrying himself with the easy, loose physical confidence of a career soldier. Xavier had imagined any number of faces under that mask, but it was hard to tell for sure; Autumn had a strange turn to his voice, an accent or possibly an affectation to put the other Senators off his scent, and he deflected questions about his identity effortlessly, whether they be subtle or overt. "The Duca is anything but a hero, and fears anyone who can catch the ear of the mob. His arrest was inevitable; his execution, however, conducted with unseemly haste and by the most ignoble means. The Court suspects that we, or someone like us, would have rescued Feron, spirited him away, had the delay between arrest and execution been lengthy. I know for certain that many among the city military and the Watch are appalled, and some have said the Lord Seneschal himself has chastised the Duca. For all the good that'll do, of course. He's another hero."

Pater Felicio shifted uncomfortably in his chair. "He'll die a hero's death, dancing at the end of a rope, then. Old fool. This is no time to speak openly against the Duca."

Xavier dragged his attention back to the matter at hand. Moon was still watching him, amusedly. He leaned forward, determined to at least give the impression he was following the conversation. "If indeed he did – we have only the word of the Court for that and I suspect there's something in Moon's suspicions about spies. I have more to say on that later. Besides, can we not use this to foment an open revolt among the masses? The Rookeries are already astir..."

"Not yet." For the first time during the debate, the great Black Sun spoke. None knew who lay behind the Black Sun; she (or he, for her sex was indeterminate) seemed to know the true identities of all. "Let us not forget ourselves; let us not see the passing of a Senator without paying the respect due. Raise your goblets and mark him. To the Pole Star…" Sun raised her goblet once more, and stood, awaiting the others.

"To Lord Feron, our bravest and best." Pater Felicio raised his goblet.

Autumn grumbled under his breath, then raised his goblet too. "To heroes, and the wasted opportunities that their deaths cause."

"And to the inspiration to our cause that they have been both living and dead," said Moon, quickly, as if to expunge Autumn's cynicism.

Xavier raised his own goblet, and paused before adding "…and to the city he strove to protect, as is our own sworn duty, as he would be the first to remind us."

The five turned their backs on each other, raised their masks slightly, and drank a toast; then returned to their seats again. The great black Sun Face was the first to break the silence.

"Our time is near upon us, but Lord Feron's unexpected sacrifice creates a dual problem for us. He was fully committed to our cause and our best hope; now we have no obvious candidate to succeed the Duca, but the foment in the lower city that his execution has caused may be the perfect opportunity to act. We must not waste time and effort crying over spilt milk, but must focus upon the task at hand; find a replacement for Lord Feron as a pretender to the throne. Until we have one, or a plan for one, we cannot proceed. Tragedy; your task was to assess the rumours about this actor, Abelard; are the rumours about the play true, and are the Seneschal's Men in fact spreading sedition?"

Xavier shook his head sadly. "Abelard is unremarkable; the rumours we had heard were, I think, more to do with the audience reading too much into a satire than anything to do with the actor's talents. Certainly, I saw nothing to suggest to me that he would be capable of raising the mob – and I was watching with generous eyes, hoping for a miracle. No, he's no Feron come again, and while the furore that the play has caused might be turned to our advantage, I certainly don't think there's anything useful that Abelard can do beyond what he has done already, which is distract official eyes away from us."

"Damn; I had high hopes for him." Autumn shook his head. "A man from the theatre – it would have been perfect. So in one dire week we lose both our prime champion and our best hope for a fall-back position. It begins to look rather grim for us, my friends... what are we to do now?"

Again, it was the Pater who darkened the mood; "If Feron's blood is not enough for us to launch the ship of mutiny then what is? The Duca's mad, the aristocracy obsessed with gambling, perversions and whores, the poor are taxed, crowded and disregarded in their ghettoes. Surely in the face of that a captain will arise?"

Xavier reluctantly raised his hand. "The mood of the city is getting worse and worse. The Duca's executions are decimating the nobility. His sister is keeping bare control of him as it is – but he sees threats and conspiracies everywhere."

Moon snorted. "That's not paranoia, that's just perceptiveness."

Autumn leaned forward. "That's as maybe. I don't imagine we're the only conspirators against the Duca but we are by far the best hidden and probably the most influential. But with Feron dead, who succeeds Augustin di Gialla if we depose him? There's nobody so populist as him."

"I suppose there's no chance the Seneschal could be persuaded?" Pater Felicio knew the answer but had to ask the question. Xavier shifted uncomfortably. Any new discussion of possible successors to the Duca would eventually roost closer to him than he was comfortable with...

"Schermo won't take the throne. He could have had it ten times over by now if that had been his ambition. He's a military man through and through." The Black Sun mask inclined to him again, fractionally. "The Tuffatore family is the next most prominent in terms of hereditary descent; we can control Lord di Tuffatore if we have to; he's not too far from the throne and if he marries Ophelia di Gialla we can engineer a political alliance between old Republican senatorial blood and the Ducal line, which serves our purposes just as well."

Autumn snorted. "Hereditary descent is all very well, but the Imperium fell six centuries ago and people put less stock in the old Senatorial families than you might imagine. And as far as he goes, people are *really* going to ask questions if too many of his paramours fall to their death, you know. He's well enough liked by the lower sorts but the bourgeois and the nobility have little time for him, *especially* the d'Amatos. What about Lord Prospero? The House of the Three Lions is old and respected."

Xavier gritted his teeth and quietly congratulated himself on his self control. *Thank the Gods for masks.* He shook his head. "Too uncontrollable. And too clever, too; he wouldn't be led. Never underestimate how sharp the mind behind that buffoon's exterior is; he's the cleverest man in the city, and he knows it too. Whoever it is, there will need to be something that will cut across the class divide in the city and win universal support, appeal to everyone."

Autumn leaned back in his chair. "So no military coup and none of the nobility are likely to rise to the occasion after the example made of Feron. Our list of options grows exceedingly thin. What about a religious takeover? Cult of the Father declaring a theocracy?"

Pater Felicio shook his head tiredly. This was not the first time this ground had been trodden, and his argument was all too well-rehearsed. "I'll not prostitute the Church just to exchange one tyrant for another. We've no choice but to wait for a suitable candidate to present themselves, and then to move as fast as possible to back them, and hope the people will forgive us our tardiness..."

His words chimed with Xavier. The Secret Senate was supposed to stand as a guarantor for the rule of law, not sit idly by while Cittàvecchio sank into the mire. "What? If we wait much longer there will be no Cittàvecchio for us to save! I know the tenor of the Rookeries; I have eyes there. These foul murders..."

And with their mention, an electric thrill ran round the room. Several made to speak at once but it was Moon who got there first, a salacious tang in her voice. "Yes, these murders, so vile they rise above even the run of death and misery that's to be expected from such places. Five so far, they say, cut up like butcher's sausage-meat, their eyes burst with a prick of a knife, and their faces cut clean from the bone and thrown to the cats." She shuddered, but was plainly relishing the description.

"Someone does not like masks," said Sun Face into the spreading silence, pointedly.

Xavier shifted uncomfortably, but continued doggedly with his point. "Do not underestimate the fury building in those tenements. Feron understood this; he knew the key to the city was the Rookeries and in all honesty that's probably why the Duca had him killed. There is a power rising among the most humble of the Cittàvecchi; we can harness it or be swept aside by it and see our plans brought to nothing. And even if the rest of you are unprepared to count the concerns of the city's poor, I will not let them pass unregarded. If we wait too long we risk being overtaken by events..."

Felicio leaned forward, the copper beard of the Old Man of the Sea glinting in the candlelight. "If, as Tragedy seems so certain, the key to overthrowing the Duca lies among the Rookeries, then we must seek to understand what it is that drives them – and to my eye at least, that is anger at the execution of Lord Feron and outrage at these murders. Never have I known them so united in anger. So; is anyone prepared to admit to involvement in these killings? I know naught of them save what any on the street knows."

"Nor I," said Xavier, watching his compatriots keenly.

Moon threw her hands in the air. "I neither. Though I would like to know who it is."

"I have no involvement..." Autumn sat, very still. Everyone turned to look at Sun Face, who had not moved. The great mask looked straight at Xavier, and the pause lengthened uncomfortably. Xavier was just about to speak when Sun face interrupted.

"I am aware of the motives behind the killings, and I believe I know the killer's identity."

The four other senators stared at Sun Face as if their strings had been cut. Autumn recovered first.

"Tell us!"

"I cannot. It would infringe the oath of secrecy between us."

Xavier shot to his feet. "The killer is one of *us?*"

"Or one close to us. I cannot say. But be assured – these deaths, though gruesome and unkind, serve the greater whole and will in time be shown for what they are."

Felicio joined Xavier on his feet. "Is someone here acting without the group's knowledge or permission? I will not be hanged for something I know nothing of! Are our hands to be bloodied –?"

"Already, tenfold." Moon cut him off brutally. "Now is not the time for squeamishness. Whoever it is, that has done this, I applaud your subtlety as much as I abhor your methods, but what's done is done. We must take advantage of this unlooked-for opportunity and press on. How do we hang these deaths on the Duca?"

"I like this not." Autumn shook his head. Xavier, reluctantly, took his seat again. "Nor I. I'll not sanction or support anything to do with those murders, and if I find out one of you is behind it then oath or not there will be *consequences*, understand? If you meddle with the Rookeries you play with fire."

"Then let us take full care. Your point, and your fervour is duly noted, Tragedy. Do not belabour the matter." Sun Face regarded them all in turn, staring at Felicio until, grumbling, he took his seat again. The Moon is right. The Duca's attentions are on the Rookeries, he knows not what occurs there, and with every passing murder the residents become more inflamed. Already "citizens watches" are springing up, with the usual violent results for any strangers, foreigners or unfortunates in the area. We must watch, guide the mood and the events there, use them to our various advantages. You all have your own means of doing this; do not waste the opportunity that the murders afford us. If we cannot find a candidate, then we must engineer a coup and hope that a candidate emerges that we can steer or at least influence. But the conjunction of circumstances we have now is not likely to ever be repeated – so we use it, and we move quickly. Understood?" She nodded. "Next point!"

There was a long pause, as everyone looked back and forth at each other, unwilling to leave the topic be. Eventually, with a sigh, Sun Face threw her hands in the air theatrically. "Shy kittens, you are. You cannot make an omelette without spilling a little claret. Time is short and still we have no pretender! We *must* take advantage of what we can!"

Moon stood; everyone's eyes went to her. "I have been thinking about that. It's obvious now that we have no clear contender to take the throne from the Duca – but what if we are going about this the wrong way? We need to think about not a personality, but an icon – something the entire city will be able to invest in, focus on. The successor to the Duca, whoever he or she may be, needs to have something that will draw everyone, from across the social strata of Cittàvecchio. Something that the nobility will respect just as much as the underclass of the Rookeries. And I believe I have come across exactly the thing that satisfies that requirement; an emblem of the City, of its past and of its power – because no matter from what social strata one of the Cittavecchi comes, if you scratch them they bleed pure superstition. All we need to do is acquire the cards -."

"Wait. Cards, you say?" Autumn, his voice suddenly harsh and perhaps a touch menacing. *Damn,* thought Xavier. *Where have I heard that voice before?*

"Indeed." Moon inclined her mask.

"*Specific* cards?" There was definitely a dangerous edge in Autumn's voice now.

"Aye…" Moon nodded to Autumn. *You have grasped the scheme, I see…* but it was Sun Face the breathed the words.

"You speak of the *Re Stracciati* deck."

"I do," said Moon.

Xavier stared at Moon, unable to fit what she had just said into his head. Pater Felicio, however, clearly had no such trouble. He shot to his feet with the speed of a demented jack in the box. Autumn was not far behind him. "Madness! Madness!" roared Felicio. "Lunacy! Setting aside for a moment the history of those cards and the connotations they carry, that cursed deck is guarded by the might of the Janizaries! The Grafs of Buchara would come down from the mountains like a scourge and..."

"Precisely my purpose," said Moon, primly. "Let them come if they dare. And no, I do not propose to disregard the deck's history. I propose to *use* it. This is an age of reason and science; men of knowledge and wit – such as we are supposed to be, Old Man of the Sea - will dismiss the curse of the cards as a story to frighten children. But they cannot deny that the cards are a powerful and potent emblem of this city and of its Imperial past! The soothsaying cards of the Tattered King himself - such an emblem in the hands of a pretender to the Duca's throne would not just unite the city across class divides, it would unite them against the upstart Bucharans as well! Nothing unites a city behind a new leader like the threat of war, and this gives us an opportunity to move matters at our pace; to ready the population for the inevitable and to put the Bucharans off guard."

Felicio Caritavo sat back in his chair, disbelief radiating from every pore. "And how, pray tell, do you propose to persuade the Grafs of Buchara that they wish to play their part in this drama and gift us with a great relic of Cittàvecchio's Imperial past – a relic they themselves believe they keep from us for safety's sake? Will they simply return it because you send a polite note?"

"The Bucharans don't need to know anything about this until the deck is in our hands." Moon sat, and crossed her legs demurely.

Autumn gawped at her. "You propose to *steal* them?"

Xavier shook his head in disbelief. *It's all very well to depose the Duca but you risk replacing him with foreign invaders ten times worse by this strategy, and all for the sake of a deck of cards that, unless I miss my guess, you want just as much as a change of power here in Cittàvecchio. What is your real purpose here, Moon? Because it is surely not the goal of the Senate...* "This is madness! Stealing them means outright war!"

Sun Face stood, slowly. "War is inevitable. Five, ten, twenty years. Buchara is a growing power, albeit internally unstable; we are seen as the ancient Imperial past that refuses to die. But a pretender to the Ducal throne – *any* pretender - with the cards as a symbol of the Imperial Republic reborn... that's a different matter. Buchara may not be so keen to attack immediately; they have other military commitments and other concerns. They would proceed cautiously – and their superstitious nature could be used against them." The voice, full of enthusiasm for the enterprise, sounded more female than male to Xavier, though he was still not sure... and in the voice he heard, plainly, greed. *You want the cards too. Are you in this with Moon?*

"Still madness." Felicio, at least, was dismissive of the entire enterprise. Encouraged, Xavier decided to risk speaking out. "I agree. It is folly. This and the murders too; are we thieves and madmen?"

Sun Face hissed beneath her mask and stared at each of them in turn, peering into their porcelain faces. "Need I remind you all that the Duca would kill us all in but a heartbeat for no better reason than the colour of our eyes? We are sworn to the greater good of the City and the downfall of the tyrant. Are you now squeamish at the tools to be used? Or perhaps children to be frightened by old tales? The *Re Stracciati* was a fairy tale, a story to frighten the barbarians – a man in a ragged coat, you fools. Do you fear him too, six hundred years on? Let us take a leaf from our Imperial ancestors' book – let us dress in ragged robes and pretend to be a god, the better to keep the ignorant in place."

Moon weighed in now, animated and using her arms for emphasis. "And anything that keeps the Grafs of Buchara at each others' throats keeps them away from our own a little longer. The loss of the deck will set them to infighting as they try to apportion blame. The Bucharans are a superstitious people. They might see this as an attempt to return to the old Imperial days, with all that entails. Only a fool would imagine that we would not be at war with Buchara inside the next ten years anyway; this gives us an opportunity to stall matters for a little longer, perhaps to even take control of events. Now; let us take a census. Are we resolved?" Moon raised her gloved hand.

"Aye." Sun Face raised her hand. Autumn, with a nod, did the same. All three looked at Xavier.

He mulled it over. An opposing vote at this stage would be futile anyway; "Aye. Reluctantly."

Felicio cursed under his breath. "This will be the living end of us, mark my words. But aye, since you are resolved and my opposition would be a formality."

The five took their seats again; the discussion had proven a little more heated than expected. Sun Face readjusted her robes, and then looked brightly round the room. "Has anyone an agent they can use?"

Felicio, slumped defeated in his chair, raised his hand. "I know of a suitable man, a soldier of fortune on retainer to an ally. Among those who know of such things he is renowned for his skills on the second storey. He will do as he is bid and is reliable, though not cheap."

"Money is no object," interjected Moon, swiftly. Her eyes glittered like emeralds.

Felicio barked a bitter laugh. "No? A phrase often used and seldom meant. And the chosen fence? Elizabeta Zancani?"

Moon nodded. "The Lady is known among those who are concerned with such things as something of a fence for stolen objets d'art. Once we know she has the cards, we can direct our chosen man to procure them at auction and use them as a rallying point. And Zancani can be trusted to co-operate."

Felicio shrugged. "I'll have my man deliver the cards to her within a fortnight. We can expect trouble from Buchara no more than a few days after that, so we must be ready to move fast, and we should probably meet soon after to set things in motion."

Sun Face clapped her hands three times and stood. "Brothers, sisters. We have worked for this in secret for months. Keep faith and hold fast, for the Republic is at hand." She looked from one to another; Xavier, tense and uncomfortable; Felicio slumped in his chair behind his mask, Moon bolt upright with enthusiasm and Autumn again examining his fingernails. He looked up from them and met her gaze.

"I have a problem, another piece of business."

Sun looked discomfited for a moment, then regained her poise. "You do?"

"The Duca's sister's witch. Calomena Giraldus. She has been asking… questions. Leading questions; especially since Feron's arrest. The kind that would get anyone else a dip in the canal with lovely granite slippers. But one does not just 'disappear' a witch."

Moon let out a delicate little laugh from behind her smiling mask. "No, you do not. Especially one with such connections to the palace. I too have noted her interest in my works. Do you think she is looking for us? Perhaps behind Feron's execution and looking for more? Who dealt primarily with Feron?"

"I did," said Pater Felicio. "he did not know my identity, and he did not know anyone else's. He would not have given us up under torture, but perhaps we should all be a little more cautious…"

Xavier watched the exchange narrowly, his mind on the exchange on the dockside the previous night. Suddenly, it had taken on a whole new complexion and depth of meaning. *Is she looking for us; or is she serving us notice that she's already found us?*

"I have had what may be termed a blunt warning," he said, and watched that settle on them. "I think she knows at least two of our identities. This represents a serious danger to the Senate."

Sun Face nodded. "Then we must be on our guard, and seek opportunities to remove this problem - be not afraid to take any such gift the fates offer you. It is only to be expected that as we close upon our goal the dangers we face come thick and fast."

Autumn stood, abruptly. "The sacrament is passing; we should adjourn."

Xavier looked up, puzzled; he felt no different; the familiar blurring of the senses was still on him in full force. But Felicio stood too; "Aye. Brothers and sisters, Adieu. We shall meet in a few days time to discuss how we propose to approach the task of actually removing the Duca. Festivàle Week is almost upon us and we'll likely not see a better chance this side of the solstice."

Felicio, Moon and Autumn all made their polite farewells and each took a different route from the chamber, through one of the archways that filled the eight walls. Only Sun face remained, watching Xavier carefully. She reached out and softly touched the side of the mask, along Xavier's jaw line. He froze, uncertain of what this bizarre behaviour was likely to lead to, but that seemed sufficient for Sun face; she turned and went to her own archway. Before she left, however, she looked back at Xavier, still seated in his chair.

"You will know what to do when the time comes, Xavier."

She inclined her head, and left Xavier to himself. He rose to his feet, but they were unsteady beneath him.

Something is wrong...

* * *

It was close to an hour and a half past midnight when Gratiano paid the boatman and disembarked on the small landing stage at the foot of the *via Fiore della Ciliega*, the Road of Cherry

Blossoms[2]. This close to the river, the city fog had an almost tangible presence, curling and roiling like milk in water; shying away from the great oil lanterns hung from the landing stage as if too much light exposed it for what it was. This fog, like many of the city's inhabitants, was far more comfortable in the dark where its true nature could only be guessed.

To Gratiano's left, at the very foot of *via Fiore della Ciliega*, an enormous set of wrought iron gates filled a great marble archway. A smaller postern gate set within them stood ajar, and Gratiano pushed it open and passed into the Court of the Dragon.

The great square courtyard was renowned throughout Cittàvecchio as the centre of Bucharan culture in the city; it was here that the merchants and traders of the distant northern river city clustered, here they set up their shops and foundries, their warehouses and their industries. And, of course, their restaurants. The *Priest's Hole* was one of the most desirable eating-houses in the city, both for the spiced cuisine of Buchara and for the cachet that comes with the foreign and the new.

Cittàvecchio viewed it's northern cousin with a jaundiced eye; Buchara was a rising power in trade, but the river which made it so powerful ran north-west to south-east, taking it far from Cittàvecchio's sphere of influence. In perhaps a decade or so when Buchara's expansion brushed the skirts of the older city, there would be a clash of interests but for now the only direct trade routes were by caravan through the rugged mountain passes or by long voyage around the Hellenes. Buchara's military might was on land; Cittàvecchio's at sea, and sea power controls sea trade. Buchara prosecuted a war of conquest and conversion

---

[2] One of Cittàvecchio's four longest unbroken streets without flooded sections, *via Fiore della Ciliega* runs from the Court of the Dragon at waterside all the way to the Grand Piazza over three major bridges. The story has it that it was the route by which food was brought into the old city during the Great Siege, and the cherry and lime trees which line it now sprang from fruit which fell from the disguised carts used to smuggle supplies. The combination of the trees and its status as one of the driest locations in Cittàvecchio make addresses on *via Fiore della Ciliega* amongst the most desirable in the city to this day.

among the heathens to its north; Cittàvecchio had long ago become more relaxed about its religious outlook. So for now, the older city encouraged cultural outposts like the Court of the Dragon; they fostered amity in the short term, and provided valuable intelligence in the longer view.

The Court of the Dragon itself was a wide marble square, bounded on three sides by tall buildings and on the fourth by a series of mews over what were once stables but had now been converted into a series of open-air restaurants, workshops and mercantile emporia. In the centre of the courtyard lay a great fountain bath. Rearing from its centre, stained with verdigris, was the great baroque dragon in copper-chased ironwork from which the courtyard took its name.

Gratiano looked up at the great snarling beast, the symbol of the Grafs of Buchara and like most native Cittàvecchi do he reached out and rubbed its belly for luck, his fingers moving over the metal worn smooth by the generations of locals who had performed this little rite before him.

The *Priest's Hole* was based in one of the great stone arches that had once been part of the stables, before the city's sinking made horse traffic impractical. Small, discreet tables, protected from one another by movable wooden screens, lined the walls, with larger areas for group dining in the centre. The smells of spiced cooking and the heat from the great ovens at the back of the restaurant held back the night mist and the damp like a great wall.

Gratiano signalled the maitre d' and took a seat at one of the smaller tables near the wall; and as was his wont, he fell into observing the other patrons. Such observations married to a keen awareness of the social climate in Cittàvecchio kept Gratiano in gossip; and while a man might find himself temporarily without gold, a man without gossip had *no* friends at Court.

Most of the clientele at this hour was the fashionable end of society; like Gratiano himself, out for a late supper after an evening at the tables or at a succession of soirees. Minor nobility drunk and fumbling, making slurred advances to their consorts;

single men drowning their sorrows or celebrating their fortune; here and there small groups, heads huddled together, whispering daring sedition they would not remember when sober. Earlier in the evening, one might expect to see social stars of the scene here but by this hour most had found parties to attend or company that did not require the persuasion of an excellent meal and a fine wine.

The other major activity practiced at the *Priest's Hole* was of course, espionage. Being a favoured spot for both local traders and merchants coming in from Buchara over the mountains, the café was a traditional sparring ground between the Ducal spies, those working for the Grafs and those working for independent mercantile concerns from further afield. On a good night, nobody in the *Priest's Hole* spoke with a Cittàvecchi accent save the waiters.

The tall, rugged-looking man with dark curly hair who sat alone at a wall table belonged in neither camp, however, and gave Gratiano a familiar nod of polite recognition; Gratiano wondered for a moment if this were a deliberate setup or perhaps some game of the fates. Mercutio del Richo.

Mercutio was a gentleman of moderate means, occasionally seen at the Red Lion or other gambling establishments and a "known associate" (which meant, in the oblique parlance of the Cittàvecchi underworld, partner, lover or both) of the auctioneer and art collector Elizabeta Zancani. Gratiano heard things of him occasionally; that he was out of the city often, on business for one or another of the noble families and, occasionally, one heard it whispered that if one needed something done that might not be strictly legal, then del Richo was your man. Hearsay, of course; but Gratiano's lifeblood was hearsay and the fascinating things it could be parleyed into at a party.

Mercutio did not keep his attention on Gratiano but toyed with a small knife, fiddling with the candle on the table, and did not touch his drink; clearly waiting for someone. What's more, he'd hooked his sword-belt over the back of his chair, so that the swept hilt was easily visible, and easily accessible. The kind of thing one does when used to drinking in environments considerably less refined than the *Priest's Hole,* he mused. He noted with some interest that the sword was a businesslike one; no fancy engraving or swooping design; just a serviceable swept hilt, a junior officer's sword. The kind that was designed to be *used*, not *looked at.*

He had not realised that he was watching del Richo so intently; abruptly, his line of view was blocked. A new arrival, sitting at the stranger's table, and a notable one at that. An older man, quite thickset, his hair and beard greying from their original ginger. He carried himself with the air of a man used to deference but trying to conceal it, and though he wore only the simple black velvet robes of a priest, Gratiano had little difficulty identifying him. Pater Felicio Caritavo, the Keeper of the Keys of the Cathedrale of the Holy Trinity, and one of the most senior prelates in Cittàvecchio. What would bring him to the Court of the Dragon, without his guards, in a humble priest's robes, at near two in the morning? Something about Buchara – well, that's predictable enough. And a timescale of a month. And that tone of voice suggests a negotiation over a fee.

Gratiano's attention was diverted for a moment from the two men by the arrival of the waiter. "My Lord dell'Allia? Lord d'Orlato has just sent a messenger down from the Castell'nuero; he is delayed on the Seneschal's business and will be unable to join you, but he bids you dine on his account."

Gratiano nodded, and scanned the proffered menu, selecting something light he could peck at, and a good wine. Whatever was occupying the two men, it obviously engrossed them.

As the waiter leaned in to recover the menu, Gratiano grabbed him by the arm and with a sweeping gesture, knocked the candle over on the table. The waiter jumped back, then immediately set to cleaning up the mess, apologising profusely. Gratiano stood, brushed himself down and made nothing of it; but while the waiter cleaned up the broken bottle, he seated himself – with his back to the two men – a table closer. The waiter, who was no stranger to such affairs, winked at this, and Gratiano left a half-ducat coin on the table to buy the man's goodwill. The two men paused in their conversation and watched a moment; then, once

Gratiano was re-seated, they continued as if nothing had happened. Another of the fine traditions of the Cittàvecchi; politeness dictates that one *does not see* clumsiness or ill luck.

He might be no longer able to see the objects of his interest, but by leaning back casually in his chair he was now in a much better position to hear their whispered tones. Still too far to catch their conversation in full without blatant eavesdropping, he had to make do with a snatched word here and there.

The waiter arrived with his shrimp, and while he set the plate and glasses, Gratiano lost the thread of the conversation behind him. Once the clattering and the polite fuss was out of the way, he bent his head slightly to try and catch the rest of the conversation but, to his dismay, realised that the Pater had risen to his feet.

"Lord dell'Allia. Do you mind if I join you?"

"Pater." Gratiano got to his feet. "Not at all. I was due to take supper with Lord d'Orlato but he was called away. By all means, be seated."

Felicio assumed a carefully schooled expression of regret and poured himself a generous glass of Gratiano's wine. It was hard not to notice that his hands were shaking. "I had hoped to slip in and out unnoticed; what ill fortune for me that you should spot me."

Gratiano glanced up at him over his shrimp. *Damn.* "I assumed you were conducting Church business, Pater, and would not be so rude as to enquire after the details."

"Good; good. It is a matter of, shall we say, *some delicacy*. On behalf of a young priest who has been... a touch indiscreet. Master del Richo is tidying some affairs up for me in the country."

Gratiano nodded understandingly. "It is human nature for such things to occur, alas. We live in an imperfect world. And I have employed Mercutio myself before – so I know to be incurious."

Pater Felicio smiled, and it was as if the sun had emerged from behind a cloud. "Then I can rely upon your discretion in this matter, My Lord?"

"Always happy to assist the Cathedrale in any way I can, Pater."

"Good; good. Then if you will give me leave, my Lord, I should get back. I have a night service to prepare for." Felicio rose to his feet, and gave Gratiano a formal bow; Gratiano stood, and returned it. Pater Felicio raised his mask, carved in the likeness of a bearded man with seashells and starfish in his hair and beard, and swept out into the mists.

Gratiano watched him go with some interest as the bells sounded two. He craned his head around to check, but Mercutio del Richo had left silently at some point during the conversation.

A pretty pack of lies, Good Pater. What on earth are you up to? Gratiano mulled the conversation for a moment or two, then smiled to himself. *So; Mercutio's out of town for an evening or two on business. That explains a great deal.*

He finished his shrimp with every evidence of enjoyment, and then set off across town. It was not that far to the Palazzo di Zancani, and the Donna was a notorious night-owl. Besides; he felt the urge to admire some *late-night art.*

*   *   *

Xavier shook his hair free of the mask, then stumbled a moment, disoriented. The sacrament, which all of the Secret Senate partook of before each meeting, usually had a mild hallucinogenic effect. The reason, so Sun Face had told him, was partly to loosen the tongue and allow for free exchange of ideas and partly to blur the eyes so that any inadvertent clue to the identity of fellow members of the Senate would be missed or forgotten.

He could still taste the hot spicy flavour of the drink in the back of his throat; normally by now, its effects would have worn off. He held out his hand, palm down, in front of him and to his dismay realised he could not even tell if it was shaking, so blurred was his vision. He gripped the back of the chair for support and the leaden mask of Tragedy fell to the floor unheeded.

Only Sun Face knew the identity of each of the Senate; they knew each other only by their masks. Tragedy, Autumn, The Old Man of the Sea, Laughing Moon and the Black Sun; and, up until last week, the Pole Star.

Something is wrong... something is very wrong...

Once there had been others; Comedy and the North Wind, but their lineages had come to an end long before Xavier took up the mask of Tragedy, Sun Face had not seen fit to pass the masks and the secret knowledge of the Senate on to any successors, and now with the culmination of the Senate's long campaign in the shadows so close, there was neither the time nor really the need to do so. Five would have to be sufficient.

Or perhaps just four.

Did you see any of the others drink?

No. Fool.

Xavier clung to the chair as his legs gave out beneath him. He saw movement on the edge of his fogged vision and reached out for it, trying to form a cry for help, but the words would not come. A sense of the most profound betrayal swept over him, all the more intense for having no object to focus on.

The movement resolved itself into a woman, standing on the edge of his vision. All he could see was a long voluminous cloak and a great beaked mask, golden spectacles painted around the eyes. *Il Dottore*, the plague-doctor.

"Puh-*puh*- poi- "

Fear not, Xavier. You are not poisoned, said *il Dottore* in a young-old voice. *Indeed, you have never been more alive than you are in this moment. It is time you saw the city as it truly is. Time you saw the Secret Commonwealth, and understood for whom it is we do what we do. Fear not, you will not come to harm, if you are wise and courteous. And if you tell no lie.*

"Father, Mother and Holy Child save me; who are you? *What* are you?"

Il Dottore leaned over Xavier and touched his face, gently, her gloved hand tracing his cheekbone. The long nose of the mask touched the end of Xavier's, and he looked into the glittering eyes behind it, full of secrets and old wisdom. Incongruously, all Xavier could smell was lacquer, camphor and the faintest hint of the night fogs; water, damp stone and moss. He tried to move his head aside, but control and consciousness were deserting him fast; and those glittering, shining eyes came closer still.

There will be no lies between us, will there? No lies between you and me, Xavier. She touched his lips, and he tasted again the spice of the sacrament.

Panic rose in Xavier as *il Dottore* swept her cloak over him and bore him up, but the sacrament had done its work. Movement was impossible, voice fled and vision, finally, dimmed. Darkness fell.

'My nerves are bad to-night. Yes, bad.

Stay with me.

'Speak to me. Why do you never speak? Speak.

'What are you thinking of?

What thinking? What?

'I never know what you are thinking. Think.'

I think we are in rats' alley

Where the dead men lost their bones.

T.S. Eliot, The Waste Land 111-116

Gratiano arrived in the courtyard outside the Palazzo di Zancani shortly before three bells; as he had suspected, there were lights still showing on the first floor of the gallery. The great courtyard before the auction-house of the Zancani family was a wide, rectangular area at the junction of three streets; it was known colloquially among the Cittàvecchi as the Court of the Lion and Serpent, for the statue in the centre of the square's fountain. A great rearing lion, entwined and wrapped by the coils of the snake it fought, cast in bronze. It depended on the time of day and the angle of the light as to whether you thought the lion or the serpent was winning – and city legend claimed that oftentimes the statue moved to represent the triumphs or tragedies of one city faction over another. All of the guilds, the great families and the city bodies had their own stories and legends about the statue.

Looming out of the night fogs, it was easy for the statue to take one by surprise; Gratiano glanced up at it as he always did, and noted that today the lion seemed to be getting the better of the serpent. Tomorrow was another day, though, and serpents were, by their very nature, tricksy beasts. Besides – it was just an optical illusion, an artefact of fog, moonlight, perspective and very clever sculpture. He wasn't a child, to be frightened by legends.

With long-practiced ease, he made his way to the corner of the courtyard and shimmied up a dangling length of vine, using the trellis behind it as support. It terminated on a broad marble balcony, with two tall windows. They stood ajar, and were lit from within, the light making the night fog boil like smoke.

He sidled up to the windows, taking the rose he had stolen from a street side flower seller out of his pocket and placing it between his teeth. From within, the scent of incense billowed out in clouds, competing with the smell of burning cedar wood and the night smell of the fog; for a moment, he entertained the possibility that perhaps the Donna Elizabeta was entertaining someone else tonight.

No – her look had been unmistakable. And finding out that Mercutio was out of town – that just confirmed it.

He moved the drape aside silently and made to enter the room; but there was nobody inside. The bed lay prepared, the covers thrown back and rose petals scattered. Incense burned in holders but there was no sign of the Donna.

Then he felt the knife.

* * *

Ever since the time of the Tattered King, before the flood and the subsidence and the Great Siege that ended the Imperium and gave the city its new name, Castell'nuero has been the centre of government of Cittàvecchio. Nowadays it was the seat of the Duca's court, the office of the Lord Seneschal and the offices of the *Vigilanza*, the Night-Watch, and it was to this latter that Lord Gawain d'Orlato came. Messengers had been scouring the city on the word of the Watch Captain; they had found him, finally, in the Grand Piazza, stood alone in the mist, in curious contemplation of the Cathedrale.

Gian Galeazzo Visconti met him at the lower postern gate of the great black fortress, his face grim and his attitude respectful but bullish. "My Lord; I apologise for the summons but I did not want to wake the Seneschal, and I seek the advice of a higher authority…"

Gawain did not break stride and Visconti fell in step with him. The fog parted for them like water before a boat as they ascended the steps to the great brooding barbican. "I assume that something of serious complexion has occurred for you to come to such a decision, Captain…"

"Another murder, my Lord."

"This is Cittàvecchio, Captain. There's a murder every night, three at weekends and that doesn't count holidays, executions and duels."

"Indeed, sir. I wouldn't trouble you for simple mayhem; this is our friend the mask maker again."

Gawain's lip curled. "You should not call him that. I do not think it is his purpose to be so called." They entered the main guardhouse to the right of the barbican entrance, and passed through several outer chambers and into the makeshift morgue.

The body lay on a hastily erected trestle, covered with a sheet already stained with the ruin of what lay beneath it. On the cold stone flags, a puddle of juices had formed, dripping from the planks. At the head of the table, on a bloodstained cloth lay the tools of the chirurgeon, still clotted with the victim's blood.

Stood behind the trestle was a tall, broad-shouldered man in polished bronze cuirass and gold-trimmed red cloak. He held a plumed helmet under his arm, leaving his close-shaven head bare. His pale eyes were on the corpse. As Visconti and Gawain entered, he glanced up at them, his face remaining impassive. Gawain met his gaze and noted with some internal amusement that his pupils were dilated; *interrupted something, did we?*

"Lord d'Orlato."

"Captain Valentin. What business has the Ducal Guard here?"

"The Duca wishes to know what steps are being taken to secure the safety of law-abiding citizens in the face of this continuing outrage. Why are you here?"

Gawain snorted in derision. "You'll be lucky to *find* a law-abiding citizen awake at this hour, Valentin." He flicked back the sheet covering the corpse and examined the ghastly injuries with cheery interest. "Just the same as the others. Did you find the face?"

Visconti gestured to a glass jar on the mantel. "The cats had been at it, as before, but we have a tentative identification from clothes and distinguishing marks. We think it's the actor, Abelard. The one from the *Revenger's Tragedy*? He was seen at the Red Lion early in the evening, but left after losing heavily to some visiting Northmen. He was found in the Quadrangle of the Red Bishop in the Rookeries."

Gawain smiled distantly. "Yes, I was in the *Lion* myself. I bumped into him at the bar. He looked quite dejected, but he was still there when I left at nine bells. The Quad of the Red Bishop is miles away from the *Lion*; how did he get there? What did the chirurgeon have to say?"

Visconti spat out the litany of ruin in short, sharp sentences. "Cause of death was loss of vital fluids through slow bleeding; he lay and died slowly without his eyes or his face. We think the murder occurred where we found him. Tongue was cut out after death. Time of death was between twelve bells and one. Sixteen separate stab wounds, all with a sharp, thin blade, straight and double-edged, about five to six inches long. Each one either cut an artery or a major muscle; he couldn't move or speak. Whoever did this is a gifted chirurgeon."

"Or a devil made flesh," commented Valentin neutrally. Visconti and Gawain both glanced askance at him, but his face was still placid.

Gawain pulled the sheet back over the dead actor. "What's the feeling in the Rookeries, Gian?"

"Bad." Visconti slumped into a chair, balancing his sword across his knees, and ran his hand through his hair. "I had to take a detachment of twenty in to retrieve the body, and I'll wager that by dawn all the Old Quarter will know of this. This is the sixth murder in as many months and as far as they are concerned we do nothing. There is nothing to do! Six bodies left in the Rookeries, mutilated, defiled and with their faces cut away and their tongues removed... and usually nobody sees anything! It's as if the night mist itself came in and cut them up itself."

"Captain; you don't carry a mask with you, I notice."

Visconti leaned back in his chair and quirked an eyebrow. "No, I don't. I don't consider it appropriate while I am on duty. The representative of the Duca's law should always go barefaced and honest when he represents that law. Why do you ask?"

Gawain nodded, lost in thought a moment. "A theory I have been mulling over, nothing solid. So what do you want with us, Captain? This is your jurisdiction, a Watch affair. There's little enough for us to do here but stare at the cooling corpse of an unfortunate actor."

"We will have mob justice tomorrow. The last few were traders, beggars, nobodies. Their families might agitate in Court for action but the Rookeries cared little for them save that they were left in their territory. Abelard was a popular actor and was from the Rookeries – one of their own made good. This might get much worse. We either need a scapegoat or I will need the loan of troops, either Ducal Guard or regular military, to go into the Rookeries and keep order while we investigate."

Gawain shook his head. "The Lord Seneschal will refuse. He won't put troops on the streets of Cittàvecchio, not for you, not for me, and, I suspect, not for the Duca. And I don't accept that the identity of the actor makes this any different to any of the previous killings. The inhabitants of the Rookeries aren't known for following highbrow theatre. This is another unfortunate dead man who strayed from the path into a part of the city he should not have, and paid with his life. Cittàvecchio is not all leafy boulevards and soirees for people like this. Behind the mask, the old lady is an ugly and vicious whore. You know that best of all of us, Gian."

"There will be *riots*, my lord. And lynch mobs. Because this time, there is a *witness*."

Valentin had been paying little attention to the discussion, instead watching the corpse narrowly as if expecting it to do something startling. He hissed, abruptly.

"The tongues. Our killer is a superstitious man. He is cutting out the tongues to *silence* them after death."

* * *

The boat was lost in a sea of mist, no features discernible to either side save the gentle lap of water against the gunwales, and the quiet ripple of the pole as the boatman manoeuvred the vessel. Xavier blinked several times to make sure the fog in his vision was the normal kind from the river and not the kind induced by suspicious drinks. He sat up slowly and cautiously. *Il Dottore* continued to pole the boat with slow, sure strokes, and did not react to her passenger's awakening.

Indistinct shapes loomed out of the mist and then faded; the ghosts of buildings dark and unlit. Sonorously in the distance, the peals muffled, the Cathedrale sounded four bells.

Xavier tried to summon up some enthusiasm for a good old-fashioned panic, but could not manage much more than a tone of mild peevishness. "The hour is very late. If you propose to kidnap me you could at least have the good grace to tell me where are you taking me?"

Il Dottore remained silent, but gestured with one hand off into the mists. The waters to the side of the boat rippled here and there, and the closer Xavier looked, the more suspicious the ripples appeared. Their shape suggested a more than random purpose in the water, and the way the long strands of weed flowed just beneath the surface could almost suggest hair…

The Undines have come to escort you to the Courtyard. Be courteous, and thank them; they will come to you in dreams and whisper secrets in your ear if you find favour with them.

"And if I do not?"

Fear death by water, said *il Dottore* flatly.

A pier loomed out of the mist, a set of weed-draped steps rising up to firm dry land along the side of a great stone pylon. As the boat drew alongside, the children of the water sank down into the murky depths, casting longing glances at the world of air. Xavier leaned forward to watch them and as he did, he caught sight of one of their faces, and muffled a cry. Not a cry of fear, or of loathing; there were other emotions at play in his voice.

Bow to her, Xavier. You owe her that at least.

With an unsure backward glance at *il Dottore*, Xavier sketched a deep if uncertain bow to the creatures of the water; for a second one of them hung in the depths, her hair a cloud of river moss around her, and nodded back. Then she sank out of sight, just as she had done once before.

Fear death by water, thought Xavier to himself, and looked askance at *il Dottore*. Was he in the hands of some kind of sorceress? This was clearly no normal abduction. The penetration of the Secret Senate's concealed chamber beneath the Cathedrale, the sure knowledge of the effects of the sacrament – indeed, the fact that it profoundly affected only Xavier and not the others suggested that this was a kidnap with a purpose, to a plan and with resource and forward planning one would not expect from those who might abduct for money or influence.

Xavier stared at *il Dottore*.

"Sun Face?"

Il Dottore inclined her head, a spark of amusement in her eyes. *Let there be no lies between us, Xavier; you may call me Orlando. For now, I am Orlando Mysterioso; this will change in due course. Tonight, I shall be Columbine, and you my Harlequin.* She danced from the boat onto the steps and held her hand out to Xavier; he took it wonderingly, and found cold stone beneath his feet. The mists swallowed the boat, the river and all sound of water; all that was left of the Undines' dance was a faint memory and the tang of salt in his nostrils.

"Where are you leading me?"

Orlando held up a finger to her lips for silence, and took him along the stone pathway. The fogs parted for her like an obliging curtain before a play begins showing a glimpse of the wonders waiting behind.

We're going to see some puppets.

Do you like puppets?

I do.

Xavier felt at his belt for his *bauta* mask, the traditional garb of any respectable Cittàvecchi out at such an hour, but found it gone.

Tonight you go before the city barefaced, Xavier. You wear no mask. There can be no lies between us, no false faces. You know that.

"Then you should take off your mask too. Fair's fair..."

Orlando just chuckled, and led him deeper into the fog. The tone of the ground beneath his feet changed from rough stone slabs to cobbles; they were ascending, climbing one of the shallow hills toward one of Cittàvecchio's remaining areas of higher ground. For Xavier, it finally became too much. He pulled his hand free, and stopped.

"No. No, look. You have given me a name but it's a name out of myth, it means nothing. You demand I go unmasked but conceal yourself. You have drugged me and deceived me, to what purpose I have no idea, and now you seem determined that I catch my death of a chill, or fall off a high ledge on what must be one of the foggiest nights of the year. It's past four bells! I-"

Suddenly, the street seemed much colder, much darker. Orlando was nowhere to be seen. "Wait – where are you? I cannot see you... aah!" He recoiled from a sharp poke in the small of the back.

You are injured. The voice hung in the air, disembodied.

"It's just a shallow graze. It's not serious. An-" He stopped.

Go on.

You were about to tell me that it was an accident.

But it wasn't, was it?

No.

Il Dottore suddenly appeared over Xavier's shoulder, coalescing like a sudden shadow on a sunny day. *No lies, Xavier. Let us have a conversation. Let us have a conversation about Sofia d'Amato.*

"The woman fell from a fourth floor balcony into the water. She drowned. Very sad. Can we move on?"

She loved you, did she not? Swore her love for you. Sent you notes. Letters.

Xavier looked away, his voice schooled very carefully. "What of it? I am a rich and popular man with many lady friends. The selfsame could be said of ten other women. Money and a title are powerful aphrodisiacs."

Did you love her too?

Xavier remained silent.

Oho. Perhaps you did, and perhaps you did not. But I do not think you love Ophelia di Gialla. I think you are playing a game, a game of brinkmanship and power and status. I think your courtship of Ophelia has very little to do with how she makes you feel, Xavier.

"You appear to be very perceptive," said Xavier, sullenly. "Though it will do you little good to try and expose me. My reputation is impeccable."

She is not to end the way Sofia D'Amato ended; I have other plans for her. No games and no competitions, do you understand?

"I will endeavour to keep her away from open windows in high buildings, then." The bitterness in his voice was open and raw.

Orlando grabbed him by the jaw with one gloved hand and pulled him round to look straight at him, tilting *il Dottore's* mask so that, like a mad bird, only one gleaming eye could be seen. *You do as you are bid, Tragedy. No games, no suspicious fall, no jealous lovers. Play your part, whether you like it or not. Your time will come.*

Xavier recoiled as if stung. "Who are you? *What* are you, that you know so much?"

Orlando laughed, took two steps back and cut a low curtsey. *I am the face the city chooses to wear a while. You have no secrets from me, no masks to wear. I am in your blood, Xavier, in the very air you breathe. Come, explore with me a while. See the city unmasked.*

She held out her hand again; reluctantly, Xavier took it.

* * *

"mmMnfPFh", said Gratiano, around the rose. He kept his hands visible and moved them slowly.

"I had wondered if you would come. You kept me waiting, Gratiano." She purred in his ear, the blade resting delicately against his ribs, just under his heart. She had been behind the drapes at the other end of the balcony; she must have seen him crossing the courtyard. So much for his career in stealth.

He gingerly took the rose out of his mouth. "I wanted to make sure I wasn't interrupting anything… or intruding on anything. I saw Mercutio leaving the city earlier, and I thought you might have made arrangements for your own entertainment this evening..."

"*Did* you," she said, her tone suddenly sharp. "Where did you see Mercutio?"

"He was in a meeting with Pater Felicio at the *Priest's Hole* and then he headed off; I think he's going to Buchara but it all seemed a bit hush-hush. Pater Felicio spun me some tale about a priest's indiscretions, but…"

Elizabeta turned him round and pushed him back through the open windows into the room. The musky smell of incense almost overwhelmed him. "But nothing, young master dell'Allia." Her hands were moving on him now and he felt himself responding to her, his blood moving faster. "What my Mercutio is up to is none of your concern – and no concern of those you report to either, do I make myself clear?"

Gratiano's legs met the edge of the bed and he fell backwards onto it. Above him, spreading across the roof of the chamber was a painted mural. Like most of the older buildings in Cittàvecchio, the Palazzo di Zancani dated back to drier times before the city's subsidence; its décor reflected the Imperial past of the city. Spreading over the roof was a depiction – rare nowadays – of the Tattered King himself, *Re Stracciati* astride the city under a stormy sky.

"Does it not disturb you, to sleep under the gaze of the Tattered King?" Gratiano lay back and looked at the great mural across the roof; at the high towers of Cittàvecchio – known by its Imperial name when this was painted – rising behind the moon, the boiling lake of fog where now lay the marshes and the bay. Elizabeta's fingers were already making short work of his jerkin; he shrugged it off and made to pull his shirt over his head, but she trapped his arms in it over his head, and pressed her lips to his through the fabric.

"Why should it disturb me? To stand in the tatters of the King is cause for joy, not fear. He made us great."

"And brought us low in the end..." Gratiano shrugged off his shirt but by now his mind was not on ancient history. The scent of the Donna Elizabeta was strong and he could not help but respond to it, skin against skin. As he lost himself in her breasts, Elizabeta watched him with an expression not of lust, but cold calculation. Her attention was not on him; it was on the full length mirror at the other end of the room, the mirror which seemed to show a shifting image that had little to do with the reflection of the room. On the floor in front of the mirror were a pair of discarded puppets and a long-nosed *dottore* mask. She watched the mirror a moment, then, satisfied, returned her attention to the boy before her.

"Mercutio is on business for me. He will be gone a few days. You keep me company while he is away, Gratiano, and we will both be happy. Now stop talking and wasting time – I must be away before dawn. I've a meeting to go to. Send me there in a good mood..."

Gratiano nodded; Elizabeta smiled indulgently. It did not reach her eyes.

* * *

"Silence them? One would think the murdering of them would be sufficient to that task..." said Visconti, with little effort to hide his disbelief. Gawain, on the other hand, was smiling openly and with some genuine humour. "A witness, Captain Visconti? A *reliable* witness?"

Valentin rumbled under his breath. "Old Rus stories. Stops a sorcerer calling them back and talking to them. Blind them and they cannot see to answer a summons in the afterlife; cut out their tongue and even if they find their way to the summoner they cannot speak. Prince Aleksandr used to have all his prisoners so treated after execution; he was a very superstitious man."

"So why cut off the face?" Visconti poked the jar on the mantel; the pallid stringy lumps inside sloshed against the walls of the jar. "So they can't be recognised in the afterlife?"

The Russian shrugged expressively. "Nothing in Rus folklore about faces. Just tongues and eyes."

Visconti turned back to Gawain. "No, not what I'd call a *reliable* witness. But definitely one the scum of the Rookeries will believe. I haven't spoken to the witness myself – he's a beggar named Black Maffeo, apparently, and under Orfèo's protection."

Gawain guffawed. "*Orfèo?* The King of the Beggars? You realise, Visconti, that this is almost certainly a scam. In the unlikely event that one of Orfèo's flea-ridden lepers saw anything of use, we will only learn of it once that razor-toothed leech has drained every ounce of advantage, gold and exposure from it that he can."

"That's as maybe. But if it gets out in the Rookeries, it will cause a riot. If you give me troops, I can go in, keep order while we locate, extract and interrogate this witness whether Orfèo wills it or no and we can ride out the worst of it – and be seen to be doing something."

Valentin shook his head. "So this is the truth of it. Even if you can guarantee a successful operation against him in the Rookeries – and I'm not sure you can, even with troops - it will be seen as Orfèo controlling the agenda. The Duca will not like the thought of a beggar, no matter how influential, dictating policy in the city. And I don't imagine the Lord Seneschal will be over-pleased at such an implication either. I know you have longstanding issues with the beggar king, Visconti, but I have to support Gawain. This would be a fool's errand."

"Not if I brought in Orfèo at the same time."

Valentin set his helmet down on the edge of the trestle table and ran both hands over his head. "Orfèo is the embodiment of smoke and mirrors, Gian. If you caught him – and I think that unlikely – he has enough blackmail on members of the Court to ensure his swift release, as you well know. It would be futile and counterproductive, and for what? This so-called witness who may not have seen anything at all."

"Then I cannot guarantee any movement on these deaths. Unless we get a moment of luck or some breakthrough, he will continue to murder with impunity and eventually this will turn around and bite us. I can't acquiesce to Orfèo's demands and without soldiers from one or the other of you, I can't go into the Rookeries and take this so-called witness off him by force. I have nowhere to go."

Gawain picked up one of the scalpels from the end of the table and examined it curiously, turning it this way and that. "What if we are approaching this from the wrong angle?"

Visconti watched him sceptically. "What do you have in mind?"

"Give me a day and a night, and I will see if I can extract this witness with a scalpel, before we send in a battering ram. If I fail to find this beggar by midnight tomorrow, then I will take your case to the Seneschal. If I do find him, I save a lot of upheaval, trouble and strife and what's more, Orfèo gets a lesson in manners he clearly needs."

Valentin nodded. "Quiet and clever. I approve."

Both looked to Visconti, whose reluctance was writ large upon his face. "Alright. You hold me to ransom, gentlemen. I'll hold off for a day, but if nothing has come of it by then, I'll take my own case direct to the Duca."

Gawain set down the scalpel with precise care and swept his cloak back around his shoulders, moving for the door. "I'm *quite* sure it won't come to that."

*   *   *

Here: The puppeteer.

Xavier had wandered the streets with Orlando, in a seemingly random pattern, for nearly an hour. Here and there a drunken reveller or late-night partygoer hurried, cloaked against the mist, from one party or another; but Xavier, barefaced, was invisible to them. One does not see such things as an unmasked nobleman in Cittàvecchio.

Those that did see them were the low folk; the boatmen, the lamplighters, the sellers of food and the lowest whores and streetwalkers. People who could not afford the luxury of disguise, from themselves or others. Those whose business of necessity kept them active through the dead hours of the night. Beggars, especially, tugged their forelock as Orlando passed, and tipped Xavier the wink.

The puppeteer was a midget, barely three feet in height. His clothes were a mass of coloured tatters and rags, seemingly sewn together into a jester's motley without regard for style or grace, and his gaze was a vivid yellow, like a cat's, as he watched Xavier approach. He nodded to Orlando, a nod between equals, which she returned. On his shoulder sat a whip-thin monkey in a tiny red waistcoat, clinging to the puppeteer's misshapen hump for balance, chittering a litany of whispered monkey secrets in his ear. It stopped, and regarded Xavier venomously a while; then it resumed its sibilant monologue.

"Is this what you have brought me to see? This mountebank?"

Hush. Watch.

The puppeteer manipulated his wooden marionettes deftly for a small audience of night people; porters and bravos, whores and those with nowhere better to go, drawn partly by the prospect of street theatre and partly by the heat of the glowing brazier which sat in front of the tiny stage where the marionettes danced. The old tale of the *commedia*, the familiar characters woven anew into another story. This one seemed to revolve around *Brighella* and *Scapino*, the drunken servant rogue and his cowardly brother. When *Pantaleone*, the employer of the two servants appeared, the puppeteer spoke his words in a thick, slow accent, mimicking the style of a Bucharan merchant; but when *Pantaleone's* rival, *il Dottore*, appeared, all turned to Orlando and raised a silent toast to her.

"I don't understand. I assume I am supposed to be one of these characters?"

Should you be?

"You told me I'd see the city unmasked, and I understand what you speak of, but I fail to see how it serves any purpose other than reminding me that there is life outside of Court circles."

Perhaps that's purpose enough in itself.

On the tiny stage, things had taken a turn for the bloody; *Brighella* had slain the maid *Zagne*, and carved her body up, the blood shockingly red on the tiny wooden platform. Xavier, with only one eye on proceedings, paid it little heed. "Well fair enough, awaken my social conscience if you feel you must. But after the river and the Undines and the rest of it I was expecting something a little more, well... *metaphysical*, I suppose. I mean, after all, this is just..."

Xavier tailed off, aware that Orlando was watching him with utter absorption. He glanced across to the puppeteer, who watched him no less intently, and then down to the puppet stage, where the marionettes continued their whirling dance.

The blood from *Zagne*'s body had pooled below the little stage now, and her shattered wooden body lay off to one side. *Brighella* had taken his knife to her face and a tiny marionette cat with great chips of amber for its eyes sniffed at the bloodstained wood shavings. *Brighella* danced triumphant; but of *Scapino* there was no sign. True to his name, he had fled the scene, leaving a trail of bloody footprints that ran straight between Xavier's boots.

Xavier looked down at the tiny red marks, then up at the puppeteer, who met his gaze levelly with eyes as yellow as rotten teeth. The monkey let loose with a shriek of cackling laughter, shockingly loud. Orlando made as if to interfere but the puppeteer stilled her with a glance and a gesture.

No. You wanted him to see, so let him see. Don't interfere.

Xavier looked from the puppeteer to Orlando, but her masked face was impassive; for the first time since believing himself poisoned in the chamber below the Cathedrale, Xavier suspected he might be in personal danger. His hand drifted casually to the hilt of the knife tucked through the back of his belt; his sword, like the rest of his effects, was still in the secret chamber.

"I want no trouble, puppeteer. Don't overreach yourself..."

The audience were all looking, now. The yellow-eyed dwarf descended from his platform, abandoning the strings of his marionettes; they collapsed in a welter of gore and broken bones. Something sharp glinted in his hand as he slowly advanced. The monkey howled with glee and jumped up and down on the dwarf's shoulder.

Xavier's knife was out and moving fast; the dwarf's first two feints met steel and drew sparks. Orlando stood silent behind her porcelain mask, but her hands clenched into fists. Xavier feinted left to give himself a little room, then lunged; the dwarf, with far more acrobatic talent than his frame implied, danced nimbly back out of the way and as he did so the monkey launched itself off his shoulder at Xavier's face like a shrieking demon. Xavier, overwhelmed by the stench of the creature, grabbed at it with his left hand, and got a grip on the whiplash tail; he flung it, as far and as fast as he could, but as he did so its claws caught along his jaw.

The pain was like a lash across his senses; he staggered, and then sat in an ungainly heap as his legs buckled under him. The scene before him was suddenly very different. Where once had been a lethal dwarf puppeteer stood a twisted and hunched beggar, muttering and menacing him with a broken bottle. The audience were ornamental statues clustered around a fountain in the centre of the square, in which he appeared to have collapsed, soaking himself - and where Orlando had stood was...

Nothing. Nothing but a coil of the night-mist, spinning itself away in the darkness. Xavier shook his head again to clear the cobwebs and kicked out at the beggar; the broken bottle skittered away and the pathetic creature mewled and cowered from this suddenly far less helpless target, blinking rheumy eyes. Of the puppet show, the monkey and the rest of the evidence of the night's strangeness there was nothing.

He put his hand to the left side of his jaw and touched; it felt wet. Blood.

Xavier picked himself up from his sprawl, retrieved his knife and, waving it unsteadily in the direction of unforeseen threats, staggered away at speed.

* * *

It took a few streets for Xavier to get his bearings and be comfortable with the distance between him and the courtyard of the fountain and the beggar. He stopped and examined his reflection in a water-trough; the cut on his jaw line wasn't serious but would need attention, and soon, or it would leave a scar. His clothes were ruined, either soaked from the dip in the fountain or covered in mud and detritus. *A fine figure I cut.*

As the flaring beacons of the torches on the *Ponte Amanti* came into view and he guessed himself less than five minutes from his own townhouse, the rain began. Gentle at first, it became more insistent and insidious, damping down the night-mist.

He crossed the *Ponte Amanti* as the Cathedrale rang five bells. Damp darkness lay over the city like a shroud, smothering everything. Between five and six bells was the only time the city was truly quiet, a great intake of breath before the dawn chorus of workers and tradesmen began to clutter the thoroughfares and the canals.

Xavier glanced behind him, conscious suddenly, fiercely, of the beating of his heart, the sensation of his own pulse in his throat. A flicker of movement on the edge of one of the pools of light cast by the flaming torches on the bridge; a tatter of something that caught the glare and then was gone in a second. Maybe the glint of light on a blade.

Don't stop and gawk.

A trickle of icy rainwater ran down the back of his collar and played a chilly dance down his spine. The rain settled to a fine mist that stained everything a strange colourless grey; it deprived the world of detail, leached away all colour. Xavier found himself longing for a sight of the colour blue, anywhere.

He could definitely sense movement behind him now, and it took an act of supreme will not to look. No more than fifty paces to the steps of the townhouse, but every instinct told him that if he ran, he'd not even see what hit him. The knife was still in his hand; he risked a glance down at it.

Twenty paces, now. He could make out the carving on the door of the house and allowed himself to relax, just for a moment. Then, behind him, he heard the whisper of cloth on cloth, the muffled creak of leather, and the soft crunch of boots on gravel. He whirled, knife at the ready, but there was nothing there.

The blade was at his throat and fingers locked in his hair before he was even aware his assailant was behind him, and panic gave him fresh strength; he kicked out backwards and both of them blundered into the doors of the townhouse, knocking them open. Xavier landed heavily on his attacker, who grunted, winded; both knives skittered across the parquet floor, in opposite directions. Xavier dived for the nearest, his heart racing and near in his throat. Before his fingers could close on the hilt, a weight crashed down on him and he found himself crushed to the floor. His free arm was trapped and twisted up behind him. His outstretched fingers were no more than six inches from the hilt of his knife. He felt hot breath on the back of his neck, and then heard an all too familiar chuckle. The pressure on his back was abruptly released and a gloved hand was proffered to help him to his feet.

Xavier retrieved his knife and accepted the proffered hand, heaving himself up face to face with his attacker. "Mother and Child. I though you were – I thought…"

His attacker had his knife back in his hand now; a long, straight stiletto blade, double edged and wickedly sharp. But it was weaving now, playfully; more interested in picking at the ruined remains of Xavier's shirt than inflicting damage. Xavier raised his hands in surrender and let fall his own knife.

"Gods, not tonight. I have no energy for it tonight."

The cloaked assailant closed with him but with a whisper instead of a knife.

"Honestly", breathed Gawain in his ear. "You should know by now it only makes victory all the sweeter for me when you *struggle*."

* * *

When Gratiano awoke, the first light of false dawn was making ghosts of everything in the chamber. He was alone; the only sign of Elizabeta Zancani was a shadow of heat in the bed and the ornate mask of the crescent moon hanging from the bedpost. The windows stood open to the night mists and the room smelled of the city and of musk.

As the warmth faded from the bed and his slowly waking mind, he realised how drained he felt. He raised his hand to his forehead to check for a fever and caught a glimpse of how pallid his arm was; his skin was cold and clammy, not feverish.

He sat up, abruptly, as the events of the previous evening assembled themselves in the correct order. Particularly, he saw himself raise his hand and mouth the words 'A hundred ducats on Lord Prospero's beast' over and over again as the bottom dropped away from his stomach.

"Oh Mother and *Child*," he gasped aloud. *I owe Barocchio Iron-Gut a hundred ducats, and I cannot pay him.* Barocchio was notorious – even more notorious than Prospero, if such a thing were possible – for his intolerance of bad debtors.

He looked around the room for inspiration or perhaps for escape, but there was none. Overhead, the King in Tatters looked down from behind his mask and passed silent judgement.

Gawain sprawled like a cat in the window seat next to the bed and watched the afternoon sun boiling the mist off the canals. Wrapped only in a sheet half-twisted around his hips, he lay, head supported on one arm on the windowsill, flicking grape seeds at passengers in canal barges and those unfortunate enough to walk beneath the window with vicious accuracy.

Behind him, sprawled face first across the bed lay Xavier, snoring gently. Gawain rolled over and got to his feet, cinched the sheet around his waist and stood a while, watching the younger man sleep. As he watched, expressions stole across his face unnoticed and unbidden, chasing each other like guileless children across territory usually fiercely guarded but now left unattended for a few moments. Covetousness and lust, and envy and affection all paused a second before moving on; but the one that lingered was a strange, lost, wild look, a look of need and possession all at once.

Gawain ran his hand above Xavier's back, close enough to feel body heat but not close enough to touch; pausing over the long shallow graze in the small of his back where a brush with a concealed knife the night before had served to remind him that too much public affection shown to others might have painful and unexpected consequences. He seemed almost reluctant to actually touch, to connect with the sleeping man, as if to do so would ruin some carefully nurtured illusion.

His hand hovered over Xavier's wild and tangled hair, seemingly about to make contact, but he hesitated, and then drew back. Xavier shifted slightly and lay now on his stomach with his head supported in the crook of one arm. The fresh cut on his jaw line, washed and cleaned now, flared angrily red but aside from that there was no sign of his night's misadventures save a few bruises here and there. He looked the picture of innocent and peaceful sleep.

Gawain went over to the water jug, wet a towel and then sat back on the edge of the bed, dabbing at the angry scratch along Xavier's jaw. Xavier shifted uncomfortably, rolling over and muttering something to himself that made Gawain's face darken briefly. "The past is another country, *Scapino*," he whispered into the sleeper's ear. "And besides, the wench is dead."

He wrung out the towel onto the tiled floor, and examined the wound minutely, before grunting to himself in satisfaction. He was no stranger to the injuries a sharp object could inflict on human flesh, and he was satisfied this was mostly superficial. He reached down to touch his lover's cheek but just as he was about to do so, from below came the sound of knocking at the front door of the townhouse. Gawain hesitated; then the bell joined the clamour as well. Xavier's servants knew better to be in the house while he was there and in all likelihood had quietly and tactfully awarded themselves the day off.

Gawain opened the bedroom door and looked down over the balcony rail into the entry hall of the townhouse; all was dark, and the persistent knocking at the door continued. Muffled shouting now, too – he could pick out his own name in it.

Cursing quietly, he dived back into the bedroom and retrieved his knife from under the bed where it had fallen in the night and threw the bed sheet hastily over Xavier, leaving only an indistinct mound visible in the bed. Then he padded down the stairs to the main door, dagger concealed, and slipped the latch, opening the door an inch or two.

"Gawain, thank the Father and Mother I've found yo-"

Gawain reached through the door, grabbed Gratiano by the neck and pulled him inside, then slammed the door and held him against the wall with the knife to his throat. "How in *Hell's* name did you know I was here?"

Gratiano, his eyes wide with fear, held up a grape pip. "I saw you in the window…"

"*Damn.* And what is so important that you have to hunt me down across half the city?"

"Ah, uh… can we discuss it once you've put some clothes on?"

Gawain glanced down, then back at Gratiano, pointing the knife at him. "*Stay here.* I am entertaining a lady upstairs without the knowledge of the master of the House and if you queer the deal or ruin my sport I will, I promise you, unseam you from your scrawny neck to your useless little cock."

Gratiano's face made an "O" of astonished comprehension and he raised both hands in the air as Gawain raced back up the stairs. "Take your time, my confidence is assured…"

Gawain ducked back into the bedroom and grabbed his clothes from the floor. Climbing with some haste into his trousers and throwing on a loose white shirt, he bundled the rest up in his cloak and grabbed his boots, sparing a glance at Xavier's still-undisturbed form as he did so. He hesitated, uncertain for a moment, then tiptoed barefoot onto the landing, closing the door behind him.

He descended the staircase, Gratiano waiting at the foot of it anxiously, and sat on the bottom step, pulling on his boots. "Now what is so urgent that it cannot wait for a natural hour like dusk? You know full well I dislike being disturbed during the hours of daylight. And how did you even know where to look for me?"

"I asked after you at the Red Lion and Prospero said you were probably entertaining someone at Lord Xavier's townhouse."

"*Did* he. I should probably have a *word* with Master Prospero, bless his informative and helpful little soul. Did he say whom that someone might be?"

"No, but he seemed to find it all too funny for words, I don't know why. Is there something I should know?"

Gawain smiled to himself. "Almost certainly not. And not a word of this to Lord Xavier. He may not take it too well that I have been plucking chickens in his bedchamber, understand?"

Gawain stood, testing his boots, and finding himself satisfied, threw the cloak with his jerkin, sword-belt and gloves bundled in it at Gratiano. "Right. Talk as we walk."

Gratiano nearly tripped over the steps in his hurry to keep up with Gawain's long-legged stride. "Well, it's a matter of some small delicacy, you see. Last night, I…"

Gawain came to a halt at the street pump on the riverside and stuck his head under the tap, before shaking like a dog and blinking the water out of his eyes. "Right, now I'm properly awake. What kind of delicacy? Give me my jacket."

"Well, Prospero said last night that he had a sure thing for the pit fight and to be fair it looked as though he did…"

"Who is into you and how much for?" Gawain examined the back of his jacket, then threw it on and took his belt from Gratiano, checking the sword hung correctly and the various pouches did not interfere with the smooth drawing of his dagger.

"Barocchio, for a hundred."

Gawain stopped and looked directly at Gratiano, raising an eyebrow. "A hundred *ducats?*"

"Yes. I was trying to impress a lady…"

"That's… unfortunate." He examined his reflection in a shop-front, and scraped his wet hair back into his preferred topknot, tying it back before turning back to Gratiano. "What do you expect me to do about it?"

"I was wondering whether you could front me for a hundred until my father…"

"And where would I get a hundred ducats from? I stopped gambling last night because I am *prudent* with my money,

Gratiano dell'Allia. No, I'm not buying your debts from Barocchio Iron-Gut. Maybe once he's broken a few of your major bones you'll learn not to bet more than you can afford and you'll listen less to Prospero and more to me."

"But Gawain," wailed Gratiano, "It's *Barocchio!* If I don't pay, he'll… He's going to…"

Gawain whipped the cloak out of Gratiano's hands and swung it over his shoulders in one smooth move. "Must get on, Gratiano, Lord Seneschal's business and I'm already late. Probably. But I tell you what; if you keep this up, you've a promising career as someone's valet. Let me know how you get on…" And with a wink, Gawain flicked a ten-*piastre* coin in the air and made off, leaving Gratiano open-mouthed, staring at the silver coin as it rang on the cobbles.

* * *

Mater Calomena leaned in and whispered in Ophelia's ear. "My lady; it is the Lord dell'Allia."

Ophelia, sat in the window seat, looked up from her guest at Gratiano advancing diffidently down the hall. Just across from her, Elizabeta Zancani sat, fanning herself lazily; she watched Gratiano in much the fashion of a lizard watching an especially juicy bug advancing haplessly along a twig. Gratiano glanced at Elizabeta and went crimson, then averted his eyes; Ophelia looked across at Elizabeta and raised an eyebrow. "Lord dell'Allia, how unexpected that you should call upon me at such an hour. I would expect not to see you until dusk had fallen."

"Ladies; forgive the unexpected intrusion." Gratiano stood, beaming, a sheen of fresh sweat on his brow.

Ophelia looked at him blankly. "And-?"

"My lady?"

"I presume you have come here for a reason, my Lord. Or are we to pass the afternoon in idle contemplation?"

Gratiano cleared his throat nervously. "My Lady, I would not trouble you, but I have encountered a few titbits of information here and there that I felt might be of interest to you..."

Calomena laughed quietly. "That *is* what we pay you for, Lord dell'Allia. What makes this particular datum so urgent that it cannot wait until the weekly report?"

Elizabeta leaned forward lazily. "Would you prefer that I gave you a moment of privacy, Donna Ophelia?"

Calomena shook her head, and Ophelia smiled. "Not at all, Donna Zancani. We have no secrets from the Sisterhood here. Speak on, Gratiano."

"It concerns the Lord Xavier, whom I believe you hold an interest in at present, my Lady?"

Ophelia watched him impassively. "Go on."

"The problem is, though, my Lady, I find myself in unfortunate circumstances; *straitened* circumstances, one might say. If you could perhaps advance me a sum against my..."

"No." Calomena rose to her feet behind Ophelia. "We pay you enough as it is, tattletale. Now speak what you know – or would you prefer I *made* you do so?"

Gratiano shied back, then regained his composure. "Lord Gawain was entertaining a lover in Lord Xavier's house – I believe without Lord Xavier's knowledge. It is likely to have only been a serving wench or some such – it is his way – but it will be the beginning of a campaign between them, a status game and you should look to yourself, my lady, for Lord Gawain will likely seek to step between you and Lord Xavier soon."

Ophelia looked out of the window and raised her fan to conceal her smile. "Then Lord Gawain will no doubt enjoy the resultant circumstance quite uniquely. *Do* go on, Lord dell'Allia."

Gratiano risked a glance at Donna Zancani, wary of that gimlet gaze. *Forgive me, Donna. But this is life or death and I will protect your interests as much as I can...* "Last night, I happened upon none other than old Pater Felicio Caritavo hiring himself the services of none other than Mercutio del Richo in the Court of the Dragon!"

Calomena glanced across at Elizabeta and then looked up, sharply. "Mercutio del Richo? Tell on..."

"I didn't catch much – the Pater was obviously aware of my presence and attention and deflected matters onto other things, but he was speaking to the gentleman in the *Priest's Hole* in the Court of the Dragon, at past two bells. He claimed it was something about a priest being indiscreet and asked me to keep quiet about it, which of course I will, it being a confidence given to a Man of the Trinity, but nevertheless gold is gold and a prior contract is a prior contract..."

"Yes, my Lord. And one does not engage the services of an *extremely* competent thief to tidy up the affairs of an indiscreet priest. Very well; an advance of fifty if you can find out more of what the Pater is up to in the next twenty-four hours. Otherwise, our prior agreements stand and you will be paid the usual fee for your next weekly report. Don't imagine you're the only gossip in town, Gratiano, or even the most adroit..." Calomena rearranged her hands neatly in her lap, and then looked up. "We're done here, Gratiano. Show yourself out."

Gratiano sketched a hasty bow to Ophelia, who had returned to her book and paid him as much attention as one would to a statue. Seeing no reaction, he turned on his heel and left, displaying as much pique as he dare in the face of Mater Calomena's vulture gaze. Once the door had closed behind him, Ophelia finally let go of her rigid self-control and burst out laughing, muffling the noise by jamming her face between pages of the book. Calomena shook her veiled head in disbelief.

"He really, genuinely *hasn't got a clue*, that boy. He's like a wide-eyed puppy that thinks itself a wolf. Sooner or later something is going to bite him and that will be an end to that."

Elizabeta looked from one to the other. "Does somebody care to share the source of the humour with me?"

Ophelia looked up. "Apparently, Lord Gawain was entertaining *a serving wench* in Lord Xavier's house." She chuckled to herself.

"Ah. Comprehension dawns. I am a little slow today. Is that still going on? I thought the Seneschal got wind of it and put a stop to it. 'Not in my army', and so forth."

"Ah, now," said Calomena. "That pair are clever and cautious and cover their tracks well. It is only obvious to you because you know to look for it; I'd wager that most don't know and would never guess, for both put themselves about as rakes and men-about-town. But it's not those two that interest me – it's Pater Felicio."

Ophelia sat up straighter. "You think the *Pater* is involved in this great conspiracy of yours?"

Elizabeta watched them from behind her fan, her gaze as deadly as one of Barocchio's basilisks.

"It may be nothing, but I've watched his movements for a long time and he is on my suspect list, yes. The *Priest's Hole*, though. Why meet Mercutio del Richo there? Unless it's something to do with Buchara or a Bucharan…"

"I think I can assist with that." Elizabeta flicked her fan and an expression of shared confidence fell across her face, a carefully schooled mask. "Mercutio was hired last night to attend to a… piece of business… in Buchara. It might be linked with this conspiracy of yours, or it might not; he will be providing me with a full report upon his return. I was going to raise this with you over dinner, but it seems young dell'Allia has stolen my thunder. Wretched boy; I shall have to teach him a lesson in good manners and taste. Either way, it's more likely to be to do with art than politics. But tell me more of this conspiracy…"

Ophelia shrugged. "It is Calomena's to tell, not mine. She has a bee in her bonnet about some things Lord Feron said under torture and some recent coincidences…"

"Synchronicities!" interrupted Calomena, affronted.

" – *Coincidences* that may well mean nothing at all. And to put not too fine a point on it, if the Duca my brother discovers the content of these conversations then we are just as likely to meet our ends as any plotters we seek to take advantage of."

Calomena paced restlessly back and forth in front of the great bay windows, punctuating her speech with sharp prods of her finger. "We *know* there is an active and dangerous secret society in the city, this so-called Secret Senate. We *know* they are plotting something, and it's as plain as the nose on your face that in the current climate any move against the Duca would enjoy *considerable* support, not just here in Cittàvecchio but from most of our major trading partners. Any such coalition of interests would have to include someone who could guarantee the support either of the Tatar Guard or of the City Levies; that means either Valentin or the Seneschal, and I think it will take more than this to break Henri di Schermo's love for his cousin, unless Lord d'Orlato plans to make it a *double* coup. But Valentin? Say what you like about the Tatars, but they are mercenaries, and mercenaries fight when they are paid to fight. Only a madman would rely on their loyalty. I am certain that one of the nobles is involved too – likely as a planned figurehead Duca after your brother is overthrown. I had suspected a man of the Church would be involved too, though I must confess I still believe it to be Fra Ottavio, not Pater Felicio…"

Ophelia cast her hands in the air. "Mater, you are going to give yourself a seizure at this rate. Conspiracies and plots and schemes left and right. If this Secret Senate exists – and I remain unconvinced – then it may be as toothless as an old cat. And even if it is not, I have my own following among the nobility. If I were to issue a call to arms, Lord Prospero would likely answer…"

"Assuming he noticed," muttered Calomena darkly.

"…as would Lord d'Amato, Lord Gideon of the Black Gryphon and Lord Castiglione. And if I have seduced him by then, even the charming and slippery Lord di Tuffatore may find it difficult to avoid declaring for me. I am sure the affections of Lord d'Orlato are *exceptionally* hard to resist, but I'm sure he'll make an effort for me once I have *explained* a thing or two to him."

Elizabeta shook her head. "This is all very well, Calomena, but there's no proof of anything here, just suspicions. And in the current climate, voicing suspicions will get people killed – possibly innocent people."

"My point *exactly*," interjected Ophelia.

"If you are this concerned, why don't you bring this theory to the Sisterhood? The assembled Priestesses of the Mother could broach it tactfully with the Duca – "

Calomena threw her hands in the air. "You know very well that the other Sisters would say exactly what you just have: show us the proof. And I have none. I only have a gut feeling, a certainty that something's afoot. I can hear the rustle of his tatters in the wind, Elizabeta, and that is never a good omen."

Elizabeta Zancani rose, smoothly. "I think this is just nerves, Calomena. It's a bad time for anyone in power at the moment. The populace is… not overly thrilled with the Duca, no. But these things come in waves; patience is the key. Yes, sooner or later a conspiracy will arise to displace the Duca. That's the way of Cittàvecchi politics. The longer we wait, the more likely it is that such a conspiracy will arise – the only thing that prevents it at present are Captain Valentin and his Tatars[3], and the loyalty the Lord Seneschal still holds for the Duca. In my opinion, those two factors are still more than strong enough to keep the city under control. Calm yourself, and worry about realities, not mist phantoms."

Ophelia turned to Calomena. "See? Even Elizabeta agrees. Now will you leave off this?"

---

[3] The Tartary Exiles, or Tatar Guards, had been employed by the (then new to power) Duca di Gialla some fifteen years before in a mercenary capacity during the innumerable skirmishes that marked the War of the Montressori Succession. They distinguished themselves at the Battle of Giovedi and the siege of Isla Bocca, earning themselves a reputation for ferocity and bloodthirstiness that continues to this day. In gratitude for their service, the Duca di Gialla offered them a permanent commission as his household guard and since the close of the war they had been based in Cittàvecchio as the Duca's personal protectors. Friction between the standing army of Cittàvecchio and its possessions and the Tartary Exiles was common and frequently violent, leading to the famous joint edict by the Lord Seneschal Henri di Schermo and the Captain of the Tartary Exiles, Valentin, forbidding duels between the two forces save on high holy days, when both forces were generally too drunk to do one another serious injury.

Calomena threw her hands in the air in melodramatic exasperation. "Let us hope I do not have to tell you *both* 'I told you so', then. Do you leave us, sister?"

Elizabeta bowed. "I have some business back at the Palazzo this afternoon – a private viewing to conduct. Perhaps I could invite you to an evening of cards? We could make it a foursome with Donna Castiglione…"

Calomena turned inquisitively to Ophelia. "You are not due to meet with your wretched suitor this evening, are you?"

Ophelia shook her head. "No, I am with my brother this evening. Assuming he does not change his mind, or decide to invade the Colombard plains or have the Ambassador from the New Colonies flogged for dressing incorrectly or one of a hundred other diplomatic disasters."

"Ah, the affairs of state. How they weigh us all down." Elizabeta's smile was brittle, but held. "Perhaps another time then. Go with the Mother, sisters."

"And you, Donna." Ophelia and Calomena waited courteously until Elizabeta had left the chamber, then the younger woman set aside her fan and turned to face Calomena. Away from the mayflies of the court, her carefully cultivated persona of flirtatious innocence fell away like dead leaves to reveal something much sharper and more purposeful; a subtle shift, but one that clearly marked the transformation from *girl* to *woman*. "Do you think she's in on it?"

"I'm not sure, but her reactions were… interesting. She was watching us at least as closely as we were watching her. That's not true – she thinks I am the direct threat, and that you are being advised by me for the moment. We should maintain that illusion."

"What of this business with Mercutio del Richo in Buchara?"

"That may be nothing – he might simply be stealing some trinket on contract; or it could be something bigger. I will investigate it in more detail. If Elizabeta is part of this Secret Senate then it would fit the pattern but if not then they are using her and her resources as well and that would potentially make her a useful ally. We need solid information."

Ophelia went to the window, her back to Calomena. "We could bewitch one of the suspects. In fact, Xavier di Tuffatore would be the most obvious choice. He plays at courting me anyway; there would be no outward difference…"

"Be careful," Calomena cautioned her student. "Don't start throwing simple charms at Xavier di Tuffatore; he has protectors and nothing I've taught you yet will be sufficient to crack that shell."

"So make me something that will. A musk, to tempt him away from the arms of his cold lover and to the flag of the Gialla. A draught that will draw him to me and make him my slave. I will not be denied, Mater. And I do not like the way he toys with me, the way he pretends to courtship."

"Ophelia, this is a dangerous and unpredictable working; and nothing to do with investigating the conspiracy. This is about your injured pride. The Mother does not look well on those who try to force the affections of others… and by doing this we may tip our hand."

"Always the cautious one. A bargain, then, Mater. If you brew a charm for me to place upon Xavier di Tuffatore, I will heed your words about this conspiracy and use it only when the time is right. I'll rally my own forces and put out word that news of this Secret Senate will be well received. Let us tip our hand and be damned, let them know that we are onto them, for it might provoke them into action where at present they sit timid as temple mice."

Calomena sat, silent for a long while, staring into the fireplace. "Very well. I'm uncertain of the wisdom of this but yes, the longer we chase shadows the more tired we will be when the real threat exposes itself to us. I'll brew you your charm; but you must use it only when the time is right or its virtue will be wasted. This will not be a toy, Ophelia."

"Toys are discarded when one is bored of them. I will never be bored of the Mysteries, Mater."

Calomena laughed an old woman's laugh, the kind that knew the lie of youth when it heard it. "Just so. Now; I must prepare your brother's evening draught in the hopes we can keep him calm enough to avoid a diplomatic incident. Do you wish to attend me in the laboratory?"

"No; I have some business to attend to before this evening's trials. I'll speak with you later."

Calomena bowed and swept out of the hall; Ophelia watched until she had gone, then went to the cage of pigeons next to the tall window. She selected one and took it from its cage, then set it on a perch next to her writing desk, and wrote a quick note in casual scrawl; *I am bored and unchaperoned for the afternoon.* She rolled the parchment tightly and affixed it to the bird's leg, then carried it to the window and let it free.

* * *

Xavier lay sleeping as the afternoon wore on. Whatever had spiked the sacrament, it had left him firmly in the grip of his dreams.

He dreamed of the sea; of deep green -

Fear death by

- water, murky like the night-fogs. Of drowned buildings; the long-submerged original port quarter of Cittàvecchio, before the sea claimed the old buildings. Long weathered stone piers, encrusted with silt and barnacles, and empty buildings, roofs long gone, lying open to the sea like shells, waiting for a hermit crab to move in and make of them something entirely different. Forests of anemones and coral, where once stood formal gardens and courtyards.

In the end, the sea always wins.

Xavier walked the drowned streets, and in his dream he knew where his route would eventually lead, though his feet would not stray from the path no matter how he willed it. He could see glimpses of her green hair in the murky water here and there, laughing at him from behind algae-encrusted gargoyles or dancing along rooftops long rotted away in the green murk. Always just beyond reach. He stretched his arm out to her but her own fingers were always just beyond his own.

He came to the foot of the tower, and knew he would have to stay the full course now. Sometimes if he managed to distract himself before this point he could move on, pass beyond this dream and into the arms of another, but once he stood at the foot of the tower he knew there was no avoiding what was to come.

He set his foot on the first step, and set the tableau in motion. The scream from above. The pounding footsteps as he raced up the tower stair.

No, I will not go back there again.

He thrashed back and forth in the bed, seeking any escape from the inevitability of it, but the inexorable logic of dream showed him no mercy.

He climbed the stairs, slow as only dreams can be. He put down his shoulder and burst through the door, remembering the pain of oak on bone.

The room, the billowing shadow he dare not look at, and there he saw her poised on the balcony as if in mid-air. Saw the shadows around her reaching out for her. Saw her, and reached for her, but too slow, too late. Much too late.

He tried to hurl himself after her over the balcony as her green hair receded into the darkening murk, but the shadows reached out and enfolded him in a great embrace and whispered to him that it would be well, that all would be well. And the shadow smiled, and Xavier saw the smile and his breath caught in his throat.

"I tried to stop her," said the shadow. "But she was gone. And now it's just you and me against the world. Just you. And me. The way it was always meant to be."

Fear death by water.

On the path below his window, a woman in an ornate porcelain *bauta* mask looked up at his balcony. She nodded, once, and passed on her way, inclining her head with grave dignity to the deformed puppeteer on the street corner, who paid her the same courtesy in return. He returned his attention to the tiny stage. Every puppeteer worth his salt knows that one must keep a close eye on *Brighella*, when he is out of the box, lest his schemes run out of control. *Scapino*, on the other hand, can always be trusted to flee from danger, no matter what that danger might be.

Xavier awoke, cold and alone. There were no tears, his face as unmoving as stone. Night had fallen on Cittàvecchio.

* * *

For the next half an hour, Ophelia sat in her window seat. She was reading tales of wild adventure in faraway places, but her mind was elsewhere. She thought of Lord Xavier and his pretended, political romance; thought of conspiracies and secrets and lies. When, in due course the door to the hall slid open, she did not look up until the soft pad of footsteps came to a halt.

He had clearly climbed the castle wall; he had ivy in his hair, his clothes were rumpled and untucked and his complexion flushed from eluding the Tatar Guards. He looked as though he was barely out of bed. He bowed low, and presented her with a single rose, presumably wrested from the gardens on the way through.

"You smell like a stable, Prospero," she said, pulling him close.

"That, my lady," said Prospero, with a wicked, raffish grin that lit up the room "…is probably because I thought you might like to play *horsey*…"

* * *

Elizabeta Zancani disembarked from the boat at the foot of the steps that led to the Court of the Lion and Serpent and the Palazzo di Zancani. In the bright light of the afternoon the great statue seemed washed in yellow; she dipped her fingers in the fountain and flicked some water affectionately at it as she passed, a gesture of long habit. The mosaic in the bottom of the fountain, barely visible beneath the layers of rain grime and lichen, swam as she did so, the crowds of people rippling and blurring as if in life for a second.

She nodded to the two guards – relics of an older time – who stood to either side of the Palazzo's main doors. Though it was a gallery and museum, viewing was by appointment or invitation and the guards were there mostly for show, old men retired from the forces seeking a comfortable sinecure. Everyone in Cittàvecchio knew better than to steal from the Palazzo di Zancani.[4]

Behind her serene porcelain mask, her mind was racing. Spreading out before her was an ocean of potential, of possibilities; a web. Whenever variables like the young Donna di Gialla entered the equation, old loyalties had to be re-examined, current allegiances weighed against future benefit. The Secret Senate was all very well and all very noble and Elizabeta was quite sure in herself that at least two of its members were in it for ethical and ideological reasons. She was not one of those two, however, and as far as she was concerned, possession of the *Re Stracciati* deck gave her the thumb on the balance of power. And the object of power was not *having* it; it was *using* it to a specific end.

---

[4] Apocryphal tales told of the second-storey man who had broken into the Palazzo when the Montressori Diamonds were shown there. It was said he was found the following morning, dead of unknown causes with the diamonds on the floor beyond his outstretched fingers; and that when they opened him up on the autopsy table, his brain had shrunk to the size of a pea and the Zancani arms were found, engraved in miniature, on the *inside of his skull*. Of course, superstitious people will believe anything, and the more prosaic of the doctors pointed to the fact that Donna Zancani was known for dusting her exhibits with a particularly virulent Sindi contact poison.

Inside the old palace she set aside her mask and lit a lantern; then, throwing aside the great woven Sindi rug that covered much of the ground floor, she hauled up the oak door set into the marble slabs and descended the dark and dripping staircase concealed beneath it.

She emerged into what once, before the rising water claimed it, was the ground floor ballroom. Now, it was a cavernous space, the floor ankle-deep in canal water throwing weird reflections and ripples up from the light of the lantern she carried. Three-legged yellow symbols raced across the great mural of the city at its height which was painted across the roof as she swung the lantern, chasing spiders into the corners; hairy multi-legged monsters hidden in the cracks and secret places of old Cittàvecchio, before the flood came. And here and there, the water looked... oily, slick, as if something large and smooth moved beneath the placid surface, hugging the old marble floor.

The ballroom (like most of the semi-flooded areas of the city) had not seen use since the days of Cittàvecchio's Imperial greatness. Back then, these hidden chambers were the heart of the Imperial City; now, they were home to damp, rats, whispers and ghosts of the old times – and to those who preferred their affairs kept out of the eye of modern man.

Along the walls of the chamber, affixed with great nails, were hundreds of masks. *Bauta* and *Dottore*, Pierrot and Punchinello, papier-mâché and porcelain and here, of course, the masks of the *commedia*, Scapino and Brighella, the brutish aide-de-camp and his brother who flees from everything. Masks of beasts and of smiling faces; masks of tragedy and comedy, of the north wind, of sun, moon and stars. And in the centre of the room, on a draped podium, the great mask of the Black Sun. Next to it, also on the podium, a large copper ewer.

An audience of empty-eyed faces stared down at her.

Behind the masks, a great cat's cradle of pins and nails, each with a mask hanging from it and string, yarn, wool and catgut running from nail to nail. Some of the nails had small paper labels written in an elegant hand; others had no such marker. Masks, connected by thread both thick and thin, from spider web to rawhide. A great web all knotting and twisting around the walls of the ballroom, the threads beaded with silver condensation and dew from the shimmering, oily surface below.

This was the true city. And this was where the City spoke to her.

"*Mascherina Pallida!*" Her voice sounded very loud in the chamber. She took the ewer and poured its contents into the water around the dais; they stained the water shockingly red for a moment.

The mask of the black sun dipped on its stand for a moment, and then focussed upon her, intelligence and vivid life sparking from nothing in the eye sockets of the mask. The residue on the surface of the water, reflecting the mural of the old city above, suddenly seemed to coalesce and fill out the space between the mask and the water like boiling mist until, robed and hooded, Sun Face stood in the water before her and inclined her cruel face to see who called upon her.

"*Yhtill, Yhtill, Yhtill.*" Donna Zancani fell to her knees before the figure, and bowed her head. "I had thought you gone."

"It takes more than a thrown knife to destroy such as I, child," whispered the ghost of the City. "And do not bow to me; I am messenger and expediter, the soft man. One greater still than I is coming. I but herald his return."

All around the chamber, the masks on the walls whispered their secrets, one to another, and the cords and threads vibrated. The falling dew made rain in the chamber, and Sun Face raised its borrowed arms and laughed to be flesh once more, even if only for a little while.

After the torchlight red on sweaty faces

After the frosty silence in the gardens

After the agony in stony places

The shouting and the crying

Prison and place and reverberation

Of thunder of spring over distant mountains

He who was living is now dead

We who were living are now dying

With a little patience

T.S. Eliot, The Waste Land 321-330

The Lord Seneschal's Offices were close to the pinnacle of Castell'nuero, overlooking the sunken courtyard. Gawain stood, resting his fists on the balcony rail, watching the troops drill in the yard below. Next to him, watching just as keenly, stood the Lord Seneschal.

Henri di Schermo was a few inches taller than Gawain, and considerably older; his hair was iron-grey with streaks of white in the severe topknot; his craggy face lined with the wear of foreign sun and sea salt. He dressed plainly in a soldier's uniform, with only a deep purple sash to distinguish him from any officer, and his weapons were always to hand and both simple and well-worn, not ostentatious or ornamented. He held a plain goblet with a dent in one side, and swirled the brandy within speculatively.

"So. There's to be trouble then."

Gawain nodded. "Gian Galeazzo Visconti may come to you tomorrow and ask for troop support in storming the Rookeries – you absolutely must refuse him."

The Seneschal snorted. "Would anyway. Not having regular troops on the streets of Cittàvecchio. Out of the question. Not a bloody tyrant."

"It's about the Rookery murders. I've a lead on the criminals, a possible witness, but I'm going to have to try and pursue it myself and Visconti stomping over all of this would be disastrous at such a delicate moment. However…"

"Always a 'however' with you. Try living a simpler life, Gawain. Fewer 'howevers'."

"…however, it's possible that if I do manage to pull this witness out, there may be repercussions. The Rookeries may riot anyway, and if they do, it's important that Valentin and the Ducal Guard go in to put it down, not you and not Visconti."

Di Schermo regarded him warily. "Why?"

"Visconti and his men are for keeping the peace; Valentin and his men are for protecting the Duca's affairs, and your men are for protecting the city. It's a jurisdiction issue. But you'll have to order Visconti to stand down, he won't take it from me. It's for his own good in the long term and his men aren't trained for that kind of bloodshed. The Ducal Guard are…"

"No, I understand all that. Not an idiot. Why would the Rookeries riot?"

"Because I may have to start a fight with the Beggar King as cover to get the witness out."

"Ah." Di Schermo peered into his cup. "Good point, well made. That'll set the Rookeries off. This witness; worth it, is he?"

"His information might stop the Rookery murders. The benefits of giving Orfèo a slap can't be overstated, though."

"Gawain." The Seneschal had missed nothing and challenged the open and honest gaze of his protégé. "This is official business, yes?"

"Of course."

The older man regarded his pupil. "Nothing personal going on here?"

"No. Why would there be?" Gawain's face held the hint of a challenge; *push on this, and see where it gets you.*

"You have history with the beggars, Lord d'Orlato. Prefer not to put you in a position where your judgement might be questioned."

Gawain stiffened. "If my Lord Seneschal has doubts, one of the other Officers of the Levies would be equally able to acquit this duty."

Di Schermo considered long and hard, staring down at the courtyard. "I'll talk to Visconti. Tell him I'm handling this personally. Matter of internal security, going over his head, no reflection on him. And I'll tell Valentin to ready his men. Don't like the idea of that wretched beggar throwing his weight around. Get the witness out, I'll provide you with cover. Operation'll start at nine bells under Captain Valentin. Heavy presence, Ducal Guard, orders to stop anything that starts."

Gawain clicked his heels and gave a precise military bow. His smile was that of a loyal servant of Cittàvecchio and nothing more, but his eyes had the gleam of a man who was relishing his night's work.

"And Gawain – keep it tidy. Professional. No prosecuting personal grudges, understand?"

Gawain clicked his heels, saluted, and left the balcony.

He made his way down through the Castell'nuero and emerged onto the top of the *Via Fiore della Ciliega* just as the sun was setting over the city and the mist was rising off the canals like smoke. As the sun set, so the city's night life began to crawl from its hiding places; the further into the lower city he went, the darker it became, the more masks on the street, the more street entertainers and the fewer traders, merchants and businessmen. The city's respectable face was being hidden behind a gaudy confection of papier-mâché and polite consensual lies. And of course, with the street theatre and the high-class Cittàvecchi came the beggars.

The Grand Piazza was thronged with them – lurking in the shadows, flitting from shadowed archway to shadowed archway. Gawain watched them with care until he spotted one who seemed alone, and plotted a route that brought him within close distance of the beggar's alcove. A wretched specimen of humanity, as they all were, this one was afflicted with a wall-eye and weeping sores; he knew there was a process whereby their severity was aggravated the better to draw pity and therefore coin from the passing nobility. He dropped a ten-*piastre* coin in the wooden bowl and hunkered down before the ruined creature. "There's more, but I want to know something."

The beggar swung his good eye to Gawain and measured him, deciding how much coin this would be good for. "What do you want to know?"

"I am looking for a specific beggar who did me a favour last week. His name is Black Maffeo. Do you know him?"

The beggar rattled the bowl; Gawain dropped another coin in it. "Aye, I know Black Maffeo. But you'll not find him tonight; he's a guest of the King in the Rookeries this night. What manner of favour would Black Maffeo be doing for one such as you?"

"A wise beggar would not ask questions, he would simply give answers and earn coin thereby. If I were to go looking for Black Maffeo this night, where would I profit from looking? And don't just say 'the Rookeries', I'm no fool."

The bowl rattled again, and Gawain dropped a *ducat* into it. The beggar looked at the gold coin with mild surprise, then back at Gawain. "If you know enough about the King, you'll know it takes more than gold to make a beggar betray him. And the King wants Black Maffeo kept hidden for the while. Seek elsewhere for your answers, I know nothing of this."

Gawain stood, giving the beggar a hard look, and strode off. The beggar swiftly made the coins from his bowl disappear and eased his way to his feet; after such an encounter, no fool beggar stayed where he sat, and Orfèo had asked that any case of questions about Black Maffeo be reported straight back to him. And any noble willing to drop gold in a beggar's bowl wanted information *badly*.

He stood, rolled up his mat and tucked it under his arm, and hobbled along the edge of the Grand Piazza to one of the innumerable back streets that connected the upper city to the warrens of decaying buildings along the old waterfront. In such streets even after dark it was easy for a beggar to lose himself in the mists; besides, the robes of a beggar were better magic than a Cloak of Thieves when it came to not being seen in Cittàvecchio.

The mists thickened as he made his way closer to the river; what was a light ground mist in the Grand Piazza was a smothering blanket further down and this far from the social hub of the nighttime city torch-boys were few and far between. Other people were few and far between on this route; the only man the beggar passed was a leering yellow-eyed dwarf, packing his puppets away as the beggar passed, his monkey chittering on his shoulder.

He was perhaps two hundred yards from the waterfront and the relative safety of torchlight and the bridges when the blow came. He was bowled off his feet and his wooden begging bowl rattled to a halt in the gutter. Winded, he tried to find his feet but his assailant was too big and too fast, landing a well-aimed kick into the centre of his chest that winded him and kept him on the floor.

When he saw the blade, for the first time, genuine fear reared up in his breast.

In the distance, a cat's chorus began; cats always know when they are about to be fed. "You should have given it up for the gold. Now I'm going to have to *cut* it out of you," said Gawain.

*　*　*

Barocchio leaned back in his chair with an expression of some considerable surprise on his face. "I'm sorry, I'm clearly going deaf in my left ear. Could you repeat yourself, my Lord?"

"I say, I'll have the hundred for you in a month, when the dell'Allia ship from Montressori comes in, but until then I find myself somewhat financially embarrassed..." Gratiano's contrite expression was well schooled, but the sweat beads on his forehead did the illusion no favours.

"Do you deny that we had a wager, Lord dell'Allia?" Barocchio selected a walnut from the dish on the side of his desk and examined it minutely. "I clearly recall accepting your wager for a hundred Ducats that the manticore would settle the basilisk's hash. Do you recall that also?"

Gratiano nodded, his shoulders slumping.

"And you accept that a gentleman settles his bets with speed and good spirit, since this is after all merely a little sporting spice on an already excellent dish of entertainment?"

Gratiano nodded again.

"I have given you a full day and night to settle and now you come to me with a tale of financial impropriety and woe. My lord, I would almost suspect that you thought that my lack of noble blood meant that you need not take me *seriously*."

"I can assure you, I take all of my debts-"

Barocchio splintered the walnut in his fist and started picking shards of shell out from among the shattered nut. "*All* of your debts? So it is not just me, but other honest businessmen who await your noble pleasure for payment, and yet you come to me and ask for a *month* in which to pay a miniscule hundred? Perhaps in the gilded world in which you live such things are acceptable, my lord, but to an honest businessman they are a matter of livelihood, of livelihood, I say. No. Out of the question."

"Master Barocchio, I have every-"

"No. No, I'll not stand for this; it's arrogance plain and simple. But let it not be said that I am an intemperate man, or that I'm not prepared to cut people in trouble a little slack. I'll allow a fortnight from today, for an additional fifty per cent. But if you go so much as one day over that, my lord dell'Allia, or if the payment is not made in full, complete and with interest owing then the consequences for you will be most unfortunate. Am I making myself sufficiently clear or should I arrange a demonstration for you to ensure the matter remains *sharp* in your mind?"

Gratiano stood. "A hundred and fifty? But I- I'll have the money with you within the allotted fortnight, without question."

"Excellent. Then we have a *gentleman's* agreement, and it won't be necessary to remind you of this closer to the time. Let us shake upon it."

Barocchio shook the remaining shards of the smashed nut out of his palm and held it out; Gratiano, reluctantly, took it. His small white hand was lost in Barocchio's meaty fist and as his knuckles ground together he was uncomfortably reminded of the fate of the walnuts. "A fortnight, my Lord, to the hour, and not one minute more. To be paid to me, in person, in gold, here. Always a pleasure doing business with a member of the Quality."

Gratiano extricated his hand and bowed curtly, aware that Barocchio's lizard gaze had not once left him. Massaging some circulation back into his hand, he left Barocchio's office for the main room of the *Red Lion*.

Early in the evening, the *Lion* was quiet; a few patrons here and there but the real party animals were only just rising from their beds. Prospero, he suspected, would not be seen for another hour or two – until he'd taken his time over his appearance, and his spies had reported back to him where the parties were forming for the night.

Gratiano settled to a seat at the bar and gestured wearily to the barman. "I might as well spend what little life I have left in a pleasant pastime. Or failing that, drunk."

"Ah, the lament of the debtor…"

Gratiano turned round; stood just behind him, smiling enigmatically, was the dapper priest Fra Ottavio. "May I join you?"

Gratiano gestured to the seat next to him. "By all means, Father. I don't suppose you'd happen to have a cool hundred and fifty ducats lying around that you wouldn't miss for a month or so, would you?"

Ottavio laughed, a deep and rich sound from such a small man. "Alas no, I don't tend to carry that kind of currency around with me. Is it Prospero or Barocchio?"

"Barocchio."

Ottavio winced. "Nasty. At least Prospero would be civil while he fed you to his crocodiles, and all the best people would witness your death. Now all you have to hope for is a beating in a back alley…"

"Well you're just a tower of hope in the darkness, aren't you."

Ottavio smiled. "I will pray to the Child for your deliverance, my friend, but with no very great hope of success. In any case, that's not what I have sought you out for. I am told that you spotted Pater Felicio out and about late last night; is this true?"

Gratiano tensed and chose his words carefully. When two people asked innocently after the same piece of information in quick succession it was generally a sign that it was valuable, dangerous or both. "I saw him taking a late dinner at the *Priest's Hole*, yes."

Ottavio smiled and narrowed his golden eyes. "I see. And was he dining alone?"

"No, though I could not for the life of me tell you the identity of his companion."

"I would expect nothing less. Should anything further come of this, do remember to include me in your distribution of any further instalments of the matter, hmm? And to seal the deal, a *benedizione* for you, albeit a small one; I have the most profound certainty, Gratiano dell'Allia, that as long as you do not shed the blood of another, your luck is about to change…" Ottavio winked at him with a twinkle in his eye, and made for the door. As he made his way out, he passed a messenger in the doorway, the man clearly winded.

"My Lord dell'Allia? A message for you…" The runner was out of breath, and looked as though he'd come flat out from the upper city. "A commission from Lord d'Orlato – he says I was to find you and tell you to meet him at nine bells on the *Ponte Amanti*. He says there's gold in it for you."

Gratiano perked up. "Where did you see him? And when?" He signalled to the barman, raised two fingers and then pointed to himself and the messenger.

The messenger sat gratefully. "On the waterfront, by the statue of the three dogs and the fallen horseman. He was washing his hands in the fountain and called me over. Told me there was an extra ducat in it for me if I found you within the hour. That was about half an hour ago. I've been up to Castell'nuero twice to try and find you, chasing rumours…"

"What was the last bell?"

"The Cathedrale tolled seven as I was making my way here."

"Then I've time for a drink, my good man, and so have you. You've done me well tonight, and a stiff drink is the least of my gratitude."

* * *

In the throng of the evening streets, nobody took any notice of two masked and cloaked figures as they stood watching a puppet play at a street corner. The misshapen puppeteer alone watched them, a gleam in his yellow eyes as the conversation turned back and forth between them in quiet tones.

Sun Face watched the puppets; one of the older, less popular plays of the *commedia*. *Brighella*, the heartless and slippery servant made good, was luring his employer Pantaleone, the good-natured fool, into a terrible trap. This, as she recalled, ended rather badly for all concerned – except, of course, *il Dottore*, who always comes out well when Pantaleone suffers.

Donna Zancani watched the pair of them, aware that something was at play beneath the surface of things. The puppeteer was a misshapen dwarf she had seen here and there about the city, but the way he looked at Sun Face – and the way Sun Face looked back at him – suggested there was more to him than just a beggar with a knack for theatre.

"Do not be so foolish as to assume I am the only mask this city wears, Donna Elizabeta. Cittàvecchio has many faces; one for each inhabitant, you might say." Sun Face turned to her. "We use the tools best suited to the task; and the task at the moment is to remove an impediment to our future plans."

Sun Face inclined her head. "You know the deck well enough. What crosses the *Re Stracciati?*"

"The Holy Fool according to the legends, but – "

"But nothing. If our Pantaleone, our Holy Fool, is abroad in the city, then this will flush him out and ruin him. You must turn your back on him, Elizabeta. He is anathema to us."

"Then why not kill him? Would it not be so much easier?"

The puppeteer spoke for the first time. "Never kill a fool. Five grow up where once there was one. There are better ways of neutering such things."

The trap was set, and *Brighella* retreated, laughing, as it closed around *Pantaleone*.

"Watch," whispered Sun Face. "No man remains holy for long with innocent blood on his hands."

* * *

The fog was thick by the time Gratiano reached the *Ponte Amanti* – he nearly missed Gawain, who was hidden in the shadows of one of the bridge supports. Over the upper city, the Cathedrale campanile tolled nine as Gawain emerged from his hiding place and with a crooked finger beckoned Gratiano to follow him. He had a large leather sack that he hefted over his shoulder, obviously quite weighty.

"The messenger said you had a job, something that might earn real money?"

Gawain nodded.

"Only my situation has got a little worse since yesterday. The debt has inflated a touch..."

"*Will* you shut your prattle." Gratiano was shocked silent, more by the venom in Gawain's tone than by the content of his statement. "Just shut up, and follow me. Don't talk."

They made their way over the bridge and down into the shrouded depths of the city's ghettoes. Here and there in the distance, muffled by the fog, the sound of an argument or a fight could be heard; now and then the flash of torches. They were well into the Rookeries now, the streets narrow and the buildings all too tall for Gratiano's liking. This was not his idea of reasonable employment; in fact, anything that took him into the Rookeries after dark wasn't his idea of reasonable. He was becoming acutely aware that he was dressed for an evening on the town, and that, to the wretched villains that lived down here, was a signal of money and a worthwhile robbery. Gawain, he noted, was dressed in sensible and hard wearing dark greys and blacks and was carrying a businesslike sword, as opposed to Gratiano's own rather fancy court sword – the very thing for duels and posturing but not so good for a wild melee. The small hairs on the back of Gratiano's neck were stood to attention, and the moisture condensing on his upper lip was as much the cold sweat of fear as it was the night fogs.

A cry, shockingly loud, off to the left; Gratiano jumped, but Gawain dropped the heavy sack behind him, caught his arm and dragged him into a doorway, his other hand over the younger man's mouth to prevent a scream. The thunder of boots on cobbles and a group of troops in the distinctive crimson of the Duca's livery stormed past.

Gratiano waited, shocked silent. Gawain had one arm looped around his neck, the other hand pressed still over his mouth and he leaned in close to whisper his words.

"We're shortly to be about our night's business. Now; I am about to ask you to do something. If you do it to my satisfaction, I'll see to it that your debt with Barocchio is quitted, in full, no arguments. Understand? Nod if you understand."

Gratiano nodded, his eyes like saucers.

"Good. Now; around the next corner and to the left there is a courtyard. On the left hand wall of that courtyard there is a climbing vine on the wall that goes up all the way to the third floor balcony. I am shortly going to create a distraction in the courtyard; you are to climb up that vine, and when I light the torch below you are to break into the room beyond the balcony, and kill the man you find there. You must do this swiftly, you understand? And you must use this knife." He pressed a long, thin stiletto into Gratiano's hand.

Gratiano swallowed, his mouth suddenly dry. "Gawain, I'm no soldier, I-"

"This isn't a soldier's job, boy. You're about the work of the Duca here, or would you prefer to just be signed into Barocchio's slavery now? I can just see you as the kept boy of some Barbary potentate, keeping your spit for when the Sultan wants his sceptre polished..." Gawain reached down and grabbed Gratiano by the balls, briefly. "Those'll be the first to go, of course, can't be having you causing trouble with the ladies of the harem..."

"Alright, alright, Mother and *Child*, Gawain. Mother and *Child*." He looked at the stiletto, then looked back at Gawain. "Who is this man...?"

"That, you will come to understand, is a question you will not ask. In this case, he is a murderer and a thief, and that's all you need know. I am charged with the Seneschal's business, as he is charged with the Duca's, and I need backup. Now are you man enough for it or not?"

"Oh, Father above, I can't do this! I've never killed anyone in my life! I-"

Gawain drew his own knife, slowly and with a cold, emotionless gaze at Gratiano. "At this point in time, what frightens you more; the prospect of doing what you are bid, or the prospect of facing me having failed to do so?"

Gratiano watched the tip of Gawain's knife weave back and forth, hypnotised.

"Good. Now remember; wait for the torch. Go! Before more troops come by…"

Gratiano tucked the dagger into his belt and edged off into the fog. He was debating running, but this deep in the Rookeries on his own he knew it would take a miracle to see him out safely, and that was assuming Gawain didn't cut him down, which he seemed more than prepared to do. He felt as though, at some time in the last fifteen minutes, his life had suddenly tipped over the edge into the abyss and it was all he could do to hold on to what tatters of sanity he could.

He had always suspected there was something a touch dangerous about Gawain; it was part of his charm. Gratiano had known him for over a year, and in that time, while he'd been aware the older man worked for the Lord Seneschal, the details of his employment had always been vague. He was never short of a modest amount of money but he shied away from the massive ostentation of Prospero; he had a reputation as a rake, but nothing compared to that of Lord Xavier. Gawain had always carried the air of espionage, of adventure in the service of the Duca about him. He had seemed an excellent bet for a young man of moderate but financially challenged family to attach himself to in order to make his way in Cittàvecchio. That blithe assumption was, reflected Gratiano as he made his way along the slimy, dripping wall, arguably the most foolish he had made in the entirety of his short and unhappy life to date.

In his head, populated by penny dreadful stories and romantic notions of heroic deeds, night-time missions such as this were always conducted with flair and panache, in the black and white of certainty. Close up, he realised, such certainties were a luxury and in the end everything was the colour of dirty, murky fog. He felt the dagger hilt jabbing into his ribs and in that moment it was more real and cold and solid than anything else; a reminder that in the next few minutes he was supposed to kill another man. He swallowed, and tasted the acid bile of fear.

He edged along, back to the wall until he found the corner, and then nervously made his way along the wall, feeling ahead with his hands until he located the vine, hanging where Gawain said it would be. The mists were so thick he could not even see the other side of the courtyard and the chill was settling into his bones. He gingerly tested the vine; it seemed secure enough. He heard slow, dragging movement behind him, and froze in terror; but it was Gawain, ghosting past him in the fog, pulling the leather sack along the ground. "Courage, dell'Allia," he whispered. "Courage, for the Duca. Your problems are about to come to an end."

He braced himself against the wall and started the slow, careful climb up to the third floor balcony. The thunder of his heart was so loud he could barely breathe; he realised he was hiccupping, and shaking with terror. Halfway up the vine, he stopped, and closed his eyes for a second; beneath him in the courtyard he could *sense* the stillness, could feel Gawain's eyes on him.

He reached the base of the third floor balcony, hooked his arm around one of the balcony rails and looked own. A spark, and then another; and then the flare of a torch.

He couldn't move.

Gawain stood in the centre of the courtyard, flaming torch in one hand. In the centre of the courtyard lay a shape that it took Gratiano a moment to identify as a body – a body in beggar's weeds, stained shockingly red.

"Orfèo!" roared Gawain, watching Gratiano. He was smiling an open and happy smile – the first genuine smile Gratiano had ever seen him give. "Orfèo!"

Then he doused the torch in the gutter and disappeared into the fog. Below Gratiano he heard the sound of people spilling out of the house, then screams; the fog swirled as if from the motion of many people, but with the torch doused he could see little from this height.

He still couldn't move. He knew if he didn't, he'd die. One of them would look up sooner or later.

He forced his fingers to unlock, and as quietly as he could, clambered onto the balcony. His plan was to hide there for as long as possible, maybe get up onto the rooftop and try to escape from this nightmare over the chimneys and gables of the Rookeries, but then the shutters were thrown open from inside and he found himself abruptly face to face with a beggar.

The boy was no older than fifteen; wrapped in grey sackcloth and thin to the point of emaciation, with a black birthmark all up one side of his face. His eyes went comically wide as he saw Gratiano, then he shrieked "Murder! Murder!" His cries were lost in similar ones from below, but the word galvanised him.

Gratiano lunged through the window, trying to muffle the beggar's cries with his hand. All he could see were the huge panicked eyes. He landed atop the boy with some force, and tried to use his body weight to hold him down, but the boy wriggled like an eel and sank his teeth into Gratiano's hand; he cursed, and snatched it back. As he did so, the boy shrieked again and he felt fire score along his side. *The bastard has a blade!*

Panic overwhelmed him; he crammed his forearm into the boy's throat, desperate to silence him, and bore down on him with his full weight, all the time frantically punching the boy's emaciated ribs with his free hand. The beggar's hands scrabbled for Gratiano's eyes, then for his throat, finding purchase only on his neckerchief, their flailing becoming weaker even as it became more frantic.

The boy was more or less of a size with Gratiano, but the benefits of regular meals and exercise were too telling, and both knew it. Gratiano watched the eyes fill with profound fear under him as the beggar boy tried to gasp out something, tried to shape words even as his throat was being crushed, batting feebly now at his assailant's face. He kept the pressure on the boy's throat for a good minute, until his heels had stopped drumming on the floor, until the eyes rolled up and the light within went out. He rolled off the boy and took a sobbing, heaving breath.

Gawain was crouched, silhouetted, in the window.

"Useless." Gawain climbed into the room, reached down and pulled the knife out of Gratiano's belt. "Go out onto the balcony and climb up the rest of the ivy onto the roof. I'll join you shortly."

Gratiano lay on his back, shaking; Gawain nudged him with his foot. "Or, stay and watch me, your choice."

"What- what did he do?"

Gawain hefted the dagger and looked at Gratiano as if surprised he could speak. "What?"

"What was it he did that meant that he had to die?" He still couldn't look at the body.

"He saw something he should not have seen and now he is dead and will see nothing ever again, nor will he tell what he saw. Now are you going to stay and see something that *you* should not see? Or would fresh air be a better idea?"

Gratiano scrambled out of the window and clambered up the vine. He made it to the roof before the wet noises of Gawain's work in the room below began.

* * *

Some ten minutes later, Gawain joined him on the roof. Below, the Rookeries were lost in an ocean of grey mist, punctuated here and there by the orange glare of a fire. Gratiano sat, hugging his knees, staring out unseeing over the roofscape.

"You have done me, the Duca and the city a great service this evening, Gratiano. And rest assured you'll be appropriately rewarded for it. There's much to do in Cittàvecchio for someone with the nerve to do it. What's this? Wounded? Ah, just a graze, you'll heal fine."

"He was just a boy."

"He was just *meat*, Gratiano. And maggot-ridden beggar-meat at that. Not like us. Not real, not true flesh and blood. Just a ghost of the city, a child of its mists and fevers. It is no crime to kill a ghost without a name, without a face. And now you are blooded and sealed in a pact with the city. Look; have you a kerchief about you?"

Wordlessly, Gratiano found a square of cloth up his sleeve and passed it to Gawain, who wiped his bloody hands on it. "Now come, lad. I think I should buy you a drink or three. You've done well."

Unsteadily, Gratiano got to his feet; the rooftops stretched away all the way to the river, above the mist. In the distance, he could see the bulk of the Castell'nuero squatting on the hill like an old toad, wise and unblinking.

"What will become of me?"

Gawain took his arm companionably. "Nothing, if you remember to keep your mouth shut. All who saw you are dead, and there is nothing to link you to the scene. Just keep your nerve. Imagine it to be a poker game for high stakes in a darkened room. Keep your face, and you'll win through in the end…"

They set off across the roofs, Gawain supporting Gratiano. But before they did, shielded from Gratiano by his body, Gawain dropped the bloodstained kerchief from the edge of the roof down into the courtyard.

It fluttered down, and was lost in the mists.

Part Two: A Wicked Pack of Cards

What is that sound high in the air

Murmur of maternal lamentation

Who are those hooded hordes swarming

Over endless plains, stumbling in cracked earth

Ringed by the flat horizon only

What is the city over the mountains

Cracks and reforms and bursts in the violet air

Falling towers

T.S. Eliot, The Waste Land 366-373

For several days after the riots, the Rookeries were silent, as if the violence of that night and the horror of the double murder had beaten them into submission.

As expected, the incursion of Ducal troops into the Rookeries had been inflammatory in the extreme; the results had been explosive. Some buildings, deep in the heart of the Rookeries, had burned for three days uninterrupted; nobody knew how many had died in the fires. The Tatar Guard had brutally put down the abortive riots, and the Duca, incensed at civic unruliness, had ordered a string of executions to drive the point home. Men whose only crime was to be in the wrong place at the wrong time found themselves chained to the pillars of the *Ponte Amanti* until high tide came in and the crabs did their work; others hung from dockside gibbets, their necks stretched to unnatural lengths and bent at unnatural angles. Those, too high for even the ambitious river crabs, the ravens saw to.

None of those who died were men of money or substance. The few of those to be found in the Rookeries during the raid had either the wherewithal to bribe their way to safety or the wisdom to keep their heads down until they were in the company of more corruptible – or biddable – captors than the Ducal Guard. And, indeed, nobody complained; for there are few things more likely to keep a civic population entertained than a round of bloody and barbaric executions, and the Duca knew the temper of his people well.

For the entirety of those few days, no man saw a beggar in Cittàvecchio. They had simply vanished.

The more callow of the gentry rejoiced; they loudly claimed that the Duca's justice and the stern discipline of the Tatars had seen the vermin off once and for all; others of a more practical mindset watched the crumbling and decaying Rookeries with concern. Among the Priesthood however, especially those who tended more to the Child than the Father or Mother, there was no rejoicing, and much concern and quiet talk in darkened cloisters. Fra Ottavio il Gatto, perhaps the most senior and certainly the most well-known of this group, went into the Rookeries himself several times – a fact that gained him no small notoriety among the social set. When quizzed on what he had heard, he simply smiled his enigmatic smile and reminded the listener of the sanctity of the confessional.

No new word on what they were calling *The Fiend in the Fog* – at least, that's what they were calling it in the salons and cafes of fashionable society, where the deaths made for entertainment and gave lurid colour to the grey autumnal days. It was whispered that on the night of the double murder the *Vigilanza* had been on the very tail of the murderer and close to catching him; some said they were co-operating with the Tatars, others that the Tatar outrages aided the murderer's escape. Some even whispered that the murderer was a member of the Ducal Guard himself, but they did not whisper this too loudly when Captain Valentin was in earshot, for in the aftermath of the riots he was high in the favour of the Duca, and those who suggested such things found themselves abruptly inconvenienced by the arrival of high tide.

Captain Visconti of the *Vigilanza*, it was said, took the double murder as a personal affront. He had defied orders and gone into the Rookeries (after the Tartary Exiles had done their work) with four of his best men and the gossip around the town was that Visconti had cut some kind of deal with the mysterious King of the Beggars whereby his men could now come and go in the Rookeries without let or hindrance. Gian Galeazzo Visconti kept his own counsel, rising at dusk and returning to his bed well past dawn on each day, and spending every waking moment with his men in the bowels of the city. Those who knew him well commented that he had taken to drink, not as a man embraces a long lost lover, but as a man grasps at a floating spar when he is drowning.

Nobody in society knew what was being said about the situation in the Rookeries save Captain Visconti; and if he knew, he kept his own counsel, or shared it only with the ever-attentive bottom of the bottle.

* * *

Among the rich, though, in their salons and their soirees, the affair of the Fiend merely enlivened the dull days. Thus far he had murdered only honest tradesmen, beggars and in one case, an actor whom all agreed was probably past his best performances. A merciful killer! Lord Prospero even went so far as to suggest that the Fiend was an art critic, cleansing the streets of Cittàvecchio of the *untidy*. And though many laughed at this suggestion, few let their mirth reach their eyes. Beneath the masks of the Cittàvecchi, all watched each other carefully. The rumours were already circulating – the *Vigilanza* had found something the night of the murders, something that suggested that the Fiend in the Fog was one of them, one of the nobility. Some said it was a kerchief, bloodstained with the gore of one of the victims; others that an ornamental dagger had been found at the scene, too fancy for the middle classes. Others still said a verse had been written in blood on the wall of the garret where the last victim was found, a verse that pointed to one of the Great Families, and that Captain Valentin had ordered it wiped away before anyone saw it and leapt to the wrong conclusion, not that the Cittàvecchi were prone to such things…

Traditionally, in Cittàvecchio one marked the Autumnal Equinox with the Grand Regatta and the masked ball following on from it; one of the four great festivals of the year for the city of mist and masks. The week before the Grand Regatta usually saw a series of increasingly outrageous events as the city's nobility competed with one another in excess and flamboyance; but the beginning of Festivàle Season this year saw an, at best, subdued response from the nobility.

In many minds, thoughts turned to the forthcoming Masked Ball – and the opportunities open to an assassin at such a time[5]. People thought of the recent execution of Lord Feron for sedition, and they wondered. In the Red Lion, the talk was all of conspiracy; of the possibility that someone was fomenting revolution. Did Lord Feron have allies, perhaps? Allies that even now killed in the Rookeries to bring the city to boiling point?

Such discussions took place only in darkened corners, though; far from the Donna Ophelia, who shone like a beacon in the gathering night. She ordered her own men down into the Rookeries to put out the fires; donated heavily to the Church fund for the area; promised Fra Ottavio that she would try to intercede with her brother for the lives of those yet to be executed. And always in the background while she did such things, young Lord di Tuffatore, with his solicitous air but his sad, sad eyes, and Mater Calomena, the Donna's mentor with her veil and her knowing air.

Few saw anything of young Lord dell'Allia in the days after the murders; it was said that he had taken to his bed with a chill.

* * *

---

[5] In Cittàvecchio, the last days of autumn, between the Autumnal Equinox and the first snows of winter, are called the *Dying Days*, because three of the city's six great masquerades take place in this period and traditionally, the great masquerades are the best time for assassins to strike at figures in public office. The number of masked people on the streets, the opportunities for disguise and deception and the traditions of the citywide masquerades are an assassin's paradise and, as is commonly observed, a hell especially designed to torment bodyguards.

While Cittàvecchio's poor lay in the grip of the night terrors that come in the fog and its rich pretended to amusement at the unsophisticated activity of the lower classes to hide their own growing unease, an altogether different mood gripped the city of Buchara, three days away over the mountains.

The great river that divided the city in two, west to east, was slow and sluggish in the autumn, choked with the silt of the mountains and girdled by dozens of long, slender stone bridges that connected the sprawling port quarter on the north bank to the steep and winding cobbled alleyways of the *Altes Viertel*. Old Buchara – the southern half of the city from whence the Grafs ruled their growing empire – was built in a series of artificial terraces carved into the cliffs of the Teufelberg. Two-thirds of the way up the towering cliffs, the gothic spires of Castle Ferenczy looked down over the sprawl of Buchara like some bird of prey crouched over a mountain nest.

Cittàvecchio was justly proud of the City Levies. Under the Lord Seneschal, they had become one of the most respected and versatile fighting forces in the south and the Military College the Seneschal had set up in his early days was still a centre of excellence; but being composed of native Cittàvecchi, and generally only being pressed into service in the defence of Cittàvecchi interests it was perhaps not surprising they were regarded so. Men fight fiercely in defence of their homes and livelihoods. Hence actions such as the storming of the Rookeries fell to the Tatar Guard rather than the City Levies. However, in Buchara, different standards applied, and different rules were in play. Buchara's army fought not for defence of home and hearth, but for the release of merciful death, and under such circumstances they fought who they were told, where they were told, without fear or favour.

The Janizaries were rightly feared by every other civilised nation. Captured prisoners of fighting age, they sought that death with a ferocity and savagery that free men could seldom match. Whispered legend told of a secret chamber within Castle Ferenczy the inside of which only Janizaries had seen, and that whatever terrible process, creature or charm hid within that chamber, it drained their blood and their soul and made them pale and fanatical slaves to the will of the Grafs. And unlike their sophisticated brethren of Cittàvecchio, who believed *benedizione* and *maledizione* alike to be the province of the Trinity and any others who claimed them to be charlatans, the folk of Buchara were a superstitious lot, and when the Janizaries came by, they got out of the way.

Mercutio del Richo kept his head down and his hood up. Like everyone else, he had flattened himself against the wall as the troop of pallid men armoured in lacquered purple scale mail had trooped past, their steps in perfect synchronisation and their eyes as cold and dead as a shark's. *They have found the break-in, then.*

The problem, of course, with troops like the Janizaries is that relying as they do on fear for a large degree of their impact, when a suitably determined man investigates the security they provide he often finds it wanting, because after all, *nobody would dare to cross the Janizaries.* But gold is a powerful motivating tool, and gold aplenty is what Pater Felicio Caritavo had promised Mercutio de Richo for this particular task. *Steal the Re Stracciati Deck from castle Ferenczy, and deliver it into the hands of the art dealer Elizabeta Zancani.*

It had been almost too easy – the deck had sat in a small wooden box, in a display case in the library. Given the politics of Buchara, attention was focussed almost exclusively on protecting people, not things – the security of the castle would have been formidable were he planning on trying to kill someone. Trying to avoid seeing *anyone* meant that all he had to do was be careful with his timing. No alarms, no traps, nothing. It had not even occurred to the Grafs, apparently, that anyone would dare break into the castle for the impertinent purpose of *stealing.* Additionally, like guards the world over, the castle guards at Ferenczy never *looked up.* Stay among the rafters, descend from them swiftly and silently on a rope, and the goal can be yours with minimal effort.

This was not the first such theft that Mercutio had performed; amongst those who knew about such things his name was always in the first five mentioned when a well-protected object had to be abruptly relocated without recourse to its owner for permission. In the shadowy circles in which he moved, people spoke his name approvingly when the matter of the Montressori Diamonds came up, or the mysterious disappearance of the Giovedi triptych from the Monastery of the Holy Birth in Lusan. All well-guarded *objets d'art* with values variously assessed as upwards of incalculable. And all, if the rumours were to be believed, now in the possession of the Duca di Gialla, a man who did not let the small matter of legal ownership impede his appreciation of the finest that the world of art could offer.

This was different, though. The triptych, the diamonds; valuable in their own right and beautiful as objects in and of themselves, they did not have the same resonance, the same significance as the eighty thin pasteboards in a wooden box that bumped against del Richo's ribs. It was fashionable among the Cittàvecchi in this day and age (unless one was of the Church) to scoff at the occult; the days of dragons, miracles, great quests and magical swords stuck in pagan altars were long gone. Even the *Bestia Fabula*, beasts such as manticores and basilisks, were so scarce now that their sightings were often years apart, and extravagances such as Barocchio and Prospero's pit fights all the more exciting for their rarity. But amongst this there were a few things of which even the most avid child of the Age of Reason would not question the occult nature, and the *Re Stracciati* deck was one such. It was too intrinsically tied to the very history of Cittàvecchio itself.

The legends around the deck's origins were many and contradictory; the few things they agreed on were that it had originated in Cittàvecchio, before its fall and renaming and at the height of its Imperial power. A Seeress had painted the cards to try and capture the *genius loci* of the place, to channel the power and destiny of Cittàvecchio itself into a predetermined course; to bring to life the very spirit of the city and of its far-flung empire.

According to legend (ah, how many sins of omission can be covered by such a glib phrase!) she succeeded, and in bringing to life the spirit of Imperial Cittàvecchio, she called forth the *Re Stracciati*, the Tattered King himself. And for a period of time, the City and the Empire ruled itself as it saw fit.

While studying for this job, Mercutio had consulted all the authorities on the deck and the period; the legends of the fall of the Tattered King are as numerous and varied as the tales of what occurred during his reign. None even agree on what brought his reign to an end. Some speak of a fool, a madman who the King could not touch; others of hubris against the Gods provoking the great flood that sank the city's lower districts; others still point to the great Siege, saying the outlying provinces, appalled at what went on under the King's ragged golden banner, rebelled. The cards, though, are a key thread to almost all of the tales; their uncanny predictive powers, the things that one could do with them if one understood how they related to one another.

After the fall of the King, the legends then become tangled, complex; the cards were stolen, or somehow tainted; a number of false cards (variously given as four, sixteen or twenty-eight) were inserted into the deck by a sorcerer or a fool to corrupt the purpose of the cards and lure their power away; and finally, ignominiously, the Duca d'Amato, a century and a half ago, had gambled and lost the cards to Graf Radislav Stechau of Buchara, and in Buchara they had been ever since, an heirloom of the Stechau family and a talisman of the rising power of the inland city.

The Bucharans, of course, still nailed garlic over their window frames, regarded concepts like *an Age of Reason* as dangerously heretical rubbish, and still remembered the rule of the *Re Stracciati* just fine. The witches of Buchara thought that the deck of cards would be much better – and safer – kept under their watchful eyes than the dangerously liberal Sisterhood of the Mother in Cittàvecchio. And since then, Buchara had resisted – usually politely, on occasion quite bluntly – every effort by the Cittàvecchi to recover this "quaint heirloom of their past".

* * *

These were not the legends that concerned Mercutio as he flitted from archway to wooden promenade through Buchara, heading for the stables with just sufficient speed to make his deadlines but not so fast as to attract attention. No; it was the ghastly fate of the Duca d'Amato, and then of the Graf Stechau that bothered him. Ever since the Duca d'Amato had lost the cards, every man who had ever owned them had come to an unfortunate end in keeping with one of the cards. The Duca himself, drowned with his foot trapped in the cleft of a submerged branch, in perfect imitation of the *Drowned Man* card; the Graf, killed in the collapse of his treasury doors; buried alive under a pile of gold that uncannily resembled the *Bounty of Avarice* card. More deaths, mirroring cards major and minor, continued right down to living memory; nowadays the cards were officially in the keeping of the ruling Graf's wife.

A Cittàvecchi would call this coincidence and perhaps bad luck; the Bucharans called it a curse, and ensured only women officially owned the cards. Mercutio fervently kept foremost in his mind that as far as the law was concerned, the Grafin Stechau still *owned* the cards and he was merely *facilitating their movement from point to point* until they were in the keeping of Elizabeta Zancani. After that, the Fates and the Furies could argue the toss for all he cared.

He had spent the day in dockside Buchara seeking out an old woman named Mama Koldana, who touted herself about as having the second sight, of being the seventh daughter of an only child, of being touched by the Lords and Ladies[6]. All of that was likely for show, dockside profit and the amazement of passing custom – but in the circles where Mercutio moved, she

---

[6] Bucharan folklore speaks extensively of those called the *Lords and Ladies*, *Those Of The Air* or *The Invisibles*; creatures who existed in a shadow-world half in and half out of our own. Some were benign, others much less so. Small rituals existed whereby Those Of The Air could be appeased and occasionally even persuaded to assist in small household tasks; the price of such assistance was that one mis-step in one of the rituals of propitiation had consequences ranging from the humorous to the ghastly. Childrens' tales and Bucharan folk wisdom has much to say about Those Of The Air; like many Bucharan superstitions, this is regarded as a quaint cultural phenomenon by most Cittàvecchi.

had a reputation as more than just a charlatan when it came to charms of protection and weavings of luck. People who had visited Mama Koldana had not regretted it and had been lucky when they most needed to be. Such things tend to build a loyal customer base and this was not the first time Mercutio had visited her for a blessing before a job in Buchara.

Mama Koldana, as ever, had not enquired as to his plans, satisfied that "a warding against ill fortune and discovery" meant the usual. To make a charm, she read his cards; her own stained and weathered pasteboards made, as so many Bucharan decks are, in imitation of those he sought to steal.

She had laid the cards out in the traditional cross and crown, and then as she turned them over, watched him narrowly.

"An endeavour with an easy beginning and a hard end?" Her voice, without the faux accent with which she lured in the sailors and gullible passers-by, was soft and lisping, and younger than her looks suggested.

He nodded, unwilling to share details. She turned over another card, and then another; made a 'harrumph' noise in the back of her throat and watched him again.

"*Ambuscado.* You'll have a rough time crossing the pass back to Cittàvecchio."

"Am I going back to Cittàvecchio?" He quirked an eyebrow, a loose grin never quite roosting on his jaw.

"Hah." She cackled. "Not if you don't have eyes in the back of your head. There are people in those mountains who look at you, and decide whether to kill you or not based on whether you look good enough to eat; and you are a plump and healthy boy, Mercutio."

"Less of the *plump,* you cheeky hag."

She turned over the final cards and scowled. "The *Holy Fool* crosses the *Hollow Man* under the shadow of the *Tattered King* himself. This is an ill-omened enterprise you embark on, Mercutio. Can I persuade you out of it?"

He shook his head. "The fee is paid and accepted and I am a man of my word."

She shrugged fatalistically. "What will be, will be. I will make you a *benedizione* to ward off the malign influences of the Invisibles, and another for luck against surprise attack. But against this…" she gestured at the cards, then swept them into a jumbled pile, obscuring the layout. "This, I can do nothing for. Far beyond me or you. Trust to your God, Mercutio. He will see you right or see you home."

"Well aren't you just full of cheer."

"All the young men say so. And I want paying in advance; your credit is no good here."

She had given him a headscarf to wear and a small bag of dried herbs to tie around his neck; he had followed her instructions religiously, visited the Church of the Father and made his devotions as she specified. He felt no different, and did not expect to; the pragmatist in him simply believed in playing the percentages.

He reached the hostelry where his horse and tack were quartered and glanced back up the mountain, over the quaint angled roofs of the houses. High above Buchara, Castle Ferenczy was framed against the sky, clouds piling up behind it. He tipped the ostler generously to ensure both speed and a degree of silence; knowing Bucharans, of course, a generous tip would earn silence in minutes, not hours, but minutes would be all that he would need. The Janizaries were still several streets away in their search and they were nothing if not thorough and unimaginative in such matters. He felt the reassuring weight of the wooden case next to his chest and swiftly and competently saddled his horse. If he left tonight, before curfew, he could be back in Cittàvecchio the night before the Grand Regatta, and just in time for his maximum delivery bonus.

He went to the wicker case at the back of his saddlebags, and from within he drew out a pigeon, with a thin streamer of yellow silk tied to its leg. He cooed into the bird's ear softly, and then released it to the wind; it set a course south, away from the storm. *Fly home, little pigeon. Fly to Cittàvecchio and herald my return to the Pater. I trust that my flight will be as trouble-free as yours.* He mounted his horse, and rode the short distance from the hostelry to the great Gates of Buchara, slipping through them just ahead of the curfew lantern. Nothing but the mountains and three days of hard, highwayman-haunted road lay between him and his delivery. He loosened his sword in its scabbard reflexively.

All I need now, he thought to himself, *is a run of lucky cards.*

* * *

The Grafin stood on the path running along the crenellated battlements of Castle Ferenczy, the wild wind whipping her translucent hair into a rippling flag. High overhead, storm clouds gathered like delinquent children around the peak of the Teufelberg, promising a night of rain and tempest for the city. The air was pregnant, potent with unbirthed thunder.

She let the functionary approach unheeded. Lord Buskovy; *Master of the Castle Stair* or some such title. Presumably he had been the first in a descending list of ministers not to find a more pressing duty than delivering the bad news to the Grafin. He would not meet her gaze; even after she had begun affecting the smoky glass spectacles, rumour and speculation still ran rampant in the castle that to meet her pink eyes head on was to be cursed. She had become used to men not meeting her gaze and now, she no longer expected it.

Lady Irina was an albino, but that did not change the fact that she was, by birth, the scion of the Stechau family and, by marriage, of the Ferencz family and those two bloodlines made her the most powerful Grafin in Buchara – or more specifically, they made her the most powerful Grafin while her husband was away at the wars in the north. And she found many ruses and reasons to keep him there, and he accounted himself happy to be so kept. Graf Nikolai fought the good fight against the pagans; his wife remained at home and governed his affairs. Both were entirely content with this arrangement.

"Where are my cards, Lord Buskovy?" Her voice was quiet, soft and almost lost in the wind. Buskovy, a small man, portly and bandy-legged, ran the brim of his hat through his hands in a frenzy of terror. "The Janizaries are still out, Grafin, but initial reports from the castle's staff suggests the thief may have already escaped the city. The cards may be lost, Lady. Report from the southern gate tells of a Cittàvecchi man who left on horseback just before curfew as if Iblis and all his ifrit were on his tail."

"Cittàvecchi," breathed the Grafin.

Buskovy nodded, once. "A charm seller from the docks has come forward and testified that the Cittàvecchi came to her looking for charms of good luck and protection for a dangerous undertaking and that he was specifically interested in something that would ward off curses."

The Grafin's face did not move. "She has unwoven her charms?"

"She is doing so as we speak."

"Good. See to it she is paid in silver, whatever she asks and three pieces in addition." She smiled coolly. "The Duca has lusted after those cards ever since he saw them here. Indeed, it's been the desire of the Dukes of Cittàvecchio to arrange the return of those cards ever since they lost them to us. It appears that the current incumbent of that seat does not know a good thing when he sees it and has decided to test the patience of the Stechau and the durability of the cards' own *maledizione*." The Grafin smiled, her lips very red against the porcelain pallor of her face.

"If he imagines I will not explore such a clumsy artifice as a theft then it will not require a mystical pack of cards to tell *his* fortune. Ready a carriage, an escort of Janizaries and my household, Buskovy. We go to the City of the Mists. I intend to get to the heart of this matter."

Buskovy let out a breath he had been holding for a considerable period of time. "As the Grafin commands." He saluted smartly and turned on his heel.

"And Buskovy?"

He winced. "My Lady?"

"The guards. The shift that were on duty when the theft was performed. I want them all executed."

Buskovy paled. "*All* of them, my Lady?"

"*All* of them, Buskovy. It is intolerable that a thief got in. I'll not countenance this kind of laxness when the assassination season is almost upon us. Any one of us might have been the target, not a deck of cards, no matter how valuable. Do we not pay them well enough? Sharpen the remaining guards' attention to duty by shortening their compatriots by one head's height."

Buskovy bowed again, and left, to carry out the Grafin's orders.

The Grafin leaned heavily on the battlements. The loss of the cards – bound to become public knowledge soon enough – would leave the other Grafs wondering if she was weakening. Much was made of her supposed powers, of her curses and her *maledizione*. Worse yet, it would shift the fragile and delicate balance of power between the ruling families – perhaps enough for one to think, as they had many times before, that they could do away with the ruling oligarchy and have one nobleman declare himself Margrave. Such things inevitably resulted in a generation of savage infighting, and an end to the influence of Buchara expanding outside the city walls.

But that's not all, is it? This is something bigger, something more. The cards had many uses, many functions; many meanings. Their disappearance – their clumsy theft – at a time like this could not be seen as just coincidence, and only a naïf would imagine that this was done purely for political gain. The elders of the Cittàvecchi, they might pretend to embrace this "age of reason" the philosophers crow about; but underneath the veneer, they still made the sign of the Trident when the name of the King was spoken and they still refused to call their city by its original name. They knew the power of the cards all too well.

The Lord of the Invisibles, the King of the Upper Air in his tatters and cloak of mist... centuries after his fall, his shadow still extended over his old empire.

The Grafin looked to the southwest, over the mountains, and wondered. Yes, she thought. There's more afoot here than injured pride and theft. You see us rising in the north, and this time you are rightly afraid, and you seek to do us down before we are strong enough to stop you. You have not changed since the days of the King; you just wear better masks nowadays.

I see your hand, Cittàvecchio. Do not imagine it will go unopposed.

* * *

Donna Elizabeta Zancani stood atop the rooftop observatory of the Palazzo. The city spread out beneath her, the night-mist rolling in waves across it, breaking around the towers and spires. Overhead, the moon rode high as the clouds piled up over the mountains, streaming down toward Buchara unseen on the far flank of the range.

She tasted the rain in the air and smiled exultantly. "Ah, Cittàvecchio. You sleep undisturbed for now, but soon enough you'll hear his soft tread as the nights draw in. '*Nothing is duller than dynasties*,' so the intelligentsia claim; but they will learn the truth soon enough."

She laughed as the first spots of rain landed on her upturned face.

In the faint moonlight, the grass is singing

Over the tumbled graves, about the chapel

There is the empty chapel, only the wind's home.

It has no windows, and the door swings,

Dry bones can harm no one.

T.S. Eliot, The Waste Land 386-390

Donna Zancani came down from the rooftop, the rain in her hair and a wild look in her eyes, and descended to the hidden chamber of the masks beneath the Palazzo's entrance hall. The great black sun face sat on its stand in the centre of the flooded chamber, seemingly watching her; the shadows swinging from the lantern she carried gave the hundreds of masks on the wall a strange kind of life. If one stopped to listen one could almost hear their gossip, just on the very edge of perception.

A paranoid woman might even imagine they were talking about her.

She waded into the oily water toward the central pedestal, holding her skirts up with one hand. She circled the mask on its stand several times, and twice she made as if to touch it, then pulled back.

She had bought the mask during a clearance sale of one of the oldest Palazzos down near the waterfront; an old Imperial building near the Rookeries, now near-submerged. The contents were being sold off by the owners to finance a rebuilding on top of the old structure; such was the way of Cittàvecchio. Never forget what lies beneath, and use it to build to new heights. Or, if you believed the poets, always build on love and death if you wish to build to last.

She had been approached by the agents of the owners to auction the more artistic of the pieces, and she had made them a great deal of money; but the mask she had held back as her fee. It had hypnotised her from the moment she laid eyes on it, the great swirling rays of the black sun; she had alternated between wearing it and her more traditional moon mask at meetings of the Secret Senate for over a year.

Then, one night, she attended the meeting of the Senate in her moon mask, and found Sun Face waiting for her. It was, if she recalled correctly, the night they found the first beggar dead on the streets of the Rookeries; but by then, of course, the rest of the senate were used to the arrival of the mask of the Sun; they did not comment at its presence, merely at the rare appearance of the Sun and the Moon together. Sun Face laughed and said that such things were often read as omens of doom by the superstitious.

Elizabeta did not laugh that night, and hurried home at the end of the meeting through streets once familiar but now laden with fogbound menace.

There was the mask, on its stand, when she got home; but in the water around the pedestal, a cloud of clotting blood.

She asked Mercutio if he had been playing tricks on her; his denials were sufficiently convincing that she wondered if she had not simply drunk too much of the sacrament that night. But then, the dreams began; the dreams of the great face of the black sun, of the things it whispered into her ear when sleep seemed far away. And at the next meeting, it was there again.

Blood called it; always when a murder took place in the Rookeries, there would be the Black Sun at the senate. Never for long, though; often it would be back on the stand before Elizabeta got home. But blood called it forth, of that she had no doubt.

She had begun experimenting with the blood of animals, street-caught dogs, birds, an occasional quart of pig's blood bought from the butcher. Nothing came of such things save a bad smell and a slippery mess on the floor of the subterranean ballroom, hidden beneath the water. It was the blood of a Cittàvecchi that called it, the blood of a scion of the city.

She raised the lantern high and examined the mask closely; some of the black stain on the forehead of the mask appeared to be peeling off. She reached forward to touch the damaged area, then drew back superstitiously; to touch it might have consequences.

She shrugged, and turned as if to go; his voice froze her in place.

* * *

The Cathedrale of the Holy Trinity was in many ways more the heart of Cittàvecchio's life than even Castell'nuero. Eventually, almost every soul in the city would pass through its doors for one of the great ceremonies of life; on high holy days the three great transepts[7] of the building thronged with people, eager to touch the sublime for a brief moment. But for all that, for much of the time the Cathedrale stood empty save for an occasional trickle of troubled souls who came here for solitude, for contemplation, for tranquillity or sometimes for confession. Even during the small hours, between two and three bells, there was life and activity in the Cathedrale; priests making private prayer, or perhaps just walking the great cloisters, or maybe even using the great pigeon-lofts that thronged the Cathedrale rooftops. As one of the most memorable locations in the city, the Cathedrale was a drop for homing pigeons from across the south; many the merchant who, though as irreligious as a stone, lurked in the cloisters for a sign, for word of the arrival of a pigeon with news of a cargo or a delayed vessel. And such activity went on throughout the night, so the arrival of a message pigeon would go unremarked even at such a late hour.

Were there to have been an observer at such an hour, though, they might have seen Pater Felicio, swathed in a deep and voluminous cloak, make his way from the cloister door of the

[7] In Cittàvecchio's Cathedrale and most of the surrounding region's churches, Trinity worship places the Father to the northwest, the Mother to the northeast and the Child to the south. Most civilised countries north of the mountains tend to reverse this plan, with the Child to the north and the Mother and Father to the south. This difference in architectural flavour has been responsible for more wars, bloodshed and accusations of vile heresy between worshippers of the Trinity than a century and a half of wars against the northern pagans.

Cathedrale to the great sunken Fountain of the Furies in the Piazza d'Erinye. The great statues of the three Furies, Alecto, Tisiphone and Megaera, could be reached from behind by a wide, curving stair that arched around the fountain to the backs of their heads; there, atop the Furies, was a small platform from where views of the bay could be taken and which led onto a raised and terraced formal garden with many nooks and crannies. It was a well-known lovers' tryst in Cittàvecchio and the arrival of furtive people after dark at the Fountain of the Furies was nothing to be remarked upon.

Pater Felicio climbed to the top of the long curving stair and looked out over the city; then, with a purposeful knot, he tied one end of a long streamer of yellow silk to the railing. The wind caught it, and it flapped in the breeze like a flag, flickering in the torchlight. He glanced around to check he was not being observed, and then hurried back down the great curving ramp.

As he made his way back across the foggy piazza, a shadow detached itself from the bushes of the ornamental garden behind the Furies and came to the railing above their heads. Mater Calomena, swathed in a great black cloak and muffler, touched the yellow ribbon curiously, and then watched Felicio speculatively as he hurried back to the Cathedrale.

When he glanced back, she had gone.

* * *

"The messenger can only come if blood calls, Elizabeta. You know that."

His voice low, abrupt and filled with rich dark humour; but an edge of cruelty nevertheless. She gasped and dropped the lantern into the water; it remained lit in its glass globe, and bobbed like some sinister luminescent deep-sea fish, sending pale yellow light through the murky water. She scrabbled to catch hold of it and held it, dripping, high in one hand to see who had spoken.

Crouched like a cat in one of the many alcoves that ringed the lower walls, the diminutive puppeteer watched her, his eyes flashing vivid yellow like a cat. He dropped lightly into the water as she saw him and advanced smoothly toward her, a cold and cruel smile on his face.

"To touch it would do no harm. Without the city behind it, it's just papier-mâché and gilt." He sketched a mocking bow.

Elizabeta moved warily around the pedestal, keeping the mask and the lantern between her and the grinning dwarf. "You are not like the others; not like the beggars. You are like her, aren't you?"

"Her?" The dwarf chuckled. "Her. So it is *Colombina,* not *Arlecchino* this time. Like her? I suppose you could say we come from the same sort of stock, yes. We are what the cards made of us, we creatures of the City. These are not the shapes we might have chosen but one makes do, in the Cittàvecchi way."

"She said her taken name was Orlando-"

"Hah. Orlando, Zagne, Colombina, Inamorata, doesn't really matter. You know her when you see her; *Mascherina Pallida,* the Phantom of Truth flitting across the face of the city as the bells toll, remembering their true master and sensing his return. Just as you know me for what I am when you see me." He danced around the central dais, sending ripples of water out against the walls of the chamber. The masks on the walls laughed silently.

Elizabeta moved quickly, warily. The puppeteer was between her and the stairway back to the ground floor now. "How is it that you are real when she is not? Is it blood that calls you too?"

"We are all called by something, Donna. But as for me? I am more of a facilitator than a harbinger. Look at the mask; look at what lies beneath the black lacquer. It may explain a few things."

Hesitantly, she raised the lantern to peer more closely at it. The black lacquer was in a thin layer atop something else entirely, and a combination of age and perhaps moisture had made it crack and peel away slightly. She touched it, and a piece of lacquer broke away into powder, revealing the papier-mâché base.

"Go on." The puppeteer retreated back into the shadows, only his shining eyes marking his location. "Brush away more of the soot of the present; reveal the face of the past."

Part of the papier-mâché, part of the very body of the mask itself, was a faded picture of some kind; intrigued, Elizabeta brushed away more of the black lacquer to try to see the picture across the mask's forehead. In faded paints and once-vivid colours it depicted *The Harbinger* - a figure in pale robes bearing the yellow symbol of the Trident, distorted by the folds of the garment; identity concealed by a simple white mask. In one hand, the figure held something that might be a spread deck of cards, or might be a fan. The other hand made a gesture for silence, one finger held up to the mask's lips. One of the cards of the *Re Stracciati* deck. The pasteboard rectangle had been carefully worked into the papier-mâché itself, made to become part of the mask.

When it stood revealed, she looked to the darkness, but only the voice of the puppeteer remained. "You know the stories, Elizabeta. When the King fell, fake cards were put in the deck to neuter its power. People always thought this meant new cards; nobody guessed it meant duplicates, and so nobody looked for the originals."

"How many such cards?"

She sensed rather than saw his smile. "I think we can safely say at least two, hmm?"

"To what purpose?" She swung the lantern about, but could not see the diminutive creature anywhere.

"Do you fear or rejoice in the coming of the King, Elizabeta?"

There was a long silence as she gazed at the mask. When she answered, the words came slowly, as if from a great distance.

"I fear but I desire to see the city great again. No Duca will ever do that while they sit in borrowed finery on a throne not theirs at all. I rejoice, for once he has come, Cittàvecchio will have a ruler worthy of the name once more."

"He is a King whom Emperors have served, and I know this to be true for I am such a one." The dwarf moved smoothly through the water and deftly climbed onto the raised dais in the centre of the room. "His harbinger has been abroad, but it is time now for more than ghosts and figures in the mists. Put on the mask, Elizabeta Zancani."

She stared, transfixed, into the back of the great mask. Then, she glanced at the puppeteer.

"What is your name, creature?"

"I go by many, but if you mean what I suspect, I am the Beggar King." He watched her keenly. "You knew that already."

"Yes." She paused. "Will I see Him?"

"*Oh, yes,*" said the King of the Beggars. His knife slipped effortlessly into his hand.

She put her face into the mask.

* * *

Pater Felicio slammed the door of the vestry behind him, the sound echoing through the body of the near-deserted Cathedrale, and leaned against it until the pounding of his heart slowed to less terrifying levels. To someone sensitive to the ebb and flow of the hidden city, a trip across night-time Cittàvecchio was more of an adventure tonight than it might first appear.

For the entire journey back from the Furies, he was quite convinced the Undines had paralleled his course, their poor drowned fingers scrabbling at the kerbstones by the edge of the water every time he strayed too close to the edge. The mist had concealed the scraping of stone on stone and fluttering; he knew that had he turned back at any point, he would have seen an entirely unexpected number of gargoyles perched on architecture not normally associated with their presence.

The spirits of the city were exceptionally restless this evening; it did not bode well. Something was afoot.

He shed his muffling cloak and scarf and locked himself into his study. The note from Buchara, still stained with the effluvia of the messenger, lay uncoiled on his desk;

Success. Coming home. Pursued.

The ribbon would summon the Senate for a meeting within the day; a strategy needed to be ready by the time he arrived back in the city, since any window of opportunity would be small at best before Buchara responded with its customary lack of humour.

He let his fingers stray for a moment over the mask of the Old Man of the Sea; back in the days when he and his kind ruled, matters of religion were much easier. Poseidon Earthshaker, when he disliked something, sent a great wave to smash it flat, then sank it. Simple. No moral ambiguity, no wiggle room; you were devout, or you were drowned.

Felicio longed, sometimes, for such clear and unambiguous guidance from his own god, but the Trinity was a distant force and the aspect of it that he chose to speak for the most distant of the three.

He felt the eyes of the triptych of ikons on him, and knew he would have to pay for his transgressions here in private if nowhere else. The Father did not approve of sedition against the authorities.

He unbuttoned his robe and laid his back bare, then took the cat o' nine tails out of his bottom drawer. Its handle was worn smooth with long use; the same could not be said for the Pater's back, which bore testament to the depth and history of his seditious and improper urges.

He remained locked in his chambers until long after dawn broke over the city.

* * *

Few chambers in the Castell'nuero were better guarded than the retiring-chamber of the Donna Ophelia. As a member of the Ducal family she was accorded the highest level of protection; as a Donna of virtue in a city full of rakes and scoundrels such security was redoubled. The chamber was huge, with great floor-to-roof windows running down the entirety of the east wall; in the centre of the room, on a raised dais, the huge four-poster bed an ocean of pillows, quilts and blankets in which the tiny figure of Donna Ophelia looked lost and doll-like.

The trek from the door to the bedside took Calomena a good thirty seconds; her shoes clicked loudly on the parquet flooring and Ophelia stirred, yawned demurely behind a raised hand and blinked in the dawn light streaming through the great windows.

"Mater – you're here early; what news?"

Calomena composed herself and then settled on the bedside. Ophelia propped herself up on a mound of pillows and bunched a pile of bedding up in front of her so that barely her head and shoulders were visible. If Calomena noticed that Ophelia seemed a little more flushed than usual, she tactfully did not comment.

"I believe I may have cracked the good Pater."

Ophelia sat up a little straighter. "And?"

Calomena looked meaningfully at the mounded quilts in the bed. "Am I free to speak, my Donna?"

Ophelia smiled evilly. "Oh, he can't hear *a thing*. Don't mind me if I seem a touch distracted though…"

Calomena hissed to herself. "Pay attention to the matter at hand, Ophelia. I am laying the groundwork for your future power here. If Felicio is up to something he'll be close to or at the heart of whatever's going on. I believe I might be able to crack this entire mess wide open by tomorrow evening – and then we can decide whether to expose them or use them."

Ophelia looked at her mentor appraisingly. "You've had three days to look into this in detail. We'll talk in detail this afternoon about what you've got so far, and then decide whether to take it to another authority or deal with it ourselves. If a move is going to be made against my brother it'll likely be during Grand Festivàle week when we're all more exposed; he's going to be making his own arrangements for security. I'll be making my own, just in case he's having one of his more paranoid moods when he briefs the guards. But Mater – I'm only going to act on *solid* evidence, not suspicion. If you have enough suspicions to pursue then I'll throw my weight behind pursuing them, but I'm not having people executed unless there's solid proof of malfeasance."

Calomena nodded. "You're not your brother."

Ophelia swiped at her with a pillow, half in play. "That's exactly the kind of talk that will get you poisoned. What about the elegantly wasted Lord di Tuffatore?"

Calomena rested her chin in cupped hands and thought for a moment. "I'm still very unsure about him. I *think* he's involved somewhere, if only because there's a powerful *benedizione* on or around him that I can neither identify or trace, but I'm still not sure where. He disappears into the night fog like a ghost. None of my spies can find him until he reappears back at his townhouse. He could be up to anything – bedding a witch, perhaps. For the moment, continue your dalliance with him, but be cautious." Calomena paused, then stared at the quilts aghast for a moment. "That's not *him* under there, is it?"

Ophelia laughed; it was a dirty, ripe laugh and not at all what one would expect from a noblewoman. "A lady does not tell tales, Mater, as well you know. Or would you like me to make enquiries about with whom *you* spent the night? Now, what of Buchara?"

"I can find no follow-up on young dell'Allia's story – clearly, Felicio is up to something but I cannot find any unwarranted connection to any Bucharan in the city. The involvement of Mercutio del Richo means that Donna Zancani might be involved too – though I am loath to suspect a fellow member of the sisterhood. If she has betrayed the city, I will work a wrath on her that children will be scared to sleep by. The Bucharans in the city seem disturbed as well – something going on back home, apparently. It might be something, so I've sent a pigeon to the Embassy in Buchara asking after the news."

"Good. And the matter of the philtre we discussed regarding my suitor?"

Calomena set her face. "I haven't had time to look into it…"

"Well make the time. I am not to be denied in this, Mater." Ophelia's face may have been impish but her voice left little room for manoeuvre. "We will have use for it; *much* use for it if your suspicions are correct."

Calomena nodded, and bowed. Her entire posture spoke volumes of reluctance, but Ophelia was unrelenting. "Thank you, Mater. You may go; I will rise presently and meet you in the gardens."

Calomena left the chamber. Once the echoes of her heels on the wooden floor had faded, the quilts shifted abruptly, and rising like a somewhat disreputable Venus from the foam, Prospero's head and shoulders emerged from beneath the ocean of blankets. He blinked at the sudden light and then rolled over atop Ophelia.

"A philtre, my sweet? For your *suitor*? Are you so swiftly bored of me that you must now have me poisoned and done away with like a character from the *commedia*?" He clutched his throat and rolled over theatrically onto his back, his eyes bugging. Ophelia cuffed him about the head playfully. "Not you, you buffoon. Xavier di Tuffatore."

"Let me just duel him for your hand. That'll settle the matter, and put an end to these clandestine meetings. Pleasant though it is to spend my days hidden under the sheets in such fine company…"

"No. For the moment, it suits my purposes and those of the di Gialla family to keep this courtship going. And you are my ace in the hole, Prospero. I don't want our relationship exposed for the moment. You'll know the time, when it comes, and if all ends well, you'll be Ducal Consort beside me. Be patient for now, and try not to be *too* jealous of Xavier… Now; tell me what you propose to do for the Festivàle. All the city's aflame with curiosity, as you well know."

Prospero sat up, a dreamy look on his face. "Well; I have been crossbreeding these *peacocks,* you see…"

* * *

The messengers had specified four bells, but Gawain arrived at the armoury fashionably late. He was in the kind of stylish disarray carefully gauged to suggest he had been torn from someone's bed in order to attend the meeting, and hadn't troubled to hide it. Valentin was already there, impeccably attired in Ducal purple and looking as though a summons to a clandestine meeting at four in the morning happened to him all the time; Visconti on the other hand had clearly been up all night and was pacing back and forth, a bundle of nerves and energy sustained by bad temper and righteous rage.

"Lord d'Orlato. *Good* of you to finally join us."

Gawain raised both eyebrows in surprise at Visconti's abrupt tone but the Captain either did not notice or did not care and continued in the same vein. "You two deliberately kept me out of the Rookeries on the night of the dual murder. Why?"

Valentin glanced at Gawain, then back to the Captain. "I did no such thing, Gian. I went into the Rookeries, on the direct orders of the Duca, to suppress a riot. I wasn't conducting a police action and I wasn't trying to trespass on your turf. I assumed your men had been pulled out because of the threat of the riots. You are watchmen and investigators, not soldiers…"

Visconti turned to Gawain. "Then it was you."

"You know, Gian, it's a little early in the morning for this degree of insolence and I haven't slept well, so my temper isn't all it could be. What, exactly are you insinuating?"

Visconti smiled grimly. "I'm not insinuating anything *yet.* Why did you order my men out of the Rookeries?"

"I didn't order anyone –"

"Spare me, my Lord. You advised the Lord Seneschal that he should order me to stand down so that you could go in and extract my witness. How did that work out for you, by the way?" Visconti's voice dripped with sarcasm. "Black Maffeo was found dead after the riot was suppressed, cut up just like all the other victims. Did you order me out so that someone could *clean up* after themselves? Do you know who it was? Are you defending them out of some kind of code of nobility?"

Valentin started away from the fireplace. "I've heard just about enough of –"

"No." Gawain stilled him with a gesture. "Gian is angry, and he has a right to be, I suppose. I went in looking for Black Maffeo, yes. It was politics. The Duca couldn't have the Beggar King dictating terms to him, especially not with the murders going on. I was sent in to extract the witness, and the Ducal Guard were sent in to suppress the trouble in case I had to crack a few beggar heads on the way in and out. I know you have an... understanding... with the Rookery beggars; I thought it would be best to keep you clear of it all, in case we needed a clean pair of hands afterwards." Gawain shrugged eloquently and held up his hands helplessly. "I never found Black Maffeo and I assumed my information on his location was bad. I only found out he was one of the victims the following morning. Now I can understand why you might think ill of me, Gian, but that's hardly grounds to accuse me of complicity in the murders..."

The *Vigilanza* Captain looked askance at Gawain. "Smooth patter, my Lord. But this time we have at least three witnesses that say they saw a man climbing up a wall near the murder site; a well-dressed man. I'm sure you can imagine the mood of the Rookeries at the insinuation that it's a nobleman that's been murdering and dumping his bodies in their patch. Plus, there's a thriving trade among the Priestesses of the Mother all claiming they've seen this or that and most of them are falling within the broad band of 'Someone from the upper city'. The Ducal Guard have put down one riot but the next one may rip the city apart."

Valentin shifted uncomfortably. "Do you have anything except these witness reports? My men had nothing on this..."

Visconti smiled a tired but satisfied smile. "Physical evidence. A kerchief found at the murder scene, with one of the victims' blood all over it. It's of Montressori manufacture, silk and quite rare. We are having it checked at the moment to see if it takes us anywhere, but it's certainly not the kind of thing I'd expect to find a beggar carrying. For a start, aside from the blood, it was clean and probably freshly laundered."

"Montressori silk, you say?" Gawain pursed his lips. "I know a few people who own such. May I see it?" He was a picture of solicitous concern, but Visconti shook his head. "The Day Watch are making some enquiries with it, I don't have it. Lord Gawain, if you can think of anyone, anyone at all, who might be short of a Montressori handkerchief, anyone of your acquaintance who knew that you might be on official business that night in the Rookeries, who might have caught wind of a witness alive – you will be *sure* to tell me, won't you?"

Visconti's tone was polite and supercilious, but his eyes were glittering. Gawain held his gaze for just long enough, then bowed.

"I have a few ideas, but I'm going to make some enquiries of my own first. I'm not in the business of *impugning* the reputations of *blameless* men in darkened rooms at dawn, so I need to be sure myself before I say anything."

Visconti nodded, once. "Then we'll meet here, again, two days hence. I expect you to have a name for me, Lord d'Orlato." The captain turned on his heel and left the armoury, his firm stride belying the exhaustion in his frame.

Valentin was the first to break the spell. "*He expects you to have a name.* Not even the courtesy of an *or else*. Damned if he didn't just front up to you, Gawain. Damn! Who'd have thought old Visconti had the blood for it? If I hadn't seen it, I'd have called you a liar."

"He certainly does seem to suffer an excess of blood. I'm sure someone will be able to help him with that, though," said

Gawain, his mind clearly elsewhere. "Buy you a coffee, Valentin? I think I need one and since we're up, it seems a shame not to take advantage of the city at dawn…"

The mists were just starting to clear as the morning sunlight hit them, giving the impression of streets filled with boiling smoke. The first signs of civic life were evident here and there as the two walked down the shallow incline to the coffee houses and bakeries of the lower city; torch boys and lamplighters extinguishing the last of the night's illuminations, deliveries being made by young lads blinking sleep out of their eyes, masked revellers from the night before making their furtive way back from an alien bed to one more familiar. And with the growing light level, slowly colour flooded back into Cittàvecchio; yellows, reds and browns, greens and then finally the blue of the sky breaking through the mist as the night's grey blanket finally drifted down through the streets to the sea and the sun struggled above the horizon.

"Do you have plans for the day, Valentin? Are the Tatar Guard at hazard this fine morning?" In spite of his rough handling at the edge of Visconti's tongue, Gawain seemed in a positively buoyant mood as the light improved. Valentin laughed briefly, and shook his head. "This afternoon is the first Ducal Promenade; His Grace will probably want to be abroad on the canal barge so I've a busy day ahead of me. There's the Duke and the Donna Ophelia to worry about; the Promenade is usually the start of the funny season; all the cranks and half-baked political assassins come out of the woodwork at this time of year. Still; it keeps me in a job, I suppose… You?"

"I had completely forgotten the Promenade[8]. I shall attend, of course, even if only to see what animal-based lunacy Prospero

---

[8] The Ducal Promenade, held annually, was one of Cittàvecchio's biggest events, combining boating, naval skills, fashion and a carnival-like atmosphere. The Gialla family had long promoted the Promenade as a means of keeping Cittàvecchio's shipbuilding facilities employed and fresh, as many owners brought smaller vessels into the naval yards for refits ahead of the day's boating. Races from point to point in the city, treasure hunts and a procession of the larger boats through Cittàvecchio's largest flooded thoroughfares were among the highlights of the day.

comes up with this year. It was barges drawn by dolphins last year, and a balloon powered solely by the exertions of geese the year before. Surely for once he's going to make it all the way through the day without ending up in the water…"

"It is Prospero. I wouldn't lay money on it."

Gawain chuckled, and conceded the wisdom of his companion's opinion.

They arrived in the Piazza d'Erinye just as the first of the Piazza bakeries was opening for business, and took small cups of thick coffee and breakfast pastries to one of the round tables that dotted the Piazza. They sat eating and drinking as the city slowly wakened around them. Indeed, because the morning was so still, and the hazy sunshine so bright, it was some considerable time after they had sat down that Captain Valentin noticed the flutter of yellow silk tied to the railing above the great statue of the three Furies in the fountain. Shortly after noticing the streamer, Valentin hurriedly made his excuses, and left the Piazza, pleading an urgent need for sleep before the afternoon's festivities.

Gawain sat and finished his coffee, and mulled over the affair of a missing handkerchief. His smile broadened and he sat back, hands behind his head. Truly, coffee and a pastry first thing in the morning were good for a man's soul.

* * *

As dawn spread slowly through Cittàvecchio, it chased away the night mists and brought a touch of reality and illumination to the city of spires and towers, burning away the layers of obfuscation and secrecy that a city night brings.

In the Palazzo di Zancani, the first fingers of dawn's light spread across the marbled floor and across the shape of the Donna Elizabeta Zancani, sprawled across the top of the steps leading down to the chamber of the masks. She was quite, quite dead.

Beyond her outstretched fingers, the broken and powdered remains of a mask; it had once been a sun face but years of neglect and rot had finally turned it into a tangled mess of wire and mushy damp. There was nothing left of value there.

Sat cross-legged, the misshapen puppeteer watched impassively as the sunlight crept ever closer to the body on the floor. When it touched the outstretched fingers, they twitched, and the body of Donna Elizabeta Zancani opened its pearly eyes.

Something else entirely looked out through them.

"Welcome back to the world of flesh, Columbine," said the yellow-eyed dwarf, and bowed long and low.

My friend, blood shaking my heart

The awful daring of a moment's surrender

Which an age of prudence can never retract

By this, and this only, we have existed

Which is not to be found in our obituaries

Or in memories draped by the beneficent spider

Or under seals broken by the lean solicitor

In our empty rooms

T.S. Eliot, The Waste Land 402-409

Xavier wiped the steam from his mirror and examined his face. The cut was not as serious as he had at first assumed; the inflammation had faded over the past few days, leaving only the ghost of a red line. He angled his jaw and examined it appraisingly; not the disaster it could have been. He smiled for a moment at his own vanity, but it was fleeting.

His servants had been in: while he had bathed, a series of letters and cards had been neatly stacked up against the corner of the mirror. He picked them up and sat down on the edge of his bed, leafing through them. Invitations to galas and afternoon soirees from some of the nobility; the obligatory invitation to the Ducal regatta; the programme for the week's performances at the city's theatres; and at the back, on cheap parchment written in an uneven hand, a single sentence:

A yellow ribbon flies from Megaera's hair.

He tapped the folded parchment against his chin. It came from a woman who worked in one of the cafes on the Piazza d'Erinye and was paid a retainer to watch for specifically such things as this and send him word when the Fury's hair was decorated in such a fashion. It betokened a change in circumstance and called the Secret Senate to meet tonight. He skimmed back through the other invitations and found the one scrawled in Gawain's casual backhand; *the upstairs room, Red Lion, three bells.* Knowing Gawain, that meant three in the morning; he was seldom abroad before dusk. Providing the Senate meeting concluded swiftly - and presuming Orlando had no more entertaining late night odysseys through the city's supernatural underworld planned - there would be no impediment to the meeting if he chose to make it. But he was growing tired of the *demands* made on him, both by the mysterious Orlando and the voracious Gawain. He needed no more scars and no more sleepless nights.

He had not seen Gawain since the storming of the Rookeries. There were matters to be *discussed* between them over that; Gawain knew full well his fondness for the poor and his sympathies for the inhabitants of the crowded tenements that the Tatar Guards had rampaged through. Such things were typical of d'Orlato – he did not react well to anything that focussed attention away from himself.

He recognised the handwriting on one of the discarded invitations; the Lord d'Amato's dance, three days hence. He had almost certainly been invited either by accident or as a matter of political form; relations with the Lord d'Amato had not been cordial since...

Well. They just hadn't been cordial for a while. His mind shied away, again, from the scene. That night with Orlando, with the dwarf, had stirred up all kinds of things he had thought buried and lost. The night in the fog had troubled Xavier deeply; the dreams that followed it even more so. He had spent three days abed, claiming a night-chill after an attempted mugging.

But now, this invitation. He turned it over idly; he would almost certainly not go, to spare the elder d'Amato's feelings. And to spare his own.

A yellow ribbon flies from Megaera's hair. And tonight the Senate would meet for possibly the last time before this scheme with the cards was put in place.

Xavier glanced out of the window, gauging the hour by the angle of the sun. *About eleven bells; still not noon.* Almost a full day.

Traditionally the first day of the Festivàle saw events beginning at around three in the afternoon, so he still had plenty of time before his absence at a public occasion would be noticed. He dressed hastily and inconspicuously; with the addition of a *bauta* mask and a cloak, few people would look twice at the figure he cut. He hesitated at the door, and then, reluctantly, grabbed his sword belt off the hook and buckled it on.

Any noble of Cittàvecchio would be taught the sword as a matter of course; it was regarded as a gentlemanly art. It was also a well-known adage that most swords were for show; if one wanted someone dead a shorter weapon was a far better option. Duelling swords were all the rage among the smart set at the moment; great ornamental swept-hilt affairs with long needle-sharp blades designed for one-on-one honour combat. Xavier's weapon of choice reflected his family's history[9]; it was a short, wide-bladed stabbing weapon in a fitted leg scabbard, of little use in a duel but nastily efficient in a melee – and easy to conceal under a cloak, down the side of a leg. A businesslike weapon designed for maximum efficiency in killing one's opponent. In daylight, the likelihood was Xavier would not need the extra insurance but after the affair of the dwarf – or the drunken beggar, depending on how seriously you took what happened that night – he was taking no chances.

He left the townhouse and made his way into the growing throng. The first early boats were out on the canals and flooded thoroughfares and children were already lining the bridges to see them sail by, bedecked in ribbons and flags. The crowd was notable for the absence of beggars, of course; still hiding away in the Rookeries, nursing their wounds and planning their response to the events of three nights before. But where the beggars left the crowds be, the street entertainers made the most of the undivided attention of the purses of passers-by. He watched the puppeteers he passed narrowly but did not see the deformed dwarf or his monkey and curiously the puppet tales of the

---

[9] The di Tuffatore family, historically, have been heavy infantry commanders in the City Levies; three of Cittàvecchio's seven Lords Seneschal have been di Tuffatores. Such a family history can tend to incline one to a more practical bent where use of weapons is concerned.

commedia characters held little allure for him of late. The air was raucous with horns and whistles and nobody noticed the passage of a man masked and cloaked in such a throng. It is always easiest to hide in plain sight.

He made his way to the Grand Piazza, skirting along the great colonnade of shadowed arches where normally one would find beggars thronging, all competing for the charity of passers-by. Today the arches were empty, cold and still; a pool of quiet in the thronging square. Xavier avoided them, and made for the great portico of the Cathedrale.

As he passed through the great leaden doors he felt very small and lost in the great vault of the transept, one of perhaps five or six lone worshippers in a space designed to contain thousands. Xavier had been expecting the Cathedrale to be busy enough for him to lose himself in the crowds, but he had misjudged the popularity of the early day boat races, for now his footsteps echoed as he made his way down the side aisle. One or two of the other worshippers glanced at him incuriously but most were lost in private prayer. The echo of his footsteps in the sacred space sounded very loud to him.

He left the shadow of the wall, briefly genuflected and hurried with long-legged strides toward the central altar and the great cloisters beyond, nestled in the crook of the two northern wings of the building. He slipped out through the postern door into the tranquillity and peace of the great triangular gardens; at this time of day a few clergy were taking advantage of the space to walk and think in solitude or in quiet pairs. One or two wandered the meandering paths through the centre of the gardens, but most kept to the covered walkways that surrounded it. The autumn sun slanting over the roof of the east Transept sent stark fingers of shadow slicing across the cloisters, distinct bands of light and dark in and out of which the occasional supplicants or priests meandered, lost in their own thoughts.

As he watched, a figure he recognised hove into view. He watched as Gratiano dell'Allia, Gawain's young friend, made his way diffidently towards the great portico into the Cathedrale proper. As usual, he felt the bitter bile of unreasoning jealousy in the back of his throat; Gawain's easy open friendship with the young man was, he was sure, cultivated almost exclusively because it engendered such unreasoning envy in him. He's never had much time for dell'Allia, a vapid creature of the nightlife; he seemed to be in reality what both Xavier and Gawain wore as masks, to be put off in company when real faces could be revealed.

He watched with some interest as the boy walked to within a score of yards of the portico, stopped and looked up at the great trident above on the Cathedrale roof.

Looking for absolution, are we? Fascinating. Something is weighing on you heavily enough to make you come here, and I'll bet it isn't just the gambling debt everyone's talking about. I wonder has Gawain talked you into doing something you find morally dubious?

He's good *at that.*

He watched Gratiano a while; the younger man had dressed in muted colours and drabs; like Xavier, deliberately trying to avoid attention. Whatever it was that was chewing at him, though, it was not sufficient to make him pass through the postern door and into the body of the Cathedrale proper; after pausing a while, turned on his heel and left the cloisters with the stoop-shouldered walk of a man with the weight of the world on his shoulders.

* * *

It had never been Mercutio's intention to even open the case.

For one thing, it was unprofessional; for another, he knew enough about the curse of the cards to know that his flimsy argument that he was carrying them and didn't own them would never stand up in a metaphysical court for a second once he'd handled the pasteboards themselves. But the further he rode from Buchara, the heavier they weighed in his pocket. He wondered if Mama Koldana had betrayed him; or if her loyalty to her craft had meant the betrayal had been forced from her by the Janizaries. Either way, he placed little faith in the bag of herbs around his neck.

The case was very heavy in his pocket. Very heavy, and growing heavier and warmer while the clouds piled up ahead of the pass, spilling over the mountains and down onto the fertile plains that led to Cittàvecchio and the sea beyond. Rain, warm and heavy, drenched the world around him painting everything in greens and greys – the higher up into the mountains he rode, the heavier the downpour as he ascended into the clouds that struggled to force their way through the pass. The road became a stream, then a river as excess rainwater flooded back down the Bucharan side of the mountains and made footing for his horse near impossible.

This is ambush weather. Don't be a fool; haste will only get you killed quicker.

Mercutio dismounted and led his horse off the path into the lee of the mountain; after a few minutes of searching he found a crevice in the rock wide enough for him and his mount but sheltered from the fierce rain. The remnants of a scattered campfire showed that he was not the first to find this spot, and the age of the ashes showed that whoever had been here last was more than a day gone. He tethered his horse, and crept as far back into the crevice as he could to escape the driving rain. He sat wrapped in his cloak watching the sky fall through the narrow opening.

A sense of threat, immediate, total and compelling, overwhelmed him for a moment; a sense of *urgency*. The creeping of hair on the back of his neck, the instinct that had served him so well on so many previous occasions. His hand was on the case and he could feel the warmth of the wood, almost like flesh, under his fingers; he hesitated for only a second before drawing the box out.

The light was fading, so the finer detail of the marquetry on the box was lost, but he knew from careful research that it displayed scenes of street life from old Cittàvecchio before the great floods. He knew the old traditions about the deck. *Look once and it might save you. Look twice and it might save you again; look a third time and it will surely damn you.*

He flipped the tiny catch on the side of the box, unwrapped the cards from their oilskin covering, and cut the deck. He looked at the card emotionlessly, and then replaced the cards in their box, and the box in his cloak. And then, from a sheath in the small of his back he drew a wickedly curved dagger.

* * *

Xavier suppressed the old thrill of jealousy as Gratiano left, then dragged his mind back to the matter at hand and scanned the cloisters, picking out his target. Pater Felicio wasn't the most popular of Keepers. Something of a disciplinarian, his attitude to the younger priests and priestesses was at times almost determinedly killjoy. And while Priests of the Father were supposed to have an element of the stern to them, such rigid adherence to doctrine didn't sit well with other priests. Felicio was normally to be found walking alone in the cloisters before noon, "setting an example" of quiet and pious contemplation. Xavier waited for Felicio to come closer to him in his perambulations, then matched speed and stride. Felicio glanced up, registered the *bauta* mask and cloak and promptly filed Xavier away under "seeker after religious advice".

"How may I be of assistance, my Son?" Felicio did not look up, or break stride.

"It is more how we may both be of assistance to the city and to each other. Or do I not speak with the Old Man of the Sea?"

Felicio missed a step, but recovered swiftly. "What makes you look for him here, my son?"

"A ribbon in the hair of a fury, and perhaps a game of cards."

Xavier felt Felicio take his elbow in a firm grip. "Perhaps we should talk inside…"

He twisted sharply and jerked his elbow out of Felicio' grip. "I think the open air suits such conversations much better; lots of witnesses at a distance not conducive to eavesdropping."

Felicio looked at him narrowly, then raised both hands in a gesture of surrender. They walked on, together, in silence for a moment. Felicio broke it first.

"I have always found *autumn* to be a most amenable season."

"And I have always found it to be a tragedy when people jump to unwarranted conclusions, Father. Are we going to talk, or continue to play children's guessing games about masks? I know who you are; you know which mask I wear. That should, for now, be sufficient."

"Sufficient for what?"

"Sufficient to discuss the matter of the cards. I presume you put the ribbon in Megaera's hair?"

"I did. I received word from my agent in Buchara, and the object of the exercise is on its way back to Cittàvecchio. If we are to move to the next stage of the plan we will need to do so quickly, hence the ribbon."

Xavier smiled coolly behind the shield of the *bauta*. "If we are to move to the next stage of the plan. Indeed. Did you notice that both Sun and Moon were all too enthusiastic about this plan? That they clearly have their own views about this deck and the purposes to which it is likely to be put?"

Felicio weighed his words carefully before replying. "This was not lost on me. What's your point?"

"I wonder whether there is an agenda that we do not perceive at work here, Pater. Whether the Sun and Moon have their own plans that may not involve us beyond the most incidental nod; and that do not in any way, shape or form involve the good of the City or that of any putative claimant to the Ducal throne. They were very quick to play down the cards' supernatural reputation, were they not?."

They walked on in silence a while.

"The cards are cursed, Tragedy, make no mistake. And it is wisest by far that they are kept far from Cittàvecchio; the city remembers its Imperial master in its stones, in its very mortar. Those cards are a strong echo of him and yes, I agree, there was too much glib disregard for their occult properties. Only a fool would claim such things were irrelevant." Felicio glanced at him speculatively. "You suggest withholding the cards? Running against the will of the Senate?"

"I suggest no such thing, and I certainly don't suggest an open split in the Senate. We two against those three? I think not. No – this must be done by coincidence and stealth, in the fashion of the cards themselves. The weak part of the chain of course, is you, because you have to see the cards delivered to the Palazzo di Zancani... When do you anticipate the cards' arrival in Cittàvecchio?"

"Two nights hence, three at most, assuming all is well. What do you propose?"

We see to it that the Senate never get the cards. Your messenger is intercepted before he can deliver the cards to the Palazzo di Zancani and relieved of the cards – and we make arrangements, via an intermediary, for the cards to be returned to the Bucharans quietly and without fuss. The Duca could be blamed for it further damaging his reputation and the loss of prestige from having to back down to the Grafs would be all his... and the cards would be back where they can be kept safe. Our personal goals would be achieved – albeit a little more slowly than the others envisage – and Sun and Moon would be thwarted for now. The question is - are you prepared to trust me?"

Pater Felicio laughed out loud, then hastily smothered his guffaws behind a raised hand as several other priests looked over to see what had drawn such uncharacteristic mirth from the dour Father. "Trust you? Mother and *Child* what a question. Of course I don't trust you."

"If those cards aren't returned, don't for one moment imagine Buchara won't go to war over it. Have you ever seen the Janizaries at work, Pater? Seen what they are capable of?" Xavier took the *bauta* mask off and shook his hair loose from his hood, fixing the Pater with a surgical gaze. "And now?"

Felicio looked at him appraisingly. "I must admit, I had not thought it would be you, though it seems obvious in hindsight. I am… surprised at the trust you put in me."

"So repay it."

Felicio turned so they were both facing one of the cloister walls. "The agent is named Mercutio del Richo; he will be arriving by the landward gate. His instructions are to deliver the cards to the auction-house of Elizabeta Zancani; I have no way now of rescinding that order."

"Do you want Mercutio kept alive?" Xavier asked the question casually, but Felicio' eyebrow rose at it nevertheless. "*Yes*, Lord di Tuffatore, I do. Good agents are not easy to find and definitely not easy to replace."

Xavier shrugged eloquently. "Then I'll arrange for him to *lose* the cards before he gets to Zancani. You brief him to carry on as though he had made the delivery, and I'll see to the rest – including fronting up to the rest of the Senate. They won't expect it from me. Do we have an agreement?"

"Not so fast. Where do you propose to hide the cards?"

Xavier smiled, and raised the *bauta* mask to cover his face once more. "I think they should be left in the custody of the Holy Father, here in the Cathedrale. In the short term, they can sit on the high altar where none but you and the other Primates go – in the medium term, I had Fra Ottavio in mind as a go-between to protect us both."

Felicio whistled softly. "Full of surprises, my Lord. *Full* of surprises. An excellent hiding place. Very well; you should probably go – our conversation is starting to attract attention from the other walkers. I seldom speak to anyone for so long, or indeed smile so much. We have an agreement, my Lord." He extended his hand, and Xavier shook it.

Felicio smiled and turned to go back into the vestry to the west of the cloisters, and Xavier waited a while, artlessly wandering the cloister walkways, seemingly deep in thought or religious contemplation. He sat a while in the shadow of the cloister roof and watched the other walkers as they went to and fro, wrapped in their own problems.

To entrust the deck to the Priesthood – especially with the city's politics as they were at the moment – was a dangerous proposition but Xavier's instincts told him that leaving the deck in the hands of avaricious Moon, or worse yet manipulative Sun, was a danger far more explicit. Sun had shown him the Invisible Republic and it was astir; even if the surface life of the city was placid, those who hid in its mists and waters were awaiting the return of those cards with keen anticipation and that suggested nothing but ill for the city and for the wider region.

And if he, he alone, did not start *acting* rather than *reacting* then any chance to influence the events of the next few days was going to be torn from his grasp. The trick was going to be getting the cards safely onto the high altar without alerting any of the people looking for the arrival of the agent from Buchara.

* * *

The Palazzo had been, up until about ten years ago, a private home. Uffizi Zancani had been a successful speculator in the silk and spices business with offices on the Sindi coast and a string of ships that had brought him more wealth than a man of modest tastes and sober habits could find a way to spend. Being an efficient businessman, he sought to spend his money in a way that would safeguard his investments, and he began amassing a collection of art and antiquities to rival those of the Duca himself.

With art come those who appreciate it, and with money come those who appreciate that too, and Uffizi's betrothal and swift wedding to the widowed Donna Elizabeta Bellamondo, who had inherited much of old Enrico Bellamondo's fortune when *he* died, came as no surprise to anyone. And Uffizi's death in a boating accident came as no real surprise either, after the legal papers were all settled correctly and the will was lodged with the city magistrates.

Donna Elizabeta Zancani, now the inheritor of a thriving import business, a massive art collection, a large palazzo and the pointed interest of the authorities, made a substantial donation to the pension fund of the *Vigilanza* and turned the Palazzo into the city's most famous public art gallery and auction house. With the Duca's patronage, Donna Zancani became one of the most influential and sought-after women in the city after Donna Ophelia herself; but Donna Elizabeta, after two marriages, accounted herself content with her widowed state and took only lovers. And to those lovers, she gave the location of the key in the lion's mouth, and an injunction to come only when Mercutio del Richo was out of town on business.

Gratiano cupped his hands around his eyes and peered up at the façade of the Palazzo, seeking any signs of life within. High above, the drapes stirred from an open balcony window in the late afternoon breeze but nothing else suggested any signs of occupancy.

Since the night of the Rookery riots, he had more or less isolated himself from everyone; he had stayed in bed for most of the first two days, hiding under the covers from his staff, the outside world and from the things he saw when he closed his eyes and the beggar came out of the dark, his eyes bugging out and his tongue forcing its way through teeth clenched with panic.

The afternoon light did him no favours and the rings around his eyes, the drawn features and the wan colour of his face all betokened many nights avoiding sleep; what little available money he had, he invested in strong spirits. They, like hiding under the bedclothes, proved useless in the end; weight of guilt hung round his neck like a ship's anchor, digging into the ground and dragging him to a halt no matter how much he tried to flee.

He'd gone to the Cathedrale seeking something; some kind of solace, absolution or even just someone to confess to, someone to tell what he had done, but at the back of his mind always was Gawain's voice; *nobody knows. You'll be fine if you just keep your nerve.*

He had kept his nerve thus far but he did not feel fine.

He glanced around at the street, and then felt inside the mouth of the stone lion to the right of the door; within, where it usually was, the spare key to the front doors. He fumbled it into the lock, slipped the doors open and vanished into the cool darkness within. Surrounding Gratiano as he slipped silently into the building were some of the greatest works of art in the history of Cittàvecchio; sculpture regarded as incomparable in this city that so loves its statuary; tapestries from Sind, tribal carvings from the New Territories, Montressori glass, paintings, carvings, jewels, idols, things of beauty from a hundred countries across a dozen lands. But none of them were what he was looking for.

"Donna Elizabeta?"

Up above him, on the wide sweeping balcony around the hall he heard a whisper of cloth, but saw nothing. He took the staircase two by two with a long-legged stride and scanned the wide sweep of the first floor; the balcony arced around the central rotunda gracefully, dotted with small statues, ceramics and vases but all the doors were closed and there was no sign of life.

"Elizabeta? Are you there?"

"Gratiano…"

The whisper caught him by surprise, and he started at how close it sounded; almost at his shoulder. When he turned, though, he saw only her veiled silhouette against the great first floor windows. She crooked a finger at him to follow her, and moved into one of the side rooms.

"Elizabeta… I need to talk with you…" Gratiano glanced down at the floor. "Something has happened… something has gone wrong. I can't talk to anyone else." His eyes were on the floor; he did not see how pale her skin looked, nor that her movements were a touch stiff. Absorbed in his own woes, he did not think to look for anyone else's.

He reached to doorway and saw her, standing by the bed in silence. She affected a papier-mâché mask in the style of *Inamorata*, one of the ladies of the Commedia, and from behind it, her eyes glittered to see him; she wore only a silk retiring-robe, loose and voluminous. She beckoned him in.

"I have done something terrible, Elizabeta. I do not know what to –" He did not finish the sentence; she came close, and touched his lips *sshhh* with one finger. She took his arm silently and led him to the bed; he started at how cold her fingers were as they fumbled with the fastenings of his shirt. "Elizabeta… are you unwell? You seem so cold." He sat on the edge of the bed, her icy fingers leaving trails over his back, raising his hackles.

"Then I must borrow a little of your warmth to bring me back to life, my sweet," she whispered. "You won't mind, will you? You are so young and full of heat, you will not miss a little of it."

He made to protest, but she pushed him flat on his back and straddled him, and he felt himself respond to her in spite of himself. "Elizabeta, I came to talk, to tell you –"

"Shhh, now, my holy fool. I know why you came." She pulled the silk sheet for among the tumbled covers and pressed it down over Gratiano's face; everything in the room became an ill-lit blur to him. "You came to confess to a sin. I understand, and I forgive you. The city forgives you, Gratiano. You will not suffer for it."

He saw her through the veil as she cast aside the mask she wore and leaned down over him, and something indefinable struck a missed chord in his heart; something profoundly not right. He made to pull the sheet away, to see clearly, but she held his arms down in claws suddenly much stronger than he remembered and leaned forward to kiss him, separated by the thickness of a single sheet of silk.

He felt an unreasoning panic rise in his breast a moment, but he smothered the tiny misgiving as his flesh responded to her long, lingering kiss. He closed his eyes and fell into her cold embrace.

* * *

Xavier stood and stretched, then replaced his hood and mask before leaving the Cathedrale cloisters. He had almost reached the great gate at the north end of the cloisters when one of the other walkers threw back their own hood and looked straight at him. He met Calomena's gaze, and in that instant, knew that she had watched the entire exchange – watched, and watched knowing the gist of what was discussed even if not the detail. Alarmed, he looked over his shoulder but Felicio had gone inside already; he glanced back to her and her coy and knowing smile told him everything he needed to know. He caught a whiff of Ophelia's perfume from her veil.

He froze – caught in the open and for all the good the porcelain confection he wore did he might as well have been barefaced.

"My Lord." She curtsied; knowing arrogance in every move, in every gesture. "Meeting with the Pater? A discussion of the Bucharan adventure, perhaps?"

Xavier stood still as a statue, watching her.

"Your movements and purpose are known to me, Lord Xavier, and perhaps we are not so distant from one another as you might think. We both want what is best... for Ophelia, do we not?"

"Do not play games with me, witch." Xavier's voice was frigid. "And don't presume to imagine you know my feelings on the matter of Ophelia di Gialla or anything else."

Calomena smiled a wicked smile and curtsied again. "Carry on with your scurrying plots then, Lord di Tuffatore, but remember: I know you, and Pater Felicio, and that is guarantee that whatever your plans may be, they will bring no harm to my ward. Carry on your courtship if you must – we both know it is a sham – but remember that no ill befalls Ophelia. Dishonour her or cross me, and you, the Pater and the rest of your conspiracy will be given over to the Duca, and shortly thereafter you'll be crabmeat."

"I wish nether Ophelia nor the city any ill will. If you've an accusation to make, make it."

"Brave words, my Lord, but we both know there are things going on beneath the surface you don't want brought to the public eye. And as long as you continue to play the game fairly, so will I."

Xavier turned on his heel abruptly and walked away. The swirl of his cloak barely concealed the fact he was shaking with a combination of rage and fear. The fact that the Senate was compromised so badly was one thing – but to be confronted so... and right on the heels of plotting a betrayal of the Senate itself. Xavier glanced up at the great Trident atop the Cathedrale; the Gods were mocking him today.

*   *   *

On the roof of the Cathedrale, on one of the long widow's walks that lined the structure, a tall woman in a mask all peacock feathers and mirrored sequins put the finishing touches to a sketch on a great artist's pad. Next to her, crouched on the low wall watching the figures in the cloisters below was a misshapen dwarf, his yellow eyes narrow as he squinted at Xavier and Calomena below.

She finished her sketch with a flourish. "It's always sweetest when they struggle, don't you think?"

He kept his own counsel, but the faintest of smiles crossed his face as he watched Xavier leave the cloisters. "Perhaps."

She looked down at the tiny figure of Calomena, below. "The Witch is interfering; she may represent a genuine threat."

The dwarf showed his teeth. "I do not think we need concern ourselves *overly* about Mater Calomena."

The peacock mask showed no emotion, but her voice was smiling. "Calomena is not the *only* witch in this game, Orfèo. And not *all* problems may be solved with a knife..."

He turned to look at the sketch and smiled a crooked smile. "Though that one, it seems, was solved with seven of them. One would almost think it was an omen."

She fussed over a detail of the central figure's curved knife. "I am quite pleased with it; a good likeness. Strong enough to call. It was always one of my favourites; the poor brigands looked so *surprised*."

The dwarf watched Calomena below, and chuckled.

Here is no water but only rock

Rock and no water and the sandy road

The road winding above among the mountains

Which are mountains of rock without water

If there were water we should stop and drink

Amongst the rock one cannot stop or think

Sweat is dry and feet are in the sand

If there were only water amongst the rock

T.S. Eliot, The Waste Land 331-338

The mountain passes between Buchara and the plains leading down to Cittàvecchio were a favoured haunt of gentlemen who had found themselves temporarily embarrassed for riches but had a horse, a dab hand with weaponry and a refreshingly flexible take on ethics as applied to the principles of crime and punishment. These gentlemen were an important part of the regional economy – their presence in the difficult passes meant it was often more economical, if more time consuming, to send cargo by sea around the Hellenes than it was to send it overland in half the time but risk its theft. Sea captains and river boat pilots whose livelihood depended on the sea routes between the two cities often prayed for "*...bad weather and highwaymen in the mountains*" in the hopes of keeping the lucrative traffic on their vessels.

If goods had to be transported overland between Buchara and Cittàvecchio merchants usually waited until a sizeable body of them were ready to set off, and then pooled their funds and hired an escort from the thriving mercenary companies that based themselves in Cittàvecchio and Buchara - the captains of successful mercenary companies had risen to high rank in both cities in the past. Speed costs money and is high risk in these endeavours. But of course, sometimes time is of the essence; and the overland route, in good weather and without problems, took between three and four days as compared to a week minimum for the sea journey, and that with a favourable wind all the way around the islands. And it was on this reliance that the highwaymen made their living.

Their methods were much the same whether they were of Cittàvecchi or Bucharan origin – they would block the road, then ride out in ambush on lone travellers or small groups. Romantic tales of highwaymen who would spare a beautiful lady in return for a dance on the wild mountain moor, or who deliberately chose the carriages of the rich and bloated rather than honest merchants abounded[10], but in reality the vast majority of them were cut-throat brigands and the fate likely to await a beautiful lady who fell into their clutches was nowhere near so romantic as a dance on the heath.

But no highwayman in their right mind – or even in a wrong one – would attack a column of twenty Janizaries and a coach emblazoned with the Stechau Arms. For while there might well be riches beyond compare within, your chances of surviving to enjoy them were nil.

The great purple plumes on the heads of the horses nodded and whipped in the keen wind that blew through the pass. Lord Buskovy, perched atop the carriage and huddled in sufficient fur to make him appear a great bear of a man, peered warily out from within his hood, a rheumy and nervous tortoise testing the air for danger before exposing his wrinkled neck.

---

[10] Much was made in song of the exploits of the famed highwayman of Buchara, Maxim the Razor. He would (according to the tales) stop a coach and upon determining to his satisfaction whether the occupants were of sound moral fibre or of dubious nature, either slit their throats or give them an honest and most excellent shave and a haircut for the price of a silver shilling. The truth of the matter, if the truth of such matters can ever be discerned, is that he was apprehended by a regiment of the Tatar Guard sent out after him in revenge for the murder of the youngest scion of the d'Amato family (whom, as far as anyone could tell, had barely had time to grow into his moral fibre, let alone determine if it were lacking). The Tatars caught him, used his own razor to cut anything off that looked dangerous, and then dragged him back to Cittàvecchio tied to the back of a galloping horse. And for all the popularity of the songs in the taverns, few, if any, spoke up against this punishment. Romantic tales are all very well, until the wheat shipment is delayed and people begin to go without bread.

The Grafin rapped on the coach roof from within. "Buskovy; why have we stopped?"

"Dead men in the road, lady. Many dead men."

"*Touch nothing...*" The Grafin's voice was electric, and shortly thereafter she emerged from the coach, unfolding like a perfect snowflake from within the carriage's warm confines. A pair of the Janizaries formed up behind her, shadowing her every move.

A tree had been brought down across the path; by the looks of it, rolled into place from a nearby hiding place, suggesting that this was a favoured ambuscade. Not, however, a fortunate spot for the highwaymen this time, for scattered about the tree and its immediate vicinity were six bodies. The Grafin circled the scene carefully before settling on a point just downwind of the scene; she squinted at the arrangement of the bodies, and then peered over her smoked glasses. Buskovy watched her in bewilderment from the top of the carriage.

"My lady?"

"This one has a touch of power about him, Buskovy. He's much cleverer than I thought. Did you ever see the cards out of their case?"

"Once, my Lady. I saw the Lady Anastasi perform a reading for the old Graf with them when I was a boy."

"Did you ever see the card '*Ambuscado*', the one they call the seven of knives?"

"No, Lady, though I've seen an illustration of it in the philosopher Giereck's treatise on the deck."

"Come down here, and see if you can see what I can see."

Buskovy clambered down reluctantly from the top of the carriage, and toiled up the hill toward the Grafin, obviously reluctant to be away from his warm nest. He stopped next to the Grafin, peered at her curiously and then looked up the hill toward the fallen tree. His mouth made a perfect "O" of astonishment.

"It is the very image of the card!"

The bodies of the highwaymen lay where they had fallen, but might as well have been artfully arranged. The only thing missing from the scene was the central figure, a wickedly curved knife in hand, silhouetted against the sky.

The Grafin smiled grimly behind her opaque glasses. "I wonder if he even knows what he's doing."

Buskovy pulled his furs closer around him in the suddenly chill wind. "I wonder if it's even him doing it."

*   *   *

A few hours ahead of the Grafin, a man sat in the lee of a great rock while overhead the skies grumbled and threatened a hard rain from clouds the colour of ugly bruises. Funnelled by the narrow pass, the thunderhead spread through the gap in the mountains like ink in water. The first of autumn's great storms was about to fall upon Cittàvecchio, sweeping down from the high passes like a broom, driving the summer's detritus down the rivers to the great marsh where the scavengers would find it, drag it back to the Rookeries and put it to what use such things may be put to. Broken carriage wheels, carcases, fallen trees, all such things ended up in the great lowland marshes and eventually someone from the city or its outlying satellites would find such things and create a purpose for them. The families of the poor in Cittàvecchio learned to be inventive with the cast-offs of others and the mountains were a rich source of such modest treasures in the autumn.

The marquetry box lay open to one side; the oilskin cloth, spread out on the ground in a great semicircle. Mercutio sat, cross-legged before the cloth, and held the deck of cards in his hands, his eyes shut and his face a picture of absorption.

He was a child of just such a poor family, made good; his father was a painter, one of the itinerant artists that flock to Cittàvecchio from across the Low Countries in hope of a commission, a sinecure or a great public building work on which to make a mark. The elder del Richo never got to paint the

Cathedrale roof or a great mural, though he made a living painting pornographic friezes for the bedchambers of the nobility, a vogue he was perfectly timed to exploit. It provided enough money to have his son schooled and trained, given the skills required to move among the middle classes of the city. The elder del Richo swore his son would not be an artisan but instead a gentleman.

Alas, or perhaps fortunately, the father never lived to see the career the son eventually chose. In Cittàvecchio, to be a footpad, a cutpurse or a brigand was a low, mean thing, deserving of an end tied to the bridge pillars; but that is not what Mercutio was, not the role he had carved for himself. As with all such things in Cittàvecchio, it wasn't what you did, it was the way that you did it, and the difference between *cutpurse* and *gentleman thief* was vast.

The pasteboard rectangles - each individually and painstakingly painted - were longer than normal playing cards; too long to comfortably hold in the span of one hand, or to shuffle with ease. They had the feel of expensive, thick paper stock, covered with a thin layer of lacquer to protect them from handling, and smelled of old books, oilskin cloth and something quite other. He rubbed them between his hands, savouring the odd, slightly greasy feel of the cards as he cut the deck and then cut it again before awkwardly shuffling them back together.

For Mercutio, life opened out like a rare bloom when he fell in with Elizabeta Zancani during his education. The Donna Zancani was well-known in the city; rich but not of noble family, she was a connoisseur of art and literature, retained by the Duca di Gialla as a critic and assessor of his collection. Given the Duca's flexible policy on other people's ownership of *objets d'art* that interested him, it was only a matter of time, between the Duca's backing, Zancani's training and Mercutio's natural athleticism and physical talents, before his "education" with the lady moved from the artistic to the criminal.

His exploits on behalf of the Palazzo di Zancani earned him both a comfortable living and a quiet reputation amongst those in the know; like the highwaymen of the mountain passes, a certain romantic cachet attaches to the gentleman thief, especially when he makes himself available at balls and in polite society. An "agent of change of ownership" rather than a thief; he was uninterested in profiting from the value of the stolen object, instead seeking the challenge of stealing it. This suited Elizabeta Zancani, whose interests were solely in profiting from the value of the stolen object, just fine. Indeed, the pair of them made a most credible and effective partnership – until now.

Mercutio had read the most famous books on the *Re Stracciati* deck - Giereck, Mantegna - before leaving for Buchara; indeed, he already knew them well, since any study of Cittàvecchi art history would touch at least briefly on them. But he had not imagined that they would feel the way they did – illustrations of the cards, reproductions, did not communicate the *feel* of the pasteboard, the tang of them.

He laid the first card down to the left of the oilcloth, face up, and let his fingers run lightly over the paint. The *Red Queen*, sometimes called the *Queen of Knives* or the *Warrior Queen*; she stands in profile and the predominant colours of the card are red, brown and black. She holds a two-handed sword before her, blade upwards, in a purposeful grip. Her curly red hair and scarlet cloak smoke and billow; lions are concealed in the shadows and folds. Her cuirass is of burnished brass, or perhaps blood; her skin might well be the same. There is a gleam in her eye that suggests watchfulness, wariness and the lions in her cloak and her long cascading hair stand guard like ghosts in the darkness; a play of shadow on a folded cloak one moment, nature red in tooth and claw the next. As with all of the cards of the *Re Stracciati* deck, she means many things depending on where she stands and with whom; but normally, blood is shed before her tale is over.

The second card he placed to the centre of the oilcloth, a little higher than the *Red Queen*; he knew it all too well – it was one of the most famous in the deck. Legend spoke of an indeterminate number of "fake" cards, later designs included in the deck by artists trying to either duplicate the original magic of the deck or perhaps dilute it somehow. Arguments raged between the scholars of the deck's history as to which cards were fake and which original but there were a handful of cards – the

"incontrovertibles" – that all authorities agreed were original –
and *Down Among the Dead Men* was one of them.

The card bore no number and no suit designation; its colours
were primarily blue, white and grey. A man, a sailor perhaps,
reaches up for the unseen surface of the water, dressed in simple
clothes. His attitude is as of a man sleeping stretched out or
dreaming of flight – but his outstretched ankle is caught in
tangled driftwood, or perhaps in a tentacle, the painting is
deliberately unclear. His eyes are marbled white and shine –
perhaps with excitement, perhaps with the glazing of death. An
ill-omened card; fear death by water, as any who live in a port
city will be the first to tell you. Do not go to sea, my son; do not
dare the things that live in the depths for they are cold,
implacable and know nothing of mercy. An ill-omened card in
an ill-omened deck.

*   *   *

Someone had replaced Xavier's robes and the mask of Tragedy
in the secret chamber behind the statue of old Saint Niccolo and
his toad. Xavier did not even remember where, on his nighttime
odyssey with Orlando, he had abandoned the mask; he knew he
was no longer wearing the robes by the time he had got home
that night. Yet here they were folded neatly and pressed; here
laying on top of them the leaden mask. A yellow ribbon had
flown in Megaera's hair and now as midnight approached, the
Secret Senate convened to discuss the final stages of the plan.

Xavier's heart hammered in his chest so loudly he was
convinced that it must be audible to anyone within ten feet of
him. Behind the mask, he could lie in a way he found near
impossible to achieve when barefaced; but he was in no way sure
if he could look Orlando in the eye, with that cruel black sun
before her face, and tell her the necessary platitudes to bring her
plan to ruin.

He descended into the smoky chamber beneath the Cathedrale;
for once, he was not the last man to arrive. Sun and the Old

Man of the Sea were already present – he exchanged a long, meaningful look with Pater Felicio – but no sign yet of Moon or Autumn. Felicio held the great jewel-crusted goblet out to him, and he turned away, lifted his mask and let his lips touch the smoky liquid- but no more. He placed the goblet on the central table, and felt eyes on him; glittering like jewels behind the Black Sun, Orlando watched him. It took every ounce of willpower he possessed to match her gaze, and take his seat.

Autumn arrived at last, shrugging into his robes and muttering of delays and business to attend to; he swept up the goblet, half-turned and took a swig from it, then hurried to his seat. Orlando watched him, relieving the pressure on Xavier, who had sat near-paralysed with fear for a moment.

"Who tied a ribbon in the fury's hair?" her voice was soft, but steely.

"That would have been me." Pater Felicio got slowly to his feet. "Should we begin without Moon?"

"Moon is on my business and not in a position to attend this extraordinary meeting, though she is aware it is taking place. We were not due to meet, Old Man of the Sea. What has prompted this?"

"I have news, important news, and we need to discuss it, and indeed to discuss what we are going to do next, where we go from here."

Xavier followed the exchange carefully, marvelling at how much detail he missed under the influence of the sacrament. Things like the large diamond ring on the Black Sun's thumb that he had seen a hundred times before at auctions and parties; like the boot knife scabbard in the colours of the Tatar Guards on the side of Autumn's boots. Things that were obvious when clear-headed. Sun leaned forward to speak, and he listened to the voice carefully; yes, it was Zancani herself, he was sure, though the mask muffled her voice a little. So who the hell was Moon, and where was she?

"You have news from Buchara?"

"I do," Pater Felicio confirmed. "The theft has been successful. I received confirmation yesterday, which prompted me to tie the ribbon; then this morning I received another pigeon confirming he had successfully crossed the mountains. He will be arriving in Cittàvecchio by the landward gate tomorrow evening at just after one bell, best guess."

"Then I will... notify Elizabeta Zancani to expect his arrival by two bells," whispered Sun. Xavier was certain he would never have noticed the hesitation normally.

Autumn rumbled in his chair. "And then what? The Bucharans will be hot on his heels. Do we even have a plan yet? Who is to succeed the Duca?"

Felicio interrupted, sharply. He was watching Sun Face unblinkingly. "Then we are resolved that it is to be done?"

"What?"

"That the Duca is to die."

The Sun Face matched his gaze. "Yes."

"And that he is to die at the Regatta Ball or immediately after?"

"Yes."

"And that it is to be us that strike him down, no agents, no remove, no assassins in the dark?"

Xavier watched the exchange, wondering if he had been the only one who had shared night-time sojourns in Cittàvecchio with the creature that called itself Orlando, and what promises and inducements might have been made to others to win their co-operation and agreement.

"Yes."

"He will die?"

"I have said it, have I not?"

Felicio nodded, once. "I wish us to be clear on what we discuss. This is no longer a game of plotting clever sedition in a cellar. We propose regicide or near to it for the good of the city and the consequences of a misstep will be unpleasant for us to say the least. Are all comfortable with that?"

Autumn nodded without hesitation. "I expect to be the one with the blade."

Sun Face turned to look at Xavier, who shrugged. "I have my own reasons for wishing to see things change in Cittàvecchio. They are sufficient to motivate me to take the risk."

"Then we are resolved. Now let us stop wasting precious time hand-wringing and proceed to the meat of the matter." Sun Face's tone was dismissive. "Whoever has the cards and is in position to seize the moment once the Duca is removed. And, of course, whoever ends up marrying the Duca's sister. We have an agent in place who knows to play his part once he receives the cards… all we need is to ensure that they are at the auction-house for the night of the Regatta Ball." The Black Sun watched them all, one by one. "We use our influence in the Ducal Guard to strike the Duca down during the ball; there will be a few hours of instability before our man Lord di Tuffatore emerges as a civic champion."

"Di Tuffatore?" Autumn's derision was plain. "I hardly think *he* will make a convincing Duca!"

"He will with us behind him," said the Old Man of the Sea neutrally. "He is already courting Ophelia di Gialla. He seizes power in the chaos surrounding the Duca's assassination, supported by the Tatar Guards. He shows the cards, wins the populace. Di Tuffatore is not unpopular among the Rookeries, and that will be vital on the night. The question is how we get the cards to him in a fashion that does not look contrived." He looked at Xavier, who took his cue smoothly.

"That is for my part; leave it to me. I will approach Ophelia directly regarding an *objet d'art* of interest for private auction, arrange for the cards to pass into her hands and plant the idea in her head that revealing them will stabilise the city. Events will be moving so fast by that point that she will be swept along by them." *How can you not realise it's me based on that? Are your senses all so numbed?*

If your senses are numbed to this, what else are they numbed to?

Pater's eyes met the glittering sparks behind the Black Sun. "Any dealings with Ophelia di Gialla run the risk of falling afoul of the witch Calomena. Can we not find another route?"

"Too dangerous now. She is clearly onto us." Xavier hurriedly interjected. "She's confronted me without my disguise and the Old Man of the Sea too – she knows the identity of two of us, perhaps of a third too. She is far too dangerous to use as part of the plan, we need to work around her."

"Or remove her." Pater Felicio left little doubt of the course he would prefer.

"Or, indeed, *recruit* her." Orlando's voice was quiet, but amused. "You two who have spoken with her – does she seem inherently inimical to us?"

Xavier chose his words carefully. "If the approach was made carefully, and with the correct inducements, I suspect she would see the wisdom of our approach; but I think at this short notice – " he glanced across at Pater Felicio, but the Old Man of the Sea was looking at Autumn, who flexed his knuckles and cracked them, loudly.

"*I* think," he said, loudly into the spreading silence, "that we should concentrate on the *matter at hand*- is she going to be useful when we make our move? The answer, of course, is yes she will. She has the best control over the heir, the current Duca trusts her and she's a well-known public figure, a respected priestess of the Mother – and would be a powerful figure to calm the populace when calming words are needed. And make no mistake, before we are done, they will be needed."

"Very well. A show of hands. Shall we make an approach before signing a death warrant that may not be needed? The motion is to give the witch a chance to join the Senate. If she refuses or tries to have us exposed we can arrange for her removal in due course as part of the coup plans. If not – well; perhaps it is time to fill the old Mask of the North Wind again. Those in favour?"

Orlando raised her hand and looked around; Autumn joined her.

"Those against?"

Felicio raised his hand, and so did Xavier. "That will make us six, Sun." Pater Felicio sounded amused. "To vote we must then be seven. If she accepts and takes up the North Wind, I move that we seek to fill the Mask of Comedy as well."

Orlando sounded equally amused. "Do you have a possible candidate in mind, Old Man?"

"Perhaps," he said, and would not meet Xavier's gaze. "Perhaps."

"If I concede this, will you change your vote?"

Felicio nodded, and then so did Sun Face.

"Fair enough. Motion carried, gentlemen. Tragedy – you are best suited to make the approach. Let it be for, say, two bells tomorrow night – let us ensure the cards are safe and sound before we begin making new friends."

"Do we have any preference for a meeting place?" Autumn leaned forward. "If not, I can recommend the Court of the Gryphon on the north side of Castell'nuero Hill. It is high, dry, easy to get to, surrounded by a maze of streets for a fast escape, and full of places to hide in an emergency. It is also in plain view of the Castell'nuero, which may encourage her to believe herself safe."

"Very well; two bells, Court of the Gryphon, tomorrow night. I shall make the offer, though I believe it to be foolish. I will also place in hand the process of the deck reaching the Duca di Gialla. The auction must be organised swiftly though – the following morning, I would recommend."

"That," said Sun Face, "is no significant problem. Assuming the cards arrive as planned we will hold the auction at midday the following day. Any earlier after a ball night would arouse suspicion. Let us meet again, then, tomorrow morning at six bells, just before dawn, to confirm the safety of the deck, the situation regarding our dear Calomena and the timing of the exposure to the Ducal court of the Bucharan threat and its cause. Until tomorrow night, adieu." Orlando stood, and the other Senators stood with her, and filed out to their respective doorways.

"Tragedy," called Orlando. "Will you not stay a while?"

Xavier turned from the archway that led up to the secret robing room and thence to old Saint Niccolo and his toad. "I have an appointment I do not wish to break, and must forego your company, Sun."

She regarded him a moment in silence, a vision in black and gold, like one of the statues atop the Cathedrale, or a picture from a playing card.

"Of course you do." There was a laugh in her voice. "And it would take a greater force than I to keep you from it. But have a care, Xavier – have a care what you say, whom you say it to, and make sure, always, that you know the motives of those in whom you place your trust."

"Whom do you mean, lady?"

She inclined her head, turned on her heel and left him alone in the chamber.

* * *

The third card, laid to the right of the oilcloth, was one which had excited much debate from scholars over the years, who were either absolutely convinced of its authenticity or completely adamant that it was a fake. In Giereck's numbering system, it was called the Two of Fates – in Mantegna's more rigid structure it was listed as ninth of the seventeen Court Cards. It was colloquially known as *Fever Dream* or *Night Terrors* – a foetal figure, viewed from above, curled in a bed, half-covered by a sheet as if thrown aside during a fever dream. Everything is black and white, save only the yellow light of the moon spilling through a window, bisecting the scene diagonally. The angles and lines, the lie of the shadows, everything in the card was somehow subtly wrong; a normal scene, a sleeping man yet one of the most uncomfortable cards to look at in the deck.

Mercutio already knew what the fourth card would be, and had known it from the moment he saw the Red Queen. He glanced at it, just to confirm for himself, and smiled a cold and weary smile. Then, carefully, he placed the cards back in the centre of the oilcloth and folded it back into a small rectangular bundle. He replaced it inside the wooden box. Secrets inside secrets. The box disappeared inside his coat pocket, and he paused a moment before heaving himself to his feet. Where he had been leaning against the rock was a spreading patch of vivid red.

He had sent his last pigeon aloft this morning with word of his arrival time; all that was left to him was to live long enough to reach the city, and to pass the cards on. And to pass on with them that there is no escaping a curse this old and subtle.

He limped to his tethered horse and stroked the beast's nose for a moment, whispering reassurance into her ear. The worst of the mountain was over now – but the path through the marshlands was tricky, especially in fading light, and by then he'd either be delirious or unconscious through blood loss so little help to her.

"Follow your nose home, old girl, and don't hang about – the longer this takes, the more chance that whatever's behind us is going to turn us both into things for the scavengers to find." He braced himself awkwardly against the wall, and cried out as he swung himself into the saddle – gripping his side and cinching his cloak more tightly around himself to try and staunch the flow of blood. He put spur to flank and as the horse sprang forward, griped her not by the reins but around the neck, clinging on now for dear life.

The problem with the *Ambuscado* card, as he had realised the moment he saw it, was that for all the six ambushers are slain, one of them no longer has his knife – it is in the back of the central, seventh figure. And there's no arguing with the cards once you have accepted them.

No arguing with them at all.

* * *

Xavier lay on his back, staring at the frescoed roof of the chambers at the Red Lion. Gawain lay next to him, his head on Xavier's outstretched arm, running his fingers aimlessly up and down the curve of the younger man's neck and chest. His eyes didn't leave Xavier's chiselled profile, thrown into sharp relief by the flickering candles. The shutters stood open to the night mists and the first chill of autumn crept through the room, putting an edge on the air that bested the meagre heat of the candles and braziers, but which went unnoticed in the face of a different heat that permeated the room, a heat centred in that unblinking gaze.

"You are very far away tonight."

Xavier closed his eyes. "There's much on my mind. The next few days and weeks are going to be busy ones for me."

"Ahh, yes." Gawain's fingers continued to wander, lightly tracing patterns across Xavier's chest. "Escorting the Donna Ophelia. The Festivàle. Keeping up *appearances*." The tone of his voice was playful, but there was an edge to it.

"It's not all parties and dances; I've got to broker a meeting between some friends of mine and that old sow of a chaperone, Calomena Giraldus."

"You have friends other than me? I'm *hurt*." For a second, Gawain let a nail scrape playfully, drawing a sharp breath from Xavier. "I thought *I* was the only one in your thoughts. Clearly I'll have to make an effort to focus your mind purely on me…"

The younger man smiled, his eyes still shut, but a faint frown crossed his face, as if a recollection were struggling to surface. "It's just politics – she's in the way of something. It's just a matter of tidying up – but I detest the woman so. I'd prefer not to have to deal with her at all. It's souring the Festivàle week for me a little."

Gawain's fingers continued to wander artlessly but his gaze was an inferno now, unblinking, fixed on Xavier's profile. There was a terrible hunger in his eyes. "When is your business with the Mater?"

"Tomorrow night, after midnight." Xavier opened his eyes and turned to look at his bedfellow. "Why are you so interested? You had already said you had plans for tomorrow night anyway – off whoring with your wretched little catamite Gratiano no doubt… or perhaps planning another burning of the homes of the civic poor. Do you do these things deliberately, Gawain? Do you try to make me hate you?"

Gawain reached over to the candles and snuffed the wicks out, drowned in pools of liquid wax between his fingers. In the darkness, he loomed over Xavier and straddled him, silhouetted by the diffuse moonlight spilling through the open shutters with the mists. To his lover's eyes he looked the part of an ancient god of the city, swathed in coils of fog, a primal creature of the urban darkness; carved from granite and smoke. He looked down at Xavier and smiled a crooked smile.

"I am always interested in things that keep your attention away from me. I like to know my enemy."

Xavier laughed bitterly, and pulled him closer, hands on bare skin in the darkness. Gawain leaned right in and whispered in his lover's ear, but the time for conversation and word games was long past now, and other imperatives were taking over. Xavier was no longer listening.

"And for another, if I thought you were being given any real trouble, there'd be *murder*."

O City city, I can sometimes hear

Beside a public bar in Lower Thames Street,

The pleasant whining of a mandoline

And a clatter and a chatter from within

Where fishmen lounge at noon: where the walls

Of Magnus Martyr hold

Inexplicable splendour of Ionian white and gold.

T.S. Eliot, The Waste Land 259-265

Prospero whistled a jaunty tune as he ambled along the dockside, tipping his most excellent hat to dock hands and ladies of negotiable virtue alike. Everything from his stride to the broad and beaming grin on his face spoke of a man positively radiating good fortune and well-being. For Prospero, being as he was a true scion of Cittàvecchio, relished the Festivàle Week as possibly the most perfect excuse to *show off* ever invented.

But this year, it was not enough that he should arrive to the ball in a great porcelain seashell drawn by dolphins. Not enough that he should have a gondola full of naked dwarves disguised as cherubs drawn through the air by teams of tethered geese (and a few strategically placed balloons). This year, he would redefine the very *meaning* of the word excessive.

The great trading sloop had arrived from the Barbary Coast on the morning tide, the three lions of Prospero's coat of arms proudly displayed on the mainsail. As Prospero arrived at the foot of the gangplank, his captain hailed him from the deck.

"Ho, my gracious Lord, just wait until you see what we have found for you. It is no exaggeration, my Lord, when I tell you that your eyes will start from your head, and your very heart from your breast!"

Prospero hopped from foot to foot with fizzing impatience. "What is it?! A roc's egg? A catoblepas! You found a genuine swamp donkey and brought it all the way home for me! No? Tell me! No, don't, I must guess... a breeding nest of salamanders?

A giant pilot fish, with spider's eyes, and *antlers!* Or a Thracian gorgon-bull, I've *always* wanted one! Tell me, *tellmetellmetellme*!!!" He tore his hat from his head and waved it in the air. "In your *ear*, Barocchio! This'll teach you to sneak a basilisk into the city without telling me... is it a wyvern, perhaps? A little *tiny* small one? Will it fit in the pit?" He raced up the gangplank and seized the captain's lapels in a frenzy of anticipation. "Show me!"

The captain rolled his eyes, long used to his employer's enthusiasm where new acquisitions were concerned, and led him down the ladder below decks.

The below deck area smelled of wild animals that had not been allowed out of their cages for some time. Here and there a low growl or snarl signalled a dissatisfied occupant of a cage, but it was the large central cage secured under a massive shroud that drew Prospero like a moth to a candle. He held both fists up in front of his mouth, wide-eyed, and looked askance at the captain. "The cage is much smaller than I expected, Josiah. From what you said I thought you might have a *dragon* down here."

The captain laughed. "No dragons this trip, my Lord. But I'm confident you'll enjoy what we have found for you."

With a loud crack, the main hatch cover was lifted away, flooding the hold with daylight. Tigers and camels and strange birds whooped and hollered at the sudden rush of light and air, and Prospero wheeled about, entranced. "Magnificent... magnificent... but nothing *unusual*, Josiah. No *Bestia Fabulae*. That's what I sent you out there for; what I pay you for. Surely you have not disappointed me, not in Festivàle Week..."

The captain smiled broadly, and gestured behind Prospero, to the great central cage, still covered with its tarp. One did not work for the Lord Prospero of the Three Lions for long without acquiring a certain flair for the dramatic.

The tarp was winched away, and what lay within the cage stirred, and opened its eyes lazily.

"*Ohh*," said Prospero. "*Ohh...*"

His hat fell to the deck from nerveless fingers, forgotten. He stumbled forward, one hand reaching out as if to touch, then drew back. He could not tear his eyes from the vision before him.

"Captain," he said, not even glancing away. "You have earned your bonus and twice again over. My factor will pay your fee without question, and you have earned my... earned my undying..." the words tailed off. The captain smiled a quiet and satisfied smile to himself, the smirk of a man who knows he has done his job all too well.

"I shall call you *Caliban*," said Prospero, touching the white fur in wonder.

*   *   *

Gratiano had been walking to try and escape the shadows in his own head, but he had not even escaped the shadow of the Cathedrale before a shadow of an entirely different and more sinister kind fell across his path.

"Hell-*o*, Gratiano. Nice to see you out and about, I was getting a little worried about your *health*." Barocchio moved smoothly off to the landward side of Gratiano, preventing him from fleeing into the side streets; to the other side, a canal, and behind, two extremely large shaven-headed gentlemen in ill-fitting doublets with arms that looked like sacks full of watermelons.

"It hasn't even been four days, Barocchio; you gave me a fortnight. You gave me your *word* on a fortnight."

"Steady on there, now. I am a man of my word; this is merely a social visit, between two fellows who have the good fortune to meet on the riverside. You look *terrible*, my Lord dell'Allia; rumour had it you had taken a chill but I can see from your eyes you merely need rest and probably the attentions of a good cook. Little bit of an upset stomach is it? Has life given you a hard time? Is Dame Fortuna turning her fickle face from you in your time of need? It has happened to us all in time, my young and unhappy friend, one just makes the best fist of it that one can..." Barocchio's expression of solicitous concern sat poorly with the avaricious light that illuminated his eyes like a lighthouse beacon.

"You will have your money, Barocchio. I've already made the appropriate arrangements. I'm just making sure you have to wait for it if I'm paying so handsomely for the time." Gratiano's words contained a confidence he did not feel; since that night in the Rookeries he had seen neither hide nor hair of Gawain and his promised payoff. Without it, Gratiano's life was rapidly becoming a study in fiduciary misery. Word of a deferred debt payment spreads fast and all those people who would normally be more than happy to extend a line of credit to a nobleman – tailors, bakers, cooks, factors, owners of warehouses and brokers of shipping insurance to name but a handful – emerge from the woodwork like hungry termites and demand immediate payment on past debts without any prospect of extending further credit. Gratiano was damn near cleaned out and even if the expected dell'Allia ship arrived from Montressori, unless it was laden with gold and diamonds it would barely cover his expenses.

Still; he reflected bitterly. *At least I won't be in debt to anyone.* He looked Barocchio up and down with an expression more tired and dismissive than fearful.

Barocchio may have been expecting one of a number of reactions, but boredom clearly wasn't one of them. "Tish tish, my cheeky Lord. So rude when I have been so understanding of your temporary financial embarrassment. Which reminds me – will we be seeing you at the opening ball tonight? The good Donna Zancani apparently has a selection of tribal nonsense from the New Territories for the delectation of her audience. It would be a shame not to see you there…"

Gratiano started at the mention of Elizabeta. He stopped, and faced Barocchio squarely. "I would doubt it, good Barocchio. I should not really be out of my bed now, suffering as I am with such *virulent* influenza." He faked a sneeze with a goodly gob of mucus behind it; Barocchio nimbly danced back out of spatter range, but he did not risk coming close again once he had done so, and his hand hovered over his kerchief. "Best, then, that you get yourself back to the bedroom, my good Lord. I would hate for anything unfortunate to happen to you before you had paid your dues." He sketched a bow and retreated, his pair of men-mountains in tow.

You are such a snob, Barocchio, thought Gratiano. *More a snob than anyone born to rank ever is. And not content to climb the social ladder, you insist on kicking those you have just climbed over.*

Gratiano hawked, and spat bile deftly into the canal. *I have more to worry about than you.*

For the past few nights Gratiano had not slept, staring at the roof of his chamber and playing things over again and again. Gawain's smooth patter, his explanations... the blood. Fog, swirling through everything, through the night and through his brain like an airborne madness, The beggar, and the look of terror on his face. What, in the final analysis, could a beggar have done to offend the great and the good? *He has seen what he should not.*

Twice, now, Gratiano had got as far as the cloisters of the Cathedrale, planning on unburdening himself in confessional. Twice, he'd reached the doors, frozen, and turned back. He had gone to Elizabeta Zancani, but could not confess to her either – though that was as much to do with her strange behaviour as anything else. He had not felt right since he had seen her – drained, a touch feverish – and he half suspected that he had caught some flux from her. She had been so cold, her flesh freezing to the touch; never before had she been so ferocious in the bedchamber, keeping him there until near dawn, keeping her face veiled and calling him her holy fool. He had tried several times to talk with her but her attentions were on other things than the confessional, and he, being but weak flesh, had conceded to the inevitable. But away from her touch that gave him no aid, and this secret that he carried had grown from an anchor to a millstone until it felt as though he dragged the very foundations of the city around with him.

He had convinced himself that it was loyalty to Gawain and the city that turned him back, but it was becoming more and more difficult to believe that. Whatever business he had been on, it wasn't that of the city government unless that government revelled in clandestine murder – and the Duca had never been clandestine when he had wanted a man dead in the past. The dozens of crab-gnawed corpses tied to the pillars of the city bridges attested to that.

But Gawain d'Orlato was a nobleman of Cittàvecchio. The honoured aide (and some would say chosen successor) of the Lord Seneschal himself. Lord Gawain would not have so acted without good reason...

Childhood stories of high adventure – of dashing agents, of cloaks and daggers. Would the heroes of those youthful tales have run to the church bleating of their bruised consciences after a little claret was spilled? No. They were diamond-hard, sharp-edged, suave, witty and sophisticated. Everything he wished to be. Everything that he could be – if he could only get the image of the light fading from the beggar's eyes out of his mind.

Preoccupied as he was, he tripped and nearly fell over the black cat, weaving between his legs nimbly. He cursed and aimed a kick at it, but it was up a gatepost and sat atop it long before his clumsy swipe connected, staring at him with great amber eyes like lanterns.

* * *

Prospero's menagerie was based in a large walled estate in the lower part of the city. Once, it had been a manor house surrounded by elegant gardens, defended from the hoi polloi by a wall and a shallow moat. He had converted the manor house into a central building for the more difficult animals and divided the grounds up into enclosures for his various creatures. A not inconsiderable fortune had been ploughed into a series of aqueducts, terraces, cages and pits, with water routed in from the bay to provide a fresh water environment for the animals requiring it. The moat had been deepened and reinforced and was now, famously, home to an irascible and baleful crocodile which rumour suggested was a *special* favourite of Prospero's.

The well-being and day-to-day maintenance of the animals was the province of *Miranda*, who was generally reckoned to be one of the wonders of Cittàvecchio by all who had seen her. Prospero had won her from the court of one of the Rajahs during a trading trip to Sind and as far as anyone knew she was unique. Shaped like a Sindi woman but carved from dark mahogany and inlaid with marquetry lacquers, she was an *automaton*, like those spoken of in the old legends of Hephaestus and Athena. Whether there was sorcery about her or just cunning engineering nobody knew; Prospero had expressly forbidden anyone from opening her up to find out. It was a common rumour among the more salacious of the gossipmongers of the city that the frequent late night parties at the Menagerie saw Miranda pressed to duty in a fashion that her original designer would likely have found *quite* surprising. Fortunately for the dignity of scandalmongers and partygoers alike, Miranda's many wonders did not include a voice.

Prospero arrived back at the Menagerie ahead of his precious cargo; still almost dazed, he had fair floated home from the dockside. Carts laden with his precious cargo would be arriving within the hour, and he had several important logistical decisions to make about cages, ponds, and whether he could afford to put the tigers in the manticore's old pen.

He burst through the front doors still full of ideas and plans, and bellowed for Miranda at the top of his voice; much to his surprise, she did not appear. Somewhat nonplussed, he wandered out into the main atrium.

"Miranda? Miraaaaan-*da!*"

She was stood in the centre of the main courtyard, still and lifeless like a marionette with cut strings. Her carved wooden smile was as enigmatic as ever, but her jewelled eyes seemed dead and her arms hung limp. The top of her head was flipped open on a cunningly designed hinge; within, a cavity where something had clearly been removed. Prospero peered into the space within, bafflement giving way to a sudden sense of foreboding.

"Who's there? Who's there, I say! I'm armed, I warn you…"

"Good afternoon, Prospero. I thought we should have a little talk…"

Gawain sat cross-legged on top of one of the kennels. Until he spoke, he had looked like part of the shadow of the building. Prospero started at the sound of his voice, but sheathed his sword. "Gawain. What's happened to Miranda? What are you doing here?"

"I disabled Miranda so that our little chat wouldn't be interrupted. I think we need to get a few things straightened out, you and I." The man's smile put Prospero in mind, suddenly and incongruously, of a shark that has suddenly noticed the jolly little remora swimming along under its jaw.

It is always a startling thing when one lives so long and so close to the shark to be reminded what sharp teeth it has.

"Do you recall, a few days ago, directing young Gratiano dell'Allia to find me at the di Tuffatore townhouse?"

"Ah." Prospero smiled weakly. "Yes, I recall. Quite keen to find you, so he was. Matter of money, I thought…"

Gawain unfolded his limbs slowly and patiently, like a spider emerging from a burrow in languid and implacable pursuit of a prey all paralysed by venom and sticky web. "And do you recall what you said to him when you directed him to find me there?"

"Look, Gawain, what you and di Tuffatore get up to in your spare time is entirely your own affair, I'm hardly one to complain after all. But don't imagine that it isn't known in certain circles that you pair are *at it* like a pair of oiled Hellenic wrestlers every chance you get-"

Gawain landed on the floor noiselessly and padded slowly and methodically toward Prospero, who found himself involuntarily walking backwards to maintain a distance with this new, menacing figure. *I see you, little fish.* He felt the low wall of the raised shrubbery bump into the back of his knees, cutting off his avenue of retreat. Gawain continued to advance silently, a strange distant smile on his face. "Look, I didn't say anything to dell'Allia that's not deniable. I'm an old hand at this. I mean, if you're giving them both the nasty and want them kept unaware of each other that's fair enough, Mum's the word..."

Prospero sat down, abruptly, in the shrubbery. Gawain leaned in close over him, his right hand closing softly around Prospero's throat, just enough pressure to make its presence felt. Prospero's hand went instinctively for his knife, but Gawain's left locked around his wrist and he moved in closer, his mouth right next to Prospero's ear. He spoke in a breathy whisper, barely audible; each word was punctuated with a gentle squeeze of Prospero's throat.

"You don't speak of Xavier and me.

"You do not, *ever,* laugh about Xavier and me.

"If you do not do these things, I will not cut off your diseased and rancid prick and choke you to death with it.

"Do you understand? Nod once if you understand."

Prospero nodded, once.

"Good. Then we have an understanding. No more amusing yourself at my expense."

Prospero nodded, again. Gawain could feel Prospero's pulse racing in his neck. He leaned in close again and whispered. "Don't imagine there is any place, any thing that I cannot reach, Lord Prospero. Do not imagine that I cannot *touch* you. You would be foolish and wrong to base a course of action upon such an assumption. And Cittàvecchi society would be so much the lesser were I to be forced to teach you a more *practical* lesson in manners. So I will *accept...*" he squeezed Prospero's throat again, harder and longer this time, "...your apology, on the understanding that such a situation will not occur again." He released Prospero and stepped back. The older man gasped for air, his hands to his throat,

"You'll find the gyroscope I took from Miranda's head amongst the peacocks, Prospero. Consider this a warning. I don't tolerate those who cross me, and you have received this warning only because I like you. Anyone else I'd have killed out of hand."

By the time Prospero had recovered himself, Gawain had gone. He touched his throat gingerly, and composed a blistering curse under his breath. *Arrogant bastard; who does he think he is?*

He picked himself up and dusted himself down, buttressing his wounded dignity with every passing second. By the time he had found his way to the peacock enclosure to find Miranda's innards, he had a good head of steam building up.

The peacocks had been a long-running project of Prospero's; careful interbreeding and incubating of eggs, control of diet and not a little praying to the Trinity or to any old deity that might have been in the mood to dispense a miracle as they passed. The birds were of unusual size and their plumage, prismatic and translucent, had been intended to catch the fading rays of the sun and provide Prospero not just with an entrance to the Ball that would be talked about all month, but with talking points all night and with startling meals the following day to amuse and amaze at the banquet.

Prospero fell to his knees at the gates to the peacock pen. All bar two of the birds lay, their necks twisted at unnatural angles, trampled into the mud of the enclosure. The two remaining alive blinked at Prospero and came forward, expecting seed; it was all that he could do to caress their poor heads. Gawain had *plucked* them. Not a single feather remained on their bodies, and the birds shivered in the breeze. Their once-magnificent plumage blew through the enclosure, mud-spattered and ruined.

Sat in the centre of a bed of the feathers, weighing them down was the missing gyroscope from Miranda.

"You wretched, vile, evil, cruel, vicious *bastard!*" shrieked Prospero in a rising falsetto, sending the two surviving birds skittering across the pen. He clutched a double handful of the ruined plumage and hurled it in the air. Weeks of planning lost. Beasts killed for no good reason. The pointlessness of it all near drove Prospero mad; Gawain could have achieved the same effect with a stern *note*.

The sound of heavy carts rumbling to a halt outside brought Prospero back to the now, and he carefully scooped up the gyroscope. He examined it closely, but could find no obvious damage; he pulled a few mangled feathers out of its innards, peered at it critically and then carefully refitted it into Miranda's gaping skull, and closed the lid on the automaton's head.

With jerky movements growing increasingly smooth, she stuttered back to life, her posture and body language conveying a brief moment of confusion, though when she registered Prospero's presence she calmed down. He imagined the surprise she must have suffered, being so rudely assaulted and absently patted her on the arm. The automaton tottered, stiff-limbed, to the peacock enclosure, looked around and raised both wooden hands to her carven face in an eloquent expression of mechanical dismay.

"I know, I know, Miranda. It's a terrible thing. A terrible thing, but we must make the best of it." Prospero patted her awkwardly. "I shall call the cooks immediately. Gather as much of the plumage as you can, m'dear, and we'll work from there. The costumes will be somewhat less gaudy than planned, and the banquet perhaps a little more generous, but one works with the tools one is presented with."

The cage containing Caliban was so large it barely fitted through the ornamental arch over the gateway; and as Prospero looked at it, he smiled an evil smile to himself, thoughts of his ruined peacocks fled for the moment, chased away by bright and gaudy delight, and cheery revenge, whose claws were no less vicious for being painted in jolly colours.

You may smile your smug superior smile for now, Gawain. But you are not the only one who knows how to hurt the things that other people love.

* * *

It was late in the day when Gawain finally found Gratiano, stood on the platform above the Furies, looking out over the city. The young man looked a picture of misery, shoulders stooped and mud splashed up his britches. Were Gawain given to pity, he reflected, he would probably feel some stirring in him for the condition of the poor naïf.

"You have been absent from the social scene for a few days, Gratiano. I have been *worried*."

Gratiano started abruptly, then shook his head, his face a combination of alarm, relief and wariness. "How do you move so quietly? I thought myself alone until you spoke."

"It's a gift. Besides, you were so sunk in misery I could have arrived atop one of Prospero's elephants and you would have been none the wiser."

"I've been ill."

"No, you've been moping because you squashed a beggar's windpipe, and now you're wondering if you did the right thing."

Gratiano started, and what little blood remained in his face fled for warmer climes. He looked around in a panic, watching for eavesdroppers. Gawain barked a short, sharp laugh. "Be calm, Gratiano. I'm no fool to jabber within earshot of the bushes. We are alone save for two courting couples back in the gardens and both of them, I can assure you, have more on their minds than our conversation. Be still, and calm down. You might as well be wandering the streets with a flag saying 'Reluctant Murderer' above your head."

Gratiano looked down at his feet, then darted a glance back at Gawain. "I haven't been able to sleep… I didn't think it would be like this. It's eating me alive."

Gawain draped his arm companionably around Gratiano's shoulders. "You haven't yet mastered the art of looking unconcerned when all around you is falling apart. It's a vital skill, and one that I suggest you learn quickly."

"Gawain, I don't think I'm cut out for this kind of thing; I –"

"Whether you are cut out for it or not is a moot point now, my friend. You cannot unbloody a hand once it's been in the wet and red stuff. You simply have to make the best of it, and make sure that nobody gets wind of what goes on beneath the surface. Walk with me."

The pair of them crossed the Piazza d'Erinye and headed back across the city as the afternoon sun lengthened shadows everywhere and the mist began to rise. "What you must understand, Gratiano, is that what passes for law in this city only holds true for those who let it. For others, the law is just an inconvenience, an impediment to be worked around - people like Barocchio or Prospero. Do you imagine for one moment that if someone were to die during one of Barocchio's pit fights or someone were to be trampled by one of Prospero's elephants during a parade that either of those worthies would suffer the consequences? No. They would wriggle out of it with some kind of official slap on the wrist. It is my duty – and will be yours – to ensure that those who are above the law do not go unpunished. You must understand the concept of justice and set aside this old notion of law."

"But who decides-"

"Ah-ah." Gawain touched his finger to his lips. "Who do I work for? Whose word is the guiding principle of my actions and of my life? I do not question those who offend him or his propriety, I merely trust, implicitly, that his judgement is correct because the love I bear him is due no less. Now; listen to me with care. Visconti of the night watch has asked me about the whereabouts of my associates the night of the murder. I think he suspects the involvement of a member of the nobility and this means his attentions may fall on you."

Gratiano started like a hare. "But you said – "

"*Hush*, and listen. He has nothing – a few bits of whimsy and suspicion. You must brazen this out and behaving like a schoolboy in a sulk just makes it look all the worse and solidifies his suspicions. You, act as you always have – play the parties, gamble, act the rake and dissolute. He'll be looking for changes in behaviour, and if he sees none, his eye will move on. If he finds you behaving as you are at the moment he'll have a letter of authority from the Duca to reel you in for questioning and then a few lost fingernails will be the *least* of your worries. Can you do that?"

"I am without cash, Gawain. All my creditors have come out of the woodwork – Barocchio included – and have left me without so much as a penny. Everything depends on my ship coming in now. I cannot afford to gamble, or to party – I can barely afford to live day to day."

Gawain sighed theatrically, and held out a purse. "There are twenty in there. Consider it a loan for the time being."

"You said you'd settle-"

"And I will, be patient, you are not the only one who must mind the flow of his coin." Gawain smiled a broad and reassuring smile. "Now go to the opening ball tonight, act as you normally would and do not draw attention to yourself the way you have been. All will be well, and the eye of the *Vigilanza* will pass on in due course. Trust me in this."

Gratiano hesitated, and then took the purse. "Very well. I'll do as you suggest. But it will not be easy to put a brave face on things."

Gawain clapped him on the back. "You will manage. I chose you for just such fortitude. Have confidence in your own abilities!"

Gratiano bit his lip, and then nodded. He tucked the purse into his doublet and with a little more of a spring in his step, set off into the gathering twilight gloom.

No sooner had the rising mists claimed him, than the broad smile fell from Gawain's face like rain sliding from a window.

"There is not a lot of use left in you, but some yet, I think."

Above him, on the eaves of a house, a black cat lay along a gutter pipe and watched, unblinking, as Gawain turned and walked back into the fog. It stood and arched its back in that way cats have, and padded silently along the gutter in pursuit.

The senses of a cat are often believed to be preternatural; perhaps it was that edge which saved the black cat as it sniffed the air. It stopped, abruptly, where it would perhaps have carried on, and a split second later, a throwing knife thudded into the guttering in front of it. The cat reared and hissed, and climbed the roof tiles with a scrabble of claws; from the rooftop, it watched with affronted amber gaze as Gawain shimmied up the gutter pipe and retrieved his knife.

He balanced at the top of the pipe and matched the cat, stare for stare.

"Keep your distance. If I see you again, I'll put an end to your arrogance."

With a flick of its tail, the cat was gone, over the roofs. But by then, Gawain was gone too, and all that was left to mark his passage was a widening eddy in the golden fog.

Part Three: Death By Water

As the Festivàle preparations swept the city up, the less affluent side of the city began to crawl, slowly, back to life. Beggars were seen again around the docks and by the sunken spires of the old church that marked the edge of the Rookeries; though they did not return to their haunts in the arches along the edge of the Grand Piazza. Fra Ottavio and several other priests of the Holy Child preached sermons of tolerance and charity that were gauged sufficiently that nobody was in any doubt of their aim – appeals to the Duca to leave the Rookeries be, lest he provoke a tempest he could not control.

As for the Duca, who can tell if he even heard the sermons? The better angels among his advisors were sufficiently persuasive that the pogrom of executions came to an end and permission was given to take down the bodies that festooned the piers of the city bridges. The crabs would have to look elsewhere for their meals during Festivàle Week, and the city would have to do without the festive dashes of colour that the unfortunate victims had provided to the bare stone piers. Few indeed were those who complained, especially those downwind of the bridges.

The day of the Opening Ball was a strange one in Cittàvecchio; the night mist did not disperse, but hung in the air all day, turning the weak autumn sun into a faint watery glow and painting the entire city in shades of yellow and orange by turns warm and sickly. All-pervasive damp soaked into the bones of the buildings, and the daily bustle of life was somehow muted, as if beneath the concealing blanket of the mists foul deeds took place with only a thin veneer of smoke to conceal them from the common view. The traffic on the streets and rivers was much lighter, as every soul with the money and inclination prepared their costumes, their boats and their spirits for the first of autumn's great carnivals.

*　*　*

He could no longer feel his legs, and had to simply assume they were still serving the purpose of keeping him upright on his horse. He had stopped feeling the pain of his wound in the small hours of the night, stopped feeling hungry by dawn. Now as the sun rose toward zenith he felt it warming him, softening the crusted blood and loosening the wadded cloth jammed against the gash in his lower back. He could barely move for stiffness, and every jolt of the road or uneven step from the horse gave him a moment of giddy disorientation. Blood loss, he suspected, in a devil-may-care fashion.

A moment of panic swept over him as he reached for the cards, only to be reassured by their presence still within his jacket.

The little water he had left in his canteen he drained in one gulp; there were pools of brackish water here and there in the marshes but any child of the Cittàvecchi knew better than to drink from such pools. Legend claimed that the marshes were the graveyard of the army of the *Re Stracciati* himself, drowned during the great flood; more prosaic warnings included the disease-ridden mosquitoes and stagnant water. Besides, stopping and boiling water would be a waste of time and dismounting from the horse would almost certainly ruin the illusion that he was not a ruptured bag of guts precariously glued together with dried blood.

He squinted up at the sun; afternoon already, and he was barely a third of the way across the great floodplain. He would be lucky to make it inside the Landward Gate of Cittàvecchio before it was closed for the night; luckier still to live to see the inside of the Palazzo di Zancani again. He imagined, for a moment, the sensation of soft silk, of clean sheets and a feather mattress, of a lover's kiss and the feeling of a statue's cheek against his fingers. Just for a moment, he closed his eyes, a gift to himself for his skill and dedication thus far. A place of peace and silence; bright sunlight and the scent of flowers. The faintest rustle of a tattered robe over a marble floor.

He did not hear the distant cries of the carrion birds overhead or the drone of the mosquitoes drawn by such unexpected bounty. His horse patiently and sure-footedly picked its way across the treacherous marshes, heading for the south and home.

* * *

"Lord Prospero, what an unexpected surprise at this *unconventional* hour. Rumour has it you have suffered a misfortune over at the menagerie earlier today – a break-in? I do hope nothing valuable has been harmed..." Barocchio's face displayed exactly the correct solicitousness, but he could barely keep the glee – and the curiosity – out of his tone. One seldom saw Prospero less than perfectly dressed, yet here he was with muddy knees and clothes all covered in brambles; one saw him even less often in the middle of the afternoon, the dead hours for the *Red Lion*.

"Oh, *do* try to contain your mirth, you wretched man." Prospero flung his crumpled hat casually at one of Barocchio's muscle-bound bodyguards, who scrabbled to catch it, and perched on the edge of the wide desk, craning his head to read the paperwork in front of his rival. Barocchio hastily scrabbled to cover it up. "I'm here for a favour, not to allow you to wallow in my misfortune like a well-fed sow in the mire, though I will concede that the metaphor suits you nicely."

"You come seeking a favour with one hand and dispensing insults with the other. One day, Prospero, you will go too far and someone will object to your wit with a foot of sharp steel."

Prospero smiled his sunniest smile. "But not you, and not today. Not while we two own the only menageries in town, anyway. I have a new champion."

Barocchio leaned back in his chair. "Better than the Manticore?"

"Oh, *oceans* better. *Oodles* better. You're going to have to come up with something pretty damn special…"

Barocchio steepled his fingers. "I have a ship due in from the New Territories within the week; word from the captain suggests he may have excelled himself. There has been mention of *giant lobsters*. Shall we set a date?"

"Patience, my dear Barocchio, patience. There is the small matter of that favour first… Gawain d'Orlato, he keeps a set of rooms here at the Red Lion, does he not?"

"He does. He pays handsomely for them, and on time too, almost uniquely among my tenants. So no upsetting him."

"Oh goodness me no – I wouldn't *dream* of *upsetting* him." The malicious gleam in Prospero's eye was hard to miss. "I just want to *surprise* him a little. I need access to his rooms for five minutes."

"Out of the question." Barocchio crossed his arms. "I never invade the privacy of a guest, it would be unprofessional."

Prospero smiled the happy smile of a man to whom opposition was spur, not impediment. "His privacy is of singular disinterest to me. I know he is not within, because I have just left his company on the other side of town, so there's little to worry about on that account. Turn the other way, Barocchio, and it'll get you three days access to my buck Gryphon for stud."

Barocchio's face crumpled up in dismay. "I couldn't possibly… *three days?* No. Unprofessional."

"…and the pick of the amphisbaena's eggs, just as soon as it works out which end is going to be the *lady* end."

Barocchio winced. Prospero sighed theatrically. "*Oh* well, I shall just have to seek opportunity elsewhere. Always a pleasure to see you, Barocchio…"

"*Wait*." Barocchio shot to his feet, red in the face.

"Aah…" Prospero smiled beatifically. "I *knew* you'd come round."

"Five minutes, not a second more – and I deny all knowledge of this, you understand? All knowledge. He and… he and *a guest* were here not half an hour ago – they have both gone now, but I'll not be responsible for the consequences if he comes back and catches you… I'm not having d'Orlato on my back." Barocchio came round the desk, unhooking a large ring of keys from his belt, and led Prospero up the back stairs of the Red Lion, deserted save for the staff cleaning up the evening's excesses.

"On your back? Heavens no, Barocchio. I don't think you're his type. A little too *round*; a little too *hairy*." Prospero took the offered key, and tripped up the stairs. Barocchio waited anxiously at the bottom of the staircase.

Prospero reappeared barely two minutes later. "What a terribly *messy* boy. Still – I have what I need." He waved a hand towel in the air, sniffing it elaborately. "*Oh* yes, no mistaking that."

"You are a *sick* man, Prospero. This is a new depth of perversion, even for you."

Prospero proffered the key back with an elaborate bow, and straightened with a beaming grin. "Ah, friend Barocchio, you have no idea. No idea at all. I shall be in touch about scheduling a meeting between your new champion and mine in due course." Prospero had nearly reached the door when he stopped, and with a theatrical flourish, swivelled on his heel to face Barocchio again. His face was a picture of innocent surprise. "Oh – I *knew* there was something else. I will need to call upon the services of your capture team; one of my beasts is going to need recovering after an unauthorised jaunt in the city. "

"One of your beasts has escaped?" Barocchio turned serious immediately. "Mother and *Child*, Prospero! Why didn't you say so to begin with? I will summon the capture team straight away. It serves neither of us to have a *Bestia Fabula* rampaging through the city at night, especially not with things the way they are in the Rookeries..."

"Oh – don't rush, old bean. No hurry, no harm's going to be done just yet. I won't need them until, say just after midnight tonight..."

Prospero sniffed the towel again, and then burst out laughing.

* * *

The carriage jolted to a halt in the driving rain, and the Grafin emerged, unfolding herself from the carriage like a bloodless origami crane. Buskovy fussed over getting an umbrella up and hurried along behind her waving it vaguely in the direction of the sky while she, regardless of the rain, picked her way over the rocks to where the three Janizaries stood.

"Here?"

She crouched down, felt the rock and touched the red stain on the side wall of the crevice. "He stopped here, for perhaps an hour. Tended his wound, took some rest..." she looked at the blood on her pale fingers with a hypnotised fascination, turning her finger this way and that to examine the redness of it against her skin. "He has lost a lot of blood; perhaps his injury is more serious than we at first anticipated. He is weakening, fast. He may not live out the day; I will be surprised if he reaches the city alive. In any case, time is against us now. Onwards at double speed. Try and catch him before he reaches the city precincts – and if you run him down, do not kill him until I have spoken to him. Do you understand?"

The Janizaries nodded silently and resumed their positions as outriders around the carriage. The Grafin sat down inside in brooding silence a while; Buskovy joined her inside as the carriage set off. He knew better than to try to make conversation; his very presence within the carriage as opposed to perched atop it like a miserable, cold and portly gargoyle was an unexpected concession to the rain. A less shrewd man, a man less versed in the ways of the Bucharan court might have imagined that the Grafin invited him to ride with her because she feared for his health being stuck in a howling gale and driving rain atop a carriage; Buskovy, knowing the family he served all too well knew that if he had been invited in it was because the Grafin wanted him for something, not because she gave a damn whether he froze to death or drowned.

So he waited in companionable silence and was grateful for the chance to try and warm up out of the driving rain.

"He has started using the cards; started letting them lead him. The deck is awake and besides, he knows he has little to lose now."

The abruptness of the statement startled him; the Grafin was not even looking at him, instead staring out of the carriage window at the driving rain outside. "He has crossed a bridge, and knows it. That makes him dangerous and gives him real power in the short term."

"I do not understand, my Lady…"

A nerveless smile flitted across the Grafin's face but found the territory inhospitable and moved on. "No, of course you don't. I would not expect you to. He knows he is dying, Buskovy; he knows it, this thief and that makes him very dangerous indeed. The deck likes a willing sacrifice."

"Is he somehow tapping the power in the cards?"

"That's not how it works, Buskovy. One does not tap them - they are not like a sword, or a hoe; not a tool. They are… almost alive; certainly, there is a will behind the cards, one that most of the time is quiescent or imprisoned. We knew how dangerous it was; we've always known. That is why the old Graf Stechau went to such lengths to secure it and carry it to Buchara."

"But that act brought the curse down on his own head!"

"Curse? Not exactly, no. The deck looks for ways to influence the world around it, to recreate what it was created to be an occult allegory of. And better it try to do so at Buchara, where we were wise to its cause and able to suppress it, imprison and control it, than in Cittàvecchio where the Ducas were ever more prone to its whispers."

"Giereck says the deck was painted to *represent* Cittàvecchio – "

"No. Not Cittàvecchio – or not the city as you presently understand it. The deck was painted to hold the soul of the capital of the *Regno dei Stracci*, the city before the floods came and washed away its corruption. Giereck was a clever man, to hint but not to say aloud; the cards and their protectors have ways of keeping their own secrets." The Grafin huddled further into her furs. "Even then, his caution didn't avail him – he died like every man that meddles with the deck eventually. It is a very *jealous* lover."

* * *

Early evening was the worst time imaginable at the offices of the *Vigilanza*, as the night shift came in and handed over from the sleepy day patrol and at the same time the city's night life began to awaken, bringing with it the ticks and leeches of the criminal underworld that infested the body urban. Today of all days with the opening ball – traditionally the signal for the beginning of Assassin's Season – on top of the last few days' unrest, the need for public order was paramount, and co-operation between the Tatar Guards and the *Vigilanza* closest.

Visconti had the haggard and unshaven look of a man who knows it will be a long time before he next sees his bed for anything other than a fleeting lover's kiss. He sat slumped in his chair, listening with one ear to Captain Valentin's lengthy discourse on last-minute security plans for the ball.

"Ho, Gian. Gian!"

He sat upright abruptly; with the look familiar to schoolteachers the world over. *I was awake, I was awake. I was just resting my eyelids.* Valentin was looking at him with half-smile, half exasperation.

"You have not heard a single word I have said for the last five minutes, have you?"

Visconti slumped, his head in his hands. He was saved from the embarrassment of responding by one of the Tatars rapping smartly on the open door and leaning into the room.

"Captains, forgive the intrusion. Captain Valentin, an urgent summons to the Castell'nuero. Captain Visconti – Lord d'Orlato is here to see you on a matter of urgent business."

Valentin raised an eyebrow to Visconti. "We can catch up during the opening presentations. Just make sure your men know that patrolling the landing stage is their lookout, not my lads', alright?"

"Landing stage, yes, of course, fine. I'll meet you at the *Vecchi Punti*[11] at eight bells to greet the guests. You can brief me on any last-minute changes then." As Valentin left, Visconti signalled to the Tatar at the door. "Be good enough to ask Lord d'Orlato to come in, would you?"

Gawain had clearly stopped in on his way to the ball – dressed in tailored black leathers and grey silks, his hair scraped back into a fierce topknot and powdered grey-white in sharp contrast to his eyes. In lieu of a mask, his eyes glittered from eye sockets blacked with make-up, and dark grey lines accentuated his cheekbones. He looked, thought Visconti incongruously, like his own ghost.

"My Lord; what can I do for you. As you can imagine, time is short at such a critical stage of the evening – "

Gawain cut him off. "The handkerchief."

---

[11] The *Vecchi Punti* or the Old Staircase was once a grand stepped colonnade leading downhill to the old water gate of the Castell'nuero. Rising water covered not only the great stone piers but the bottom two-thirds of the staircase, resulting in a massive arc of stairs which simply descend into the water on the eastern flank of the Castell'nuero. This is now a favoured disembarkation point for any visitors to the Castell'nuero arriving by water, as it provides a fast route straight into the heart of the fortress.

Visconti froze, and watched Gawain very carefully out of the corner of his eye. "What of it?"

"I believe I may have traced the owner."

"And?"

"Here are the caveats: I have no proof that will stand before a magistrate. I want my name kept out of it. The Court and especially the seneschal's office will deny any knowledge or involvement whatever he says under confession. And as far as I am concerned, this conversation never happened. Clear?"

"Absolutely clear, my Lord. Just give me the name." Visconti looked at the floor carefully to conceal his impatience.

"I cannot account for the movements of Gratiano dell'Allia during any of the periods under question."

Visconti risked a look at Gawain; his face was even, his eyes glittering from their dark pits.

"My Lord is sure of his information?"

"Sure enough to suggest that if you are going to apprehend him you might consider doing so tonight."

Visconti managed a brittle smile. "My Lord has my thanks – and of course, a promise that we will speak further on this matter and on the delays that have plagued this investigation once the immediate threat to civic amity has been dealt with appropriately."

Gawain met him stare for stare, and it was Visconti who looked away first. "I shall look forward to it with *keen* anticipation, Captain. I always enjoy a vigorous exchange of sharp debate."

"I'm sure you do. If you will excuse me, my Lord, I have matters to attend to." Visconti left the room, barely able to resist breaking into a run.

Gawain remained in the centre of the room a moment, alone and still. Then, with a broad smile, he turned on his heel and left the barracks, whistling a jaunty tune.

It was, he reflected, going to be a *busy* night.

*   *   *

From Ophelia's balcony, the city looked soft and magical, like the inside of an opium dream. The late evening mist lay in a thick, waist-height blanket over the flooded streets and rivers, and the gaudily-decorated boats of the Regatta all bore yellow lanterns and torches, the smoke of which added to the haze and gave it a distinct smell of wood smoke and pitch. The strange light distorted distances and angles, turning the surface of the mists into a luminescent mirror, reflecting, muffling and distorting. Familiar thoroughfares suddenly became alien; the carved prows of ships looming out of the mist took on the aspect of great snorting beasts, breath boiling, smelling of damp and polished wood. And the city's smoky breath muffled and distorted the distant music from the harbour and the sound of the bells, tolling to summon the ships of the flotilla to the opening Regatta, the great ball held on the decks of the ships in the harbour.

Ophelia's maids and attendants fussed around her like ducklings, pinning, knotting and teasing, while she stared down into the dream of the city, lost in a reverie. The sound of Calomena's voice jolted her back into the world of the moment. "...Ophelia!"

She turned abruptly, the architectural folly of her wig swaying ominously, causing several maids to squeal in terror as the ship wedged into the cleft in her coiffure wobbled ominously. "No sudden movements, milady! The ship isn't properly buttressed yet"

"I swear," said Ophelia in a long-suffering tone, rolling her eyes at her mentor, "than before they are done I will be able to enter the Regatta as a float rather than as an observer..."

"I *said*, your suitor is here, early, offering to escort you to the ball. What do you want to do?" Calomena's face was a cross between incredulity and asperity. Much of the former and not a little of the latter was directed at the woefully unprepared state of Ophelia's costume for the night.

"He's *here?* He can't be here, he's early!"

"Actually, my chicken, you are an hour late, and he's on time. Shall I keep him busy for you?"

"Please, Mater. I shalln't be long… and Mater – the philtre?"

Calomena stopped, her back to Ophelia. "Are you *absolutely* sure you want to take this path, Ophelia? Such things have a way of rebounding on those that use them. If I have taught you nothing else I have taught you that, surely?"

Ophelia hid a brief flash of genuine irritation behind a coquettish twirl. "If he is as much trouble as you claim, then better I have some insurance, no?"

"And what of those who love you without the aid of magic, girl? What of your secret Lord Prospero?"

"If Prospero truly loves me for myself and not for the power I could bring him then he will understand that a political marriage will be a necessity. Better a political marriage with one that loves your name, to allow one who loves your soul to do so without the interference of politics, no?"

"You, girl, should take up law." Calomena produced from within her sleeve a tiny glass phial, stopped with a blob of red wax. "A drop or two in a drink should produce the desired effect for an hour or two; increasing the dose will only increase the intensity of the sensation, not the duration. Too much will produce spasms and nausea, so don't be over-generous. And understand that I will take no responsibility for what happens when you use it."

Ophelia examined the phial curiously. "You spoke of Xavier having 'defences'; what of them?"

"You will have to navigate them yourself…" Calomena was cut short by the appearance of a servant at the door, waving to attract her attention. She left Ophelia to her toilet, and made her way across the great balcony of the townhouse, watching Xavier pacing back and forth in the atrium below. Sweeping down the long staircase, she felt cold grey eyes track her. He was dressed in plain, simple black, tailored to fit, with a half-cloak and, unusually, no mask. Calomena met his gaze, and saw cool hostility there.

"Lord di Tuffatore. Donna di Gialla is delayed at her toilet, and will be with you presently."

Xavier coolly inclined his head, but his gaze did not leave Calomena as she continued down the stairs. If she was waiting for a response, he gave none, but remained, poised like a dancer, in the middle of the great marble hall. She spoke again, into the spreading silence.

"You, sir, wear no mask?"

He inclined his head gravely. "Indeed."

"Indeed? Is it not time, though? All will be wearing disguise but you."

Xavier's smile was fleeting, but clearly the exchange amused him. "I choose to wear no mask. When everyone is wearing a mask the best disguise is often to go barefaced. Besides; this seems to be a time for the laying aside of disguises. Wouldn't you agree?"

Calomena rounded the banister-post at the end of the staircase. "The Festivàle might be seen as a place where deception is commonplace; under such circumstances, any unmasking would be viewed with a healthy scepticism by any who witnessed it, I am sure."

"Ah; but when everyone is actively seeking to deceive, surely to play the barefaced fool is the way to rise above the crowd and be noticed?" Xavier paced warily around the edge of the hall, keeping his distance from Calomena.

"Lord Xavier; one would almost imagine there was some double meaning to your words. What purpose would anyone have to deceive? We are all friends and loyal citizens are we not?"

"This is Cittàvecchio, Mater. Here, everyone wears masks. It is as common as breathing, and as hard to live without."

"So what would your purpose be, oh dead man walking, to wander barefaced through the carnival? You are aware that people will talk, and that some will be scandalised?"

Xavier laughed. It was a hollow sound completely unlike his usual chuckle. "The only thing worse than being talked about..." Slowly, finger by finger, he pulled off his gloves, paying minute attention to the process.

"...is not being talked about, yes. Well, I'm sure you're going to be talked about, my Lord. But I wonder what they will say."

One glove off now, Xavier arched an eyebrow and gave Calomena a sideways glance as he methodically pulled the other off, finger by finger. "And who, pray tell, are 'they' when they are at home?"

"Let us say, a few interested parties who watch the progress of the ship of state with some concern about the proximity of the rocks." Calomena watched Xavier narrowly, but the young man made no move save to smile gently to himself and tuck his gloves into his belt.

"I would have thought that your concerns would be exclusively for your ward and her family affairs."

"They are; and those family affairs, lest you forget, consist of the good governance of this city."

They circled each other, like wary tigers.

Xavier clasped his hands behind his back and with a half-smile and a curious look, stopped pacing and turned to face Calomena.

"Good governance is a matter close to my heart. Perhaps you and I and some friends should discuss it."

"Would Pater Felicio number among these friends?"

"You are a perceptive woman, Mater. But you are not as clever as you think you are. Let us say, the Court of the Gryphon above the Castell'nuero, at two bells. It will be quiet and we will be undisturbed."

"Have I a guarantee of safety?" Calomena met Xavier's gaze directly; he smiled broadly. "No member of the Secret Senate will offer you one whit of harm, so long as you come alone and our own safety is assured. If, between now and the meeting, any offence is offered to me or to anyone else of the Senate you may have identified then the consequences of that will be... unfortunate. Do you accept the terms of the meeting?"

Calomena paused and thought furiously. Here was Lord Xavier, practically confirming everything she had suspected for months – that there was a society working to overthrow the Duca, that Xavier's courtship of Ophelia was probably part of it, and that they were close to achieving their goals. And this was close to being an offer of a truce, or at least an armistice.

It was almost certainly a trap of some kind – ever since she had seen Xavier and Pater Felicio talking in the Cathedrale she had known that something like this was coming. But trap or no it was still closer to the conspiracy than she had come to date.

"I accept," she said. "The Court of the Gryphon, two bells."

"Then we have an understanding," said Xavier, with a courtly bow.

"An understanding about what?"

Ophelia swept down the staircase like a man-o-war under full sail, a great creaking explosion of silk and whalebone and taffeta and brocade, all topped off with a wig that could have kept four people alive for a week after a shipwreck. She held up a filigreed mask on a wand before her face but it did nothing to conceal the mischief glittering in her eyes.

Calomena turned and intercepted the comment smoothly. "About the time that I expect to see you returned safely to your brother's house, young Lady. I hope you do not expect to be allowed to gallivant around the city until all hours of the night."

"Mater, you are such a prude. I will be quite safe with Lord Xavier; my virtue is beyond question in the company of a gentleman of such reknown."

Xavier bowed low. "Even my gentlemanly manners would be sorely tried by such a vision of beauty as I see before me. How am I to resist?"

"I'm sure you'll manage," muttered Calomena, low enough for just Xavier to hear. "Now; you two enjoy yourselves at the ball, and remember to avoid eating anything without making sure it's been tasted first. I have a few things to finish up here, but I shall be along shortly to act as chaperone. You run along…"

Calomena ascended the stairs again. She watched with every evidence of benign protectiveness as the couple left the hall and climbed into a boat at the front dock to take them down to the *Vecchi Punti*. That benevolence drained from her face as soon as they were out of sight.

She turned to one of the house servants. "You. Run to the Ducal Barracks *immediately*. Tell Captain Valentin that he is summoned in the name of the Donna Ophelia on a matter of state security."

The time is now propitious, as he guesses,

The meal is ended, she is bored and tired,

Endeavours to engage her in caresses

Which still are unreproved, if undesired.

Flushed and decided, he assaults at once;

Exploring hands encounter no defence;

His vanity requires no response,

And makes a welcome of indifference.

T.S. Eliot, The Waste Land 235-242

The Castell'nuero was lit beyond the *Vecchi Punti* with thousands of candles, illuminating the evening mists and turning the waterway in front of the stairs into a rippling mirror of brass, throwing dancing yellow ghosts onto the ancient walls of the fortress. One after another, boats disguised and decorated arrived at the great stairway and let their passengers disembark to the sound of elegant music from within; swan boats, miniature warships, boats that looked like carriages skimming over the waves, one boat that looked like old Poseidon himself, his scaly tail arched over the occupants as a canopy. To either side of the great gateway into the Castell'nuero, ushers announced the new arrivals to the gathered throng beyond the stairs.

Xavier leapt nimbly from the boat, then turned and proffered his arm to Ophelia; such acrobatics were impractical given the complexity and inflexibility of Ophelia's costume.

Competition among the Cittàvecchi nobility was never fiercer than when costume was at stake. Amongst the men, everyone knew that there would be no beating Prospero so few tried; competition was much more fierce amongst the ladies of the court, and more than one tailor, milliner or wigmaker had their reputation and fortune made or broken by the opening ball.

All eyes were on Ophelia di Gialla as she disembarked with as much grace as possible from the boat. Her coiffure drew gasps; the barefacedness of her consort for the evening drew yet more.

"I do believe we have made an impression, as the Donna required," commented Xavier in an aside. "Donna di Castiglione has just fainted."

"How delightful. Walk very slowly," said Ophelia through gritted teeth. "I feel like I'm balancing a monkey on my head."

Xavier pursed his lips diplomatically. "A very fetching monkey it is too."

They moved into the great ballroom, moving down the centre of the aisle toward the dais at the far end of the room. Hanging above the dais, a massive tapestry stretching almost to the roof; the golden trident of Poseidon, on a field of black velvet. The heat haze of the candles and the many people already thronging the margins of the hall made the trident writhe and dance on its velvet field, drawing the eye to the dais below. There, sat at the foot of the banner was the Duca himself, surrounded by a group of his officers and functionaries. For a man who commanded such strength of feeling in his subjects – whether it be loathing or love – he was a nondescript man, balding and moustachioed, seeming lost in the pomp and ceremony. His ceremonial uniform gave the appearance of being a size too large for him. Ophelia and Xavier presented themselves before him; he nodded boredly and made a vague gesture with his hand. His eyes – and mind – were elsewhere, on the whispered words an advisor leaned forward to pour into his ear. Something about the New Territories, and corn harvests.

Ophelia spoke quietly out of the corner of her mouth as she smiled and nodded to acquaintances and political enemies to either side of the processional carpet.

"You know my brother expects you to ask for my hand in marriage either tonight or at the closing ball – and if it is not tonight other suitors will take that as a signal to present themselves to me."

"Were I to ask for your hand, would you object overly?" Xavier's voice was coy, but there was an undercurrent of chill in it. He was carefully observing the officers of the court around the Duca – the two Tatar Guards with their ivory death masks, the priests – yes, there was Pater Felicio in his mask, nodding gravely to Xavier in recognition - and Captain Valentin, just arriving on the dais, with an all too familiar mask of bronzed autumn leaves. What could have kept him from the start of the ball? Xavier revelled in his secret knowledge. *I know, but you don't, and you don't know that I know.*

"I think we should discuss a number of matters frankly and openly; not least, any designs you may have hatched with my chaperone." Ophelia waited a reply, but got none; turning to look, she saw that Xavier's attention was focussed on a woman in a magnificent ball gown; one side in shimmering gold, the other in moonlit silver. She wore a magnificent filigreed mask of gold depicting the solar face of Apollo, inlaid with chips of amber and topaz; when she inclined her head, he saw that the back of her mask was a crescent moon of beaten silver and lapis lazuli. She curtsied elegantly as they passed. Laying supine along her arm was a black cat, regal and Egyptian in aspect, its amber eyes following Ophelia's every move. It licked its lips, slowly and insolently.

For no reason she could place her finger on, a shiver ran up Ophelia's spine.

* * *

Something drew Mercutio back to the real world.

For the last hour he had been dreaming of his mother and of childhood games in the streets; of the scavenger hunts out in the marshes and the strange treasures that one could find if one looked. It was a secret of the street children which somehow became forgotten as they moved into adulthood that the best places to scavenge were either on the far side of the marshes where the runoff from the mountains formed great pools or the points where the city's sewerage system – flooded and partially inoperable – disgorged its burden into the swamp outside the landward walls. Here all the lost coins and trinkets, everything that fell from a windowsill or a pocket, would be washed and would settle to the bottom of the great pools that abut the wall.

A child who could hold his breath for more than a minute under water could be guaranteed a find of worth; the older children knew where to look, knew where the currents washed the heavier refuse, and used to dive with small nets, bringing clumps of mud back to the surface that by the time they reached the air had somehow magically transmuted into a bundle of coins.

Sometimes, of course, a child would underestimate the strength of the currents, or the treachery of the underwater weeds. Those children would be quietly and briefly mourned; the street parlance was that they had gone to dance with the Undines, the spirits of the water.

To a child, of course, the smell of the great pools outside the walls was the smell of adventure; a combination of rotting vegetation, swamp gas and effluent that in the summer could blister your nose with its power. Adults normally just avoided the entire area if they possibly could – it was yet another hazard of landward travel from Cittàvecchio and yet another reason to take the boat.

But to Mercutio it was the smell of home. He rose from a bed of memories and, blinking, regarded the world around him. As darkness had fallen, the mists had risen over the marshes and now his horse seemed like some fantastical boat afloat on a smoking sea, an equine entry in the Regatta. And in the distance ahead of him, the lights of the city twinkled – almost within reach.

The smell was vile, but unmistakable. He was nearly home.

* * *

The news rippled through the ballroom like a stone dropped in a millpond – *Prospero is here*. It reached Ophelia at the same time as the sound of trumpets from outside and what sounded suspiciously like an elephant's roar.

Guests crowded toward the top of the *Vecchi Punti* partly from curiosity and love of spectacle but not a little to see if Prospero's annual feat of planning a wildly over ambitious entrance ended up, yet again, with him in the water. It had over the past few years become something of a Festivàle tradition.

Descending from the sky outside was a massive balloon of yellow silk, buttressed with bamboo and painted with Sindi characters. Hanging from its base in lieu of a basket or gondola was an elephant, caparisoned in white chiffon, trumpeting as it descended toward the steps, where two columns of five trumpeters, each with a great fan made of albino peacock feathers, saluted it and played a fanfare. As the elephant landed on the steps – *mostly* out of the water – the supporting ropes fell away and the great balloon, now no longer counterweighted, shot up into the sky, swiftly consumed by the flames which had held it aloft in a great burst of fire and light overhead.

While everyone's attention had been focussed above, the trumpeters had rushed forward and formed a shield in front of the elephant with their fans; now the elephant reared high above their heads and crashed back down on the steps with a roar as they scattered in a complex choreographed dance. Stood on the elephant's back was Lord Prospero of the Three Lions, and he had really rather excelled himself this time.

He wore wide and flared trousers composed solely of the translucent albino peacock feathers; his mask a spray of the same shaped like a peacock's tail in miniature. His top half was bare save for a tiny bolero jacket made of small overlapping plates of ivory, displayed to full effect as he struck a dramatic attitude atop the elephant's head, like some exceptionally badly dressed climber stuck up to his waist in feathers atop a large grey pachydermic mountain. Dancing around his feet, to the clear consternation and irritation of the elephant, were several monkeys; each dressed in miniature versions of Prospero's costume.

"*Behold,*" bellowed Prospero in his best baritone. "*The Genie of Sind!*"

The elephant reared up again, and trumpeted; as it landed on its forelimbs, Prospero slid down its extended trunk, fell to his knees on the marbled floor and skidded to a halt, scattering onlookers, at the very feet of Ophelia, a train of dancing, gibbering monkeys in his wake.

"My lady," he said, taking her hand as she, like almost everyone else, watched the display dumbfounded. "From the heart of the darkest continent, I bring you apes, ivory and peacocks..."

Xavier on the other hand watched the display with an expression of polite distaste, the lingering way in which Prospero kissed Ophelia's hand in no way lost on him.

As the shouts and applause for the entrance mounted, he pointedly did not clap.

"You might have at least waited to see if I was going to ask," he pointed out coolly to Ophelia.

She smiled a coy smile. "These things are always a little more vital when one injects an edge of competition to the game. You of all people should know that, Lord di Tuffatore."

She took Prospero by the hand, raising his arm to the assembled guests. "An entrance with spectacle but no incident; my Lord of the Three Lions, you are spoiling us!"

* * *

Calomena disembarked from a small boat at one of the less well-known water gates of Castell'nuero. She had delayed her arrival to speak to Captain Valentin, briefing him at length on her suspicions and arranging for a troop of the Tatar Guard to be in position at the Court of the Gryphon from one bell onward. Xavier, Pater Felicio and his conspirators could make their explanations to the Duca – if Valentin and the Tatars could be trusted. And if not – well; on the one hand, another conspirator would be exposed, and on the other one did not become a Mater in the faith of the Mother without learning a trick or two.

An old but potent *benedizione*, woven into a rare and expensive oil would turn any metal blade from her skin – a secret of the Mother, and one of the primary reasons that she maintained her influence so close to the ever-paranoid Duca. Let Xavier's conspiracy do their worst – and indeed, let the Tatars do the same if they intended to turn coat. As a measure of insurance, she intended to brief the Duca – and he would almost certainly insist that a squadron of the *Vigilanza* go along as well – just to keep the Tatars honest. Either way, someone's secrets were going to be exposed.

Muffled in a heavy cloak and concealed behind a white porcelain mask in the shape of a swan's head, she tipped the boatman heavily for his incurious nature. Once he had vanished into the night mists she used a large old-fashioned key and unlocked the heavy wrought iron gate that protected access to the upper precincts of the castle via a long, upward-sloping corridor.

She secured it after her, glancing to either side; normally, there would be at least two guards on the gate. The alcoves to either side of the gate were empty.

Surely the *guards* hadn't deserted their post to watch Prospero's entrance?

"Hello? Guards?"

Something was not right – something in the air, a texture to the floor, to the reflected sound from the walls. Calomena knelt down and touched the ground; her fingers in the reflected light from the canal showed vivid red.

She stood, and let her stiletto slide from its concealed sheath on her arm into her hand.

"I know you're there. Come out."

"Hello, Mater," came a sibilant whisper from all around her. "It will be much swifter if you don't struggle…"

A death's-head coalesced from the shadows and moved fast, low and to the left; Calomena dodged back but in the confines of the corridor there was little room. There was a sharp snapping retort, and the sound of metal ringing on the stone flags. The broken blade of a dagger lay between them on the floor.

"*You*," she breathed. "I had not thought it would be you." She stepped back and raised her own blade warily.

Gawain gave ground and threw the hilt of the broken dagger to one side. "I always wondered if there was any truth to those stories about you and your witcheries. One has to test these things just to be sure, you understand."

"Stand down, Lord d'Orlato; your knives hold no fear for me."

In the slanting light from the canal, Calomena saw a twisted grin flash across his face. "I'll have to use my *bare hands*, then," he said.

* * *

Buskovy's heart leapt into his throat. He had been dozing in the coach, as they picked their way across the foggy marshes, when the Grafin had grasped his hand, fiercely and so hard he felt the bones of his knuckles grind together and gasped involuntarily with the pain.

The Grafin sat bolt upright in the carriage, unaware of the strength of her grip, staring into space.

"Tell them to hurry. Tell them to hurry, Buskovy. Something is happening. Something terrible."

"My lady – the marsh – the fog…"

"To *hell* with the fog and the marsh!" She rapped on the roof of the carriage. "Faster!"

* * *

"My Lord dell'Allia, may I join you?"

Gratiano froze in an instant. A tiny bead of cold sweat made its way slowly down the nape of his neck. From somewhere, he found the courage to incline his head and gesture to the seat opposite.

Captain Visconti sat down opposite, laying his sword across the table between them. Around the table, the early bustle of the Ball continued unabated. Visconti spoke quietly; to ensure the background music drowned his words out to any eavesdroppers.

"Enjoying the ball tonight, my Lord? Only I notice that you seem to be displaying little in the way of enthusiasm."

"I- ah, I was considering..." *Don't act out of the ordinary.* "Considering my options for the evening. I like to be spontaneous when it comes to the early stages of the Festivàle Week; things get so bogged down in formality later in the season, you know?"

He was doing well, but there was no hiding his blanched expression and the sweat dribbling down his nose. In a leap of logic, he decided to make a virtue of a necessity. "To be honest, I dined heavily on oysters last night and I think they have disagreed with me – I believe I may be sickening for something. I may have to give the opening ball a miss."

Visconti's face was unfathomable, his eyes giving nothing away. He looked as though he had not slept well for weeks. "My Lord, your family is in the silk trade, am I correct?"

"Amongst other things, yes, we have a weaving business in Montressori, and some trade presence in the Sindi states. Why do you ask?"

"I am looking for someone who can tell me something about this." He pulled the kerchief out of his sleeve with a flourish, and held it out to Gratiano.

The blood looked especially fresh to him. His mind danced back to the night time rooftop, to Gawain. "*Have you a kerchief about you?*" His bloodied hands. His solicitous care.

Damn, he's clever.

Gratiano managed, through a supreme effort of will, to move his hands, take the proffered kerchief, and unfold it on the table. He felt distant and light-headed, almost an observer, an unwitting passenger in his own skull as reflexive action took over. His own voice sounded very far away to his ears.

"My, what a gory thing. Yes, it's one of ours – I have one much like this myself. Montressori silk. Can't mistake it."

"Common amongst the fancy, are they?" Visconti's gaze remained inscrutable, implacable.

"Oh yes. Very popular. Almost everyone has one." He could barely hear for the drumming of his heart in his ears. How obvious this must look! How transparent!

"Any distinguishing marks? Any way of linking them to a particular person?"

"Not really, no; unless a monogram has been embroidered onto the corner – no, I see nothing here. Some people like them to be personalised but it looks as though this one is plain. I'm sorry, Captain; this could be anyone's."

He looked brightly at Visconti, who looked back at him levelly. The silence between them stretched well beyond the point of comfort, and his nerves stretched along with it. Sweat pooled above his eyebrow and dribbled down the side of his nose; the only thing preventing him from mopping his brow was the fact that the kerchief he was holding was encrusted with gore.

He knows.

He doesn't know.

He had almost reached breaking point when Visconti stood, abruptly, his chair scraping the marble flags loudly. Gratiano almost shrieked with relief, muffling it at the last with a cough. The Captain smiled cruelly and plucked the kerchief out of his nerveless hand.

"A great pity; I was hoping that you might be able to offer me some lead, some clue as to how to proceed next, but I see this is another dead end and I must simply *muddle on* as best I can. Thank you for your assistance, my Lord. Just in case I need to speak to you again... you're not planning on *going* anywhere in the next week or two, are you?"

Gratiano looked at the Captain's smile, and knew that the guttering hope that his performance had been sufficient to protect him had been extinguished. He looked away. "No, I am as poor as a church mouse, Captain. Until my ship comes in, anyway. I have no plans to travel."

Visconti nodded, and turned to go; then, as if on an afterthought, he turned back. "One last thing, Lord dell'Allia – have a care if you are travelling down by the dockside. According to Lord Prospero, a large creature escaped from his menagerie during the break-in today. It answers to the name of Caliban, and he thinks it might be dangerous to lone travellers. He's offered a substantial reward for the beast's return unharmed. But then – if you are not going anywhere, and your ship is not due in for a few days, and you are too ill to consider any of the post-ball parties – well; there's no need for you to risk it by going anywhere near the docks, is there?"

Visconti tipped a salute to the young nobleman, picked up his sword from the table and set off. Gratiano watched him go, and waited for the clutching, paralysing terror in his heart to fade.

He has no proof, but he thinks he knows anyway. It's all over.

This wasn't his life. His life was a cosy, happy game of chance and circumstance where the worst injury ever done to anyone was a mild discomfiture of the pocket, and the sharpest weapons ever used were cleverly timed bon mots. He realised in that instant that he would give up everything just to be allowed to return to that life and pretend the last week had not happened – that he had not made the bet with Barocchio, that he had not taken up Gawain's offer in the night fogs. That he had not killed at the behest of the laughing monster.

Everything in this city, now, was poisoned. Every time he struggled, he became caught deeper and deeper in the web, and he knew that unless he did something drastic, the spider was going to emerge from the darkness, and soon. He came to a decision, and stood.

* * *

Ophelia circulated among the guests, keeping one eye on Xavier, who had retired to the edge of the ballroom closest to the windows. Her conversations were brief, anodyne and impeccably worded; offers to dance declined with grace and regret. She kept one careful eye on Xavier, and if those she spoke to noticed, they were too polite to comment, and the impression given served her purposes elegantly anyway.

She glanced at the great water-clock at one end of the ballroom – past eleven bells. Calomena should have arrived over an hour ago – no doubt about her own secret business that she would deny all knowledge of later.

She watched Xavier carefully enough to notice when, without fanfare or herald, Gawain simply appeared at his side; she watched the silent interplay between them – a touch, a glance. So obvious when you knew what to look for that it was a wonder the world did not know and a credit to the efficiency with which they had kept their secret. To Ophelia, though it just served as a barb, a reminder of the clinical way in which Xavier intended to play her affections.

Gawain turned to Xavier, and made a gesture with his free hand – *a drink?* Xavier drained his glass and nodded; Gawain headed off toward the row of tables against the wall where the best vintages were displayed.

Prospero knew well enough not to approach her in public at the ball in any capacity other than politely; nevertheless, she felt his eyes on her for much of the evening as he circulated among the younger bravos and nobles, showing off his clothes and his monkeys, which proved massively popular – all the more so when they descended on the fruit-laden wig of the Donna di Castiglione and devoured it within seconds.

The shrieking of the affronted noblewoman – near as loud as that of the enthusiastic monkeys – provided her with a moment of cover; she swept two glasses of wine off the tray of a passing servant and while all eyes were on the unfortunate simian-beset wig, flicked the top off the phial, and shook the contents into one of the glasses. She dropped the phial, and ground it under her shoe. Gawain was still at the wine tables, discussing the relative merit of two vintages with the servant at the table. She moved fast, covering the ground as swiftly as dancing shoes, impractical headgear and marble floors would allow.

"My Lord di Tuffatore."

Xavier chuckled. "I was watching the unfortunate Donna di Castiglione's wig being violently deconstructed by a horde of small and angry monkeys dressed as albino peacocks. I have a suspicion that she is threatening to sue Prospero. Only at a Festivàle Ball would I be unsurprised at such a thing."

Ophelia smiled coyly. "Only at a Festivàle Ball indeed. Here, all things once regarded as impossible are regarded as normal, all natural laws stripped of their immutability. Will you drink a toast with me, Xavier?"

Xavier looked directly at her. "If we are moving to a more informal footing might I have permission to call you Ophelia?"

Ophelia proffered the glass. "For the moment, yes."

Xavier took it. "And what will I call you after the moment has passed?"

"Who knows?" Ophelia's eyes glittered with the moment, and she pitched her voice to carry just as far as Gawain, returning with two glasses. "Perhaps even wife."

"Then I will drink to the impossible made manifest." He clicked glasses with her. "To impossible futures."

"To impossible futures," she echoed, and sipped as he drank. Her eyes met Gawain's across the room, and she smiled.

* * *

241

Orlando watched Xavier toast Ophelia from across the room, and whispered softly to the cat she carried. "Any moment now, my sweet. You know what to do." The cat leapt from her arms, watched her a moment with its lambent eyes and disappeared into the shadows. From behind her own masks, Orlando looked upon the gathering without fear or favour; they did not know how close he was, did not know what was to come.

Xavier sat down abruptly, and made a comment to Ophelia about the drink going to his head. He glanced around for Gawain, but his lover was mysteriously absent. Ophelia watched him with cold amusement; then she too turned on her heel.

"Ophelia!"

She turned back to him and cupped his face in her hand. "Don't worry, my sweet; I'm just going to find the Mater Calomena. I'll be back presently."

"I will await your return," avowed Xavier.

"I know," smiled Ophelia.

"Perfect," whispered Orlando, to herself. She turned to the water clock, and watched the minutes ticking away towards midnight.

* * *

"Ho, Gratiano! I've been looking all over town for you. What kind of miserable face is that for a man! It's the Grand Opening of Festivàle Week, the first great Ball of the Season, damn it all; you can't be *glum*!" Prospero broke into a trot to intercept Gratiano's long-legged stride toward the doors and freedom.

Gratiano half-turned, but didn't break stride. "Prospero. I need a favour. A big favour."

"What a coincidence! So do I." Prospero hooked his arm through Gratiano's and dragged him to a halt. "Is this about Barocchio's wager-"

"No." Gratiano cut him off. "It's much bigger than that. I need to find someone I can trust, someone who can get me out of the city... I'm in a lot of trouble, Prospero. Serious, hung-by-the-neck trouble."

Prospero pulled him between two of the pillars and out onto the terrace of the shadowy ornamental gardens that surrounded the great ballroom. He looked ostentatiously around, but the only people anywhere near were couples who had crept quietly away from the ball for the cover of the ornamental plants, and who were engrossed in their own illicit activities. Having satisfied himself of their privacy, Prospero sat on the low balustrade opposite him, eyes gleaming. "Trouble? What kind of trouble - is this serious?"

Gratiano cursed quietly to himself. "I should not have said anything. I should not be here." He made to get up, but Prospero's hand on his arm stayed him.

"Why not? What is it that weighs on you so?"

"I have... done something I am not proud of, Prospero. And from that has come such consequences..."

"I am surprised, Gratiano – I had thought you long past guilt."

"Guilt isn't anything to do with it," snapped Gratiano. "I mean real consequences, deaths. I mean those poor bastards on the bridge being eaten by the crabs." He stopped, abruptly. A terrible fear rose in his chest and for a moment all he could see was Gawain's eyes. Then other eyes took their place; eyes bugging out of a face gasping for air, eyes with light fading in them as he watched.

Prospero's voice was abruptly low and silky. "You speak of the Rookery riots. The murders."

Gratiano's heart froze in his chest. *Keep your nerve.* "Prospero, I am not behind the Rookery murders. You must believe that if you believe nothing else. I am not the fiend in the fog. But I know who is, and I think that if I speak, I will die by his hand." Once the words were out, it was as if a dam had burst. "And I have done something wrong myself, something that means my own testimony would be questioned. I have been led into folly. I have been stupid, and I have believed what I have been told, and now I doubt. And at least one man for certain is dead, and perhaps others too. Prospero, I do not know what to do. I have led a useless life but I never thought I would end my days a killer."

"I don't understand, Gratiano. You know who the killer is? Then summon the *Vigilanza* and tell them, have them arrest him!"

"Oh Father above, Prospero, I can't! They think it's me – and if I try and spin them a tale, they'll look at the evidence and they'll think I'm trying to incriminate an innocent man – he's been so bloody clever and I'm only just realising how utterly, utterly screwed I am."

"*Who,* damnit! Who has set you up? Who is killing in the fog?" Prospero hissed the words low, but Gratiano was silent, his eyes wide.

"Hello, Prospero. Barocchio tells me you called round for me," said Gawain from behind him. "I do hope I didn't miss anything *important.*"

Prospero turned, very slowly.

"Nice trousers," quipped Gawain. He watched the slow dawning of realisation of Prospero's face, the beautiful spreading of illumination through the fog of deception. Prospero turned to Gratiano, still stood paralysed like a mouse before a cobra; then back to Gawain, the smiling deaths' head in the mists.

"Do excuse the interruption, Prospero, but I need a word with young dell'Allia. A *private* word."

Prospero looked back over his shoulder at Gratiano. "Run," he whispered. The young man didn't need telling twice. Prospero looked back to Gawain, and smiled his cheeriest smile.

"Oopsie," he said, sunnily. "I *do* hope I haven't just done something I'll regret."

"Visconti!" called Gawain. "Quickly!" He pulled his knife, and pointed it at Prospero while heading in pursuit of Gratiano. "We're not finished this night, Prospero. We're not done yet *at all*."

Prospero watched Gawain vault the low stone balustrade and set off in pursuit of Gratiano across the gardens. He put his hands on his hips and chuckled to himself. "*Damn* right we're not done. We're not even *started*. Mir-*aaaaanda!*"

He looked down at the balustrade; it was spotted with blood where Gawain had been standing. For a second, Prospero stumbled as a black cat suddenly dived between his legs in pursuit of Gawain, but then he regained his balance.

With a faint click and whir, the automaton appeared at the ballroom windows in a cloud of peacock feathers. "Find Barocchio. Tell him we're leaving. Tell him *now*."

* * *

Orlando watched the clock chime twelve bells, and turned to the high balcony above the ballroom just in time to hear Ophelia's piercing scream.

To be posted to guard Cittàvecchio's landward gate was, depending on your point of view, either one of the worst punishment duties in the *Vigilanza* or one of the best. If excitement and adventure were your game, then the Landward Gate was not for you; what adventure there was happened a considerable distance away from the gates out in the swamps, or in wild rooftop chases through the city – little or nothing ever happened at the gate. It was where retiring officers of the watch saw out their twilight years.

If you wished for a quiet life of methodical rhythm, an occasional opportunity for graft from merchants wanting in after curfew and a duty schedule that owed more to indolence than to industry then the Landward Gate was the career for you.

For Serjeant Bremchas, the Landward Gate was a sinecure earned by long service. A veteran of the City Levies, he lost his foot in the War of the Montressori Succession and eschewing a soldier's pension had asked the Lord Seneschal for a position that would allow him to continue to serve, albeit without standing up too much, with a comfortable view and definitely without any dangerous running about. The post of Serjeant of the Gate was practically made for him.

Traditionally the gate was closed at midnight and opened again at six bells; in fact, during Festivàle the gate often stood open until as much as a quarter to one, as the night shift on the gate traditionally celebrated the beginning of Festivàle Week with a slap-up meal at midnight, cooked for the entire shift in the guardhouse by the most experienced officer. Serjeant Bremchas had saved a sack of lemons, a half-kilo of Sindi spices (paid as a bribe by a caravan-master who had arrived at ten past midnight one night and did not relish a night on bare stones when a bed was for the taking) and a hank of prime mutton. The smell of his famed lemon curry filled the gatehouse, and few were the watchmen whose stomachs were not vocal in complaint upon smelling the dish, tart and spicy, cooking in the great pot over the guardhouse fire. Vocal stomachs lead to wandering attention, and soon the entire shift was in the gatehouse, circulating around the pot and commenting on the fine smell with avaricious eyes.

Perhaps that is why none of them noticed a lone horseman, slumped over the neck of his mount. The horse tiredly walked in through the great bronze and cedar wood gates as the last stroke of twelve rang over the city; and by the time a lone guardsman had come out to push the gates shut and drop the great bar that locked them, the horse and his rider had disappeared into the fog.

Captain Bremchas turned from his cooking duties with ladle in one hand and mug of wine in the other and toasted the Duca's health, to the roared approval of his men. The arrival of the horseman passed unremarked and unnoticed by all.

* * *

The smell of the mutton and lemons roused Mercutio one last time. The smell of the great city cesspits had faded now, to be replaced with the faint mildew of old, wet stone and wood; of the city. He saw the mists, and knew that he was done; he slapped the horse twice on her shoulder, and whispered "Home, girl..." with the last of his strength.

He passed through the gatehouse unchallenged; the city swept him into its embrace with anticipation. He felt the wooden box hang, heavy and potent, in his pocket. His wound had long since scabbed over, and he could barely move for pain; the hot, itching bite of infection. Even if he had not lost so much blood he knew that feeling; men who had that feeling in a foot soon after learned to walk with crutches. Men who had such a feeling in their guts made what peace they could with the Mother and Father, put their affairs in order and commended themselves to the afterlife. Nothing now mattered except getting the deck to Donna Zancani's house, but in the fog and the delirium, he mistook one bridge for another, and became lost in identical, misty streets in the shadow of Castell'nuero.

The horse, tired unto death, knew the last few minutes of the journey were on her, but for Mercutio, it was simply too much, too far. His horse reared unexpectedly and he did not have the strength to hold on; he slid nerveless from the saddle and fell into the mists.

* * *

Xavier raced up the stairs three at a time, at the head of a crowd of partygoers suddenly turned sober. The awful, cracked screaming had stopped, and now as he turned the corner of the staircase he saw what caused it.

Ophelia stood frozen like a marble statue on the landing, her hands before her face as if to stuff the broken noise she had been making back into her mouth. A spatter of red on her cheek, and her eyes were large and wide, staring at the thing hanging upside-down by one leg like some ghastly festive ornament from the upper railing of the balcony.

Mater Calomena.

No blade had cut her skin; the vicious livid bruises around her throat and the gouged scarlet pits that were once her eyes showed how death had come upon her. There was surprisingly little blood; some had spilled from her ruined eye sockets, run down her forehead and spotted the marble stairs beneath; it gave her a look of startled surprise, as if she had found herself in this odd situation and could hardly believe it.

It was some of this fallen blood, landing unexpected on her pale cheek that had prompted Ophelia to look up as she climbed the stairs looking for her tutor.

Xavier moved as if to take Ophelia in his arms, but she recoiled from him. "*Keep away from me!* This is *your* doing…"

"Ophelia…" He looked back and forth, plainly at a loss. "Cut her down! Someone *cut her down,* I say!" he bellowed over his shoulder at the gathering crowd. "And get a surgeon!"

Pater Felicio at the top of the stairs unmasked before the horror, his face ashen. "I think she is well past the need for a surgeon…" He made the sign of the Trident, his hand shaking.

"This is your doing, your doing you and your little circle of secrets… did she threaten you then?" Ophelia's face, ashen and waxy, took on an ugly twist as she advanced on Felicio and Xavier; the former recoiled in horror; the latter simply stood dumbfounded, unable to reply. "Did she threaten to expose your sordid little knitting circle? Is that it?" Her voice ended on a shriek, her hands in fists so tight that her own nails drew blood from her palms.

The landing was full of Tatars suddenly; two of them lowering the drape that was knotted around Calomena's ankle, two more supporting her body. The Duca, on the lower landing, turned to Captain Valentin and pitched his voice to carry. "The perpetrator of this outrage must be brought to justice, Captain; you are to employ the Tartary Guard to expedite the process where necessary." His face was flushed with wine, his speech slightly slurred; several of those around him clapped politely and he smiled indulgently at them and waved his hand. "I will not have my sister so distressed."

One of the braver courtiers ventured an opinion. "I saw a man fleeing the gardens, your Grace; the young dell'Allia boy. Captain Visconti and Lord d'Orlato were after him like hounds, though."

The Duca made his way up the stairs, his Tatars fanning out, keeping the guests more than an arm's length from him. "Ah, there; see the efficiency of our servants and our loyal kinsman's staff! The perpetrator is pursued by the very best of men already; calm yourself, Ophelia. The beast that did this will be back before us in chains soon enough."

Xavier took her hand; she snatched it back, an expression of horrified disbelief on her face. "Listen to your noble brother, Ophelia; Captain Visconti will run the murderer to earth soon enough."

"NO!" Ophelia spun herself free of the press of guards, of Xavier and of her impractical wig. "You with your wretched schemes and conspiracies; you may not have done the deed but you have done this – and *you*," she rounded on her brother "…you think nothing of the fact that my Mater is dead and imagine you can make it all good by throwing your hired thugs onto the streets *again*? It is a wonder that you have lived as long as you have and I swear it is nothing less than a *miracle* that we come from the same womb.

"You are nothing more than a poisonous jumped-up little *popinjay* blinded by your own madness and kept in power by a foreign mercenary force and the good graces of your cousin, who is *ten times* more loved than you will ever be. Now *get out of my way*."

She elbowed her way past the Tatars and slapped the Duca full across the face, hard enough to snap his head back; then she stormed down the staircase toward the *Vecchi Punti* with tears of grief and rage streaming down her face and making a sad mime's face of her elaborate make-up. Her wig and her mask lay abandoned on the stairs where it had fallen.

"Ophelia, wait! Forgive her, your Grace – she is mad with grief…" Xavier clambered up onto the banister rail and danced past the knot of guards around the Duca; he set off in single-minded pursuit of her. Pater Felicio called after him, but he was oblivious.

As a consequence of this, he missed what happened next on the stairs. From a certain point of view, this was the single greatest mistake of his entire life.

* * *

Prospero sat atop the cage and watched as the towel was proffered to the thing within the cage to smell. Barocchio stood to one side with his capture team, stern brawny men with heavy leather armour and many scars, watching disapprovingly.

"Nothing good will come of this, Prospero. Nothing good."

Prospero looked down from the top of the cage and his face was closed. "He hurt my beasts. He hurt the most *defenceless* of my beasts. I'm just evening up the odds a little." He jumped down from the top of the cage, landing next to Barocchio on the low wall. "A hundred says Caliban catches him within the half-hour."

"Taken." Barocchio spat on his palm, and they shook on it. A growl came from within the great cage, and Prospero signalled for the gates to be opened.

Something massive, white and silver lumbered into the mists with a sound like the restless thunder of an angry god. Prospero turned to the capture team. "Give him a half-hour, then deploy and if you find him, bring him down and bring him back but remember: *no harm to the beast.*"

Barocchio shook his head in disapproving wonderment. "I would not be the Lord d'Orlato for the next hour; no, not for all the spice in Sind."

* * *

Gratiano could feel his heart climbing up his windpipe and politely knocking on the back of his throat, asking to be let out. He was under no illusions whatsoever that he was running for his life. If Gawain caught him, he'd die "resisting arrest"; if Visconti caught him he'd likely be hauled off to the Ducal torturers – a set of men whose sadism was only exceeded by their pride in their work – and made to confess to the Rookery murders and anything else they could hang on his ruined frame by the time they had finished with him. And then: the bridge and the crabs, or the gibbet and the crows.

No. For Gratiano the only hope now was escape; either stowing away on board a ship leaving harbour or making it outside bowshot of the city walls.

Once outside the precincts of the Castell'nuero he had a choice to make – southwest to the Landward Gate or east to the docks. He commended his fate to the Child and headed east, following the smell of the sea, always alert to the sound of running footsteps behind him. In fact, he was paying so much attention to what was going on behind him that he collided with a horse, slowly walking up the centre of the street. The horse reared in surprise, throwing its rider who landed on the cobbles with a solid thump and a cry.

Gratiano paused for a fatal second, and let curiosity get the better of him. That was all the time it took for the prone man to grab his leg in a vise-like grip.

"*Gra- Gra-* "

He knelt down, moved aside the hood concealing the fallen rider's face and started to see Mercutio del Richo; all the more so for the state of his injuries. He was dying, clearly; the fall had opened an older wound on his back and judging by the smell, gangrene had already set in. He looked like he had been on the road for weeks, not the scant few days since Gratiano had seen him last.

"Mercutio, Mother and *Child!* What's happened to you!"

"...*za*... *za*... *Zancani*... *take*... *to*..." With his other hand, he guided Gratiano's hand to the wooden case in his inside pocket. "...*deliver*... *urgent*..."

"You want me to take this? To the Palazzo di Zancani?" Guilt flushed his face red at the mention of her name.

Mercutio nodded, scarlet froth bubbling from the corners of his mouth as he strained to speak. Gratiano slid the wooden box out of the prone man's pocket. "I'll do my best, man. Lie still; I'll try and get help."

Mercutio's eyes were knowing, and he did not let go. Gratiano held up the box; "I have it, and I'll deliver it, you have my word of honour. I swear it on the Child."

Mercutio nodded, once, and let go of Gratiano's wrist; and as simply as that, he was gone. Gratiano paused for long enough to close Mercutio's eyes, then found his bearings; but that small delay was more than enough.

"Caught in the act…" said Visconti, advancing out of the mists sword point first. "And, caught before you could mutilate the body, you *bastard*."

Gratiano raised both hands. "This is a friend of mine, Captain. I suppose it will do me no good to tell you that it is Lord Gawain who has been murdering under your very nose, Lord Gawain who has set me up as his patsy, Lord Gawain who kills without compunction in the Rookeries? Lord Gawain with whom you confer on your enquiries, who knows where the witnesses are, who ensures there are never any left alive long enough for you to talk to?"

Visconti scoffed, but Gratiano saw a tiny seed of doubt in his eye. His sword point didn't waver, and Gratiano backed slowly away into the centre of the courtyard and pressed his point home. "Come on, Captain. You've known me since I was six. Do you really think I am a criminal mastermind? I blush scarlet when I'm overdue with my tailor's bill. *I am no murderer!* I have been set up…"

"*Shut up*. You can tell it to the Duca's inquisitors." Visconti kept his sword in line with Gratiano, but crouched down and with his free hand checked for a pulse on Mercutio. He found none, and his face hardened. "Down on the floor, on your knees."

"I won't *live* to see the inquisitors. Gawain will see me dead long before I can tell anyone anything. That's how he works – don't you see?" Gratiano dropped to his knees, his hands still above his head; Visconti, still holding his sword, used his free hand to awkwardly wrap a rope from his belt several times around Gratiano's wrists. "If all of this is true why did you run? And why didn't you come forward with this long ago?"

"You wouldn't have believed me and I have little proof. It's my word against Gawain's and he's not on his knees in the street."

Visconti was clearly having trouble securing Gratiano; he drove his sword point first into the ground between cobbles and tied the knot with both of his hands.

Stepping back, he drew his sword out of the ground, and pulled on the end of the rope, jerking Gratiano's arms. "On your feet. You can tell it to the Court."

He pulled Gratiano awkwardly to his feet; the younger man stumbled, and looked up. There, over Visconti's shoulder was the leering death's head in the fog.

"You *really* should have listened to him, you know," whispered Gawain conversationally into Visconti's ear. His knife sang as is slid out of its scabbard.

* * *

"How dare she speak to me so? How *dare* she so speak to me? Who is she to so speak to me? I will not countenance it. I will *not* countenance it, I say!"

The Duca was near purple with apoplexy on the landing of the stairs. The ballroom was practically empty of guests and servants now - most of the guests of the ball had already fled for less dangerous climes, knowing what it was to be near His Grace when his temper was out of control. The Tatars had formed a near-impenetrable steel ring around him; Calomena's body lay forgotten not ten feet away. The only things moving in the great chamber now were scattered monkeys in bolero jackets, grazing the buffet and watching the tableau on the staircase through impassive simian eyes.

"I will not let it stand. I will not let it stand! Valentin!"

He turned to Valentin, but the Captain was suddenly not at his side. Pater Felicio had been trying to calm him down, but his cheek still burned from the impact of Ophelia's hand, and four clear read weals ran across his cheek, vivid against his face otherwise white with unbounded rage. The Pater's words were at best a buzzing in the background; the Duca told him so.

"Your Grace. Your *Grace*."

The voice was quiet, refined; it cut through the Duca's ranting like a scalpel. "You must be silent now. All the guests are gone, and it is but you, and us, and the Tatar Guards now." The woman wore a great filigreed mask of gold depicting the solar face of Apollo, inlaid with chips of amber and topaz. She stood between Valentin and Pater Felicio, who had donned his Old Man of the Sea once more.

The Duca's hackles rose, too late, much too late.

Valentin looked to Orlando; "I know Moon is occupied elsewhere, but Tragedy is absent."

The woman in the sun mask laughed out loud; it was a rich sound, full of life and promise, coppery and red. "Oh, I think that has never been less true, Valentin. Tragedy is unfolding before us like one of the best plays of the year; slow, inexorable, fated. Besides – he would not begrudge us this moment of opportunity. Tragedy is unfolding elsewhere, and that is as it should be..."

The Duca looked from one to the other, and for a moment, flickering in his face one could see the man he once was before the politics and the price of power made him less than he once was. Zancani and Pater Felicio cast aside their masks, and Felicio, quietly, said "Augustin di Gialla, for crimes too numerous to mention, for tyrannies uncounted, for judicial murders and sundry other crimes against the civic good, I place you under arrest. Will you surrender to the new Republic, your Grace?"

The Duca looked from side to side, at the impassive, unsmiling faces of the Tatar Guard, once a wall keeping those who would threaten him out but now, he saw, just as effective at keeping him in. Fool, to have trusted men who can be bought.

"I am betrayed," he said, without animus. He did not dignify Felicio with a reply.

Orlando laughed again. "You are in the way of the future, your Grace. Can you hear Him coming?"

He looked Valentin in the eye; the Captain met his gaze a moment, and then courteously looked down. Felicio' face contained nothing but ugly triumph and anticipation; the Duca spared it barely a glance. His gaze lingered longest on the great golden mask of the sun, and when he looked away from that, the beginnings of an awful comprehension and resignation were spreading across his face.

Nevertheless; he was a scion of his House and a Lord of the City, and it was not in him to end badly. He drew his sword, and as he did so the Tatars stepped back, forming a widening ring around him and the three conspirators.

"I will not sell myself cheaply."

Valentin drew his own, and saluted the Duca formally before striking high guard. "I do not expect you will, your Grace."

Orlando turned her back on the combatants, and left the circle before steel rang on steel. The Tatars closed the circle behind her, and within the fate of the Duca was decided in the way these things always are, by treachery and with two men against one.

* * *

Gian Galeazzo Visconti was the veteran of hundreds of late night street fights, and no stranger to fog, wet back alleys or desperate criminals. His sword was already in motion before Gawain had even finished speaking. *First mistake, my Lord; do it, don't talk about it.*

Gawain was too close in and the knife was already flying; Visconti spun fast and felt the blade grate against his ribs, but not penetrate. The burning sting woke him up and gave him the energy to gain a little distance; he let go of Gratiano's rope, ducked, dodged and brought his sword around in a sweeping scything motion to take Gawain's legs out from under him.

Gawain jumped lazily over the blow, and in one smooth motion swept his long, wicked knife in an arc across Visconti's throat. Red followed.

Stunned, he dropped his sword and both hands flew to his neck to try and stop the arterial spray; Gawain draped his left arm companionably about his shoulder and steered him around to face Gratiano. With his right hand, still holding the knife, he repeatedly stabbed into Visconti's guts, twisting the blade enthusiastically each time; it made a noise not unlike filleting a fish. He whispered into Visconti's ear, lovingly and almost sensually as the strength fled from the captain's legs and his life pumped out of the wide red grin below his chin, spraying Gratiano with gore as he moaned with fear and turned to run.

"Should have listened to young dell'Allia, Captain. Wouldn't have ended up bleeding out on the cobbles. Wouldn't have died a dog's death. You came very close; very close indeed. That's why I'm going to spend a while on you; that's why it's going to take a long old time. Victim of the very murderer you so doggedly pursued; perhaps they'll put a statue of you here. You do not *demand* things of me, Captain; you do not play *games* with me. If you do, I *kill* you."

With one last, almost contemptuous stab and flick of his knife, he split open the Captain's guts, wet, shiny and red and suddenly all over the cobbles. He let Visconti slump to the floor and picked up the trailing end of the rope; Gratiano's flight was brought to an abrupt halt.

"Finally worked it out, did you? Too late for you, of course. You've been an elegant decoy, though; your attempted confession to Prospero, that was a beautiful touch. And running – half the city will think you the Rookery murderer by morning. Especially given what I have left for them to find in the Castell'nuero. And especially what they will find here in due course. I was only expecting one body; two, I suppose, will have to do. Did you kill this one yourself, then, Gratiano? Finally accepted that you have a taste for it?"

He looped the end of the rope around a hitching post, and knotted it tightly; Gratiano crawled to the far edge of the courtyard at the fullest extent of the rope, and sobbed as he watched Gawain go to work on the bodies of Captain Visconti and Mercutio del Richo. Between the cobbles, blood ran like water.

A black cat with eyes like chips of amber danced among the cobbles and nosed at the rope; its gaze swung from Gawain, kneeling at his work, and Gratiano.

* * *

Xavier stood in the mists, listening sharply, every sense alert. *There;* a whiff of her perfume. He set off at a flat run down the street, rewarded with a glimpse of Ophelia at the end of the street. He caught up with her and tackled her to the ground a few scant feet short of the dock, and a boat tied up awaiting partygoers who had likely fled out into the mists.

"Ophelia, you are being hysterical; come back to the Castle, come talk with me…"

Ophelia kicked out at him, and wriggled to her feet. "So you can kill me as you killed her? Get *away* from me, you *bastard!*"

"Ophelia, *listen* to me. We didn't kill Calomena – we were going to offer her membership of the group after the ball tonight! Why would we take such a risk if we were planning to murder her? I made the offer tonight, as you were coming down the stairs!"

She still kept her distance, but she was calming down. Xavier stayed on his knees. "Ophelia, how could I have a part in something that would cause you such pain? Have I not sworn my love for you enough?" There were tears of genuine emotion on his cheeks; his voice cracked.

She stopped and turned. "Do you love me, Xavier di Tuffatore?"

"You know I do with all my heart."

"Enough to betray the rest of your conspiracy to me?"

"More than life itself. Ask it, and it will be yours."

Ophelia's eyes were wide and unfocussed, and the first hints of a smile lingered at the corner of her mouth. She stood directly before Xavier. "Do you love me more than you love Gawain d'Orlato, Xavier di Tuffatore?"

She saw the *maledizione* do battle in his eyes, and he stuttered. She smiled. "Come, Xavier. Tell me *which of us you love.*"

* * *

Gratiano watched the cat; the cat watched Gratiano.

It came over, slowly; sauntering as if it had all the time in the world. Sniffed at his wrists, looked at him with its lambent golden eyes. Then, with a flash and a whip of its tail it was gone into the fog.

"Be very, very quiet," whispered a voice into Gratiano's ear. "Do you have the cards?"

Gratiano made to look round, but could see nothing. "Cards? What cards?"

"Did you take a wooden case from the fallen man?" The voice was low, rough; it lacked courtly airs and graces. "Quickly now; the Prince of Knives will be done with his work soon enough."

"He asked me to deliver it somewhere…"

"To Zancani, yes. I know. Show me your hands so I can untie you."

"Who are you?" Gratiano tugged the rope around and looked at his mysterious benefactor; a hunched dwarf of a man, dressed in entertainer's motley. His eyes were the most vivid yellow. He wielded a vicious straight razor with deft agility, slicing through the ropes binding Gratiano's wrists.

"You can call me Orfèo, young man. Don't bow, it'll just attract attention. Just give me the wooden box."

"I swore…"

The dwarf shifted impatiently, one eye on Gawain. "I know what you swore. Give me the box and I'll deliver it to where it was due to go. Or, continue arguing and die bleeding out like the Captain over there when Gawain remembers that you're here."

Gratiano reluctantly drew the wooden case out of his inside pocket, and passed it to the dwarf. He deftly opened it and checked the oilskin wrapped bundle was still within, then closed it and tucked it inside his motley.

"Run, Gratiano dell'Allia. Run as far and as fast as you can and be outside the city limits by the first bell of the night. Never come back. And look on this as your very great good fortune that you will not be in the city to see His return."

Gratiano did not need telling twice; he vanished into the fog at speed. Gawain looked up from his butchery and flung the ragged tatters of a face into a corner, all red to the elbows, and cursed softly. He walked over, and poked at the cut ropes with his foot, looking back and forth through the fogs.

Nothing, save the mew of a black cat with amber eyes, sat atop Visconti's corpse, watching him with knowing eyes. It was gone by the time his knife was half out of the scabbard, up a wall and away into the mist-shrouded roofscape.

"I will catch you, and I will kill you, cat. I do not like the way you watch me."

High above on the rooftops, the yellow eyed dwarf watched Gawain below. "No, I do not think you will, Gawain. I do not think you will catch me at all."

He hefted the wooden box, and set off, agile as a cat, over the rooftops. He knew where he had to go. Destiny was calling, and he was a slave to his nature. He could not ignore such a summons.

* * *

Xavier buried his face in Ophelia's dress with a cry; "I cannot!"

"So only sorcery makes me even *equal* in regard to your lover? To *hell* with you, Xavier. You think I'd be content to be a *trophy wife?*"

She kicked out at him and shook him loose; he fell back onto the pier and looked up at her with an expression of incredulous horror. "Ophelia…"

"Don't even speak to me, you wretched catamite. Crawl back to your lover, and I'll go back to mine. Prospero is ten times the man you are; and it will be he that rules Cittàvecchio beside me when my brother is gone!"

Xavier held out his hand, still looking up above Ophelia. "Ophelia, *shut up* about the city. Just take my hand and *shut up* a minute."

From behind her, she felt hot breath on her neck, and a low growl. She froze.

"Ophelia," said Xavier, with the faintest hint of a quaver in his voice. "Stay *very, very still.*"

* * *

Prospero and the capture team had been following Caliban at a safe distance; watching as the great ape had picked up the scent and clambered over rooftops and walls to pursue it. Now, the ape had cornered its prey – and Prospero wanted to be there for the kill. This was, unfortunately, not what he had originally had in mind.

"Oh gods…" he turned to the capture team. "That's the wrong bloody man. Get in there and bring Caliban under control!"

Barocchio shook his head and crossed his arms as his men rushed forward with nets and clubs. "I *told* you nothing good would come of this."

Caliban towered over Ophelia; a great ape from the jungles of the south, but twice, three times the size of the monkeys favoured by the keepers of menageries. Even hunched he stood at over twelve feet; his hand alone was as large as her body. His fur was snowy white, and his eyes, showing an almost human intelligence, a vivid flaring scarlet. They were fixed on Xavier.

Xavier stumbled to his feet, and tried to interpose himself between Caliban and Ophelia, who stared dumbfounded at the creature. The great ape snarled and showed his teeth; Xavier drew his short stabbing sword and without hesitation slashed for Caliban's eyes.

"No!" screamed Prospero, running for the fray. "Xavier, *no!* Don't hurt him! Ophelia, *run!*" She turned, tried to locate the shouting, saw Prospero and his men running to her aid, but her reactions were just a little too slow.

Xavier's aim was good, but not perfect; he carved a scarlet slash across Caliban's left eye socket. Caliban roared and dodged back out of range of Xavier's blade, and with one savage backhand, swiped him off the pier and out into the mists. There was a great splash as he skipped across the water and slammed into the far wall of the canal and a smaller one as his sword found a new home amidst the river weeds as well. He sank without trace. With a roar and a shaken fist at Prospero, Caliban seized Ophelia about the waist in one great fist and thundered off between buildings into the fog in a long, loping run.

"Caliban, *no!* Come back! Ophelia…" Prospero turned to the capture squad.

"Find that ape and *bring him down.*"

Once, when six years old, Xavier had been kicked in the chest by a runaway horse in the street. For almost a minute afterwards he simply could not get his lungs to work; and then, when he did, all he could manage was deep, whooping breaths for nearly an hour. Since then, he had dreaded suffocation with a passion.

Caliban's swept arm hit him full across the torso with the force of a charging bull. He registered blankly the sound of ribs snapping; he did not connect this with his own chest.

It took a second or two for his brain to catch up with events while his body hurtled through the air over the canal, his sword flying from fingers suddenly made of rubber. Oddly, it was not the blow from Caliban's arm that really stunned him; he was too surprised by the speed of the great ape's reactions. It was the bone-jarring, tooth-rattling impact with the far wall, colliding with the frontage of the townhouse opposite the dock and blasting every breath of air out of his lungs.

Ah, he thought, as they made their presence quite prominently felt. *That would have been my ribs I heard breaking back there.*

He did not even have the air left to scream; he hit the water gasping. The shock of the cold immersion jolted him back to full consciousness and then as his lungs screamed for air he saw Her and Her sisters down below him, rising through the murky water to meet him with open arms, hair spread out around Her like great clouds of weed. Her shimmering green skin, her pearlescent eyes; the very dress she wore as she cast herself from the high tower window proclaiming her love for him, now fouled and twisted with reeds and the slime of the canal floor that was her bed.

He had fallen, and now the Undines had come to claim their dance. *Fear death by water,* Orlando had said, and she was right to say so.

He saw her face, and screamed; took in a lungful of green and cloudy canal water and tried to scream again against the spasms of drowning. The Undines rose around him in a cloud; they watched impassively as he clawed at his throat and gasped, kicked frantically toward the fading light of the surface up above.

His feet touched the bottom; the old road surface of the flooded street. He was in an older Cittàvecchio now, a crueller one, more imperial. The city before the flood. She caught him by the hand, and as the last fading sparks of awareness dimmed around him, she took him up in a great embrace, and kissed him with her cold, dead lips.

* * *

Deep beneath the Palazzo di Zancani, the thing that had once been Donna Elizabeta, the thing that called itself Sun Face, Orlando, came one last time to the room of masks.

She had left the Ballroom just as Valentin and the Duca had come to blows; from the moment the Tatar Guard had turned against him, the Duca's reign was over and the rest was academic. If truth be told, the best outcome – in terms of keeping things tidy – would be for the Duca to kill Valentin, though that was unlikely. No; it didn't matter. Who needs a Duca when one awaits the arrival of a King?

She looked up at the hundreds of empty-eyed faces staring down at her from the walls, connected by their strands of thread and yarn, beaded with dew and glittering; she touched a thread and watched the dance as the entire city sprang to shimmering life as the threads sang to her.

Orlando stroked her finger along a thick, green thread that terminated around a nail; the mask that hung from it was a polite, smiling cream bauta that barely concealed the fangs of the black monster beneath. With some satisfaction, she cut the last of the threads that connected it to a handsome pale porcelain mask crying a single tear of golden filigree with a bleeding cut along the side of the jaw, now isolated from almost all of its neighbours.

"Poor Tragedy," she whispered, from behind her own mask. "Forgive me, but it must be done."

A noise, behind her; the clearing of a throat. The dwarf stood in the doorway, holding a small wooden box in both hands.

"The Holy Fool delivered the cards unto me of his own free will; and now I deliver them unto you, Lady." He placed the box on a low table, and stepped back. Orlando had eyes only for the box. He retreated into the shadows, his yellow eyes aflame.

Orlando paused before the box then with a decisive movement opened it and unfolded the oilcloth within. She let her fingers caress the cards for a moment, a light touch like that between two secret lovers in a public place; just enough to reassure, to make a presence felt. Behind the great sun mask, her eyes fluttered a second, and she allowed herself a small gasp. When her eyes opened again, the pupils were wide with excitement.

She shuffled the cards deftly. "The Prince of Knives is loose?"

"He has killed and killed again tonight and his thirst is not slaked; the knife isn't done for the night yet."

"And Tragedy?" She lay them out in a pattern; swift, sure. The air in the room felt thick, oily; greasy somehow.

"Is unfolding. He is with the Undines now." The dwarf shifted uncomfortably. "My part in this is over, spirit; you must be about your own work, for I have other calls on me this night..." His eyes, deep in shadow, flickered once and were gone; Orlando did not notice.

She turned the central card over and regarded it; a peculiar shudder, half anticipation and half excitement, ran up her spine. *The Prince of Knives* - a figure poised like a dancer against a night cityscape, bearing a long, straight dagger in each hand; instead of a face, there is a death's head, sketched out in subtle tones. Scattered around the feet of the figure are broken masks and puppets with their strings severed; none of the puppets have faces. On the eaves of the buildings behind the Prince, dozens of cats, naught but black shapes with shining eyes, watch. The crescent moon high above laughs down at the Prince's mischief. The entirety of the card is in sharp blacks and whites except for the vivid flashes of blood on the Prince's daggers.

She gathered the cards back together, setting aside the one she had drawn, and wrapped them in their oilcloth again.

She raised her hands to the vaulted roof above, and cried out. "Can you hear him coming? *Yhtill! Yhtill! Yhtill!*"

She set aside her own pale mask, and folded the card she held in half; then, with every evidence of delight, she ate it.

* * *

Serjeant Bremchas jolted awake at the thunderous knocking at the door of the gatehouse. Like the rest of the gate shift, he had drunk more than a little of the Duca's good health and eaten perhaps more than good sense or easy digestion might have recommended. Unlike the rest of the shift, he hadn't drunk so much that he could barely move – the other three guards in the gatehouse were out for the count, delivered a knockout blow by a potent one-two of strong spiced lemon curry and repeated enthusiastic toasting.

Now, barely fifteen minutes after the gates had closed, this great thunder of knocking; someone who did not know the rules of the gatehouse and seemed to think the curfew did not apply to them. Typical. It always happened on his shift.

Grumbling under his breath, Bremchas staggered to his feet and limped to the doorway of the guardhouse.

"Who goes at this ungodly hour? It's past curfew and the gates are closed until morning!"

A blurred shape resolved itself out of the mists; a face as white as a ghost, eyes as red as blood. "Open the gate for me, Serjeant. I have to be out of the city before the first bell..."

"Who goes? Lord dell'Allia, is that you? You know the curfew rules, no exit until dawn. The gates are closed, my Lord."

"Bremchas, I don't have time to argue the toss of the legal niceties with you. Just open the bloody gate."

Bremchas folded his arms and stuck his jaw out pugnaciously. "I'll tell you the same as I told the Bucharans not ten minutes ago – wait until da-"

Gratiano was not in the position to wait until even the end of Bremchas' sentence. As soon as the old guard Serjeant folded his arms, Gratiano punched him full in the jaw with a rattling crunch. The jangle as Bremchas' elderly armour clattered on the cobbles was drowned out by Gratiano's ill-concealed blasphemy as he shook his hand in disbelief and cursed fluently under his breath at the mischief done his knuckles by an elderly jaw less brittle than vitrified.

He hurriedly pulled at the windlass that controlled the great bars across the gate, aware that Gawain might be behind him at any moment; as soon as the bars were out of their grooves, he rushed to the gate and pulled it back far enough to slip through the gap.

His relief at escaping the city was short-lived – no sooner was he through the gap than cold steel rested against his throat.

"Hold," said the Grafin, raising her arm. "Do not kill him."

Gratiano looked from the apparition in white fur to the grey dead faces of the Janizaries surrounding him, and wondered for a moment if Gawain's knife might not be preferable.

The Grafin approached him and peered closely into his face, holding his jaw and looking at him from both sides at the Janizaries stared emotionlessly at him.

"You are the Holy Fool," she whispered. "*What have you done with my cards?*"

* * *

Gawain wiped his hands on the end of his cloak and scaled the wall of the courtyard effortlessly, turning to regard his handwork. The bodies of Visconti and the stranger both arrayed in the style of the Rookery murderer and evidence enough for any enquiry that Gratiano was the killer.

He smiled to himself with the satisfaction of a craftsman who takes honest pride in the quality of his work. Even the shallow knife wound that old Calomena had managed to get in on him while he was squeezing her eyes out would work to his advantage – he could claim he came upon the killer in the act and that Gratiano had stabbed him while making good his escape.

Something made him turn to the south; to the brooding bulk of the Castell'nuero against the moon. An unerring sense of where his lover was; it had never failed him. An instinct that told him when Xavier wanted him, needed his presence; sometimes he chose to ignore it until it became an inferno that threatened to consume him with need. But tonight; tonight he could not afford to ignore the calling. Xavier was with Ophelia, and in Ophelia he could see the same thing he had seen in another woman – a rival. Gawain did not care for rivals, and he did not care to leave Xavier unattended in the company of such a woman for too long.

Accidents, after all, could happen.

He thought, for a moment, of Ophelia di Gialla.

The scent of blood was still strong, and he closed his eyes a moment; pictured his lover's face, his touch. For a moment, his breath caught in his throat, and he gave an involuntary shudder. He raised his hand to his face and licked the back of his hand absently; as it always did, blood washed away the taste of jealousy. He wiped his dagger on his sleeve and then did a swift trick with it that made it disappear; another pass of his hands and suddenly it was back; again, and it was sheathed. The simple pleasure of it made him laugh for a moment.

He came to a decision. *Now everything will be right. Nothing will trouble us now.*

He stood atop the roof and surveyed the city a moment, a vista of gabled and red-tiled islands in a sea of moonlit mist – a kingdom of cats and murderers. In the distance, a bloom of crimson and amber erupted around one of the towers of the Castell'nuero – as is often the way, fire heralding the dawning of a new order. Already the sound of crowds loose in the streets; the Cittàvecchi have an innate sense of when theatre is occurring, and will leave their beds at any ungodly hour for a great fire or the passing of princes. In times of crisis, the great and the good of Cittàvecchio would always find a large open space to mill aimlessly and panic; it was bred into them.

They'd discover the bodies soon enough and that would just add spice to the evening.

He set off towards the scent of his lover on the midnight air.

*   *   *

Consciousness slid away from Xavier as he felt the beat of his own heart slow, trapped in the Undine's kiss. Time slowed, the instant between heartbeats expanding out into an eternity in which he grappled with the Undine that had once been Sofia d'Amato - that had once been his lover. He heard her voice, between beats, down here in the old and drowned streets of the old and drowned city, where once the legions of the Tattered King had walked.

Xavier, listen.

He struggled weakly in her cold embrace, until he realised he was no longer drowning, or indeed breathing. The beating of his heart slowed even further; he became fascinated with the sensation of it, the deep bass sound as it pounded in his chest.

Listen, we do not have much time.

There it goes again. Deep and loud, like a great leaden bell. Like footsteps.

Can you hear me, Xavier? Can you hear me over the sound of your own death approaching? That is his tread you hear, shaking the ground you stand on. Let us wait a little, let him come a touch closer before we have the conversation we must have.

He tried to turn from her, tried to get free, but her embrace was all-encompassing. There was nowhere left to run now. Another beat, pounding through his head.

You do not understand, do you? You never did, you were blind to it. But this potion, this potion has blunted the edge of your blindness and now here in the dark I can show you things as they really are, without the veil you draw over them.

He felt his blood, rising like a tide, pound again; the veins in his neck stood out like cables and he lost his footing for a moment, carried along by the deep current. The undine was merciless, her lips clamped to his. Cold, green water in his mouth, in his lungs. His legs, trapped in her train, tangled in the net of weed that was her dress. No escape.

Come down with me. Come down among the Dead Men. Come back and see it for what it really is, not for what you remember it to be.

He remembered the dream he had dreamed in drug-fogged sleep after Orlando had shown him the Undines, and he realised that this flooded street was the very one he had walked in his night terrors. Long weathered stone piers, encrusted with silt and barnacles, and empty buildings, roofs long gone, lying open to the sea like shells, waiting for a hermit crab to move in and make of them something entirely different. Forests of anemones and coral, where once stood formal gardens and courtyards.

In the end, the sea always wins.

In his dream he had known where his route would eventually lead; and now, he saw, he was being taken there again, as the foot of the tower that abutted one corner of the Palazzo d'Amato came into view through the greenish murk. His struggles gained a new energy of desperation but the Undine was implacable.

See. See truth, with the veil ripped from your eyes once and for all.

The scream from above. The pounding footsteps as he raced up the tower stair. Dread clutched his heart, awful, cold dread like a smothering blanket.

He climbed the stairs, slow as only dreams can be. He put down his shoulder and burst through the door, remembering the pain of oak on bone. The room, the billowing shadow he dare not look at, and there he saw her poised on the balcony as if in mid-air, and time stopped, as her future self whispered in his mind and held him in a green embrace at the foot of the tower.

Do you see it?

Saw the shadows around her reaching out for her. Saw her, and reached for her, but too slow, too late. Much too late.

Look closer, Xavier. See what you have not let yourself see.

The shadows reached out and enfolded him in a great embrace and whispered to him that it would be well, that all would be well. And the shadow smiled, and Xavier saw the smile and his breath caught in his throat because this time he saw it all. He saw the hands; saw not a jump but a push.

Again.

He reached the top of the stair, and saw Gawain retreating into the shadows as Sofia d'Amato fell from the high balcony; what he had thought was tragically just too late was not too late at all. Gawain had thrown her to her death.

And then he saw himself, two days earlier.

"I think she loves me, Gawain. I think she loves me." His simple joy blinding him to the black shadow of jealousy that flickered across Gawain's face for a second before it was so adroitly concealed. "I intend to propose to her. We'll be married, and you'll be my best man!"

Again.

"*I tried to stop her,*" said Gawain and now the satisfied lie was open on his face for all to see. "*But she was gone. And now it's just you and me against the world. Just you. And me. The way it was always meant to be.*" And Xavier saw himself collapse in grief and take the easy way out, not seeing it, the lie in the dark, because to stay blind was to keep hold of something.

Again.

"*She's in the way of something. It's just a matter of tidying up – but I detest the woman so. I'd prefer not to have to deal with her at all.*" The image of the Mater Calomena hanging by her twisted ankle from the balcony rail, her eyes gouged out and the marks of a strangler's hands on her throat. He knew the touch of those hands well; almost as well as his own.

How many other times? "*I was expecting a man who could transform the very world in my imagination. Instead, I found an unremarkable hack who stumbled over his lines and was far from the best thing in the play. And I do so detest disappointment...*" – his own words to Gawain, less than a week ago in the Red Lion, and then, the actor brutally murdered, one of the Rookery Murders. What of the others, the beggars?

He recalled drunken conversations about being accosted in the Grand Piazza by beggars, how Gawain detested their pestering and their arrogance. He recalled the times he had tried to defend them, the times he had spoken of his love of the Rookeries, of the old city and its people... How many beggars had died for the insignificant error of being noticed? For the crime of drawing his attention away from the beast?

How many had died because he had tried to share his love of them with Gawain?

"*I intend to propose to her.*"

Gawain's face, in that instant. *Oh Gods, did I know?*

His own heartbeat was slow and loud as he thought back coldly of all the times he had complained of someone in Gawain's hearing and just how many of them had ended up dead not long afterwards, one way or another. And down among the dead men in the drowned streets of the city, the scales fell from his eyes and he saw his lover for what he truly was.

Here be monster.

The Undine let go her kiss, lovingly, with great sadness in her eyes. *Now you see. Now you know. You loved him, and only with the witchery of the Mother in your veins to make you love another could you even see what it is that you love.*

She touched his cheek. In her milky eyes was only sadness, and resignation.

I loved you once, but he killed me and now I am something else.

Everything changes in the end, one way or another.

There is no room in his heart to share you and I think no room in yours either.

I am sorry for you, and for what you must become.

You should go now. You cannot stay long in the Old City, not without the kiss of the Undine. Not yet. Your time will come soon enough. Her eyes were pearls and full of sorrow for him, but he did not see. His eyes were turned inward, as with new urgency he examined everything he had said to Gawain these past few days.

Ophelia.

He struck for the surface, new panic fuelling his veins, but it was so far away, and he had already taken a lungful of the river, of the old silt of the streets that had not seen the tread of man since the time of the King In Tatters.

Fear death by water.

He reached for the dim green light above, but it was so far away.

* * *

Gawain reached the dockside to find a crowd of late-night revellers, some fled from the Castell'nuero, others coming to see what the commotion was. The dockside was alight with gossip spreading from a knot of the older Lords of the City, masked and dressed still for the Festivàle Ball - The Lord Seneschal, so it was said, had called the City Levies together to put down an insurrection. The Duca was dead, slain by the Tatar Guards; the Duca was not dead but injured; Captain Valentin had declared himself the new Duca; the Castell'nuero was aflame; this, that and the other person was dead or fled. A rain of toads had fallen on the upper city; or worse yet, a rain of toads had fallen on the upper city and Lord Prospero knew nothing of it. A night of high confusion when people's movements would be concealed by the panic as much as the fog.

He pushed through the crowds, following his sense of where Xavier should be, but could not find him; though he could smell blood. Several men had gone out in boats, and one, in the canal, surfaced holding a familiar short stabbing blade, snagged with weeds.

Gawain grabbed one of the boatmen watching on the dock. "You; that is Lord di Tuffatore's blade. How did it get there? Where is he?"

Fear spasmed across the boatman's face at Gawain's look. "He was knocked into the water, my Lord, by the runaway beast some five minutes ago. He's not surfaced yet."

"Runaway. Beast."

"Yes, my Lord. Lord Prospero's beast; it hit Lord di Tuffatore a cracker, sent him clean across the canal, and made off with the Donna di Gialla with half of Cittàvecchio in pursuit, so it seemed. They say they have the beast cornered two streets along, but it has eaten ten men so far and Lord Prospero himself has gone to wrestle it into submission."

"Gods bless Lord Prospero," added another bystander. Gawain looked at him, and he found other business elsewhere.

"Xavier. In the water. Where?"

The clipped tones – or perhaps what they concealed behind their control – were finally making themselves felt with the boatmen. One simply pointed to the wall of the building opposite, the wet mark where Xavier had hit the wall after Caliban had backhanded him.

Gawain shrugged his cloak off and dropped his sword belt, and then dived straight off the edge of the pier into the green water.

As the boatman watched him dive, his eyes flashed, yellow like lanterns, or chips of amber.

*   *   *

Caliban's break for freedom didn't last for long; the alleyway he had chosen for his escape led to an enclosed courtyard surrounding a tall, sculpted fountain. Even had he managed to make good his escape, Ophelia's loud and angry imprecations would have led the capture team to him. She had managed to catch hold of one of her shoes and was proceeding to use it to try and batter the great ape into submission, adding to the beast's confusion and anguish. It howled furiously into the mists and tried to protect its injured eye from the beating.

Barocchio's men fanned out through the courtyard warily, holding nets and short clubs; Prospero and Barocchio entered last of all, the former in a lather of panic, the latter with a look of world-weary indulgence. Prospero made to run for Caliban, but Barocchio held him back; "Not until we've restrained him."

"But look at him! He's terrified!"

Ophelia, still trapped in Caliban's great fist, waited until the creature turned at bay and then with her free hand pulled a long, slender needle out of her hair. Like any Donna of the Cittàvecchi, she knew when to go armed and when to go armed in concealment. She did not, and would never understand any circumstance where it was permissible for a lady to go unarmed; one never knew when one would find oneself in exactly this sort of situation.

She raised the blade, and drove it into Caliban's arm just above the wrist, right up to the hilt. Scarlet flowered against his white fur, and as he let go of her he let forth a scream so human that

Ophelia recoiled in horror from the noise. Caliban shrieked again, and then made a straight run for the exit of the courtyard.

Barocchio swiftly made himself scarce as the capture team pursued the beast, but Prospero, squarely in the entranceway of the courtyard, stood his ground against the charging simian. It was his instincts that proved true; Caliban came to a skidding halt in front of him, howling, screaming and beating his chest, but he did not flinch.

The capture team froze, their clubs and nets raised and ready but a gesture from Prospero stilled them.

Caliban howled in his face again, the feathers on his hat streaming out behind with the force of the sound; then, meeting Prospero's unflinching gaze, the beast collapsed and then tried with every appearance of seriousness to hide behind him from Ophelia, crying and wailing and holding out the injured arm for attention.

She got to her feet, and dusted herself down, sparing a malicious stare for the cowering ape.

"Kill it! *Kill the beast*, Prospero! Kill it before it attacks me again!"

* * *

All was darkness, then a blinding, almighty pain as his broken ribs ground together. Someone had struck him in the chest, hard. He made to gasp, but every movement was heavy and slow, like moving through thick, gluey mud; *what is this?*

Again, this time the jagged spikes of pain awoke a near-forgotten reflex and he coughed, gurgling on the slimy water. He rolled to one side and retched again, the contents of his lungs heaving painfully out of his mouth. He opened his eyes, and watched in some bemusement as a small fish, no longer than his fingernail, flopped back and forth in a pool he was more or less sure had just come from inside him.

He was lying on a slimy paved dockside, below the level of the main piers; great wooden beams rose off to one side to support the pier, covered in barnacles and worn away by decades of water and rot. A little further out into the canal, chains hung from the blackened beams.

An execution dock. Not so long ago, men had hung from those chains and died at the Duca's pleasure; some swiftly through drowning, others, chained higher denied that luxury and left for the creatures of the shoreline to eat alive.

Someone was calling his name; insistent, but from a long way away. He rolled back onto his back and focussed at the shape hanging over him, waiting for the shadows to resolve themselves.

Gawain held him by the shoulders. "Xavier! Xavier! Come back to me. Look at me; look at my eyes. Focus. Can you hear me? I thought I'd lost you there for a moment…"

Xavier gave a cry dredged from the very pits of hell and writhed desperately to be free of his grip but his traitor muscles were still weak, and Gawain just held him all the harder. "You are safe now, safe." He pulled him up into a sitting position and held him tight.

"Safe? Safe? With you?" Xavier shook Gawain's hands off and staggered to his feet, leaning against a wooden support and retching again. Gawain made to support him but as he got close, Xavier straightened again and in his hand was his knife, wavering but pointed straight at Gawain.

He looked down at the blade and then at Xavier's blanched face; his expression betokened honest confusion. "What's this?"

"You killed her. You killed her. Sofia. I told you I loved her and you killed her." His voice slurred and he retched up more bile and river water, doubled over but still keeping the knife between himself and Gawain. In his eyes, hysteria hovered like a solicitous relative, ready to take his arm and guide him into the gentle uplands of shrieking madness at a moment's notice.

Many things flashed across Gawain's face in a short period of time. He carefully and slowly spread his hands in plain view. "This is... unexpected. Xavier... I tried to save her. You were there..."

"I *saw* you. She was down there. She was down there among the dead men with weeds in her hair and she showed me. I *saw* you throw her from the window." He wiped his hand across his face, his eyes shining from the midst of a mask of muck and slime from the canal bottom, tears carving streaks through the mess. "She showed me. I saw. I saw *true*."

"Xavier... she was using you, she was no good, no good for *us*." Gawain took another step closer, everything about him in an attitude of humility, of begging almost. The words came reluctantly, torn from him. "You couldn't see it, you were blind... I had to do something to save us."

"Us? Save *us*? And the actor? The beggars? Mater Calomena? What was that, Gawain? What the *fuck* was that? A *Holy Mother*, Gawain?" Xavier's voice cracked.

"Wasn't that what you wanted? 'I wish she was gone,' you said, so I made her gone. 'He disappoints me,' you said, so I made sure he would never do it again. How can I deny you anything that you ask? You cannot say you have not known this, you have not used it. I have been your knife, your hidden hand, and you have never questioned nor complained before. I love you, Xavier, as no-one has ever loved another. You know it to be true. You *know* I speak true." Gawain fell to his knees in front of him, his eyes shining and wet. "My knife and I make our wishes and dreams come true, for love. It makes us safe. You know it. You have always known it."

Xavier closed his eyes, and covered his mouth with both hands to stifle the sob of horror welling up within him. His knuckles were white around the hilt of the knife.

"There is only us," whispered Gawain, looking up at him. "Only us. Nothing else." He knelt there, his face shining with need, raw, open and mercilessly honest. He reached out to Xavier, his hands touching, exploring in old and familiar ways, and for Xavier, there was nowhere left to run now.

Xavier looked at his kneeling lover and knew with black despair that he spoke nothing but the truth. He felt his body responding to his lover's touch; but in his mind was nothing but the sad drowned face of the Undine.

Something within him snapped.

He lunged forward with the dagger, swift and certain, for his lover's eye. And perhaps, perhaps, he might have even wanted to strike true; perhaps in that moment, he truly wanted nothing more than to end the horror he had wrought. And perhaps, as the realisation dawned on Gawain that this was no game of knives, no edge play to be relished later, he too wanted it all over, wanted nothing more than to welcome the six inches of steel that would pay all debts and put an end to the circus. But years of training and instinct are not so easily overcome; Gawain dodged left, lightning-fast, and the blade scored a line across his eyesocket instead of finding a home in it. He lashed out instinctively at Xavier's wrist, and the dagger skittered across the mud, finding a home wedged into one of the old rotten beams just above the waterline.

Xavier recoiled from Gawain's kneeling form, cradling his wrist and staggering backwards, toward the end of the pier. His voice was emotionless, but cracked; quiet, but threatening tempests. "Stay away from me," he whispered. "You stay... away... from me." He scrambled through the criss-crossed wooden pylons, panicking, until his feet touched solid ground on the other side; then he ran along the dockside, unheeding. He did not look back. Had he done so, he might have seen the figure in the golden sun mask step from the shadows atop the pier and parallel his course into the fog.

Gawain remained kneeling beneath the pier a while, his hand pressed hard against his bloodied left eyesocket. Then, calmly, he pulled Xavier's knife from the wooden beam where it had wedged itself and tucked it into the small of his back through his belt. His face was utterly emotionless.

Caliban wailed at the tone in Ophelia's voice and tried to hide his head beneath great leathery fingers. Prospero, with the tenderness that only a doting father can summon, threw his arms around the great ape, soothing and calming the troubled beast, and then cast a malevolent glare over his shoulder at Ophelia.

"I had *everything* under control and then you have to go and stick a *hatpin* in poor Caliban's arm, and now you want me to *kill* him? Are you *unhinged,* you evil witch? I should sue you for distress!" He grabbed Caliban's injured arm and held it out for Ophelia to see. "*Look* at the mischief you have wrought!"

Caliban wailed woefully. Ophelia was, for a second, at a loss for words. But only for a second.

"*Damn* you Prospero," she breathed quietly. "You too?"

Prospero was cooing over Caliban's arm, wrapping the injury in a kerchief, when Ophelia grabbed him by the shoulder, wheeled him around and slapped him full across the face as she had earlier done to Xavier. Her face was mottled with rage. "You too, Prospero? Even you? Xavier di Tuffatore may prefer his lover to me but at least that lover is *human*. Does this craven beast's injuries matter more to you than mine?"

Prospero looked her up and down. "What injuries? Aside from your wounded dignity, of course... You had no need to harm him! I was on hand and no harm would have befallen you; but you had to show your *noble strength,* your *independence*, didn't you? Had to demonstrate how much *better* you were..." For a brief second, the bright and gaudy carousel behind Prospero's eyes died, the lights went out and the music stopped, and there was nothing but awful, yawning blackness in him. A cloud passed before the moon.

"Cruelty has ever marked your bloodline." He spat, off to one side. "Cruelty and malice. You care nothing for the *beasts*..." and Prospero flung his arms wide, to take in not just Caliban, but the gathering crowd and the benighted bulk of the Rookeries over the river too. "…nothing for those who have the most to expect from you. Silks and new fashions and art and who cares for the bodies hanging like fruit from the bridges…"

As the scene had played itself out a crowd had begun to gather; the Cittàvecchi instinct for drama. And Ophelia was in no wise immune either; as Prospero's temper rose, so did hers to match it.

"You wretched treasonous little *shit*. Are you behind all this, then? I hope you catch the flux from your own filthy beasts. Come no more to me, Prospero of the Three Lions. You are not welcome in the house of the Gialla. Guards!" She wheeled on her heel, looking to the slowly gathering crowd. "Guards!"

"The House of the Gialla? *A house of bile, plague and madness.* I hope it ends with you. Go home to your cold and lonely bed, Ophelia di Gialla. Go there and birth your plots like vipers. I'll not trouble you there again."

Prospero's eyes were black holes; then, abruptly, they lit up again like fireworks and he gave the crowd his dazzling smile, like the full moon emerging from behind a thunderhead. "Why trouble myself with such a woman when I have the crowd, a giant lovable albino ape, trousers made of feathers and a party to be had! To the Menagerie, friends, and free beer for all! If the city is to burn let us toast it appropriately!"

Amid the shouting and cheering of the crowd Barocchio stepped forward smoothly, ever ready to take advantage of his rival's misfortunes and never willing to miss a chance for social betterment. "Donna, forgive the intrusion. The guards are all still up behind the *Vecchi Punti*, putting down some trouble or so they say. Perhaps my men and I might escort you back to the Castell'nuero?"

Ophelia gave a little gasp; she looked at Barocchio, her eyes wide, but she did not make a sound, though her mouth moved. He looked over her shoulder and blanched at what emerged from the fog.

"That won't be necessary, Barocchio" whispered Gawain, one arm suddenly supporting the Donna di Gialla. "I will be the Donna's escort on her last journey this evening."

'What is that noise?'

The wind under the door.

'What is that noise now? What is the wind doing?'

Nothing again nothing. 'Do

'You know nothing?

Do you see nothing?

Do you remember 'Nothing?'

I remember

Those are pearls that were his eyes.

'Are you alive, or not? Is there nothing in your head?'

T.S. Eliot, The Waste Land 117-126

Gratiano, flat on his back, watched the point of a wickedly curved blade hovering millimetres from his eyeball. It concentrated his wits wonderfully, though it wasn't doing wonders for his bladder control.

"Cards? Cards? Cards in a wooden case? A man on a horse gave them to me but he died — well, he was dying anyway and then Gawain finished him off, or he might have died anyway, he was badly injured and it smelled like something quite unpleasant had got into the wound and quite possibly had laid eggs, which is the second most unpleasant thing I have thought about in the last five minutes. Cards? Cards? I don't know — it was the dwarf, the little man with the yellow eyes who untied me and said he could complete the delivery to the Palazzo di Zancani, and so I gave them to him, because one should always try to honour the word given to a dying man, don't you think and speaking of honouring words given to a dying man and given that I have had a terrible day could you possibly see your way clear to not killing me, please?"

Buskovy kept his arm in the air. The Janizaries watched Buskovy, waiting for the signal to gut this fish. The Grafin watched Gratiano impassively as he gasped for breath; then she leaned in close.

"The yellow-eyed man. The dwarf. Dressed in beggar's motley?"

Gratiano nodded, but slowly for fear of the point of the blade. "He said I could call him Orfèo. It is the name that the King of —"

"That the King of the Beggars goes by in Cittàvecchio, yes, I know. And the Palazzo di Zancani?"

"It's an art gallery – there are auctions there of pieces every so often. Elizabeta Zancani is a broker and a fence for stolen goods…"

The Grafin stepped back. "You will lead us there. Get him on his feet."

"I was told by the dwarf to be out of the city by one bell…"

Buskovy raised his arm again, and Gratiano was once more closely acquainted with the blades of the Janizaries. They came so close he could smell the mould on them; the charnel scent concealed by perfumes. "Who do you fear more, these or the dwarf?"

"Right," whispered Gratiano carefully. "To the Palazzo di Zancani, then."

Buskovy nudged Bremchas' still form with his toe. "What of the gate guard?"

"Leave him," said the Grafin. "If he is lucky there will still be a meaningful gate to guard in an hour or so."

* * *

Orlando followed in Xavier's wake through the murky streets, and as she did so every so often she would select a card from those she held, and would fold it in two and pop it into her mouth. And as she did so, the fog billowed and coalesced briefly, forming shapes by tricks of light and shadow, silently joining in her train, moving like ghosts in the mists.

Here was the train of skeletal beggars and their mangy dog all following the fat, smiling and vacuous priest. Once, they might have been the fawning lackeys of the *Beggar's Banquet* card but now their eyes were filled with hunger and their knives sharp. And here was *The Red Queen*, her hair and cloak black like blood in the moonlight. She held a great sword that seemed almost to be made of the fog itself and her cloak fumed and roiled like smoke over water. She took up position on Orlando's shoulder and followed her, step for step. Or perhaps... perhaps these figures were just shapes in the mist, phantasms conjured out of Cittàvecchio's night fogs to exist for a moment whole and solid, and then to dissipate through the city like the smell of smoke.

Orlando selected *Night Terrors* and regarded it a moment; the figure, curled on his side amidst the twisted sheets of a bed, with a leering full moon visible through the open window behind.

"Poor Tragedy," whispered Orlando, and ate the card. Up ahead, Xavier coughed, shuddered, and let slip a sob. Dripping wet, he staggered along the street unseeing, his feet moving of their own volition. The grip of the draught that Ophelia had slipped into his drink was fading now, but its task was done – and so was the damage.

Orlando turned over the next card; a son turns his back on a weeping father, a sack on a stick over his shoulder. The house behind is empty. *A Son's Betrayal*, the card said. She felt it reach out and take hold of the fabric of the city.

He was very close, now.

In the river water alongside the path, the weeds stirred with the passage of the Undines.

* * *

On the rooftops above, one-eyed Gawain watched Xavier stumbling along, and the masked figure following behind. He had been shadowing her for two streets now, watching her taunting Xavier, watching her slowly work her way through the cards she held.

"Her name is Orlando, you know. She is the Harbinger of *Re Stracciati*; the herald to announce the return of the Last King. Can you feel Him coming? His tatters are brushing against the very shutters of our world."

Gawain did not move, but a curious half-smile crept across his face. "I did wonder when you would put in an appearance. Friend of yours, is she?"

"Only insofar as we are both creatures of the old city." The yellow-eyed dwarf leaned against the balustrade next to Gawain. "My involvement with this is over, now; irrespective of what happens next, the Rookeries will endure. There are always powers greater than the Last King – that is how he fell in the first place. There will always be those who watch, and know, and beg; those are my charge, my people. Are you ready to beg yet, proud Gawain?"

His boot knife was fast, but it met only air. Up on the peak of a roof, a black cat with chips of glowing amber for eyes regarded him coolly. The unseen dwarf's laughter echoed around the rooftop. "Ah, *Brighella*. When you have a hammer, every problem is a nail, no? And when your friend *Scapino* cannot escape, what do you do then? You think you can solve this with a knife? No."

Gawain watched the cat through cold eyes, but stayed his hand.

"You've served me well, Gawain. Served me, and served Orlando too, though you did not know it. Now decide how to serve yourself and those you love."

With a flick of the tail, the cat was gone. Gawain turned back to the tableau in the street below.

* * *

It was the City Levies under the Lord Seneschal that found the bodies, on their way back from the port quarter up to the Castell'nuero where the scarlet bloom of fire already shone against the night mists. Old Schermo had been one of the first out of the Castell'nuero when the Tatars had struck and he had ridden post-haste to the barracks and raised what forces he could. He knew, of course, that he was almost certainly too late to save the Duca, and in his old soldier's brain that fact was probably weighed in the balance and accounted a virtue made of a necessity.

But to Schermo, loyalties to the city and to the ruling family were nearly the same thing. He had served the di Giallas for nearly forty years and Cittàvecchio for longer even than that, and when they called him down to the *Ponte Amanti* to see the corpses he struggled, a moment, to keep his vision clear and his voice steady.

In Cittàvecchio, if you wish to build to last, build on love and death.

Ophelia lay composed and calm; her face had not been touched, but she had been stabbed six or seven times in fast succession, piercing most of her major organs. She would have died of blood loss and suffocation. Arranged around her with conscientious care, like corpse-guards, Barocchio and several of his men. These, the murderer had not been so gentle with, nor so surgical in his attentions.

Schermo reached down and picked up the knife that had been placed so prominently and with such care atop the ruin that had been made of the last scion of the House of Gialla. He turned it over in his hands, admiring the smooth simplicity of it; a long straight blade, double-edged, good for slashing or stabbing. An unadorned hilt; a knife to use, not to wear. He knew it well, for he had given it to its owner himself.

It's amazing what you can do with a knife when you put your mind to it, you know.

One eighteen-inch piece of metal, two sharp edges. It can be used for work, for play. For eating, for peeling skin... off fruit, of course. Amongst other things. It can be palmed from hand to hand, the quickness of the blade deceiving the eye. It can be concealed, in a boot, in a hat, up a sleeve, inside a pocket. It can be sheathed and pass unnoticed, or it can be carried naked and bare.

But best of all, of course, it can be used to kill. And given that, really, that's what makers of knives have in mind when they make them, it's really rather surprising that people are so startled when they are stabbed. After all, it's what the knife was made for and after all, one cannot deny essential nature.

Slowly, like the awakening of a rare and poisonous night-blooming orchid, comprehension was dawning on the old Lord Seneschal.

He had spent years inculcating into Gawain every trick he knew, every military stunt, every ruse and manoeuvre that might keep him alive in a fight. Trained him like the son he himself would never have. Invested in him all his hopes, all his sense of duty, his sense of honour. But most of all, he had taught Gawain how to kill. Under the circumstances, Schermo thought numbly, neither he nor anyone else should really be surprised that Gawain kills people. After all, it is what he was made for, and after all, one cannot deny essential nature.

But he had never intended that Gawain should take such obvious pleasure in it.

He unbuckled his cloak and covered over the ruin on the bridge.

"Litter duty. Secure her somewhere that we can recover her later and arrange a proper funeral. And assign the body an honour guard. The rest of you; come with me."

He set off for the Menagerie.

*   *   *

By the time Prospero reached the gates of the menagerie he had a following of approximately fifty hardcore partiers carrying him on their shoulders on the strength of promises of free beer and entertainment. Behind, watched carefully by some of Barocchio's trained handling team, came Caliban enjoying his baffling but not unwelcome status as hero of the hour. Of Barocchio himself, there was no sign.

Outside the gates of the menagerie, a crowd was waiting with stern faces and weapons drawn. No partiers these. At their head, Lord di Schermo; the Lord Seneschal. His face was streaked with tears.

Prospero stopped, and raised his hand for silence; the cries of the revellers died off slowly, and he stepped into the spreading pool of silence.

"Lord Seneschal?"

Schermo dropped to one knee, slowly and carefully like the old man he was. "Your Grace."

The blood fled Prospero's face, and he took the old man by the shoulders, forcing him to his feet once more. "You make some mistake, my Lord. The Duca – "

"The Duca is dead by treachery; the Tatar Guard were suborned. They hold the Castell'nuero and I seek one of the Lords of the City to retake it for Cittàvecchio before these usurpers seize power."

"What of the Donna di Gialla?" Prospero shrugged eloquently. "Surely she succeeds her bro…"

The Seneschal would not meet his gaze. Prospero faltered a moment.

"There is some mistake. A mistake, yes. Easy to make in the mists; especially at a time like this. I left her in the safe keeping of Barocchio and his men. I left her with Barocchio, to escort back to the Castell'nuero." His voice rose to a near-hysterical pitch, then dropped away to a stunned whisper. "How can misfortune have befallen her?"

Schermo looked at the floor. "Perhaps Barocchio himself sought out someone to escort them. And perhaps he did not make the wisest of choices to protect the lady." Schermo showed him the dagger, still scarlet with Ophelia's blood. "Perhaps he put his trust in the wrong man. As I did. As I do not intend to do again."

They looked at each other in silence a moment. Prospero closed his eyes and seemed, just for a second, a much smaller man in a smaller, dimmer world.

"Barocchio too?" He covered his mouth for a second with both hands as if holding in a wail. "I never wanted this. I never, ever wanted this." His voice was low, pitched for Schermo only. "Not without Ophelia. Is there no-one else?"

"No," said Schermo. "d'Orlato is tainted; di Tuffatore vanished. Lord d'Amato was in the Castell'nuero when the Tatars struck. All the di Gialla save me are dead and I am too old. But most of all, you do not want it. That is what makes you the only choice." Slowly, Schermo got down on one knee again, and this time, Prospero did not stop him. "The City Levies await your command, your Grace. The *city* awaits your command."

Silence spread out in ripples from the scene; then as realisation dawned, more and more people dropped to one knee. Prospero looked round; seeking something. Escape, perhaps.

His face twisted, and for a moment it seemed he might sob. He looked down at the floor, lost in thought; then he smiled cruelly to himself. "Perhaps circumstance which appeared to be our enemy at first will become our friend before dawn." He let his voice rise, to take in the troops gathered outside the Menagerie gates and the crowd of revellers he had brought with him too. "Let the Castell'nuero burn; we cannot stop it now, and we can pen the Tatar Guard up inside the walls. Schermo – take a detachment and blockade all exits to the Castle – slay any Tatar you find in the streets, trap the rest inside. And you, my friends – we have a chance, now, to catch the Rookery Murderer; but first, we must lure him out and bait the trap. Are you with me?"

The crowd cheered, ragged and uncertain at first but growing in strength. Drunken partygoers are always happy for a spectacle, and often for a fight. Anything involving Prospero and the troops would likely include both.

The new Duca in his feathered trousers turned once more to the giant albino ape.

"Caliban, dear Caliban..." He hugged the beast, pressing his face into the white fur. "I must ask one more service of you tonight..."

* * *

Xavier stood before the great statue in the courtyard before the Palazzo di Zancani and stared up at it.

The Tuffatore family had always identified with the lion; and now, to his eyes, the serpent had him in its coils beyond any redemption. He slumped against the edge of the fountain and covered his head with his hands as the mists coiled through the square like smoke.

Carried on them, implacable, like some awful doom from a tragedy of the Classics, came Orlando. She held only two cards now; from beneath the sun mask, drool the colour of the inks and paints on the cards ran down her chin. In the weird misty moonlight her skin had taken on a weird pallid sheen, like damp pasteboard.

"Sofia d'Amato loved you, and she is *dead*," said Orlando in a sing-song voice. "Ophelia di Gialla loved you and now she is *dead*. Gawain d'Orlato loved you and you turned him *away*. And now you have *nothing*."

She held up the second to last card; it depicted a man in clerical vestments, his face cold and impassive. He holds his robe open, and where his body should be there is nothing but a great empty space, pillared, stretching off into infinity. In the far distance, between the pillars, something is visible. Something toiling, slowly, across the great intervening space toward the surface of the card.

"You have nothing left now, Xavier. Nothing left. Hollow man. Shall we fill you?"

She crumpled the card between her fingers, but instead of folding up it exploded into a puff of mist, lost in the city air. Then, with her left hand, she reached up and removed her mask, and looked straight at Xavier. He let loose one great shuddering cry, and then was silent.

She held up the last card.

"I think you know what to do."

* * *

Gratiano stopped at the corner. "Around here there's a fifty-yard stretch of street, and then the courtyard at the end of it with the statue. Can't miss it. Big marble building…"

"Show us, Holy Fool." Buskovy gestured, and the Janizaries' blades whispered out of their scabbards. Gratiano drew a deep breath and rounded the corner. The tableau was laid out before them like a stage performance; Xavier, on his knees before the fountain, his hand outstretched to the woman in the sun mask, who held the last card.

Gratiano stopped, dumbfounded. "Elizabeta? Elizabeta, what's going on?"

With a curl of her lip and a muttered obscenity in Bucharan, the Grafin swept past him, the Janizaries in escort, and rapped out her orders to them without breaking stride. "Kill the man, before he is possessed. Destroy the woman if you can. Do not look at her face." From within her robes, she drew out a plaque with the twisted trident of the Trinity inlaid in gold into its blackened surface, and she held this out before her like a shield.

"*Fantasma di verità!* I name you *Mascherina Pallida!* I name you and I abjure you, step away!"

Orlando whirled on her heel and looked straight at the Grafin, who averted her eyes and shielded her face with her free hand, all the time holding the seal of the Trinity up before her; Buskovy was not so lucky. He was staring straight at Orlando as she turned, and as he saw her face, he made a terrible cracked scream and fell to his knees. Gratiano looked at him, then following age-old instinct turned to look at what he was staring at, and saw what had become of his lover. His breath caught in his throat.

"You are *far* too late, jailer," said the unmasked thing. "Can you hear His footsteps?"

Orlando made a great sweeping gesture, and the night mists boiled into solidity around the advancing Janizaries; a horde of gnawing rats overwhelming them, figures looming out of the mist with blades solid only for a crucial second – but a second is all you need.

The Janizaries fought like dead men possessed against the mist suddenly alive with lethal menace; forming a fighting cordon around the Grafin, whose attention remained focussed solely on the unmasked figure in the courtyard.

Beneath their feet, the ground trembled, rhythmically. The Grafin, her eyes still averted, spat; where her spittle struck the cobbles, they glowed cherry red and cracked. "I name you and abjure you; return the card to me! It is not his time, and it is not the messenger's task to bid a King whom Emperors have served! Lay down your hubris, Pallid Mask, and *let him go*!" She reached down, and grabbed the broken, still smouldering cobble where her spittle had struck.

Orlando cast her arms wide and her terrible face to the swirling tumult of the skies: "He comes! *Yhtill! Yhtill! Yhtill!*"

The Grafin hurled the smouldering cobble straight at Orlando in a low, flat trajectory; it struck her in the solar plexus, and she collapsed in a weirdly boneless fashion; cards exploded from the folds of her garments like some street magician's trick, as if they had been hidden within.

The phantasms besetting the surviving Janizaries became, abruptly, night mist; for nine of the twelve guards this respite came too late. The dead men, gnawed by rats or laid low by great gashes and rents in their flesh, lay on the cobbles, leaking out the pale watery blue fluid that served them in lieu of blood. The remaining three formed a cordon around the Grafin again, blades outward, pale eyes scanning the mists for the next assault. It did not come.

All was silent save for Buskovy's awful cracked wheezing scream and the fixed, equally awful rattle of breath in Gratiano's throat as he stared at what was once Elizabeta Zancani. The Grafin fell to her knees over the prone body and tore open her robes, searching among the cards; discarding first one and then another. Beneath the court dress and the discarded sun mask, there was nothing but rotten meat; a long-dead corpse. Cold, and motivated only by will and borrowed heat.

Gratiano retched his guts out.

"The messenger of the King is soft," whispered the Grafin. "When one shakes her hand, one should be careful one does not come away with more fingers than one began with." She scrabbled among the cards, but she already knew the one she sought was not there.

The subterranean pounding was becoming more rhythmic, like the stride of giant footsteps, running, Then, abruptly, they stopped. She looked up, fearing the worst.

But the worst was not yet. Not quite, anyway.

*   *   *

Xavier clambered up onto the fountain's surround and then into the water as the Grafin attacked Orlando; he was transfixed by the card he held.

He has no face. He wears pointed shoes under his tattered, fantastically colored robes, and a streamer of silk appears to fall from the pointed tip of his hood. At times he appears to be winged; at others, haloed. He holds a smoking torch, head downwards, behind his back. The smoke from the torch forming the impression of both the wings and halo.

Re Stracciati; the King In Tatters, the Last King of Cittàvecchio. Xavier touched the surface of the card in awe, and felt the movement beneath it.

"Xavier. Give me the card. Give me the card and we can straighten all of this out."

He looked incuriously at the shadow from behind the statue of the lion as it coalesced into Gawain. He had wrapped a black rag around his head to conceal the ruin of his left eye; blood still stained his cheek. He had jumped across to the top of the statue and then clambered down; he held his hand out, open. "Give me the card, Xavier, we can fix this."

Xavier moved in close to Gawain, under the shadow of the coiled serpent and the stricken lion. The water in the fountain trembled as the footsteps grew closer. He touched the blood on Gawain's cheek a second, then drew him in close, until he could whisper directly into Gawain's ear.

"Do you love me?" His tone was high and eerily calm.

"You know I do. You know I do, Xavier."

"Then why did you kill the woman I loved?" Xavier's eyes met Gawain's, and each of them saw only a yawning abyss in the other.

"Xavier, I – "

Gawain never finished the sentence; Xavier pushed him, hard, in the centre of the chest. He stumbled, his footing uncertain for a second on the slick marble, and staggered back into the fountain; as he did so, the sound of the thunderous approaching footsteps stopped, and there was briefly the sensation of something massive moving through air in near-silence.

Then, with an unearthly howl, Gawain disappeared in a flurry of white fur and simian rage. Caliban had taken Gawain around the waist in a mighty tackle. The raised lip of the fountain broke under the weight of Caliban's impact, and water spilled out over the courtyard; they both skidded to a halt on the wet flagstones, the great albino ape sat atop Gawain, whose knives were already at work, but not fast enough. Blow after blow landed from those great leathery hands.

Xavier watched impassively from the shadow of the statue in the fountain, tapping the card against his chin, as Caliban tried to pound his lover to death against the cobbles.

* * *

Prospero and his men spilled into the square; the Grafin was swiftly surrounded by men made nervous and scared sober by the events of the night, her Janizaries disarmed; she signalled to them not to resist. Prospero's immediate concerns, though were not for unexpected foreign visitors in the city.

He rushed over to Caliban. The great ape had outpaced everyone once he had Gawain's scent; broken into a great loping run that had shaken the very ground. But now Caliban's fur was stained crimson; he lay slumped in the courtyard over Gawain, pinning him to the floor. He had driven both of his daggers deep into Caliban's chest, but the beast's dead weight pinned him to the ground. Blood bubbled at the corner of his mouth, but his one un-ruined eye glittered still.

Prospero, tears streaming unashamedly down his face, touched the great beast. "Poor Caliban. We did not even have time to get to know one another properly. You are a hero of Cittàvecchio, though you do not yet know it."

He kneeled down next to Gawain and took the trapped man tightly by the throat. "Well; how curious that we should find ourselves here with the positions reversed, hey? You have much to answer for, d'Orlato, and the death of this noble beast is the least of it. Anything to say?"

"Be wise, Prospero. Kill me now." Gawain blinked, and spat scarlet at Prospero's face. It missed, and spattered his feathered trousers, bright red against the white.

"Oh, *plenty* of time for that later. *Plenty* of time. There's something we should discuss, since we're both here and I have you where I want you." He tightened his grip around Gawain's throat until bubbles of crimson froth appeared at the corners of his lips..

"You do not threaten me in my house

"You do not, *ever*, harm my animals.

"If you do, I will *make you suffer*. Understand?" He released his grip. Gawain's gaze shone with malice, but Prospero's was black with hate.

"Who leads here?" The Grafin's imperious tone cut through the courtyard like an icicle. "Stop him!"

"I do." Prospero stood, dusting himself down. "Stop who? Who are you, that gives orders in Cittàvecchio?"

"Time for that later! Stop him! Stop him, you fools!" The Grafin lunged for a crossbow held loosely by one of her guards; the man fought back, and as they struggled, Xavier emerged from the shadow of the statue, holding the *Re Stracciati* card. Over the city, the church bells tolled, once.

He folded it in half, and ate it.

* * *

Across the city, the winds picked up; the mists swirled in a great wheel around the courtyard of the Lion and Serpent, and towered up above the fountain like a pillar of cloud, centred on Xavier, before collapsing around him like tattered robes, like wings, like a great halo.

"*Yhtill, Yhtill, Yhtill*" said a voice much deeper and louder than Xavier's, and suddenly, every bell in Cittàvecchio gave voice simultaneously. The very ground trembled; the air full and pregnant with potential malice.

The Grafin wailed and threw herself flat to the floor, averting her eyes; Prospero pressed himself back against a wall to avoid the billowing cloak of fog. Xavier – or whatever he had become

- walked slowly to the edge of the fountain and then stepped down, mist and winds holding him clear of the ground. Loose rubbish, discarded weapons and detritus was picked up in the winds and tossed around the courtyard like toys; Prospero's men scattered, leaving him a clear path. Most of them, anyway; some were neither fast nor lucky enough, and the mantle of the Last King passed over them, leaving them pallid and wan, and following nerveless in his train.

He advanced along the street, his mantle spreading further, feeling out the city, feeling out *his* city. The Old City. Imperial Cittàvecchio. He spread wide his arms, opened his mouth, and every bell in the city gave voice again; the very fabric of the buildings trembled with the noise.

The Grafin scrabbled among the windswept cards around the ruin of Orlando's body and seized upon one; she offered a swift prayer to the Mother that it would be enough. Then she turned the card face outwards and tore it clean in half.

The two pieces of *The Holy Fool* fluttered away on the King's winds. Prospero seized upon the abandoned crossbow and sighted down it at Xavier's back, but the Grafin raised a hand no; *not yet.*

Gratiano knelt in the courtyard amidst the maelstrom. Elizabeta was dead; Mercutio was dead; everyone was dead. Everyone who this madness had touched, dead or broken. He was not a student of the mysteries, knew little of the occult; cared less. All he had wanted was to enjoy his life in the city, not to be its pawn in some ghastly scheme.

As the torn halves of the card fluttered away, he decided to be a fool no longer, and his fingers touched a piece of wood, broken from a hitching-post by the tempest. He stood up.

The Grafin, on her knees, prayed hard, her eyes screwed shut, her hands raised before her, asking every spirit and God she knew for an intercession, for just one small chance for the deck to be it's own undoing, for the Holy Fool to lay low the *Re Stracciati…*

Xavier stood at the end of the street, listening to the echoes of the bells, listening to the tale the city told him, its voice freed at last. And he smiled, and turned back to face the Grafin and Prospero. His eyes were terrible; more full than any human's soul could ever be without being torn asunder, full beyond measure of ancient malice and cold, cruel amusement and terrible, endless wisdom that stretched until the very end of time. The eyes of *Re Stracciati*, of the Lord of the Invisibles, The Last King come back home again.

Xavier extended his arms and smiled a terrible smile, and the fog billowed up behind him and around him, coalescing into a form far taller and greater than the shell of flesh which formed the gateway. And all around him the city trembled – not in fear, but in anticipation, as beneath the centuries of floodwater and mire, the grime of Cittàvecchio, the Old City was rising once more.

"Behold," he said, "Carcosa awakens, and all invaders and usurpers must fall before it."

He made as if to step toward the stricken figure of the Grafin and Prospero, stood transfixed by the spectacle; but between them and him stood Gratiano, side on; and his hands were concealed behind his back. The King's mantle engulfed him like smoke on water but he stood there, unconcerned and seemingly unaffected by it.

"I'm so sorry, Xavier," Gratiano said in a whisper. "I'm so sorry for everything. For Elizabeta. But you see, whatever it may have been once, this is Cittavecchio now; this is my city too."

And with that, he swung the length of wood with all the strength he had and struck Xavier full force on the side of the head. It made an awful sound of wood on bone.

For a second, it seemed as though Xavier, fuelled by the King's mantle, would shrug it off; but when he turned back to Gratiano, his eyes were unfocussed and he stumbled. Gratiano staggered back and let the spar of wood drop from fingers suddenly dead. He stared at his hands in horrified disbelief as the life and colour fled from them, and he slumped to his knees in the middle of the street.

Something whistled past his cheek, close enough to move his hair; close enough to sting. And Xavier, suddenly no longer in the mantle of the King, catapulted over backwards with a crossbow quarrel lodged in his shoulder. The mists swirled around the courtyard like a caged beast, and then dissipated as abruptly as they had formed to begin with, but the great oppressive air remained. Xavier lay unmoving, in a spreading pool of blood. The Grafin kneeled, shocked silent. Gratiano collapsed onto his side, his hands pallid and shaking, making faint retching sounds.

Prospero lowered the crossbow, and put his hands on his hips.

"Would *somebody* kindly tell me what in the name of the Mother and *Child* just happened? It's not as if I'm supposed to be in *charge* or anything!"

*   *   *

"Your Grace Prospero. Congratulations upon your ascension of the Ducal throne, et cetera. I came to the city in pursuit of stolen goods in hopes of preventing this very catastrophe from occurring; it appears that only the greatest of good fortune has saved us all today." The Grafin and her three surviving Janizaries were being given a courteous but suspicious honour guard of a dozen of the City Levy, all armed with crossbows. In the aftermath of the events in the courtyard, half the city had poured into the area; now onlookers were being held back from Gratiano and Xavier, both still prone, by cordons of guards who themselves were hardly certain what was going on. A doctor attended to Gratiano, examining his numb hands, shaking his head in bewilderment; but nobody attended to Xavier. He lay, unconscious, surrounded by a ring of guards whose weapons pointed solely at his prone form. The courtyard was on the verge of chaos; Only Prospero's natural talent for making everyone look at him was keeping the situation even remotely under control.

As the Grafin finished her tale of following the cards over the mountains, the new duke beamed at her. "Jolly well done by you, then; and the city owes you a great debt of thanks." He was already thinking of something else – looking at Caliban's corpse where the King's winds had tossed it. "Nor is it just you that the city owes a debt to this night."

"Perhaps," she growled. "But this is far from contained yet. You will need chains – lead or wrought iron are best – to contain him. While he lives, the King will lie within him awaiting his chance. There are precautions that can be taken, charms I can weave to keep him asleep until he can be shackled with the metals of earth and fire..."

"Take them then, Grafin." Prospero waved his hand. His attention was already moving onto the next problem. "But for the moment, excuse me; there is another matter I must attend to. Hoy, you!" He signalled to some of the onlookers. "Do as the Grafin asks. She has my full authority, understand? And somebody, *get me a drink*. Am I not the Duke?"

He walked over to Caliban. The great beast had been thrown against the courtyard wall by the winds. Where Gawain had lain, there was only a pool of blood, and a trail of crimson spatters leading to a drainpipe. He looked speculatively at the moonlit rooftops.

"Your Grace! We will need a strong cell..." The Grafin, stood over Xavier's prone form. She held a handful of the cards, and had people collecting the others from where the winds had scattered them.

"I have the very thing," said Prospero, sadly. "Caliban will not be using it again, after all..."

* * *

The new Duca looked through the grating in the cell door. Xavier – or what was once Xavier – sat calmly on a chair in the centre of the cell, staring straight ahead at nothing. He was manacled in dull, heavy metal, and his shoulder was bandaged where Prospero's bolt had struck him. His face was still livid with bruising from the blow that laid him out. A faint suggestion of a smile hung around his lips, as if he knew Prospero were watching.

He turned to the Lord Seneschal. "No change?"

"He has been like this ever since the night of the ball. The Grafin said he's unlikely to change, unless it's for the worse. Young Gratiano hit him a corker with that plank; he's still blind and the doctor thinks he'll likely stay that way for good."

Schermo looked at Prospero sideways. "You should probably kill him, you know. Mercy, and all that."

Prospero shook his head. "My reign has already begun in a welter of blood. I'll not shed more unless I have good reason. Well; with one exception. Did you find him?"

Schermo shook his head. "No."

Duke Prospero smiled a cold and humourless smile. "Well. While we have Xavier, he won't stray far. I can be patient. Keep a twenty-four hour guard on him. If he tries to harm the animals, kill him. If he tries to slip his manacles, kill him. If you see Gawain…"

The Seneschal nodded.

*　*　*

Inside the cage, Xavier smiles. His hands move in the endless rhythm of shuffling, dealing and laying the cards out in the age-old pattern of solitaire.

Patience is, after all, a virtue. He is at peace, and he can wait.

Here, in the darkness, he listens to the song of the King in the wind and in the whispers of the city. He understands at last, truly, what it is to be loved.

He will never be alone again.

Epilogue: This Card, Which is Blank

PHLEBAS the Phoenician, a fortnight dead,

Forgot the cry of gulls, and the deep seas swell

And the profit and loss.

> *A current under sea*

Picked his bones in whispers.

As he rose and fell

He passed the stages of his age and youth

Entering the whirlpool. Gentile or Jew

O you who turn the wheel and look to windward,

Consider Phlebas, who was once handsome and tall as you.

> *T.S. Eliot, The Waste Land 312-321*

Duke Prospero, on the advice of several mystics and religious authorities, gifted the remainder of the *Re Stracciati* deck to the city of Buchara in the person of the Grafin Stechau. Alas, as far as can be ascertained, she did not make it back to Buchara alive. When a search party was sent out to find her, the abandoned coach was found in the high pass between the cities. The three surviving Janizaries were all slain; the murder weapon was a single thin-bladed double-edged knife perhaps eighteen inches in length. Their faces had been cut away.

The deck of cards, and the body of the Grafin were never found. Or if they were, the Bucharan authorities never admitted it.

* * *

Gratiano dell'Allia lives still in Cittàvecchio; he does not attend the party circuit any longer, and though Lord Prospero will have no ill said of him, neither does he invite him to court. He has moved to a small walled estate on the edge of the Rookeries and seldom leaves his house nowadays. He keeps himself company, it is said, with cats.

Rumour has it he does not sleep so well.

*   *   *

In the judicial investigations following the night of the Festivàle Ball, responsibility for the Rookery Murders and the deaths of Captain Gian Galeazzo Visconti, the Duca di Gialla, Donna Ophelia di Gialla, Mater Calomena Giraldus and Lord Gawain d'Orlato (whose body remains obstinately missing) was placed upon the rebellious Captain of the Tartary Guard, Valentin of Rus and his co-conspirators, Pater Felicio Caritavo and Donna Elizabeta Zancani.

The surviving conspirators were tried swiftly and executed publicly by the new Duca.

*   *   *

The fires in the Castell'nuero were brought under control, but the grand ballroom at the top of the *Vecchi Punti* and the associated apartments were damaged beyond repair. Duke Prospero declared them a graveyard, and instructed the new Pater Ottavio to consecrate the ground to allow the Duca di Gialla to rest in peace. Plans have been put forward to convert the entire wing into a mausoleum for the Gialla family.

*   *   *

Lord Buskovy resides now in the Hospice of the Holy Child in Cittàvecchio, as the informal Cultural Attaché for Buchara. His attendants all wear masks, and providing he does not see their faces he is quite composed, rational and calm. On the occasions that one of his attendants forgets and shows a bare face, the screaming generally lasts only an hour or two.

He has taken up painting to calm his nerves and pass the time; the Duke buys all of his new canvasses for a very generous fee. What happens to them after that is unknown.

*   *   *

Lord Xavier di Tuffatore remains a guest at Duke Prospero's pleasure. Those who enquire after him are told that he has chosen a life of monastic contemplation.

He does not receive visitors.

*   *   *

Whilst all of the other cards of the deck save the *Holy Fool* were collected after the incident in the Court of the Lion and Serpent, the card depicting *Re Stracciati* was never recovered.

*   *   *

In Cittàvecchio, life continues as it ever did. It's said (by those who live safe and far from the old quarter) that every night the Tattered King throws his cloak over the city that the old Gods tried and failed to drown; and that in the fog that clings to the water in her flooded streets and canals things not entirely of this world sometimes occur.

This, though, is an age of Reason and such myths and legends are dismissed by the intelligentsia in their salons and their cafes on the edge of the Grand Piazza. The mists come up in the spring from the marshes and smother the city a while on their way out to the open sea. Simple weather, nothing more, they say, and raise laughing masks to hide their faces from their fellows.

But in the dark places of the city, people remember the old ways and the old fears, and respect the things they do not understand. And everywhere, if you know where to look, there are reminders that this is still Cittàvecchio, the Old City. Once, it had an Imperial name, and not a title; and once, it had a King, not a duke.

Every night, Duke Prospero stands alone on the balcony as night falls, and watches the cloud-waves roll in from the lagoon and break against the sunken buildings of his dreaming city.

He knows in his heart that he sits upon a borrowed throne.

Afterword

The inspirations for Cittàvecchio are many and varied, and some more obvious than others. Venice and the Carcosa of Bierce, Chambers and Tynes play their parts, but so do medieval Verona and Victorian Birmingham, Lieber's Lankhmar and London, that wicked and raddled old whore, and Thomas Ligotti's dream of Zagreb; Amsterdam and an old port city by the sea that I was once all too familiar with.

But that was long ago, and in another country; and besides, the wench is dead.

For liberties taken, licence granted and faces kept straight special thanks go to Arwel Griffith, Neil Parker and Richard Polley. Gentlemen and Lords of the City all, and of a calibre rarely seen in this day and age. For generosity with support, enthusiasm and advice and for the uphill battle against my eccentric understanding of the rules of grammar, my gratitude goes to Sarah Hinksman, Kat Quatermass, Smittumi (whose nature is irrepressible), Boglin (who was more worried about the peacocks than about the people) and the inestimable Thomas Ryng, esq. But most of all, to Paul Snow, for generously allowing me to make merry with the fruits of his genius. Here Be Monster.

Had it not been for Simon Brind going down into the dark place with a lantern before me, you would not be holding this in your hand. Envy and admiration as ever to a man who has successfully become an adult without ever becoming a grown-up.

And of course, for Tony John Cooke, without whose patience and gentle encouragement this undertaking would not have been completed, or indeed possible.

Thanks are owed to many more, not least those who came to a country house in Derbyshire in the dying days of 2004 and made these names more than just ink on paper. This is mostly for you; you know who you are.